英語閱讀技巧完全攻略 1

作者 Michelle Witte / Zachary Fillingham / Gregory John Bahlmann **二版** Success With Reading

譯者 林育珊 / 劉嘉珮　審訂 Treva Adams / Helen Yeh

全英文學習訓練英文思維及語感
可調整語速 / 播放 / 複誦模式訓練聽力

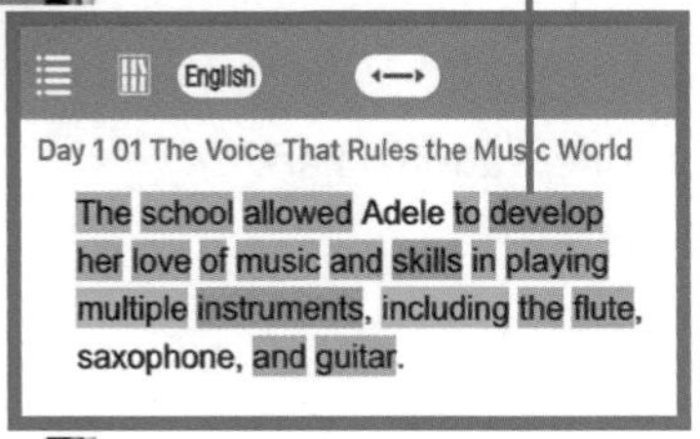

◀全文閱讀

◀單句閱讀色底表示單字級等

◀單句閱讀

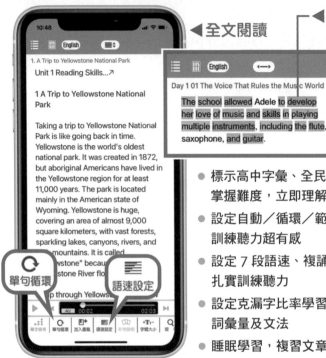

- 標示高中字彙、全民英檢、多益字級，掌握難度，立即理解文章
- 設定自動／循環／範圍播放，訓練聽力超有感
- 設定 7 段語速、複誦間距及次數，扎實訓練聽力
- 設定克漏字比率學習，提高理解力、詞彙量及文法
- 睡眠學習，複習文章幫助記憶

快速查詢字義
理解文章內容

課後閱讀測驗檢驗理解力

強力口說練習

◀錄下發音和原音比對辨識，精進口語能力。

單字分析掌握單字力

◀提供全書總單字量及單字表，掌握單字難易度，針對不熟單字加強學習。

目錄 Contents

目錄 Contents

簡介 Introduction

本套書共分四冊，目的在於培養閱讀能力與增進閱讀技巧；每冊共有 100 篇文章，不僅網羅各類主題，還搭配大量閱讀測驗題，以訓練讀者記憶重點與理解內容的能力。

本書依據不同主題劃分為四大單元。每單元主要介紹一種閱讀攻略。讀者不僅能透過本書文章增進閱讀能力，還能涉獵包羅萬象的知識，包括藝術與文學、動物、歷史、科學和運動等主題閱讀。

主要特色

• 包羅萬象的文章主題

本書內容涵蓋各類多元主題，幫助讀者充實知識，宛如一套生活知識小百科。囊括主題包括：

社會學	科學	其他主題
藝術與文學	動物／植物	體育
歷史	健康與人體	神祕事件
地理與景點	網路或科技	
文化	科學	
政治／經濟		
語言傳播		
環境保育		
人物		
食物		

• 全方位的閱讀攻略

本書以豐富的高效率閱讀攻略，幫助讀者輕鬆理解任何主題文章的內容。書中閱讀攻略包括：

1 閱讀技巧（Reading Skills）

幫助你練習瞭解整體內文的技巧。此單元涵蓋以下項目：

❶ 明辨主題（Subject Matter）

文章主題是文章中最概括的含意。瞭解文章的整體概念，可幫助你理解文中的細節內容。

❷ 歸納要旨（Main Idea）

文章要旨代表的是文章想傳達的大意，有可能是一種想法或事實。文章要旨通常會以主題論述的方式表達。

❸ 找出支持性細節（Supporting Details）

支持性細節是作者用來支持文章主題句的說明，例如事實、直喻、說明、敘述、比較、舉例等，或是任何能佐證主題的資訊。

❹ 情節排序（Sequencing）

瞭解文章內容的事件順序，能培養你整理來龍去脈的能力。當你試著了解資訊順序時，記得尋找 before（之前）、after（之後）、next（接下來）、then（然後）、later（待會）、previously（以前）等字詞或其他時間標記。

❺ 理解因果關係（Cause and Effect）

為了完全了解事件始末，重點就是清楚事件的發生原因以及最後結果。事件發生的原因就稱為**「因」（cause）**，最後結果就稱為**「果」（effect）**。because of（由於）和 as a result of（因而）等片語用於說明「原因」（cause），as a result（結果，不加 of）、resulting in（因此）和 so（所以）等片語則用來說明**「結果」（effect）**。

❻ 釐清寫作技巧（Clarifying Devices）

釐清寫作技巧包括瞭解字彙、片語的應用，以及分辨作者用來讓文章大意與支持性細節更加清楚、更引人入勝的寫作方式。有時候，最重要的釐清技巧就是要能分辨文章類型和作者意圖。

❼ 進行推論（Making Inferences）

「推論」意指運用你已知的資訊，來猜測未知的情況。作者通常會透露訊息，讓讀者能自行推論文意。

❽ 批判性思考（Critical Thinking）

批判性思考指的是「**提問問題**」。閱讀的時候，一定要在心裡質疑「為什麼？」（why）、「何地？」（where）、「何時？」（when）以及「如何做？」（how）這幾個問題。針對你所閱讀的資訊，和作者為何選擇透露該資訊而提問，能幫助你建構對文章的看法，以及了解寫作過程。

❾ 分辨事實與意見（Fact or Opinion）

判斷某種說法是「**事實**」（Fact）或「**意見**」（Opinion），是很好的思考方式。「事實」可經由其他資訊來源來驗證。只要是事實，就有對錯之分。而「意見」是某人對某事物的感覺。因此，你可以不認同他人「意見」，卻無法否認「事實」。

2 字彙練習（Word Study）

能幫助你練習累積字彙量與理解文章新字彙的技巧。本單元涵蓋以下項目：

❶ 同義字（意義相同的用語）（Synonyms: Words With the Same Meaning）

英文的詞語十分豐富。事實上，許多看似不同的詞語，其實意義都相同。如果你想表達正在享用的冰淇淋很好吃，你可以輕鬆地運用 acceptable（可接受）、excellent（很棒）、nice（很不錯）、pleasing（令人心曠神怡）、super（超讚）或 amazing（好吃得不得了）等用語。

❷ 反義字（意義相反的用語）（Antonyms: Words With Opposite Meanings）

英文的字彙十分豐富，並有許多詞語的意義恰好相反。有些反義字表達出兩種可能性的其一意義，例如 dead（死亡）和 alive（活著）；也有其他不同變化的詞彙，例如 huge（龐大）、giant（巨大）、big（大）等詞，都是 small（小）的反義字。學會越多反義字，你的字彙量就越能有所增進，也能讓寫作內容更加生動有趣。

❸ 依上下文猜測字義（Words in Context）

如果不認得某字，再怎麼與生字大眼瞪小眼，也無法猜透它的意思。但是如果你瀏覽上下文，也許就能很快意會這詞彙的意思。詞彙的上下文能讓你理解其意義。

3 學習策略（Study Strategies）

幫助你理解文意，並運用文章中不同素材來蒐集資訊，培養查詢資料的基本能力。影像圖表和參考來源等資訊，不會直接呈現出文章的含意，而是以圖片、編號清單、依字母順序編列的清單，和其他方法來展示資訊。本單元涵蓋以下項目：

❶ 影像圖表（Visual Material）

表格、圖片、圖表和地圖，比文字更能呈現繁複的資訊，例如事物的關聯性與其模式風格。要理解這類的素材，必須先仔細閱讀標題、查看圖說，然後閱讀表格行列的表頭，以及圖表上的座標軸說明。瞭解影像圖表的版面陳列後，即可解讀所含的資訊。

❷ 參考來源（Reference Sources）

字典、百科全書和地圖冊等參考來源，能讓你的閱讀問題迎刃而解。圖示、表格與圖表，能幫助你在閱讀的時候，更快理解複雜的資訊。學會運用內文裡的不同參考來源，可大幅增進整體閱讀理解力。

4 綜合練習（Final Reviews）

以豐富的閱讀素材和推敲式問題，幫助你有效複習學過的內容。此單元目的在檢視你對本書所提供之學習資訊吸收的程度。為了檢測你理解內文的能力，請務必於研讀前述單元之後，完成最後的綜合練習單元。

• 最佳考試準備用書

本書適合初學者閱讀，亦為準備大學學測、指考、多益、托福及雅思等考試的最佳用書。

使用導覽 How Do I Use This Book?

全方位的閱讀攻略

每單元主要介紹一種閱讀攻略，幫助讀者更加輕鬆理解任何主題文章的內容。

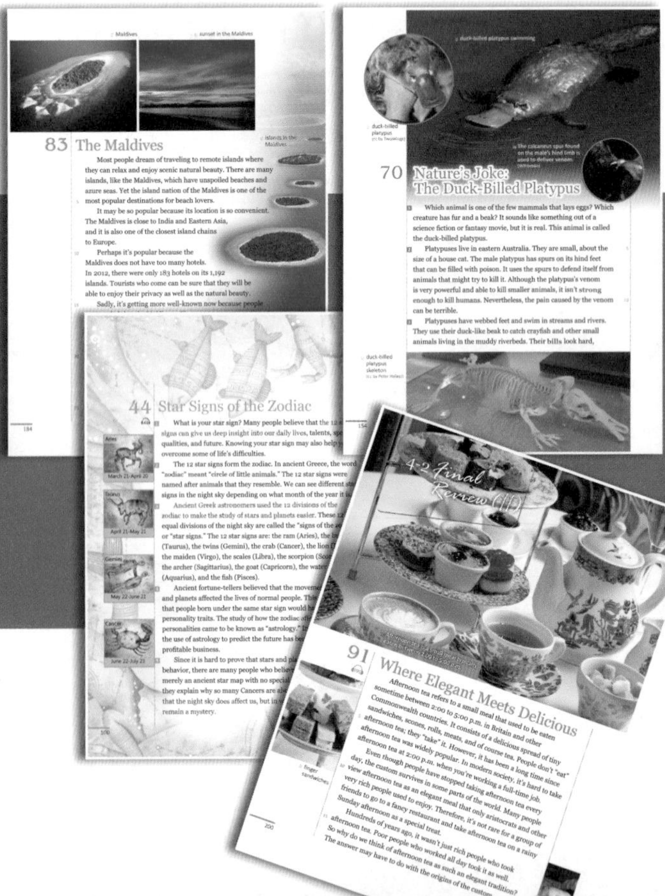

包羅萬象的閱讀主題

內容涵蓋各類多元主題，包括藝術與文學、歷史、文化與科學，不僅能充實讀者的知識，亦可加強閱讀能力。

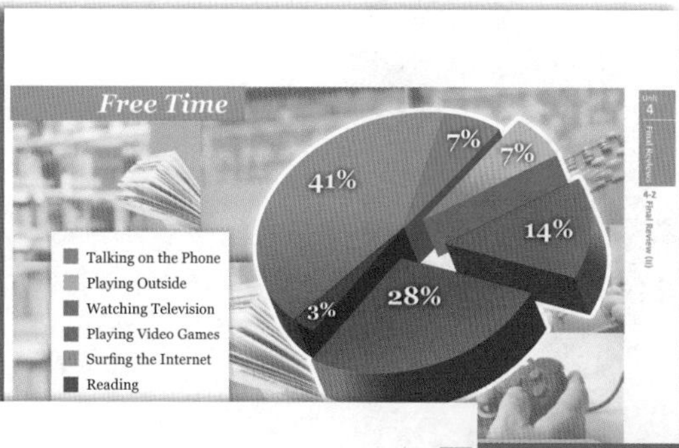

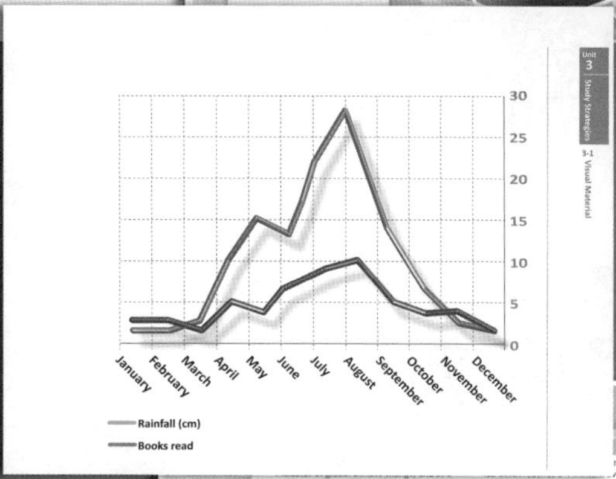

琳瑯滿目的彩色圖表

琳瑯滿目的彩色圖表，有助於讀者學習使用圖表，幫助快速理解文章內容，增加閱讀趣味性。

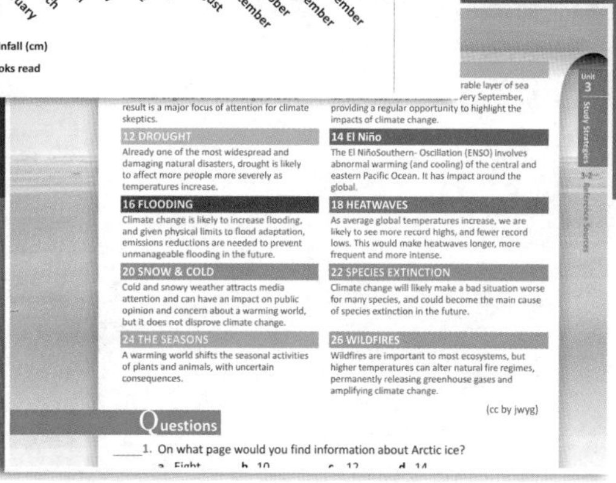

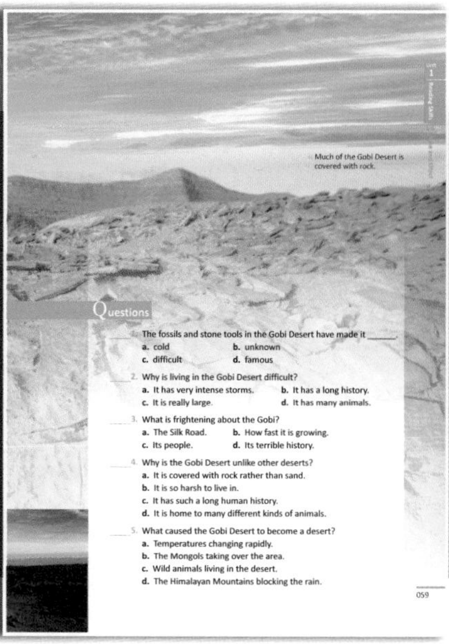

實用的主題式練習題

每篇文章後均附有五題選擇題，用以檢測閱讀理解能力，並加強字彙認知力。讀者可運用此類練習來有效評估自己的程度，以作自我實力之檢測與提升。

Unit 1

Reading Skills

This unit will help you practice some skills for understanding a text as a whole. The unit covers subject matter, main ideas, supporting details, ordering, cause and effect, clarifying devices, making inferences, critical thinking, and fact or opinion.

The skills covered in these sections will help you understand the message of a text, when events in it occurred, and why things happened. You will also learn how to make educated assumptions about information that isn't included in a text, about how an author feels about a text, about how facts can be used to support opinions, and how details can be used to support main ideas.

1-1 Subject Matter

Subject matter is the most general concept of a text. When you read, you start from a large topic and move on to "smaller," specific details. Subject matter is the large topic that contains the details. Knowing the overall concept of an article helps you understand the details in context.

1 A Trip to Yellowstone National Park

001 1 Taking a trip to Yellowstone National Park is like going back in time. Yellowstone is the world's oldest national park. It was created in 1872, but aboriginal Americans have lived in the Yellowstone region for at least 11,000 years. The park is located mainly in the American state of Wyoming. Yellowstone is huge, covering an area of almost 9,000 square kilometers, with vast forests, sparkling lakes, canyons, rivers, and high mountains. It is called "Yellowstone" because the Yellowstone River flows through it.

2 A trip through Yellowstone can show you what America looked like before we human beings arrived. You can see large herds of bison and elk in the park. Not all of Yellowstone's wildlife is harmless. You need to be very careful in Yellowstone: the park is home to wild grizzly bears and wolves. A bear is capable of quickly killing a human and should be avoided. There are also stories of wolves attacking individuals. You should not feed bears or wolves. If you feed a wild animal, then it will be less afraid of humans and more likely to attack you and other people.

grizzly bear in Yellowstone National Park

3 When you visit Yellowstone National Park, make sure to stop and see Old Faithful, one of the park's most amazing sights. Old Faithful is a cone geyser. Although it is not the tallest or the largest, it is the most famous of the over 10,000 natural springs and geysers in the national park. The spectacular geyser shoots boiling hot

« a herd of bison in Yellowstone National Park

» natural springs and geysers in Yellowstone National Park

water 44 meters on average into the air about every one and a half hours. Imagine seeing that!

4 This famous geyser was named "Old Faithful" because of its consistent performance for members of the Washburn Expedition in 1870. Though its average interval of eruptions has lengthened over the years, Old Faithful is still as fantastic and predictable as it was a century ago.

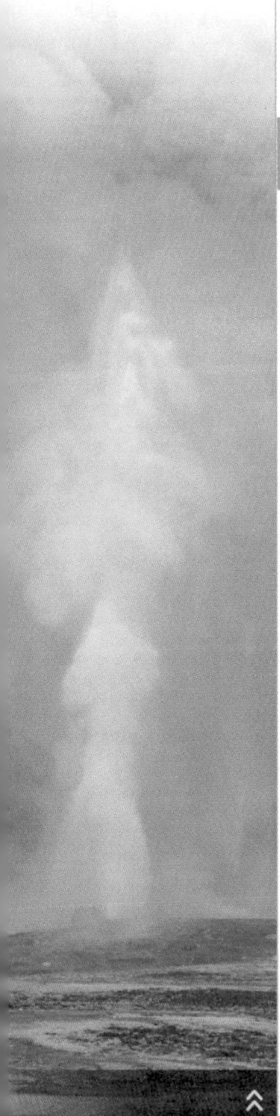

Old Faithful geyser

Questions

_____ 1. What is this article about?

a. A river. **b.** A group of people.
c. A natural area. **d.** A state.

_____ 2. The second paragraph is mostly about ______.

a. animals in Yellowstone **b.** Old Faithful
c. the age of Yellowstone **d.** directions to Yellowstone

_____ 3. The third paragraph is mostly about ______.

a. cone geysers **b.** the Washburn Expedition
c. aboriginal Americans **d.** Old Faithful

_____ 4. **Yellowstone** is the name of what two things?

a. An aboriginal American and a park.
b. A river and a park.
c. A park and a geyser.
d. A geyser and a river.

_____ 5. What would be another good title for this article?

a. Seeing Old Faithful for the First Time.
b. Going Back in Time at Yellowstone.
c. Yellowstone's Most Dangerous Animals.
d. My First Trip to Yellowstone.

002 2 The Amazing Butterfly

monarch butterfly

1 My Uncle Matt used to collect butterflies. He would catch them and display them in glass cases in his study. I was often amazed when looking at those beautiful winged insects. One of my hobbies today is watching butterflies flying free in the wild and enjoying the many patterns formed by their colorful wings and graceful flight.

2 Uncle Matt told me lots of interesting facts about butterflies. For example, he told me that butterflies have four wings, not just two. They flap their wings more slowly than many other insects. However, this means that they can fly farther. During the summer, butterflies flying through the Arctic, where the sun never sets, will fly 24 hours a day. Many butterflies migrate very long distances. Monarch butterflies, for example, can travel 4,000 to 4,800 kilometers from Mexico to the northern part of the United States in a single year.

3 Adult butterflies do not grow. They also don't chew. They can't because they do not have a mouth. They use a long proboscis that is like a thin drinking straw. They use this long "straw" to sip water from damp patches, and they feed primarily on nectar from flowers. Some butterflies also derive nourishment from pollen, tree sap, rotting fruit, dung, and dissolved minerals in wet sand or dirt. Butterflies are also delicate. During storms, they must hide from the rain in trees and shrubs, or they may get killed.

4 There are over 15,000 species of butterflies in the world today. Unfortunately, that number is decreasing. Their declining population is due to pollution and loss of habitat.

life cycle of a butterfly

Butterflies feed primarily on nectar from flowers.

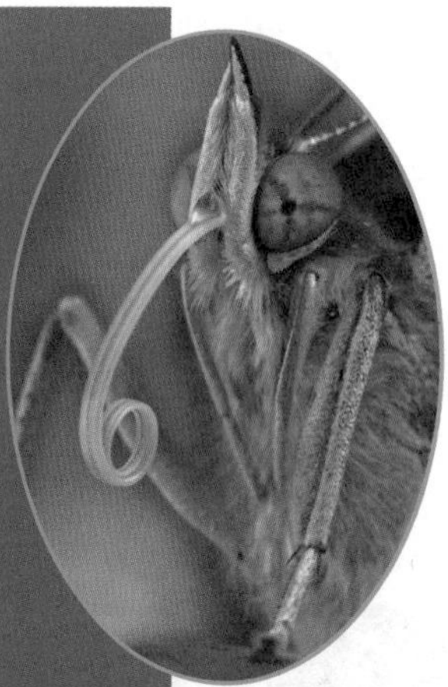

Butterflies have two compound eyes and a proboscis.

Questions

_____1. What is this article mainly about?
- **a.** A family relationship.
- **b.** A personal opinion.
- **c.** A type of insect.
- **d.** A past experience.

_____2. The second paragraph is mostly about ______.
- **a.** Uncle Matt
- **b.** butterflies' flight
- **c.** butterflies' homes
- **d.** how to catch butterflies

_____3. The first paragraph contains ______.
- **a.** some personal history
- **b.** scientific facts
- **c.** questions
- **d.** a thesis statement

_____4. The third paragraph is about ______.
- **a.** displaying butterflies
- **b.** where butterflies live
- **c.** how butterflies fly
- **d.** how butterflies live

_____5. Another good title for this article would be ______.
- **a.** Butterflies and Other Travelers
- **b.** My Hobby: Butterflies
- **c.** How to Protect Butterflies
- **d.** Butterflies in Danger

003 3 The Battle of Midway

1 The surprise bombing of Pearl Harbor on December 7, 1941, forced the United States into World War II. At that time, Emperor Hirohito's Japan seemed invincible. It already controlled a large part of China and could attack almost anywhere in the western Pacific Ocean.

2 In early May 1942, the United States fought back desperately at the Battle of the Coral Sea. Japan lost two aircraft carriers, two destroyers, about 100 planes, and approximately 3,500 men. The United States lost an aircraft carrier, a destroyer, a tanker, 65 planes, and 540 men.

Admiral Yamamoto (1884–1943)

3 Still, the Japanese controlled most of the Pacific Ocean. Admiral Yamamoto was in charge of the Japanese Navy, and he believed America's navy had been largely destroyed. He planned to lure America's few remaining aircraft carriers into a trap, sink them, and occupy the Midway Islands.

4 On June 4, 1942, the Battle of Midway began. The grimly determined American pilots sank four Japanese aircraft carriers, two cruisers, and three destroyers, and also shot down 200 experienced naval aviators. The United States lost one aircraft carrier and one destroyer.

5 This was the turning point in the war against Japan. After the Battle of Midway, the balance of power in the Pacific Ocean shifted

burning oil tanks on Midway Island after being hit by Japanese bombs

atomic bomb mushroom cloud over Hiroshima

in favor of the United States. Soon after that, the huge scientific, technological, and economic strength of the United States was better organized for war. Japan wasn't able to compete with the United States in building aircraft carriers, battleships, cruisers, destroyers, submarines, supply ships, airplanes, torpedoes, and bombs.

6 In August of 1945, an atomic bomb destroyed Hiroshima. Another destroyed Nagasaki, but Japan still wouldn't surrender. They finally surrendered only after America's President Truman allowed Japan's Emperor Hirohito to remain in place.

7 You may argue about President Truman's decisions to drop the atomic bombs and to protect Emperor Hirohito from the legal charge of war crimes. But whatever the merits of those later decisions, the Battle of Midway in June 1942 ended Japan's plan to control the Pacific Ocean.

atomic bomb mushroom cloud over Nagasaki

Questions

Midway Island (photo by Shealah Craighead)

_____ 1. This article mostly discusses ______.
- **a.** a place
- **b.** a period of history
- **c.** a person
- **d.** a piece of technology

_____ 2. The third paragraph discusses ______.
- **a.** a plan
- **b.** an island
- **c.** a result
- **d.** a date

_____ 3. Another good title for this article would be ______.
- **a.** Pros and Cons of the Atomic Bomb
- **b.** Japan's Victory in the Pacific
- **c.** A Turning Point in the Pacific War
- **d.** My Experiences at the Battle of Midway

_____ 4. The fifth paragraph describes ______.
- **a.** an agreement
- **b.** a person
- **c.** a battle
- **d.** a change

_____ 5. The final paragraph mentions ______.
- **a.** the start of a war
- **b.** a treaty
- **c.** a controversy
- **d.** a city

004 4

HARVARD UNIVERSITY

Charles William Eliot (1834–1926)

1 According to *Newsweek*, the best university in the world is Harvard University. You probably know its name, but do you know much about the school itself? Do you know what hobby could help you get into Harvard?

2 Harvard University is a private university in Cambridge, Massachusetts, and it is the oldest institution of higher learning in the United States. Harvard was founded in 1636. It was initially called New College but was renamed Harvard College in 1639 after a young clergyman named John Harvard. It was not called a university until 1780.

3 Between 1869 and 1909, Harvard's president was Charles William Eliot. He changed Harvard and made it the first modern American university with elective courses, small classes, and entrance examinations for all students.

4 Today, Harvard has about 2,400 professors, 6,700 undergraduate students, and 15,250 postgraduate students. It is more difficult to get into Harvard than any other university in the United States. In 2018, the school accepted only 4.59 percent of the people who applied, the lowest acceptance rate in its history.

5 Harvard's library system is made up of about 80 individual libraries. With over 18 million books, Harvard's library is the largest academic library in the United States and the fourth largest library in the world.

6 A huge library is useful because extensive reading is how you can greatly increase your vocabulary and improve your writing skills.

Harvard University Library
(cc by Jessica Williams)

Harvard is the oldest institution of higher learning in the United States.

A massive amount of reading is an essential part of a Harvard education. Being a highly skilled reader is the key to becoming successful in the Information Age. If you want to attend Harvard or some other famous university, your main hobby should be reading.

7 One hundred and fifty-seven Nobel Prize winners are affiliated with Harvard. Since the beginning of the 20th century, 124 Nobel Prize winners and 43 winners of the American Pulitzer Prize have served on the Harvard faculty. Some of Harvard's most famous graduates include Presidents John F. Kennedy, George W. Bush, and Barack Obama, as well as author Michael Crichton and poet T. S. Eliot.

Harvard's Most Famous Graduates

George W. Bush (1946–)

Jurassic Park author and *ER* creator Michael Crichton (1942–2008)

Questions

_____ 1. The article is mostly about ______.

a. a town
b. a school
c. a person
d. an event

_____ 2. The second and third paragraphs mostly discuss ______.

a. Harvard's future
b. Harvard's facilities
c. Harvard's current president
d. Harvard's history

_____ 3. The final paragraph is mostly about ______.

a. people
b. books
c. buildings
d. degrees

_____ 4. Another good title for this article would be ______.

a. How to Get into Harvard
b. The Founding of Harvard University
c. The Best University There Is
d. My Story of Harvard

_____ 5. The sixth paragraph is mostly about ______.

a. courses at Harvard
b. a library
c. a Harvard teacher
d. a useful skill

005 5 Bitten by a Snake!

milking a snake for the production of antivenin

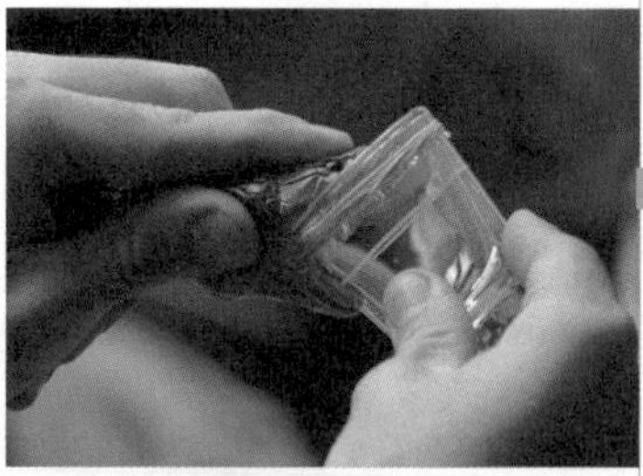

Venomous snakes often have brightly colored bodies and triangular heads.

1 Rob Coulter worked in South Africa as a game ranger. He knew the animals, insects, and reptiles of Africa very well. Rob knew them so well that he became careless.

2 One night, while camping alone, Rob reached out to pick up a large piece of wood and felt something hit his arm. Rob didn't think much about it, but a little later, his arm began to ache. When he looked closely at it, he saw two fang marks in the skin of his arm. He realized that a venomous snake had bitten him. His pulse became rapid.

3 Rob's mind raced as he thought about what he had to do to survive. Rob knew that he should remain calm, stay still, keep the injured arm below the level of his heart, and avoid eating or drinking anything, especially anything with alcohol in it. He also knew that cutting the wound to suck the poison out was a bad idea.

4 He used his two-way radio to call for help. As he waited, he washed the bite with soap and water. To help slow the spread of the venom, he wrapped a bandage around his arm two inches above the bite. The band was loose enough to slip a finger under it so that it would not cut off the flow of blood from the veins. After about half an hour, his friend Mike arrived. Mike took Rob to the local hospital, where Rob was given antivenin—an antidote to snake venom.

5 Rob still enjoys camping, but he is now very, very careful not to disturb snakes.

How to Treat a Snakebite

Avoid eating or drinking anything.

Keep the wound below the heart.

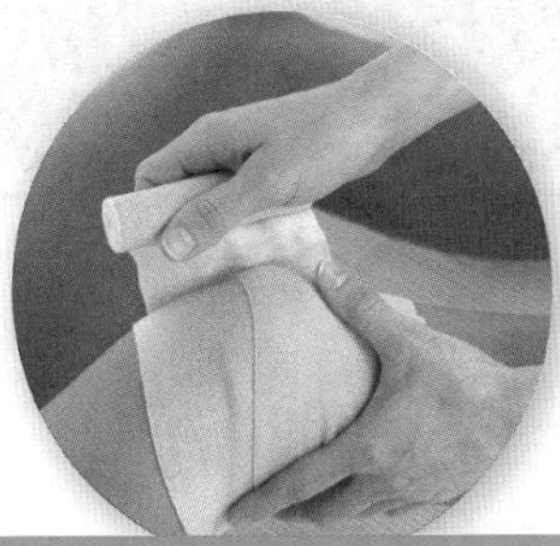
Wrap a tight but not uncomfortable bandage two inches above the bite site.

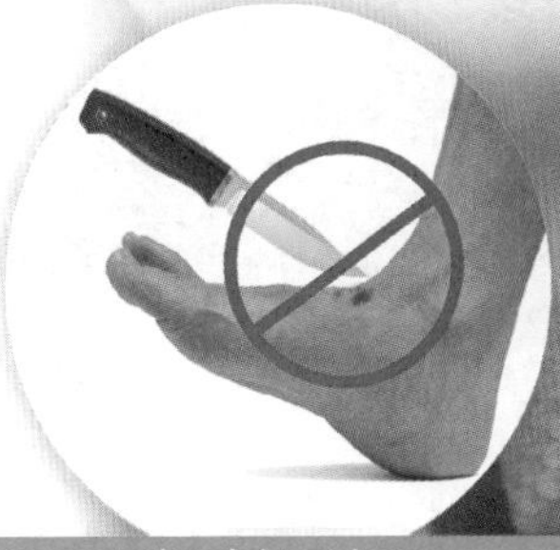
Do not cut the bite site or use your mouth to suck out the poison.

Questions

_____1. This article is mostly about ______.

a. a place **b.** a person
c. an event **d.** a type of animal

_____2. This article deals mostly with ______.

a. Something negative or unpleasant
b. Something positive or pleasant
c. Something neutral
d. Something that could be positive or negative

_____3. The information in this article is about ______.

a. the future **b.** the present
c. the past **d.** the past and the future

_____4. The first paragraph is mostly about ______.

a. an event **b.** a person
c. a place **d.** a time

_____5. Another good title for this article would be ______.

a. When Danger Strikes
b. The Life of a Game Ranger
c. Snakes in South Africa
d. How to Avoid Snakes

1-2 Main Idea

The main idea of a text (whether an essay or a paragraph) is the key message it tries to convey. This might be an opinion or a fact. A text about cats could have different main ideas: "cats are good pets" or "cats are mysterious." The main idea is often expressed in a thesis statement.

BattleBots is an American company that hosts robot competitions.

6 BattleBots: Let the Games Begin!

006

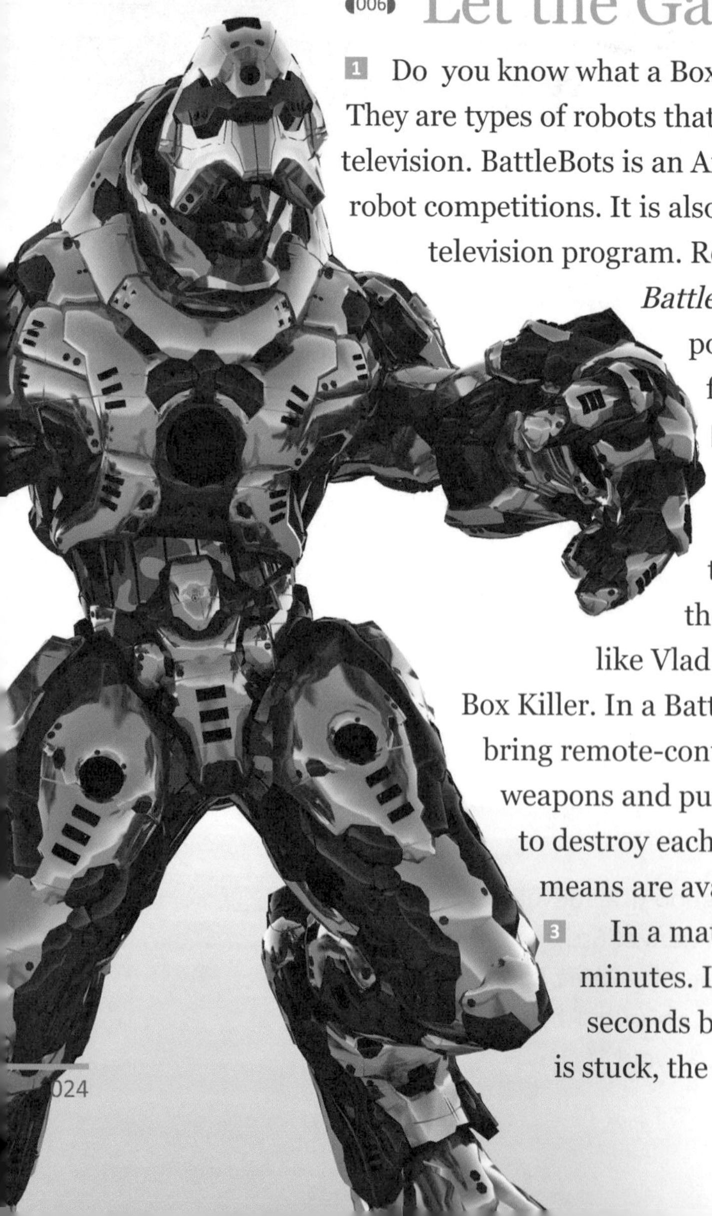

1 Do you know what a Boxbot, Flipper, or Thwackbot is? They are types of robots that are built to fight one another on television. BattleBots is an American company that hosts these robot competitions. It is also the name of a robot-fighting television program. Robot-fighting programs like *BattleBots* and *Robot Wars* have become popular all over the world. Millions of fans watch these programs.

2 Teams of engineers design and build robots that can cost up to US$50,000 and enter them into those television contests. They give their machines scary or silly names like Vlad the Impaler, The Judge, and Cereal Box Killer. In a BattleBots competition, competitors bring remote-controlled, armored robots armed with weapons and put them into an arena to do their best to destroy each other. The robots use whatever means are available in the fight.

3 In a match, the robots fight for three minutes. If one robot cannot move for 30 seconds because it has been damaged or is stuck, the other robot wins. If both robots

survive the fight, three judges choose a winner. They judge based on which robot has gained the higher score according to three categories: aggression (how bravely a robot fights), strategy (how well a robot attacks the other robot's weaknesses, protects its own, and handles danger), and damage (how much damage a robot can inflict upon its opponent while remaining intact itself). Players can call a "tap-out" if their robot is about to be destroyed. This means that they lose the competition but save their robot from destruction.

4 The popularity of BattleBots in the United States is not as strong as it was in the beginning, but it remains popular in many other parts of the world.

Questions

_____ 1. What is the main idea of this article?
- **a.** There are many robot programs on TV.
- **b.** BattleBots are dangerous and should be banned.
- **c.** BattleBot competitions are popular and organized.
- **d.** The BattleBots engineers are interesting people.

_____ 2. What does the second paragraph mostly describe?
- **a.** The fighting robots.
- **b.** The engineers.
- **c.** The TV shows.
- **d.** The BattleBots fans.

_____ 3. What does the third paragraph mostly describe?
- **a.** The fighting robots.
- **b.** The robot battles.
- **c.** The BattleBots fans.
- **d.** The history of BattleBots.

_____ 4. Which sentence from the article is closest to the main point?
- **a.** "BattleBots is an American company that hosts these robot competitions."
- **b.** "Competitors bring . . . robots armed with weapons and put them into an arena to do their best to destroy each other."
- **c.** "The popularity of BattleBots in the United States is not as strong as it was in the beginning."
- **d.** "Millions of fans watch these programs."

_____ 5. What is closest to the main point the author wants to make?
- **a.** Fighting robots are complicated and expensive to make.
- **b.** The man who makes BattleBots is important.
- **c.** The *BattleBots* TV program should be cancelled.
- **d.** BattleBots and their competitions are complex and interesting.

In a BattleBots competition, armored robots armed with weapons fight for three minutes. (cc by AnnieCatBlue)

"White noise" image

007

7 White Noise?

1 Have you ever noticed how, on a rainy night, all other sounds seem to disappear? The sound of the rain drowns them out. And even though the sound of the rain goes on all night, it doesn't keep you awake. Rain is a kind of white noise—a steady, unchanging, unobtrusive sound.

2 White noise is made up of sounds from all the frequencies a human ear can hear, with the sound at each frequency having equal power. It's called "white" because the definition is like that of white light, which is a combination of all the light wavelengths we can see. You might think that a combination of all possible sound frequencies would be terrible, but it's not—quite the opposite. The reason for this is that white noise masks other sounds. Think of it like the rain: the sound of one drop falling, like from a leaky tap, would be very distinct and annoying. Two drops would be the same. You could even tell three steady drips apart. But if there were five or 10 or 1,000, you couldn't pick out each individual drip. They'd all blend into a sort of hum or a quiet roar and probably lull you to sleep.

White noise has proved to be useful in alleviating migraines for some people.

3 The calming properties of white noise are starting to be used to treat different problems. White noise can help restless people

Rain is a kind of white noise.

sleep and help migraine sufferers sleep through their pain. It can be very useful for people with attention deficit disorders, who have trouble tuning out background noise. White noise can help them concentrate. It's even used to mask the sound of individual conversations by therapists and others who want to maintain privacy. Who would have thought that mashing lots of sounds together would actually turn out to promote peace and quiet?

Questions

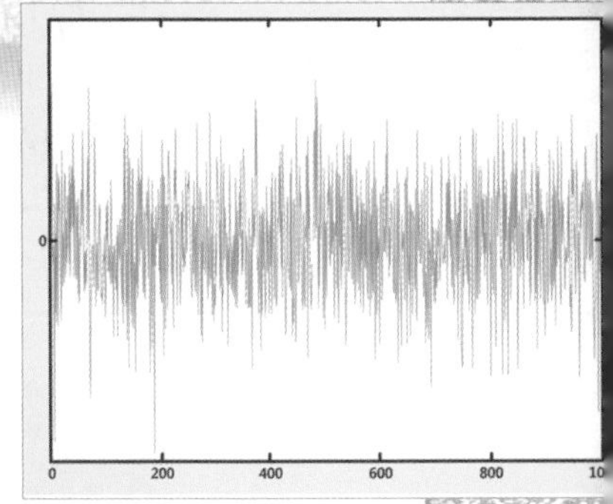

» White Gaussian noise signal (cc by Morn)

_____ 1. What is the main idea of this article?
- **a.** White noise is a soothing sound.
- **b.** White noise is important for privacy.
- **c.** White noise is a dangerous phenomenon.
- **d.** White noise is important.

_____ 2. Each of the statements below is similar to one from the article. Which statement below best expresses the main idea?
- **a.** The calming properties of white noise are used to treat sleep problems.
- **b.** You might think that hearing many sounds together would be terrible, but it's not!
- **c.** Rain is a kind of white noise–a steady, unchanging, unobtrusive sound.
- **d.** Have you ever noticed how, on a rainy night, all other sounds seem to disappear?

_____ 3. The main point of this article is ______.
- **a.** that white noise is terrible
- **b.** that white noise is a myth
- **c.** that white noise should be more important
- **d.** that white noise is positive

_____ 4. What is the second paragraph mostly about?
- **a.** Describing what white noise is.
- **b.** Describing the effect of white noise.
- **c.** Describing pros and cons of white noise.
- **d.** Describing the history of white noise.

_____ 5. What is the third paragraph mostly about?
- **a.** The effects of white noise.
- **b.** Problems with white noise.
- **c.** Studies about white noise.
- **d.** The history of white noise.

008

8 JOKES

LOL!

1 Jokes are things we say to make other people laugh. Sometimes a joke is a short remark, while other times it can be a story that can take some time to tell. There are lots of ways that jokes make people laugh.

2 Here are examples of two simple jokes:

Why do birds fly south?
Because it's too far to walk.

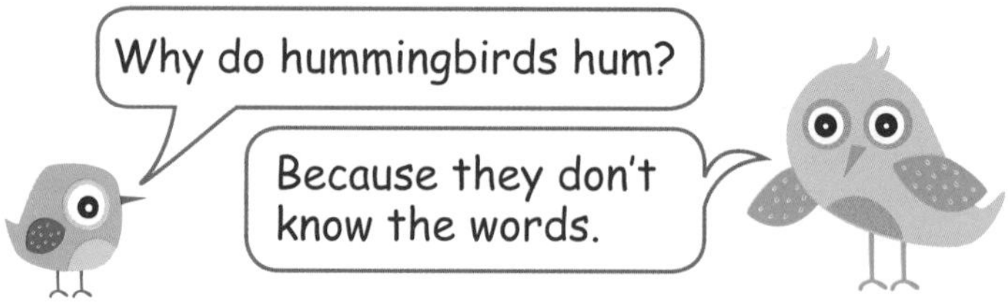

Why do hummingbirds hum?
Because they don't know the words.

3 Most people like to laugh, and people who tell jokes well are often popular. But there's more to a joke than just the words; a joke depends on the way it is told. Jokes depend on building suspense. The humor in many jokes also depends on using the element of surprise, so the joker has to be a good actor. Some people have a knack for telling jokes; others don't.

4 Not all jokes can be saved by the way they are told, however. We say a joke is "corny" if it's not funny or if it's stupid. This is a corny joke:

Why did the chicken cross the road?
To get to the other side.

Of course, some people, like me, really like corny jokes!

5 Every language and culture has its own jokes, and many jokes lose their humor when translated into a different language or

cultural context. Some jokes rely on sarcasm or irony to be funny. However, these jokes can be rude or insulting.

6 Sometimes jokes are told about certain races and religions. These are called "racial" and "religious" jokes, and they can be insulting, too. Jokes about the supposed special characteristics of a gender are often called "sexist." Hurting people's feelings really shouldn't be funny. There are plenty of other ways to make people laugh. Have you heard a good joke lately?

Questions

_____ 1. What is the main idea of this article?
- **a.** Jokes about birds are funny in every culture.
- **b.** The best jokes in the world are religious jokes.
- **c.** There are certain techniques that make jokes funny.
- **d.** Jokes have been popular throughout history.

_____ 2. What is a joke?
- **a.** Something that talks about race or religion.
- **b.** Something that people say to make others laugh.
- **c.** A way to get people to agree on a subject.
- **d.** Something that people write down for history.

_____ 3. Which paragraph has a sentence that best expresses the main idea?
- **a.** The first paragraph. **b.** The second paragraph.
- **c.** The third paragraph. **d.** The final paragraph.

_____ 4. What is the third paragraph (beginning with Most people like to laugh) mostly about?
- **a.** Joking and culture. **b.** Examples of good jokes.
- **c.** What makes a joke rude. **d.** How to tell a joke well.

_____ 5. What is true about jokes?
- **a.** Jokes are simple.
- **b.** Jokes are never insulting.
- **c.** Culture has an impact on jokes.
- **d.** Some cultures are not funny.

009 9 Cold Feet

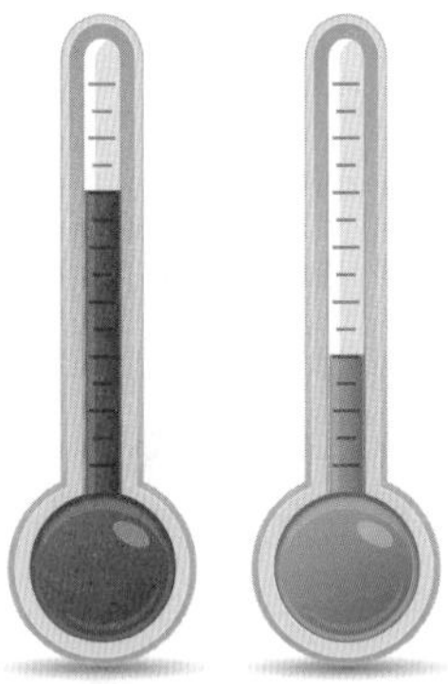

Some people may experience a drop in foot temperature when they are afraid.

1 A bride who can't make herself walk down the aisle at her wedding; a person who has paid a lot of money for a skydiving trip who then won't jump out of the plane; a person who requests a karaoke song, but then doesn't want to get up to sing: What do they have in common? Cold feet.

2 In English, we say someone "has cold feet" when they suddenly get nervous about doing something they have planned. The phrase describes a situation where someone is afraid to do something he or she was previously excited about. Usually, it means the fear is unjustified, people usually get over their cold feet because their desire is stronger than their fear.

3 The term "cold feet" is an idiom, but is it based in reality? Research says yes. The American TV show *MythBusters* put three people in situations that scared them and measured the temperature of their feet. One took a scary stunt plane ride, one was covered in spiders, and one ate some insects. For two out of the three, the temperature of their feet dropped sharply when they became afraid.

4 The researchers think this has to do with something called the "fight or flight" response. When we're scared, our body prepares to fight or run away. More blood goes to our muscles, preparing for action. In our skin and other organs, blood vessels constrict, so we'll bleed less if we get injured. When the fight or flight instinct kicks in, the small muscles in our feet get less blood. This means our feet often really do cool off when we're afraid.

5 Should we wear thick socks when we think we'll be nervous? Probably not. Push through your fear and your chilly feet will be just fine.

Someone who has "cold feet" backs out of a situation or a commitment because he/she feels afraid.

« Push through your fear, and you can overcome cold feet.

Questions

____ 1. What is this article about?

a. A strange effect.
b. A strange body part.
c. A strange place.
d. A strange culture.

____ 2. Which sentence expresses the main idea of this article?

a. Idioms are not connected to reality.
b. The phrase "cold feet" means danger.
c. This idiom is related to a physical reaction.
d. There are many ways to avoid getting "cold feet."

____ 3. Which sentence best expresses the main idea about **cold feet**?

a. Idioms can inform you about what your body does.
b. The mind and the body are separate things.
c. "Cold feet" exists in all times and cultures.
d. Research shows that "cold feet" is more than just an expression.

____ 4. What does the second paragraph mostly describe?

a. How a theory was tested.
b. The author's personal experience.
c. What a phrase means.
d. The author's opinion.

____ 5. What is true about **cold feet**?

a. They happen when you are afraid.
b. They can do you harm.
c. They are a myth.
d. They only occur in Western cultures.

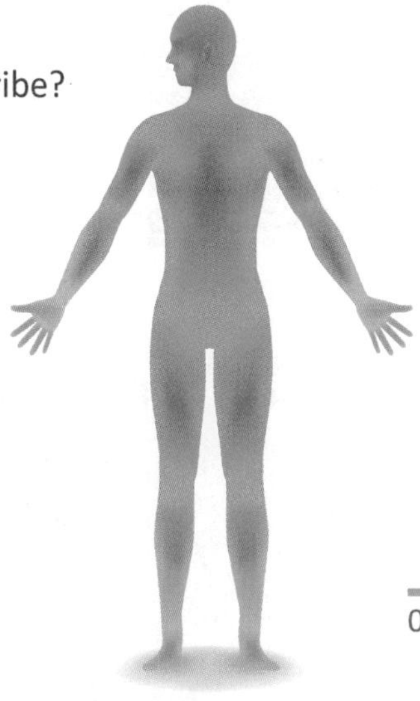

Shakespeare's birthplace in Stratford-upon-Avon, England

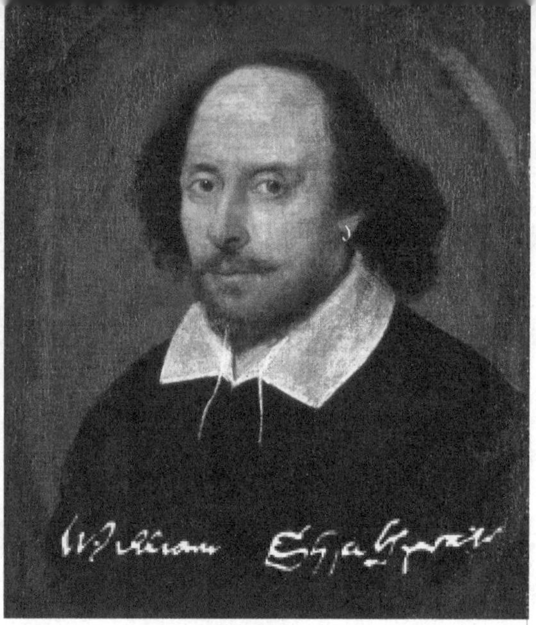

William Shakespeare (1564–1616)

10 The Life and Works of William Shakespeare

010

1 William Shakespeare is widely regarded as the most famous writer and poet in the English language and the world's pre-eminent playwright. He was born in England in 1564 and died in 1616. The works he left behind consist of 38 plays, 154 sonnets (a poem that must be 14 lines long and have a particular style), two long narrative poems, and many other poems.

2 Shakespeare is most famous for his plays, which have been translated into every major living language and are performed more often than those of any other dramatist. Some of his well-known plays include *A Midsummer Night's Dream, The Merchant of Venice, Hamlet, Romeo and Juliet, King Lear, Macbeth*, and *The Tempest*. His work remains popular with many people who enjoy reading classical English. University students who study English usually have to study at least one of Shakespeare's plays.

3 Shakespeare married a 26-year-old woman when he was only 18. Between 1585 and 1592, he began his career in London as an actor, a playwright, and part owner of the theater company the Lord Chamberlain's Men. It was in London that he wrote most of his plays. Although he was well-known and successful in his own day, he was not as famous as he is today.

4 After William Shakespeare's death, his fame continued to grow until he was considered to be the best poet and writer of his time, a status that he still retains today.

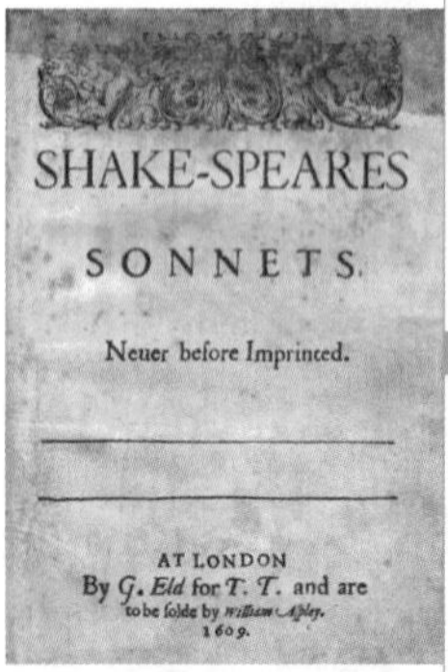
SHAKE-SPEARES

SONNETS.

Neuer before Imprinted.

AT LONDON

By *G. Eld* for *T. T.* and are to be solde by *William Aspley*.

1609.

title page of Shakespeare's sonnets

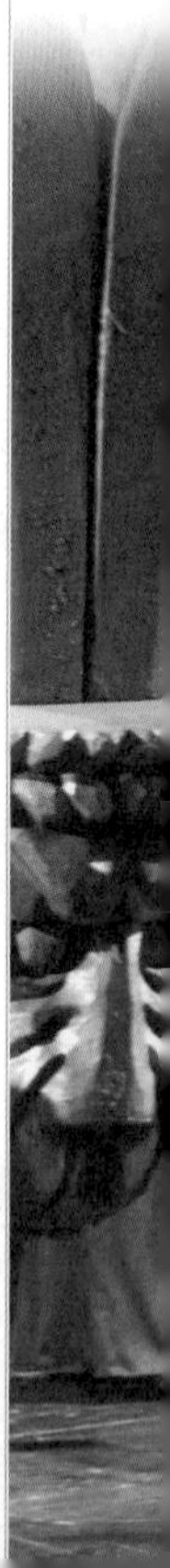

Questions

Shakespeare's funerary monument in Stratford-upon-Avon, England

Shakespeare's grave in Stratford-upon-Avon, England
(cc by David Jones)

_____ 1. What is this article mostly about?
   a. A writer's works. **b.** A period of history.
   c. A man's family. **d.** An event.

_____ 2. Who was William Shakespeare?
   a. A famous contemporary author.
   b. An unknown writer from the past.
   c. The world's best-known English writer.
   d. A writer who has inspired controversy.

_____ 3. Which is closest to the main idea of this article?
   a. William Shakespeare led an interesting life.
   b. William Shakespeare's incredible writing remains popular today.
   c. William Shakespeare is not as famous as he deserves to be.
   d. William Shakespeare's life and times influenced his writing.

_____ 4. Where can you find information about Shakespeare's life?
   a. In the first paragraph. **b.** In the second paragraph.
   c. In the third paragraph. **d.** In the final paragraph.

_____ 5. This article is intended as ______.
   a. a comparison of different works by Shakespeare
   b. a look at Shakespeare's most famous plays
   c. a detailed examination of Shakespeare's life
   d. an overview of Shakespeare's writing and life

a production of William Shakespeare's *Hamlet*

1-3 Supporting Details

Think of supporting details as the material that a writer uses to build up the main idea of an article. They can be facts, similes, explanations, descriptions, comparisons, examples, or anything else that supports the message of the main idea. Don't look for just one supporting detail in an article because there's usually quite a few.

new Agua Clara locks (Atlantic side) of the Panama Canal expansion project

11 The Canal That Connects Two Oceans

011

Have you ever wondered how ships get from the Atlantic Ocean to the Pacific Ocean? Prior to 1914, ships had to sail via the Drake Passage and Cape Horn at the southern tip of South America. It was a long trip that involved strong winds, large waves, strong currents, and even icebergs, which made the route very dangerous for ships.

A canal that would connect the Atlantic and Pacific Oceans was the logical answer to make the route shorter and safer. Panama was chosen because it was the narrowest country in the Americas. The French started building the canal in 1881 but failed. An estimated 22,000 people died from disease and accidents. In 1904, the United States took over the building of the canal. They used a system of locks to solve the problem of building a canal through areas with different levels of elevation. The Panama Canal opened in 1914. The 82-kilometer (51-mile) canal made travel by ship much safer, although a total of 27,600 people had died while building it. The United States handed management of the canal over to Panama in 1977. By then, it had long been an essential route for shipping cargo around the world.

Panama Canal locks

Panama on the globe (cc by TUBS)

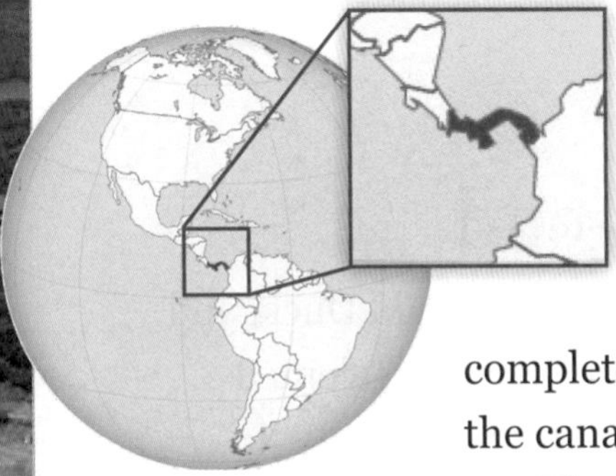

Throughout the 20th century, increasingly larger ships were being used to transport cargo. Therefore, Panama decided to expand the canal so these larger ships could fit through it. After spending US$5.25 billion, the expansion was completed in 2016. This expansion widened and deepened the canal to allow passage of the new larger cargo ships.

The Panama Canal was a bold project that sought to make travel and shipping both safer and more efficient. It also became an essential part of world shipping routes. From its inception to its completion and later expansion, the canal may be considered a modern technological marvel, which has permanently changed the pattern of sea travel.

Questions

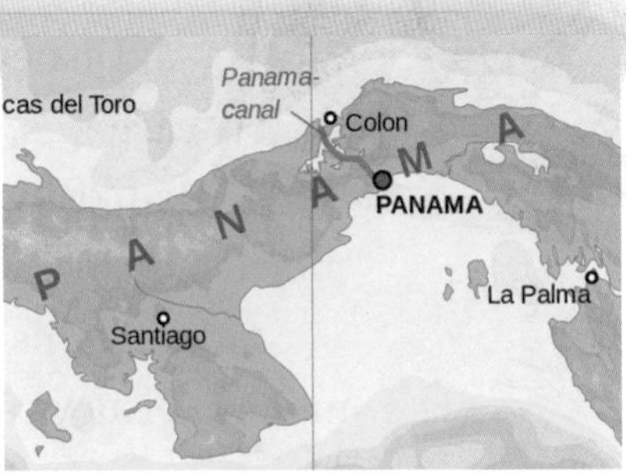

Panama Canal on the map (cc by Kaidor)

_____ 1. Which of the following is true?
- **a.** Britain built the Panama Canal.
- **b.** France completed the Panama Canal.
- **c.** The United States completed the Panama Canal.
- **d.** Panama built the Panama Canal for the French.

_____ 2. Where is the Panama Canal located?
- **a.** In Africa. **b.** In the Americas. **c.** In Europe. **d.** In Asia.

_____ 3. Which of the following statements is NOT true?
- **a.** The canal's expansion was completed in 2016.
- **b.** The Drake Passage was a dangerous sea route.
- **c.** The canal connects the Atlantic and Pacific Oceans.
- **d.** The canal is over 100 kilometers long.

_____ 4. How did shipping change during the 20th century?
- **a.** Planes became the preferred method of transporting cargo.
- **b.** Larger ships were used to transport cargo.
- **c.** Technology made the Drake Passage a better shipping route.
- **d.** International trade decreased.

_____ 5. What year did the Panama Canal open?
- **a.** 1950 **b.** 1881 **c.** 1914 **d.** 2016

12 Walt Disney — Hollywood Legend

012

Walter Elias Disney (1901–1966)

Everyone has heard of Mickey Mouse, Donald Duck, and Pluto. They are the inventions of Walt Disney, a talented screenwriter, filmmaker, voice actor, animator, and entrepreneur.

Walter Elias Disney was born in Chicago in 1901. During his lifetime, he created some of the most famous characters that have ever appeared on film. He is also the namesake for Disneyland and Walt Disney World Resort theme parks in the United States, Japan, France, and China.

Disney began his career in Kansas City making short cartoons, but it wasn't long before his company went bankrupt. Afterward, he decided to set up a studio in the movie industry's capital city—Hollywood, California.

Although his first Hollywood movies did not make much money, Disney refused to give up. In 1928, he created Mickey Mouse and a star was born. Mickey's first animated cartoon with sound was *Steamboat Willie*, and it was very successful. It was so popular that Walt Disney decided to use sound in all of his subsequent cartoons and movies. Disney himself did the voice of Mickey Mouse until 1947.

Walt Disney's animation company went on to make several masterpieces like *Snow White and the Seven Dwarfs* and *Bambi*. In 1932, Walt Disney received a special Academy Award for

Walt Disney World Resort in Florida

Snow White and the Seven Dwarfs

creating Mickey Mouse. During his lifetime he received 59 Academy Award nominations and 26 Oscars. Many doubt that any other moviemaker will ever have as much influence as Walt Disney.

Walt Disney died of lung cancer on December 15, 1966, a few years before the opening of the Walt Disney World Resort in Florida.

Today, the company he cofounded, the Walt Disney Company, has annual revenues of over US$55 billion. It has become one of the most famous and profitable motion picture companies in the world.

It's hard to find someone who hasn't seen one of Walt Disney's movies or cartoons. His creativity and hard work have brought joy, fun, and laughter to children and adults everywhere.

Bambi »

Questions

Walt Disney characters *(from left to right)* Minnie Mouse, Mickey Mouse, Donald Duck

_____1. Which of the following statements is true?
   - **a.** Walt Disney was born in Chicago.
   - **b.** Walt Disney was a Canadian immigrant.
   - **c.** Walt Disney died poor.
   - **d.** Walt Disney did the voice for Donald Duck.

_____2. Which of the following statements is NOT true?
   - **a.** Walt Disney was a voice actor.
   - **b.** Walt Disney won several Oscars.
   - **c.** Walt Disney used to live and work in Kansas City.
   - **d.** Mickey Mouse was Disney's first character.

_____3. When did Walt Disney's luck start to change?
   - **a.** When he moved to Hollywood.
   - **b.** When he started making cartoons.
   - **c.** When he created Mickey Mouse.
   - **d.** When he gave up drinking alcohol.

_____4. The first Mickey Mouse cartoon with sound was ______.
   - **a.** *Bambi* **b.** *Steamboat Willie*
   - **c.** *Fantasia* **d.** *101 Dalmatians*

_____5. Walt Disney originally provided the voice for ______.
   - **a.** Mickey Mouse **b.** Bambi
   - **c.** Pluto **d.** Donald Duck

⌃ Rieko Ioane of New Zealand is tackled by Jesse Kriel of South Africa during the Castle Lager Rugby Championship Test in 2017.

13 Rugby Rules!

013

One man carrying a large oval-shaped ball is tackled by another man, or sometimes an entire team, and no protective equipment is worn. This is rugby, a game invented in England in 1871. The term "rugby" actually refers to two similar sports: Rugby League and Rugby Union.

In both sports, a team wins by earning the most points after 80 minutes of play. Teams score by either touching the ball to the ground in the scoring area at the end of the 100-meter rectangular field or by kicking the ball between the two goal posts. But scoring is difficult in this fast-paced and sometimes rough sport.

One reason it is difficult is that to move the ball forward, a player cannot simply throw the ball ahead. Instead, he's only allowed to throw the ball backwards to a teammate, who's also trying to run forward while avoiding being tackled by opponents that want to prevent him from reaching the goal.

What happens after a player is tackled is the main difference between the two sports. In Rugby League, after being tackled, the runner just stands up and uses his foot to pass the ball behind to a teammate, and the game continues. After six tackles though, the team must give the ball to the other team. In Rugby Union, there are two other possibilities. If a player is tackled by more than one person, there can be either a maul or a ruck. In either case, the teams use their biggest and strongest players to try and push the other team backwards. The winner of the push then gets the ball.

⌃ rugby ball (cc by NikRugby23!)

There is very little time to rest in rugby. Players are either running, passing, tackling, or pushing for the entire match. The difficult challenge in trying to score and the fast pace make the sport very entertaining to watch.

Questions

Rugby League player Kyle Paterson (cc by NAPARAZZI)

____ 1. Which sentence below best supports the idea that Rugby League is a faster game than Rugby Union?

a. The game does not have a maul or a ruck.
b. The players try to run forward.
c. The field is 100 meters long.
d. The rugby ball is oval-shaped.

____ 2. Which of the following best describes the difficulty of trying to score in Rugby?

a. Points are earned by touching the ball to the ground in the goal area.
b. Teams can earn points by kicking the ball between the goal posts.
c. The runner with the ball may be tackled by an entire team.
d. The team passes the ball backwards from player to player.

____ 3. According to the article, why is Rugby entertaining to watch?

a. The players have to throw the ball ahead instead of throwing it backwards.
b. Players are either running, passing, tackling, or pushing for the entire game.
c. The term rugby actually refers to two similar sports: Rugby League and Rugby Union.
d. The field is a rectangle shape with scoring areas at each end.

a maul (cc by Clément Bucco–Lechat)

____ 4. According to the passage, what is the main difference between Rugby League and Rugby Union?

a. Players in one sport wear no protective equipment, but they do in the other sport.
b. In both sports, a team must give up the ball after six tackles.
c. In each sport, the ball has a different shape.
d. What happens after a runner is tackled is different in each sport.

a ruck (cc by Clément Bucco–Lechat)

____ 5. In Rugby Union, why do both teams send out their biggest and strongest players?

a. To play rough so that the other team will get scared.
b. To push the other team backwards in order to get the ball.
c. To shorten the game time from 80 minutes to 40 minutes.
d. To stop the other team from kicking the ball between the goal posts.

14 Augmented Reality: Better Living Through Technology

014

Pokémon GO on iPhone

Augmented reality is something you will be hearing about more and more in the future. To augment something is to make it greater. Thus, augmented reality (or AR) is a technology that lets us see the real world in greater ways.

Think of smartphones that can take a recording and add computer images or sound to it in real time. This mixing of the real world and the virtual world is AR in a nutshell. AR also appears on television sports broadcasts and some video games, such as the popular Pokémon GO game from 2016. Technology companies are turning to AR to help people connect their online and real-world experiences. Thanks to this connection between worlds, the use of AR is expanding rapidly every year.

Some of the most exciting AR technologies are still in the process of being developed. One of these is the Magic Leap One AR system. A remote control, a small computer engine, and a pair of special glasses make the setup. They let Magic Leap One users see AR in the real space around them. A user might view a product in their house, have virtual meetings, or project games into the room. With this technology, users can move beyond their smartphones and take AR to a whole new level.

But AR is not only a convenient tool for playing games or shopping. In the future, it may help save lives. Doctors might use

Magic Leap One logo

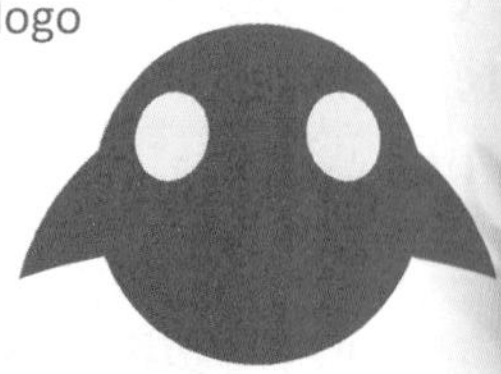

illustration of Magic Leap One

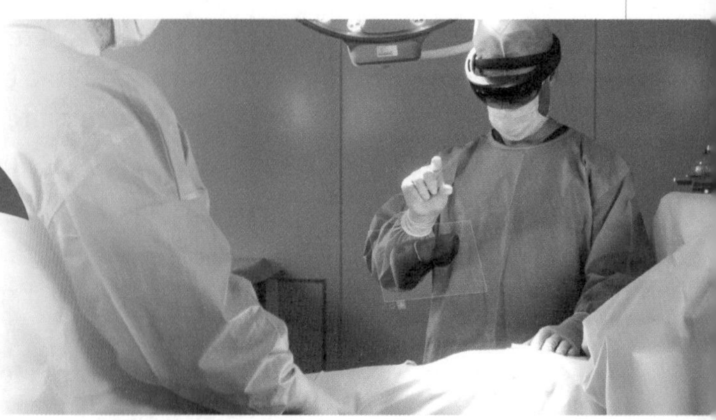

Surgeon using augmented-reality glasses to prepare for liver-tumor operation

AR to practice difficult operations without worrying about hurting a real patient. Cars can show heads-up displays that help drivers see important information without looking away from the road. What other things could AR help us do? With this kind of technology, the possibilities are endless.

heads-up display (HUD) of vehicle

Questions

_____ 1. Which of the following statements is true?
- **a.** Augmented reality has not been invented yet.
- **b.** Augmented reality is the same as the Internet.
- **c.** Many augmented reality technologies are in development.
- **d.** Augmented reality will replace reality.

_____ 2. Which of the following statements is NOT true?
- **a.** Augmented reality can be used to save lives.
- **b.** Some augmented reality technologies can be controlled by hand.
- **c.** Smartphones cannot perform augmented reality.
- **d.** Augmented reality puts computer images on top of the real world.

_____ 3. What is mentioned in the article as a way that augmented reality could possibly save lives?
- **a.** It can let doctors train for surgery without using a real body.
- **b.** It encourages you to go outside and play in the real world.
- **c.** It lets people have virtual meetings with other users.
- **d.** It can help soldiers scan the area where they are fighting.

_____ 4. According to the passage, what is another kind of technology that sometimes has augmented reality?
a. Books. **b.** Newspapers. **c.** Telephones. **d.** Video games.

_____ 5. Why are some technology companies choosing to use augmented reality?
- **a.** Augmented reality is better than virtual reality.
- **b.** Augmented reality links real-world and Internet experiences.
- **c.** Using augmented reality makes their customers happier.
- **d.** It's cheaper to use augmented reality than real world tools.

Maasai flag

Maasai men performing a traditional jumping dance

15 The Maasai

015

The Maasai tribe of Kenya and northern Tanzania is one of the most well-known tribes in Africa. Their distinct customs and way of dressing have changed very little in centuries. Many Maasai live a seminomadic lifestyle, which means they rarely settle down in one place for very long. They speak a language called Maa. Many of the Maasai also speak Swahili and English, which are the official languages of Kenya and Tanzania.

The Maasai use cattle as money.

Cattle are very important to the Maasai. They use cattle as money, which means they trade cattle to get the things they need. Cattle are also their primary source of food. Because of the importance of cattle in the Maasai society, cattle are often used to measure a man's wealth.

The Maasai believe that their god, Enkai, gave them all of the cattle in the world. If someone who isn't a Maasai has cattle, the Maasai believe that the individual must have stolen those cattle from a Maasai. Therefore, they believe stealing cattle from other tribes is simply a rightful act of taking back what is theirs.

Maasai men do a famous jumping dance to show their strength. In traditional Maasai culture, young

men have to kill a lion before they can get married. Women have their own set of duties in traditional Maasai culture. They are responsible for cooking, raising the children, and building huts for their family to live in.

There are about 900,000 Maasai living in Kenya and Tanzania. Some of them no longer live in rural areas. They, like people from other tribes, have moved into towns and cities and live like many other people around the world. However, many Maasai still try to keep their traditional culture alive.

» a mother from the Maasai tribe holding her child (photo by U.S. Air Force Staff Sgt. Maria Bowman)

Questions

_____ **1.** Which of the following statements about the Maasai is true?
- **a.** They are a seminomadic tribe.
- **b.** They only trade in chickens.
- **c.** They don't believe in any gods.
- **d.** They can be found in Sudan.

_____ **2.** Which of the following statements about the Maasai is NOT true?
- **a.** They have a unique traditional culture.
- **b.** They often speak several languages.
- **c.** Men have to kill a lion before they can marry.
- **d.** They have always built cities.

_____ **3.** Why do the Maasai believe that they can steal cattle from other tribes?
- **a.** Because they are the fiercest warriors on the continent.
- **b.** Because only they can truly understand the mind of a cow.
- **c.** Because a god declared that all cattle belong to them.
- **d.** Because they will pay the other tribe back in the future.

_____ **4.** If you want to know how important a man is in Maasai society, then count his ______.
- **a.** money **b.** cattle
- **c.** houses **d.** wives

_____ **5.** In traditional Maasai culture, men show their strength by ______.
- **a.** fighting cattle **b.** dancing
- **c.** holding their breath **d.** eating a lion

» Maasai man

1-4 Sequencing

Understanding the order of events in what you read is very important. Imagine if you tried to tie your shoes before you put them on. When trying to understand the order of information, look for words like *before, after, next, then, later, previously,* or other time markers.

Arabian camel

16 Camels: The Ships of the Desert

016

Camels are called the "ships of the desert." Why? Well, like ships that carry goods and people across oceans, camels carry goods and people across deserts. They are very important to people who live in the deserts.

Camels have been evolving for ages. The first camels appeared in North America, 40 or 45 million years ago. Around five million years ago, they crossed a land bridge into Asia and never came back. Camels have since died out in North America. There are now two types of camels: the dromedary or Arabian camel, which has one hump, and the Bactrian camel, which has two. They all eventually became well adapted to life in the desert. Their feet evolved to be good for walking on the hot desert sand, and their bodies adapted to live for weeks without drinking water. Their fur is short and thick to protect them against sunburn and against sand storms. Also, their long eyelashes keep sand out of their eyes.

Bactrian camel

These useful creatures are kept by people as beasts of burden in harsh climates. Humans quickly discovered how useful they are; camels may have been used by humans in the Middle East and China as early as 4000 BC. They were being used in Central Asia and Africa around 2000 BC. People also keep camels for their milk and meat. Camel milk is said to be richer in fat and protein than cow's milk. Camel meat has been eaten for centuries in Somalia, Saudi Arabia, Egypt, Libya, Sudan, Kazakhstan, and other arid regions. In some regions, camel blood is regarded as a good source of iron, vitamin D, salt, and minerals.

Camels are well known for their bad tempers, and they often show their anger by making a loud grunting sound. Nonetheless, they are so important that their owners don't mind. A camel can stand between life and death in the desert. Who cares about their bad moods?

Questions

_____ 1. What happened before camels crossed a land bridge to Asia?
- **a.** They were used by human beings.
- **b.** They were known for their bad tempers.
- **c.** They lived in North America.
- **d.** They were called "ships of the desert."

_____ 2. What happened first?
- **a.** Camels were eaten in Somalia.
- **b.** Camels were used in China.
- **c.** Camels died out in North America.
- **d.** Camels crossed a land bridge.

_____ 3. What had to happen before camels were used in the Middle East?
- **a.** They had to leave North America.
- **b.** There had to be two types of camels.
- **c.** They had to be eaten in China.
- **d.** They had to die out in North America.

_____ 4. Which of the following happened first?
- **a.** Camels began evolving.
- **b.** Camels were used for milk.
- **c.** Camels were used for transportation.
- **d.** Camels were called ships of the desert.

_____ 5. Which of the following happened last?
- **a.** Camels died out in North America.
- **b.** Camels crossed a land bridge to Asia.
- **c.** Camels were domesticated in China.
- **d.** Camels were domesticated in Africa.

» Grand Ole Opry House in Nashville, Tennessee (cc by Ron Cogswell)

» The Grand Ole Opry, a weekly country music stage concert in Nashville, founded on November, 1925 as a one-hour radio "barn dance" on WSM (cc by Lucashoge44)

17 Nashville: Music City USA

017

When James Robertson founded a village on the Cumberland River in 1779, he must have been singing a country tune. After all, this was the future site of one of the most musical places in the world.

Robertson's village was made an official city in 1806. It was called "Nashville" after Francis Nash, a famous general in the American Revolutionary War. Before long, the new city had grown into a major manufacturing and railroad center. In 1843, it became the capital of the state of Tennessee. And though Nashville saw terrible fighting during the American Civil War, music was always in the hearts of its people. During the war's darkest days, the Fisk Jubilee Singers was founded—a world-famous act that even performed for Queen Victoria.

^ neon signs in Lower Broadway Area of Nashville

But it was the spread of radio in the 1920s that really helped Nashville's music scene take off. In 1925, WSM was launched, the city's first full-power radio station. It was soon joined by WLAC, another station, in 1926. Together the two radio stations attracted talent from around the country. It didn't matter if you were a piano player, a singer, or a guitarist. If you wanted people to hear your music, you headed to Nashville.

Music in the region continued to develop its own style during the Great Depression years of the 1930s. We now know it as "country music." In 1947, Nashville had its first record that sold a million copies: Francis Craig's "Near You." In 1956, Elvis Presley recorded

» Cumberland River, Nashville, Tennessee

the Fisk Jubilee Singers in 1882

"Heartbreak Hotel," which quickly became his first number-one pop hit. Presley of course went on to become a country music icon and is still known as "The King." By 1958, people across the United States were talking about "the Nashville Sound." And to this day, there's a never-ending stream of hit country music with links to Nashville. Even country star Miley Cyrus was born and raised in the area, and often performs concerts there. Music was in the air at every point of Nashville's history. It's no wonder they call it Music City, USA.

Questions

_____ 1. Which of the following happened first?
- **a.** Francis Craig's record sold over a million copies.
- **b.** The WLAC radio station was founded.
- **c.** The WSM radio station was founded.
- **d.** Nashville's style developed during the Great Depression.

_____ 2. What happened before Nashville was made an official city?
- **a.** Fighting broke out in Nashville during the civil war.
- **b.** James Robertson founded a village on the Cumberland River.
- **c.** Nashville grew into a manufacturing and railroad center.
- **d.** Nashville's music scene really began to take off.

_____ 3. Which two things happened at the same time?
- **a.** The civil war, and the Great Depression.
- **b.** The founding of the WLAC radio station, and the civil war.
- **c.** The civil war, and the founding of the Fisk Jubilee Singers.
- **d.** The founding of the Fisk Jubilee Singers, and the American Revolutionary War.

_____ 4. What happened after the WLAC radio station was founded?
- **a.** Nashville was made an official city.
- **b.** Musical talent began to arrive in Nashville.
- **c.** WSM was launched.
- **d.** Francis Nash died in the American Revolutionary War.

_____ 5. What happened most recently?
- **a.** The WLAC radio station was founded.
- **b.** The Great Depression happened.
- **c.** Nashville had its first million-selling record.
- **d.** People began talking about "the Nashville Sound."

18 Obesity

018

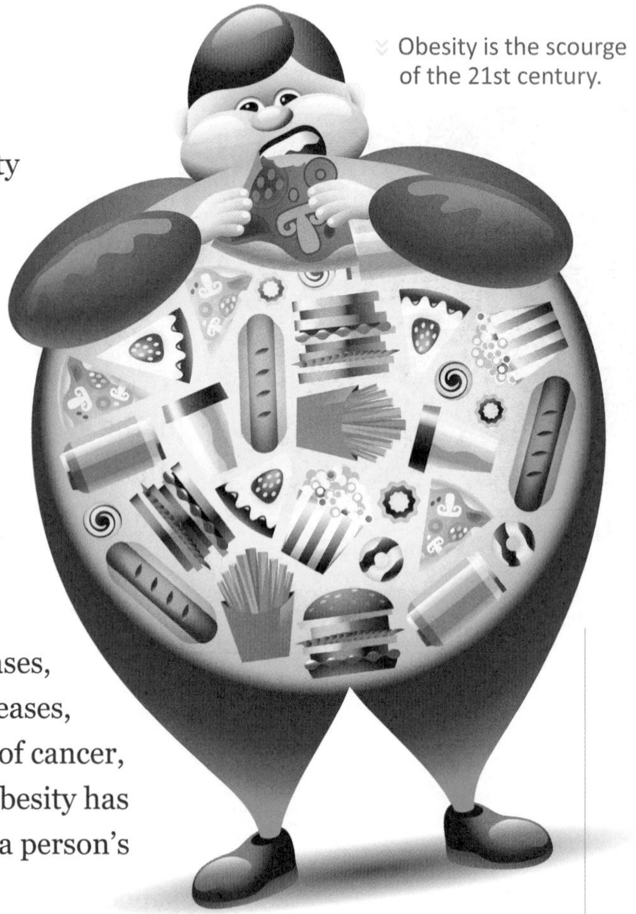

Obesity is the scourge of the 21st century.

Doctors say that obesity is the scourge of the 21st century. But what is obesity?

A person who is obese is too heavy. The problem of being overweight is caused by an excessive accumulation of fat. Research shows that obesity may cause or contribute to various diseases, such as cardiovascular diseases, sleep apnea, certain types of cancer, gout, and osteoarthritis. Obesity has also been found to reduce a person's life expectancy.

A person's "BMI" (body mass index) can show if a person is obese. BMI is calculated by dividing an individual's weight in kilograms by the square of his or her height in meters. Someone who weighs 80 kilograms and is 1.6 meters tall will have a BMI of 31.25. A BMI of between 18.5 and 24 is said to be healthy. If it's more than 30, the person is probably obese.

In the past, it was considered beautiful to be heavy, because it meant you had enough food. Now, obesity has become a serious public health problem. Between the 1980s and today, the number of obese people in the United States has jumped. For the first time in human history, there are now more overweight people than

Junk food makes us tired.

people who are starving. Obese people may need medical care more often than people with a healthy weight, so obesity is very expensive for societies.

Why are so many people obese? There are many reasons, but generally, we eat too much food and don't exercise enough. The types of food we eat also have an impact. Sugary, processed foods give us a rush without actually providing much nutrition. They can also be addictive. It's also hard to exercise when the junk food we eat doesn't give us energy and makes us tired.

But we can take control. As individuals and societies, we should take a hard look at our choices and make some changes.

Questions

_____ 1. Which comes first when becoming obese?
- **a.** A person is obese.
- **b.** A person accumulates too much fat.
- **c.** A person has a high BMI.
- **d.** A person develops cardiovascular disease.

_____ 2. What happens first in the process of obesity?
- **a.** A person lives a short life.
- **b.** A person has a high BMI.
- **c.** A person becomes overweight.
- **d.** A person develops gout.

_____ 3. What happened most recently?
- **a.** Obesity numbers went up quickly.
- **b.** We eat too much and don't exercise.
- **c.** Obesity is an expensive problem.
- **d.** It is good to be heavy.

_____ 4. According to the article, which happened first?
- **a.** More people are starving than overweight.
- **b.** More people are overweight than starving.
- **c.** Obesity becomes an expensive problem.
- **d.** Junk food leads to obesity.

_____ 5. What happened first in history?
- **a.** Obesity is expensive for societies.
- **b.** Obesity is a major public health problem.
- **c.** The number of American obese people jumped.
- **d.** It was beautiful to be fat.

Processed foods don't provide much nutrition.

19 The Brothers Grimm

019

You must have heard of "Hansel and Gretel," "Rapunzel," and "Cinderella." Although they are popular children's stories now, they were originally written for adults by two German brothers, Jacob and Wilhelm Grimm.

"Hansel and Gretel" is a warning tale for children.

The Grimm brothers were interested in fairy tales and folktales. They collected hundreds of the tales by talking to peasants and villagers. They published their first collection of 86 German fairy tales in a volume entitled *Children's and Household Tales* in 1812. In 1815 their second volume of 70 fairy tales was published. Between 1816 and 1818, they published two volumes of German folktales entitled *German Sagas*, which contain 585 German folktales.

Jacob and Wilhelm Grimm had more than just a personal interest in folk tales—they were university professors who studied folk stories seriously. A folktale, or a folk story, is a story, fairy tale, or legend that is circulated by word of mouth among the common people of a region. Folktales are usually very old stories that teach a lesson. For example, "Hansel and Gretel" teaches us not to be greedy. "Cinderella" teaches us that kindness is rewarded and cruelty is punished.

Wilhelm (1786–1859) *(left)* and Jacob Grimm (1785–1863) *(right)*

The Grimm brothers were probably the first to publish a large collection of folktales and the first to write so many of them down. Even after they were written down, the stories continued to change slightly as time passed. Some people thought the original tales were too frightening or violent for children, so later editions of the collection were edited to be more pleasant. The versions that we see today in books and movies are slightly different from the dark, original tales.

Thanks to the Brothers Grimm, these tales (in many versions) are used to entertain and to teach around the world.

Questions

_____ 1. What happened before the Grimm brothers published their book of 86 fairy tales?
   - **a.** The Grimm brothers talked to peasants.
   - **b.** The Grimm brothers published a book of 70 fairy tales.
   - **c.** The Grimm brothers wrote *German Sagas*.
   - **d.** The Grimm brothers changed their fairy tales.

_____ 2. What happened first?
   - **a.** The Grimm brothers' tales were edited for children.
   - **b.** The Grimm brothers' tales were written for adults.
   - **c.** The Grimm brothers published two volumes of fairy tales.
   - **d.** The Grimm brothers published 70 fairy tales.

_____ 3. What happened most recently?
   - **a.** The Grimm brothers published 70 fairy tales.
   - **b.** The Grimm brothers talked to peasants.
   - **c.** The Grimm brothers published 86 fairy tales.
   - **d.** The Grimm brothers published 585 fairy tales.

_____ 4. Which of the following happened first?
   - **a.** The Grimm brothers' fairy tales became world famous.
   - **b.** The Grimm brothers published a book of 70 fairy tales.
   - **c.** The Grimm brothers published a book of 86 fairy tales.
   - **d.** The Grimm brothers published a two volume collection.

_____ 5. What happened after people thought that some fairy tales were too violent?
   - **a.** The Grimm brothers' fairy tales were edited.
   - **b.** The Grimm brothers collected tales from peasants.
   - **c.** The Grimm brothers wrote fairy tales for adults.
   - **d.** The Grimm brothers published their collected fairy tales.

"Cinderella" teaches us that kindness is rewarded.
(cc by BagoGames)

Cuneiform is the first known form of written language.

20 The Importance of Language

020

Language is not just used for talking. It is our most important communication tool. Through language, we can tell other people what we think, how we feel, and what we need. Civilization itself depends on our ability to communicate.

Nobody knows exactly when people first started using language. Some scientists say that people first spoke to one another about two million years ago, while others say that the use of human language occurred only about 50,000 years ago.

Languages survive, grow, disappear, move from place to place, and change with time. Some languages are ancient; others are new. There are nearly 7,000 different living languages around the world today (though there are many different ways to count languages). Many thousands more are already extinct. These languages all sound different, but they are thought to have come from a single ancient language. English, for example, originally evolved out of the ancient Germanic language. Germanic evolved into three types, West Germanic, East Germanic, and North Germanic. From West Germanic came Old English, and then over time, today's modern English.

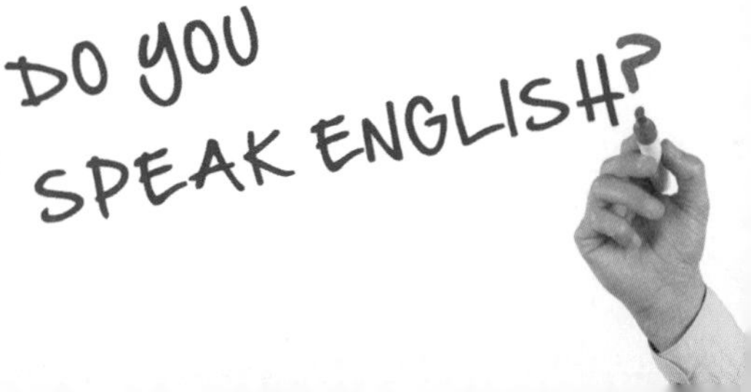

English is the most obvious example of lingua franca.

Today, languages are used not only for conversation, but also in the magazines, books, and movies that fill our libraries and bookstores. The long stories we can tell separate us from the great apes.

Throughout history, many languages have served as a lingua franca—a common language that could be used as a bridge between people of different cultures. Today, English is the main language that plays that role around the world. Over two billion people have some ability to use English. Most of these people have studied English as a second or third language.

Language helps people to cooperate, share knowledge, and build up modern societies. The development of humanity's many languages was an important process that helped humans create their civilizations.

Questions

_____ 1. What happened most recently?
- **a.** People used language two million years ago.
- **b.** People began communicating 50,000 years ago.
- **c.** Scientists disagree about the first use of language.
- **d.** Thousands of languages have become extinct.

_____ 2. Which event happened first?
- **a.** English became a lingua franca.
- **b.** Some languages became extinct.
- **c.** Languages were counted.
- **d.** One language divided into many.

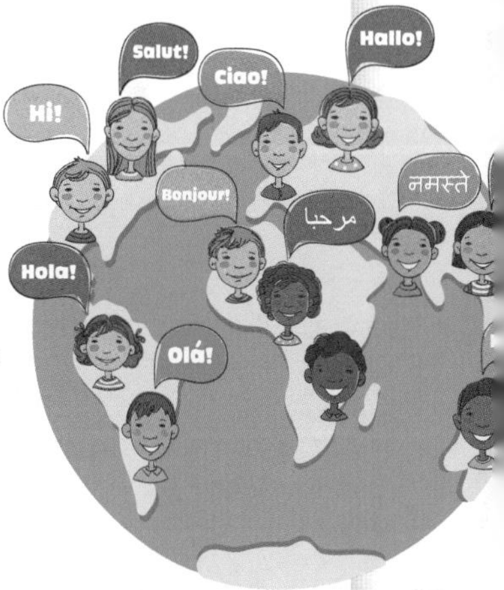

_____ 3. What happened to help develop human civilization?
- **a.** English became a lingua franca.
- **b.** Old languages went extinct.
- **c.** Language was invented.
- **d.** Scientists counted languages.

_____ 4. Which idea from the article describes the most recent event?
- **a.** Language helps people cooperate.
- **b.** Today, English plays the role of lingua franca.
- **c.** Many thousands of languages have become extinct.
- **d.** People first spoke to each other.

_____ 5. Which language was spoken first?
- **a.** West Germanic.
- **b.** English.
- **c.** Germanic.
- **d.** Old English.

1-5 Cause and Effect

In order to fully comprehend an event, it is key to know why it happened and what else happened as a result. Why something happened is called the cause; what happened as a result is called the effect. Phrases like "because of" and "as a result of" show causes. Phrases like "as a result" (without "of"), "resulting in," and "so" show effects.

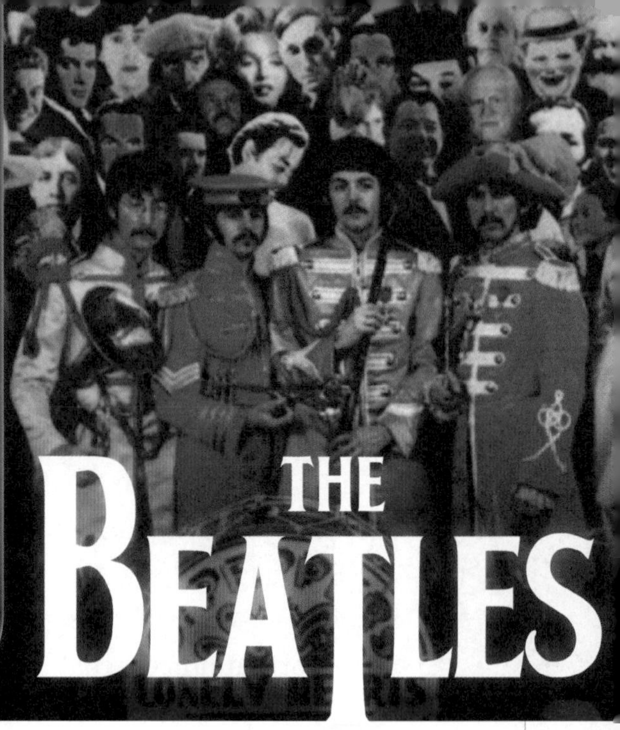

21 Beatlemania

021

The Beatles is the name of a band formed in 1960. Its members were from Liverpool, England. The Beatles did a lot to change the music and culture of the 1960s. Even today, their music continues to inspire youth all over the world.

The band was made up of four young men: John Lennon, Paul McCartney, George Harrison, and Ringo Starr. They led the mid-1960s musical British Invasion into the United States. The Beatles played rock and roll and pop music and sold more records in both England and America than any other singer or band of the 20th century. John Lennon, Paul McCartney, George Harrison, and Ringo Starr became some of the most famous people of the 1960s and 1970s, with millions of fans all over the world.

Beatles For Sale (1964, The Beatles' fourth album)

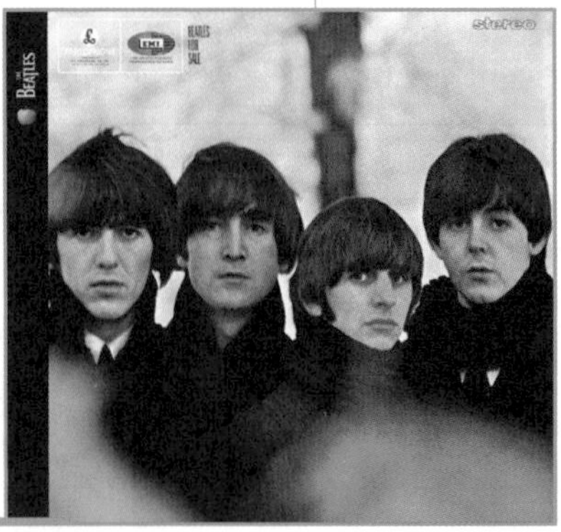

The Beatles fans demonstrated intense levels of hysterical screaming during the band's concerts and during their travels to and from cities around the world. Often during a concert, the screaming was so loud that the band's music was completely drowned out. Newspapers and magazines noticed how frenzied the band's fans became, and the term "Beatlemania" was born.

Not only did the Beatles inspire people through their music, but they also set trends with their clothing, hairstyles, behavior, and language.

front cover of *Sgt. Pepper's Lonely Hearts Club Band* (1967, the Beatles' eighth album), the most famous cover of any music album, and one of the most imitated images in the world

Because of improvements in global transportation and communication during the 1960s, they could reach out to fans around the world. Their creative influence extended into the huge cultural and political changes of that decade. Some people even credit them with helping to make English the most popular foreign language in the world.

Although the band broke up in 1970, the Beatles' impact on pop culture is still evident today, and many people remain Beatles fans. Many of the Beatles fans believe that "Beatlemania" will live forever.

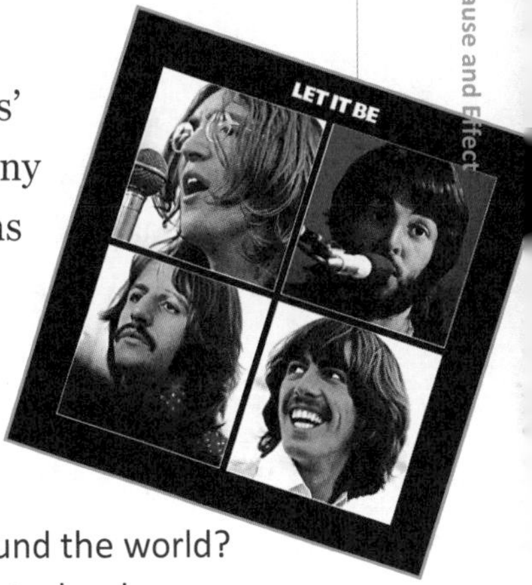

Let It Be (1970, the Beatles' final album)

Questions

_____ 1. Why were the Beatles able to reach fans around the world?
- a. Because they invested in communication technology.
- b. Because they had private cars and jets.
- c. Because of communication improvements in the '60s.
- d. Because they were style icons.

_____ 2. Why was the band's music sometimes drowned out at concerts?
- a. Because they played so loudly they broke their equipment.
- b. Because their fans screamed louder than the music.
- c. Because their offensive lyrics were silenced.
- d. Because they never played electric instruments.

_____ 3. Because the Beatles were so popular, ______.
- a. the 1960s were full of change
- b. the band came from Liverpool
- c. communication technology advanced
- d. English became very popular as well

_____ 4. What inspired the term "Beatlemania"?
- a. Beatles' fans' frenzied behavior.
- b. The Beatles' huge record sales.
- c. The Beatles' style influence.
- d. The Beatles' political influence.

_____ 5. The Beatles are still influencing pop culture, even though ______.
- a. their music is no longer popular
- b. the band broke up in the 1970s
- c. the band was disgraced in the 1980s
- d. the band's style fell out of fashion

22 JFK

022

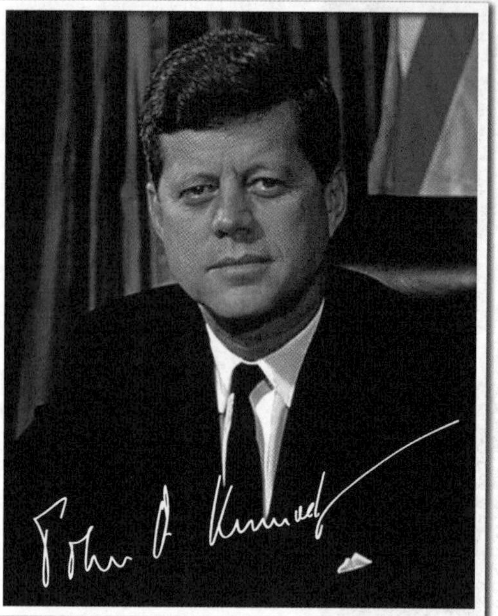

John Fitzgerald Kennedy (1917–1963)

John Fitzgerald Kennedy, or JFK, became the 35th President of the United States of America in 1961. In 1963 he was assassinated. Although he was president for fewer than three years, many Americans regard him as one of their best presidents.

John Kennedy was a liberal president. He said that all Americans should be equal and that race and religion weren't reasons to deny any individual his or her political rights.

JFK also believed in fighting to protect democracy. During World War II, he served in the Navy. He received the Navy and Marine Corps Medal for helping save the lives of some fellow soldiers. President Kennedy wanted America to be a strong defender of freedom and democracy in Europe (if not in Asia). His most famous saying is, "My fellow Americans, ask not what your country can do for you; ask what you can do for your country."

Kennedy on his navy patrol boat (1943)

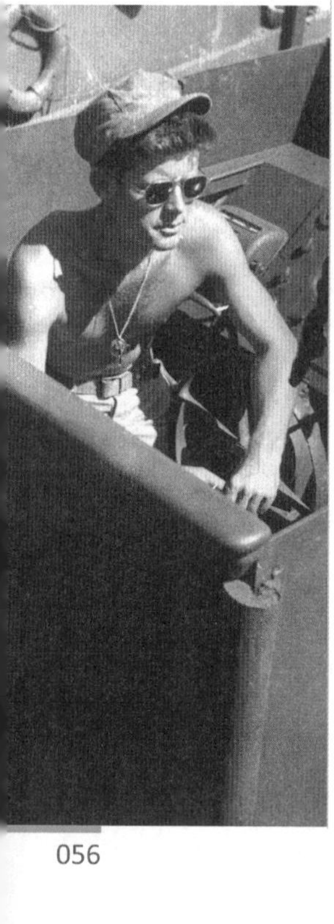

He also wanted Americans and other nations to fight "the common enemy": tyranny, poverty, disease, and war itself. To do this, he established the Peace Corps, which encourages American volunteers to help developing countries in the areas of education, farming, and health care.

In 1961, the Soviet Union was America's greatest threat. The two nations were involved in the "space race." JFK set a goal for the United States: Land a man on the moon by the end of the 1960s. This goal was also a technological challenge to the Soviet Union. Landing a man on the moon would be very expensive, but it would give prestige to the nation that did it. Kennedy said the United States should go to the moon and do other things "not because they are easy, but because they are hard." On July 20, 1969, almost six years after JFK's death, his goal was realized.

« Almost six years after JFK's death, American astronaut Neil Armstrong became the first to step onto the moon. (1969)

Questions

_____ 1. Which statement is true?
- **a.** JFK was president for too short a time for people to admire him.
- **b.** People admire JFK because he was president for such a short time.
- **c.** People admire JFK despite the fact that he was president for a short time.
- **d.** JFK was president for such a short time because people admired him.

_____ 2. Why was the Peace Corps created?
- **a.** Because of the space race.
- **b.** To fight WWII.
- **c.** Because of inequality in the United States.
- **d.** To fight poverty and disease.

« the Kennedy family in 1962

_____ 3. Why did JFK want to go to the moon?
- **a.** Because the Soviet Union did it.
- **b.** Because it was hard.
- **c.** Because it was easy.
- **d.** Because it was inexpensive.

_____ 4. What happened before JFK was given a medal?
- **a.** He helped save soldiers' lives.
- **b.** He was assassinated.
- **c.** He landed a man on the moon.
- **d.** He made his most famous statement.

_____ 5. The country that landed a man on the moon would ______.
- **a.** earn a lot of money **b.** gain a lot of prestige
- **c.** lose the space race **d.** fight poverty and disease

23 Asia's Gobi Desert

023

The Gobi Desert is the largest desert in Asia and the fourth largest one in the world. It exists because most of its rain is blocked by the Himalayan Mountains. The Gobi Desert covers parts of northern and northwestern China and southern Mongolia. It's about 1,600 kilometers at its widest point, and it is about 36 times larger than Taiwan. Unlike many other deserts, much of the Gobi Desert is not covered with sand, but with rock.

The Gobi Desert has a long history. Some parts of it are famous for the fossils and ancient tools found there. It was home to the Mongols, who built the huge Mongol Empire across China about 800 years ago. The famous Silk Road linking China with the West also runs through it. In AD 1271, Marco Polo traveled the Silk Road to China. He visited the Great Khan of the Mongol Empire, Kublai Khan, who was the grandson of Genghis Khan.

The temperature in the Gobi Desert changes quickly. The nights can be up to 35°C colder than the daytime. In winter, temperatures can go down to -45°C, while in summer it can be as hot as 45°C. There are also very big snowstorms and sandstorms that make living in the Gobi Desert difficult. Despite this difficulty, the Gobi Desert is home to many types of desert animals, including brown bears and wolves.

As big as it is, the Gobi is growing even bigger—and in a frightening way. "Desertification" is the name of the process by which a desert expands, taking over green lands at its edges. The Gobi is moving very quickly, spreading its harsh landscape even wider.

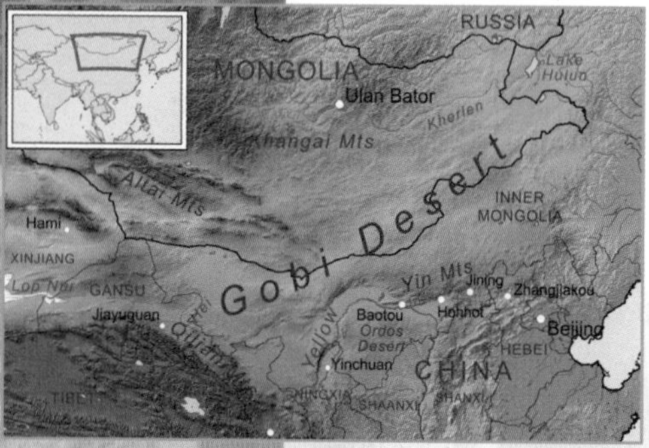

The Gobi Desert covers parts of China and Mongolia.

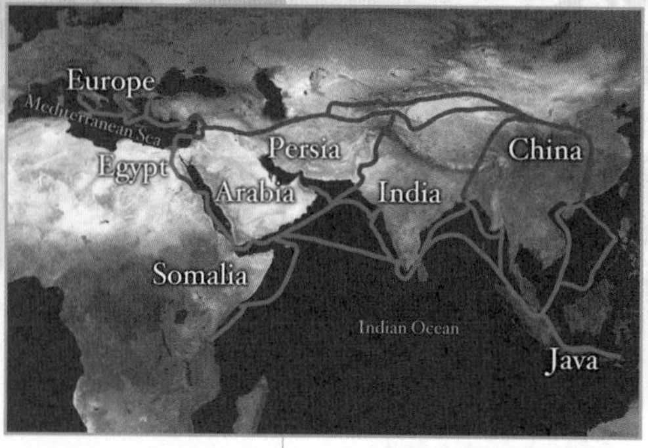

the Silk Road—land routes in red, and water routes in blue

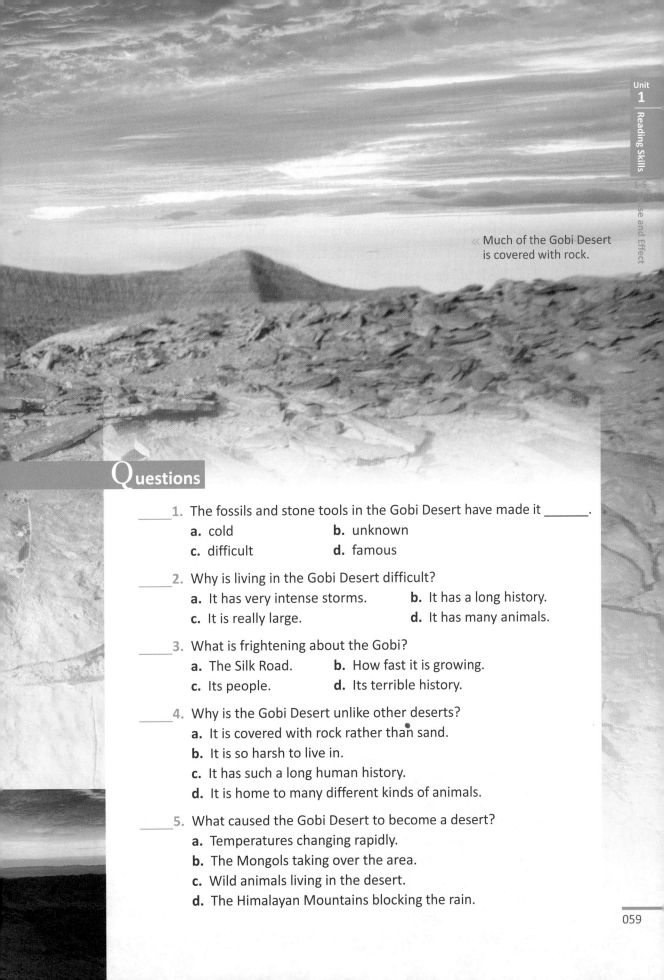

Much of the Gobi Desert is covered with rock.

Questions

_____ 1. The fossils and stone tools in the Gobi Desert have made it _____.

a. cold b. unknown
c. difficult d. famous

_____ 2. Why is living in the Gobi Desert difficult?

a. It has very intense storms. b. It has a long history.
c. It is really large. d. It has many animals.

_____ 3. What is frightening about the Gobi?

a. The Silk Road. b. How fast it is growing.
c. Its people. d. Its terrible history.

_____ 4. Why is the Gobi Desert unlike other deserts?

a. It is covered with rock rather than sand.
b. It is so harsh to live in.
c. It has such a long human history.
d. It is home to many different kinds of animals.

_____ 5. What caused the Gobi Desert to become a desert?

a. Temperatures changing rapidly.
b. The Mongols taking over the area.
c. Wild animals living in the desert.
d. The Himalayan Mountains blocking the rain.

24 The Mysterious Roma

024

The Roma are an ethnic group found in Europe, the Balkan Peninsula, the Middle East, North Africa, and the Americas. Although many people call them Gypsies, they are also known as Romanies, Roma people, or Roma. The name Gypsy was invented by Europeans, who wrongly believed that the Roma came from Egypt.

The Roma have been poorly treated and discriminated against for hundreds of years because of their culture and beliefs. Many people think that they are witches and use magic to do bad things. Others think that they are criminals who steal and kill. These wrong opinions of Roma people exist simply because most people know very little about them. For a very long time, the Roma had no written history. The only way to learn about them was to talk to them.

It is believed that the Roma originated in the northern part of the Indian subcontinent. About 1,000 years ago, they began to migrate via the Iranian plateau. As they moved through the Middle East and Europe, they mixed with the local people. There are now about six million Roma in European Union countries and at least 10–12 million in the world.

Many of the Roma still live in small family groups, away from towns and cities and modernization, and they will regularly move from place to place. Some of the Roma have given up their old nomadic lifestyle and have settled down in cities and towns.

For centuries, the Roma people were heavily persecuted, because they were different. However, they are now being gradually accepted, because people are taking the time to get to know them.

Verona, Italy, where some of the Roma have settled down

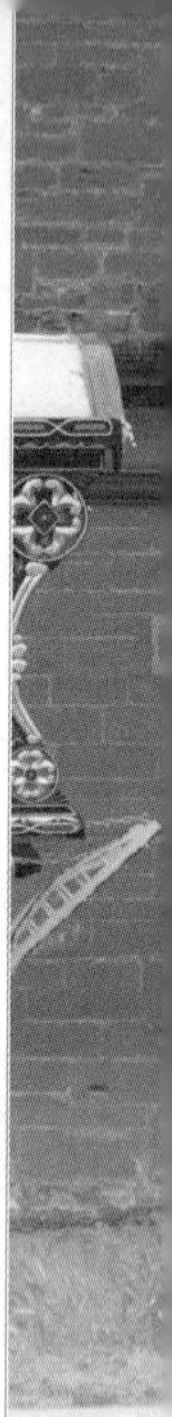

Romany vintage caravan

Questions

_____ 1. Why have the Roma people been discriminated against?

a. They look very strange. b. They live in unusual places.
c. They come from Rome. d. They have a different culture.

_____ 2. What is the reason for the many false beliefs about the Roma?

a. People don't know much about them.
b. There is too much false literature about them.
c. They live far from other people.
d. They only live in small family groups.

_____ 3. What is the reason the Roma began to be called Gypsies?

a. They come from the Middle East.
b. Their religion is called Gypsy.
c. People thought they were from Egypt.
d. The way they roam influenced their name.

_____ 4. What has happened because some Roma have given up their nomadic lifestyle?

a. They have been discriminated against.
b. They moved through the Iranian plateau.
c. They began to steal and kill.
d. They have settled in cities and towns.

Romany girls

_____ 5. For what reason was it possible to learn about the Roma only by talking to them?

a. They were very dangerous.
b. They had no written history.
c. They had traveled far from home.
d. Their history was left in Egypt.

Romany carvings

25 Disaster on 9/11/2001

025

Bin Laden (1957–2011), who orchestrated the 9/11 attacks, was the founder of al-Qaeda.

September 11, 2001, has become a very important date in world history. On that morning, 19 Islamic terrorists hijacked four passenger airplanes. They intentionally crashed two into the two tall towers of the World Trade Center, called the Twin Towers. As a result, the Twin Towers collapsed. A third airplane crashed into the Pentagon, America's military headquarters. The fourth airplane, which had been redirected toward Washington, DC, crashed in a field in Pennsylvania when some of the passengers and flight crew fought bravely to retake control of the airplane from the terrorists.

On September 11, 2001, a total of 2,974 innocent people died in the al-Qaeda suicide attacks: 246 on the four airplanes, 2,603 in the Twin Towers and on the ground, and 125 at the Pentagon. There are 24 people listed as missing. Most of those who died were civilians, including people from over 90 different countries. These deaths include the many police officers and firefighters who entered the World Trade Center buildings to rescue people.

The thousands of tons of toxic debris resulting from the destruction of the Twin Towers has led to debilitating illnesses among rescue and recovery workers.

The terrorist attacks had a significant economic impact on the United States and world stock markets. Even today, these attacks have negative effects on the airline industry around the world.

World Trade Center burning on 9/11

The Pentagon was damaged by fire and partly collapsed.

The United States responded to the attacks by launching a war on terrorism. The United States and Britain invaded Iraq and Afghanistan to capture or kill the terrorists who were responsible for 9/11 and to try to stop it from happening again. Unfortunately, the decade of war that followed has led to the deaths of even more innocent people.

Questions

_____ 1. What caused the Twin Towers to collapse?
- **a.** The Pentagon hit them.
- **b.** Two planes flew into them.
- **c.** They were shot from a plane.
- **d.** The war on terrorism knocked them over.

_____ 2. For what reason did the United States invade Afghanistan?
- **a.** To find the people responsible for the 9/11 attacks.
- **b.** To prevent the 9/11 attacks.
- **c.** To end the war on terrorism.
- **d.** To stop people from planning the 9/11 attacks.

_____ 3. What is the reason that one plane landed in Pennsylvania rather than Washington, DC?
- **a.** The pilots got lost and crashed.
- **b.** The passengers fought the hijackers.
- **c.** The Twin Towers had already fallen.
- **d.** The war on terrorism stopped it.

_____ 4. What has caused recovery workers to get sick?
- **a.** Toxic debris from the Twin Towers.
- **b.** The crash at the Pentagon.
- **c.** The war on terrorism.
- **d.** Fighting back against hijackers.

_____ 5. Why has September 11 become an important date?
- **a.** Because of the war on terrorism.
- **b.** Because of the al-Qaeda attacks on that day.
- **c.** Because of the toxic debris that exploded that day.
- **d.** Because the Twin Towers were built on that day.

new One World Trade Center under construction on October 8, 2011

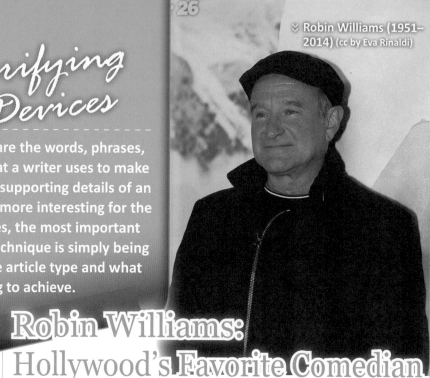

1-6 Clarifying Devices

Clarifying devices are the words, phrases, and techniques that a writer uses to make the main idea and supporting details of an article clearer and more interesting for the readers. Sometimes, the most important clarifying device technique is simply being able to identify the article type and what the author is trying to achieve.

Robin Williams (1951–2014) (cc by Eva Rinaldi)

26 Robin Williams: Hollywood's Favorite Comedian

026

Robin Williams *(second from left)* in *Night at the Museum: Secret of the Tomb* (2014) (cc by BagoGames)

mask worn by Robin Williams in *Mrs. Doubtfire* (1993) (cc by Edward Blake)

1 Over a successful 36-year career, he played an alien, an elderly woman, a teacher, and even a US president. But in the end, the role that proved most challenging was just being himself.

2 The actor in question is the incredibly talented Robin Williams. Williams was one of Hollywood's brightest stars. Younger generations may remember him as Teddy Roosevelt in the *Night at the Museum* films, or as Ramon in *Happy Feet*. Others might recall Williams dressed up as a woman to get closer to his children in *Mrs. Doubtfire*. And older generations can think back to *Mork and Mindy*, the show that gave Williams his big break in 1978.

3 Robin Williams is one of those rare actors who is loved by all. He began as a stand-up comic and had a well-known gift for improvisation. No matter what the scene was, Williams could make it work—and get a big laugh in the process. Yet Williams would not have made it as far as he did if he had relied on his comedy skills alone. There was a very genuine quality in his acting style. He was willing to reveal a vulnerable side to characters he played on-screen. This display of weakness helped people connect to Williams, because it's what we all feel sometimes in our everyday lives.

4 Williams may have been drawing from his own troubled private life during these performances. Struggles with depression, drugs, and alcohol were constant themes in his life. During his later years, a brain disease led to other physical problems like poor vision and trouble sleeping. In 2014, Williams ended his life at his home in California. It is very sad that he left the world so soon. However, he left behind an incredible body of work, one that has made the world a better place.

Happy Feet (2006)
(cc by Chao Lam)

Robin Williams's star on the Hollywood Walk of Fame surrounded by flowers and memorial tributes left by fans, August 12, 2014

Mork & Mindy (1978–1982) bubble gum picture cards (cc by Joe Haupt)

Questions

_____ 1. What does "his own troubled private life" refer to in the final paragraph?
- **a.** Williams's dramatic roles in films.
- **b.** Williams's struggles with depression, drugs, and alcohol.
- **c.** Williams's big break in *Mork and Mindy*.
- **d.** Williams's training as a stand-up comic.

_____ 2. How would you describe this article?
- **a.** A biography.
- **b.** An opinion piece.
- **c.** A joke.
- **d.** A timeline.

_____ 3. How does the author grab the reader's attention in the first sentence of the article?
- **a.** With a list.
- **b.** With a joke.
- **c.** With a story.
- **d.** With a comparison.

_____ 4. How does the author present information in the article?
- **a.** By showing contrasts.
- **b.** By using a dialogue.
- **c.** By making a comparison.
- **d.** By giving personal opinions.

_____ 5. What is the function of the last sentence of the article?
- **a.** To give a new detail.
- **b.** To surprise the reader.
- **c.** To sum up the story.
- **d.** To give a different point of view.

27 The Huge Pyramids of Giza

027

1 About 25 kilometers southwest of Cairo in Egypt, three huge pyramids stand on the Giza Plateau. This complex of ancient monuments consists of the Pyramid of Khufu (known as the Great Pyramid or the Pyramid of Cheops), the Pyramid of Khafre, and the Pyramid of Menkaure. Of the three pyramids, the Great Pyramid is the oldest and largest. It is also the only one of the Seven Wonders of the Ancient World that still exists.

the Sphinx and the Great Pyramid

2 Many pyramids were built in ancient Egypt. Pyramids were actually built to be the final resting place for pharaohs, who were the kings of Egypt. Although it is difficult to say when the first pyramids were built, many experts believe that some of the oldest ones are 4,700 years old.

3 Back then, the Egyptian people believed that pharaohs were gods. Each pyramid was built to hold only one dead pharaoh along with his gold, food, animals, and even servants. It was believed that everything buried with the dead pharaoh would travel with him into the afterlife.

the Pyramids of Giza

pharaoh's mask

It's hard not to feel sorry for the servants. They serve the pharaoh for years and instead of a salary raise, they get locked up with his dead body!

4 **Nowadays**, the pyramids aren't as marvelous as they used to be. As time passed, the sun, wind, and sand damaged the outside layers of the stone that was used to build them. Grave robbers have also broken in and stolen many of the valuable treasures that were placed inside with the dead pharaohs.

5 The pyramids are still considered to be quite interesting and a little mysterious by historians and scientists. Is it any surprise? After all, the pyramids are among the coolest landmarks ever built!

Questions

_____ 1. In the final sentence of the third paragraph, the author creates interest by ______.

a. using a foreign language b. shocking the reader
c. telling a joke d. stating a fact

_____ 2. This article can best be described as a(n) ______.

a. myth b. joke
c. narrative essay d. informative essay

_____ 3. In the fourth paragraph, the author uses **nowadays** in order to create a(n) ______.

a. contrast in time b. emphasis
c. counterargument d. added description

_____ 4. The author develops the main idea by ______.

a. recalling people's descriptions
b. explaining how something works
c. listing events
d. describing historical actions

_____ 5. In the sentence "After all, the pyramids are among the coolest landmarks ever built!", the author creates interest using ______.

a. a fact b. an opinion
c. a comparison d. a metaphor

Roswell Daily Record

ROSWELL, NEW MEXICO, TUESDAY, JULY 8, 1947

RAAF Captures Flying Saucer On Ranch in Roswell Region

Claims Army Is Stacking Courts Martial

Indiana Senator Lays Protest Before Patterson

House Passes Tax Slash by Large Margin

Defeat Amendment By Demos to Remove Many from Rolls

Security Council Paves Way to Talks On Arms Reductions

No Details of Flying Disk Are Revealed

Roswell Hardware Man and Wife Report Disk Seen

Ex-King Carol Weds Mme. Lupescu

Former King Carol of Romania and Mme. Elena Lupescu relax aboard the S. S. America bound for Cuba and Mexico in May, 1941. A member of Carol's household in Rio de Janeiro said the ex-king and his companion for 23 years in reign and exile were recently married at their hotel Copacabana Palace suite. (AP Wirephoto).

Miners and Operators Sign Highest Wage Pact in History

Some of Soviet Satellites May Attend Paris Meeting

American League Wins All-Star Game

Roswellians Have Differing Opinions On Flying Saucers

Roswell Daily Record, July 8, 1947, reporting the RAAF captured a flying saucer

28 The UFO Crash at Roswell, New Mexico

1 In the summer of 1947, during a violent thunderstorm, a UFO (Unidentified Flying Object) crashed on a farm in Roswell, New Mexico. At least, that's what some people think. Others say that these stories of a UFO crash are all just a big hoax. **Of course**, the US government won't be settling the argument any time soon. It has always denied that anything out of the ordinary happened.

2 People who claim to have seen the craft say that it was strange indeed. They describe an aircraft that is very different from an airplane. Some even insist that they saw several dead aliens inside the wreck with eyes like black saucers. Whatever this strange aircraft was, it didn't remain in the field for long. Soon after the crash, every scrap of the craft was carried away to Roswell Army Air Field. Later, it was reported that the craft was transported by a railroad flat car to Wright Patterson Air Force Base in Ohio for examination. The American government announced that the aircraft was not a UFO, but rather a weather balloon.

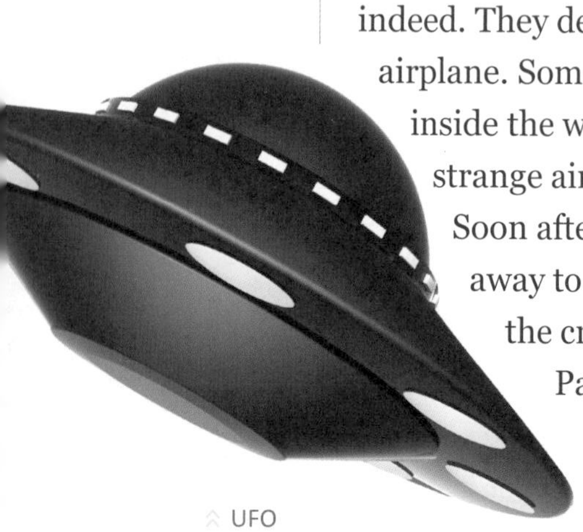

UFO

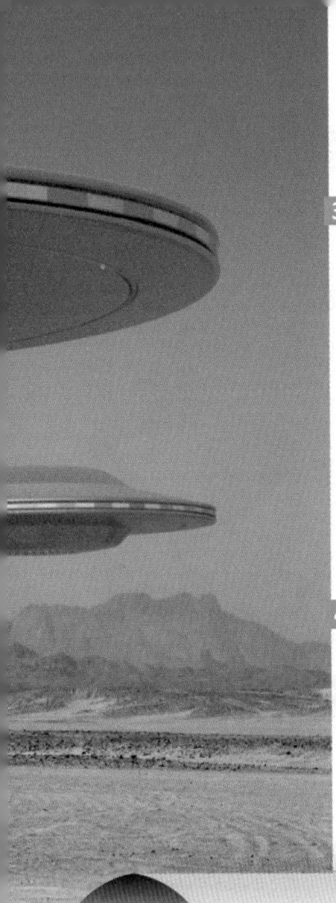

3 However, many Americans believe that their government has tried to cover up the truth. To them, there are two important questions that have **yet** to be answered: **First**, if it was a weather balloon, why was it kept at a secret military base to be examined by the Air Force? **Second**, who could possibly build a weather balloon so heavy and so valuable that it needed to be transported on a railroad car with an armed guard?

4 If you visit Roswell today, you will still find people arguing about what really crashed in that farmer's field back in 1947. You will also find a UFO museum that helps to keep the story alive.

Questions

aliens

_____ 1. In the first paragraph, the author creates interest using ______.

a. a biased viewpoint **b.** contrasting viewpoints
c. an example **d.** a joke

_____ 2. As used in the first paragraph, **of course** indicates ______.

a. an expected result **b.** an unexpected result
c. a negative result **d.** a positive result

_____ 3. As used in the third paragraph, the signal words **first** and **second** are meant to ______.

a. teach the readers a lesson
b. provide the readers with two different opinions
c. provide the readers with a contrast of time
d. organize information for the readers

_____ 4. In the sentence ". . . important questions that have **yet** to be answered . . . ," the word **yet** indicates ______.

a. a period of time **b.** a consequence
c. a conjunction **d.** a myth

_____ 5. In the second paragraph, the author uses the phrase "eyes like black saucers" to ______.

a. help the reader imagine how the alien might have looked
b. make the reader consider where the aliens might have come from
c. provide the reader with a different viewpoint
d. make the reader think about the color black

Mexican piñata

29 Take a Swing!

029

Things are more appreciated if you have to work for them. Rather than leaving candy in a bowl at your next party, you can put it in a piñata. Popular at parties for children, piñatas are decorated containers made of thin paper. They come in different forms, from cartoon characters to soccer balls.

The process of getting the candy out of the piñata is an exciting game. Kids take turns using a stick or baseball bat to hit the piñata, which is hung from a tree or ceiling. To make it challenging, the contestant is blindfolded and spun in circles before swinging the bat. Kids laugh as their friends swing wildly and miss. After a few hard hits, the piñata starts to break and the candies spill out. Kids rush to pick up candies as it falls. Finally, the whole piñata bursts open!

Although the word "piñata" is Spanish, the origins of the tradition are international. Marco Polo, the legendary Venetian trader who traveled to China in the late 13th century, was the first to describe piñatas. He witnessed people in China making colorful paper figures, which they filled with seeds. When hit by a stick, the figure broke and the seeds spilled out. Polo brought this idea back to Italy. Eventually, piñatas were used as part of Christian religious festivals.

Candies spill out as the piñata breaks.

little girl hitting a piñata on her birthday

During the same period, the Aztec people had a similar tradition, but they used pots rather than paper. The pot was made of thin clay, decorated and filled with small offerings. It was then brought to the statue of one of their gods and broken with a stick. The offerings were then left at the statue.

The piñata was once associated with religion and rituals around the world. Now seeing a brightly colored piñata is a sign of fun and celebration.

» clay pots specially made for the creation of piñatas (cc by Slevinr)

Questions

_____ **1.** Why does the author write about piñata traditions of China and the Aztec Empire?
- **a.** To show that piñatas did not originate in Spain.
- **b.** To explain how piñatas spread from China to the rest of the world.
- **c.** To let people know they can buy piñatas made of clay.
- **d.** To show that piñatas were first used at parties.

_____ **2.** What does Marco Polo's journey explain about piñatas?
- **a.** The different items that can be placed in a piñata.
- **b.** How piñatas came from China to Europe.
- **c.** How to plant seeds using a piñata.
- **d.** The use of piñatas in religious festivals.

_____ **3.** Why does the author discuss clay pots?
- **a.** To explain the spread of piñatas from the Europeans to the Aztecs.
- **b.** To demonstrate how the Aztecs made piñatas.
- **c.** To show that piñatas are no longer connected to religion.
- **d.** To teach readers how to create a piñata from clay.

_____ **4.** What is this passage mainly about?
- **a.** Games to play at parties. **b.** The best way to make a piñata.
- **c.** The history of a party game. **d.** The skills of artists who make piñatas.

_____ **5.** What does the author use to introduce the topic?
- **a.** A comparison between the types of piñatas.
- **b.** A story about a party with a piñata.
- **c.** An explanation of how to use piñatas.
- **d.** The history of piñatas.

030

30 K2: Climbing the Savage Mountain

1 Most people have heard of Mount Everest, which is the tallest mountain in the world, but the second highest mountain in the world is barely talked about at all. This mountain is K2, and it has a peak elevation of 8,611 meters. It is located in the Himalayan mountain range between China and Pakistan.

2 K2 has a **dark secret**: more people have died climbing K2 than Mount Everest. Although the summit of Mount Everest is higher than that of K2, K2 is much more difficult and dangerous to climb due to its terrible weather. These unpredictable and dangerous weather patterns have given K2 a reputation as the most difficult mountain to climb in the world.

the first K2 ascent, completed in 1954 by Italian expedition led by Count Ardito Desio

3 People have been trying to climb K2 since as far back as 1902, but it wasn't until 1954 that the first expedition reached the mountain's summit. This was a group of Italian climbers led by Count Ardito Desio. Since then, over 300 people have successfully made it to the top, while around 80

have died on the climb. This means that for every four people who get to the summit of K2, roughly one person dies trying.

4 K2 has been particularly unkind to female climbers. In 1986, Wanda Rutkiewicz became the first woman to reach the summit. By 2017, the number of successful female climbs had increased to 12, but three of these women died on the way down, and two died on later climbing trips. Some people even believe that these deaths are the result of a curse that K2 places on its female climbers.

5 **In conclusion**, it should come as no surprise that K2 has been nicknamed "Savage Mountain."

« Wanda Rutkiewicz (1943–1992), the first woman to reach the K2 summit (1968)

Questions

_____ 1. In the third and fourth paragraphs, the author conveys the danger of climbing K2 by ______.
- **a.** carefully describing the mountain's shape
- **b.** referring to all of the climbers who have died
- **c.** describing the weather in winter
- **d.** explaining the curse of K2 over the past two decades

_____ 2. In the fifth paragraph, the author uses **in conclusion** to convey ______.
- **a.** a contrast of time **b.** an unexpected result
- **c.** a funny joke **d.** a logical result

_____ 3. This article can best be described as a(n) ______.
- **a.** myth **b.** informative essay
- **c.** short story **d.** biography

_____ 4. In the second paragraph, K2's **dark secret** refers to ______.
- **a.** something good that is not well known
- **b.** a unique landscape found nowhere else
- **c.** something bad that is not well known
- **d.** a violent personality

_____ 5. In the final sentence of the third paragraph, the author captures the reader's attention using ______.
- **a.** a biased point of view **b.** a specific example
- **c.** a joke **d.** a shocking statistic

Count Ardito Desio (1897–2001) during the K2 expedition in 1954

1-7 Making Inferences

Inference is using something you know to guess at something you don't know. Every time you look up at clouds in the sky and reach for your umbrella, you're inferring that it's going to rain. Readers do the same thing. Authors provide information so that their readers can infer their own meaning.

Wikipedia logo

WIKIPEDIA
The Free Encyclopedia

31 Wikipedia: The Online Know-It-All

031

One of the best places to search for information online is Wikipedia. This online encyclopedia is written by thousands of people from all over the world. Anyone can contribute to any topic he or she finds interesting. Likewise, topics that are poorly written or incorrect can be changed. Therefore, you don't have to be a university professor to write for Wikipedia.

Larry Sanger (1968–) (cc by Larry Sanger)

Wikipedia started in 2001 by philosopher Larry Sanger and businessman Jimmy Wales. Both men wanted to create an ad-free online English-language encyclopedia that could be edited by anyone. However, Wikipedia was only meant to boost traffic for Nupedia, another Internet encyclopedia that was written by experts. Nupedia's website was shut down in September 2003. Its content and articles have since moved to Wikipedia.

Jimmy Wales (1966–) (cc by Manuel Archain)

As of December 2017, there are over five million English articles written on Wikipedia. In addition, another 40 million articles are written in one of 301 different languages that occupy the online encyclopedia. This makes Wikipedia one of the most international websites on the Internet. Many people who visit Wikipedia use it as a source for news because it is constantly updated.

Interestingly, researchers have discovered that countries with bad weather tend to have more Wikipedia pages than sunny countries. This may be because people living in warmer climates spend less time on their computers.

Nevertheless, Wikipedia has its problems. There have been complaints that some of the information on Wikipedia is not accurate. Additionally, some important subjects are not even included. Sometimes, this has led to arguments among contributors. In January of 2014, it was reported that Wikipedia had two billion fewer views than the year before.

The people running Wikipedia have listened and responded to these complaints. They say that accuracy on the website is always improving. They must be doing something right, because Wikipedia has become the fifth most popular website on the Internet.

Questions

_____ **1.** Which of the following statements about Larry Sanger and Jimmy Wales is probably true?

- **a.** They never expected Wikipedia to be so popular.
- **b.** They never had any disagreements over Wikipedia.
- **c.** They were in the same university program together.
- **d.** They haven't spoken to each other in over 10 years.

_____ **2.** What is probably true about Wikipedia?

- **a.** It became more popular than Nupedia.
- **b.** It features articles in French.
- **c.** It is only popular in North America.
- **d.** It has not been updated for years.

_____ **3.** Which of the following is probably true about Wikipedia's business practices?

- **a.** The company only hires philosophers.
- **b.** The company has gone bankrupt several times.
- **c.** The company spends all of its money on advertising.
- **d.** The company doesn't hire editors.

_____ **4.** According to the passage, which statement is probably true?

- **a.** There are more Wikipedia pages in English than Spanish.
- **b.** Wikipedia will release a print version of its encyclopedia.
- **c.** There are no Wikipedia pages in Russian.
- **d.** Information on Wikipedia is never wrong.

_____ **5.** Which of the following would Wikipedia probably not be good for?

- **a.** Learning about things that you're interested in.
- **b.** Reading news before anyone else.
- **c.** Using it as the only research tool for university essays.
- **d.** Writing articles on topics you are very familiar with.

32 Getting to Know Vincent van Gogh

032

possible photo of Vincent van Gogh (1853–1890) in 1886

Theo van Gogh (1857–1891) was a lifelong supporter and friend to his brother Vincent van Gogh.

Some people say that he was crazy. Others say that he was a genius. Whatever people think of him, there is no doubt that Vincent van Gogh was a great artist. His paintings sell for millions of dollars, and they can be seen in all of the top art galleries around the world. But behind all of this fame, there's an artist who had a very difficult life.

Vincent van Gogh was born in the Netherlands in 1853. He spent his early adult years working various jobs as an art dealer, a teacher, and a missionary. In 1880, he started painting. His life as a painter took him across Belgium and France. In his first 10 years as an artist, Van Gogh produced around 860 paintings and 1,300 drawings.

Self-portrait With Straw Hat (1887/88)

Van Gogh's paintings were never popular when he was alive. This meant that it was hard for him to earn any money. Throughout his life, he was supported by his brother Theo, who helped make sure that Vincent always had enough to eat.

This lack of success made Van Gogh depressed and anxious. In 1888, he famously cut off his ear after quarreling with another painter. After this incident, he spent some time in a mental hospital. Sadly, in the end his depression was too much to bear. He shot himself in the chest and died in 1890.

In his final letter to his brother, Van Gogh wrote that his paintings were like children to him. It wasn't long before the rest of the world started to notice them. After his death, Van Gogh became one of the most famous artists in history. Some of his best known paintings include *Still Life: Vase With Twelve Sunflowers* and *The Starry Night*.

Questions

Vincent and Theo were buried together in Auvers-sur-Oise.

_____1. Which statement about Vincent van Gogh's early adult years is probably true?

a. He could get along with everyone.
b. He didn't know what he wanted to do for a career.
c. He was the smartest student in his university class.
d. He was taught how to speak Russian at a young age.

_____2. How did Vincent van Gogh benefit from his brother's financial support?

a. It allowed the two brothers to develop a close relationship.
b. He could spend time with his brother's children.
c. He could focus a large amount of time on painting.
d. He could save up for his own art gallery.

Still Life: Vase With Twelve Sunflowers (1888)

_____3. Which of the following about the mental hospitals was probably true?

a. They were extremely expensive.
b. They were very rare.
c. They treated people with depression.
d. They only took children as their patients.

_____4. From the statement "he famously cut off his ear after quarreling with another painter," we can assume that Van Gogh probably ______.

a. hated his brother
b. had a bad temper
c. most enjoyed painting flowers
d. always lived by the sea

The Starry Night (1889)

_____5. It is quite likely that ______.

a. Van Gogh had a miserable life
b. Van Gogh studied in Russia
c. Van Gogh is a national hero in France
d. Van Gogh hid away his wealth

33 Lemurs of Madagascar

033

black and white ruffled lemur

Lemurs are cute animals that live on the island of Madagascar, the fourth-largest island in the world. Lemurs have big eyes, long noses, and long tails (except for the indri) and live high in the trees of Madagascan forests. Lemurs are quite intelligent. They are the cousins of monkeys and look quite similar. Like monkeys, they also swing through trees and live in family groups.

There are many different species of lemurs. Some lemurs (the indri) sing like a whale, and some (the sifaka) dance like a ballet dancer. Some lemurs are very small, like the pygmy mouse lemur, which can weigh as little as 25 grams. Others, like the indri, can weigh up to 10 kilograms. Some lemurs are nocturnal, which means they stay awake all night and sleep during the day. Other lemurs are diurnal. A diurnal animal stays awake during the daytime like humans. Generally, smaller lemurs are nocturnal and bigger ones are diurnal. Every species of lemur is unique to Madagascar.

Lemurs, such as this white-fronted brown lemur, are killed for bush meat in Madagascar.

Unfortunately, people in Madagascar have been destroying the forests where lemurs live to build new farms and houses. Some local people hunt lemurs for food. Other people kill lemurs because they think that lemurs are bad luck. These actions have caused many species of lemur to disappear over the last few centuries. All of the remaining lemurs are endangered, which means that they will disappear too if something doesn't change soon.

While there are still over 100 species of lemurs left, many experts fear that this number could fall very quickly. If serious efforts aren't made to protect the remaining lemurs of Madagascar, we may face a future where they are gone for good.

crowned lemur

ring-tailed lemurs

Questions

____ 1. Which of the following statements is probably true?
   a. Lemurs are smarter than humans.
   b. The pygmy mouse is the smallest lemur.
   c. Most lemurs live underground.
   d. Lemurs are very scared of the water.

____ 2. The indri species of lemur probably ______.
   a. lives in Nigeria
   b. is diurnal
   c. dances well
   d. lives the longest of any lemur

____ 3. Which of the following statements is probably NOT true?
   a. Lots of charities are trying to save the lemur.
   b. Lemurs have lived for thousands of years.
   c. Lemur meat is known for its bitter and disgusting taste.
   d. Scientists have proven that lemurs can play simple games.

____ 4. Lemurs are known for being ______.
   a. grumpy all the time
   b. expert tree climbers
   c. able to speak their own language
   d. asleep all winter

____ 5. Which of the following do people often say about lemurs?
   a. Lemurs are very violent and dangerous.
   b. Lemurs are hard to tell apart from monkeys.
   c. Lemurs can be excellent pets.
   d. Lemurs can do complex math problems.

pygmy mouse lemur

the Amazon River

34 Amazon: The River Sea

034

The Amazon River flows from the Andes Mountains in Peru across northern Brazil and into the Atlantic Ocean. It is the second longest river in the world after the Nile River in Africa, and it is the biggest river in the world by water volume. In fact, the Amazon River is so massive that people call it "The River Sea." The mouth of the river, which is where the river flows into the Atlantic Ocean, is about 330 kilometers wide. That is almost the entire length of the Thames River (346 kilometers) in England. Moreover, the Amazon River carries more water than any other river in the world, with a river flow that is greater than the next 10 largest rivers flowing into the ocean combined.

the mouth of the Amazon River

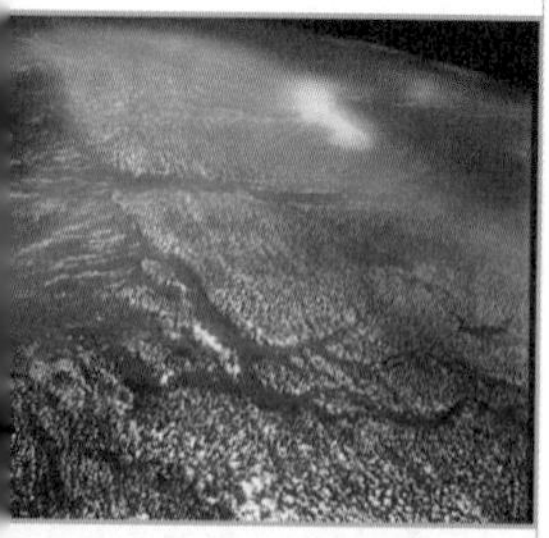

The Amazon has over 1,100 tributaries. These are smaller rivers that branch off the main river. Seventeen of these tributaries are over 1,500 kilometers long.

The Amazon is very important to people all over the planet because it drains water from the enormous Amazon rain forest, which is the largest rain forest in the world. This is where around one third of all known species can be found. The plentiful trees of the Amazon rain forest also help remove carbon dioxide (CO_2) from the atmosphere. This is why the Amazon rain forest is considered to be very important in the struggle against global warming.

the Amazon rain forest

The Amazon River contains one-fifth of the world's freshwater, and it is home to an estimated 5,600 species of fish. Some strange and wonderful species include the boto, which is known as the Amazon River dolphin. There are also various kinds of piranhas, meat-eating fish that have been known to eat livestock and occasionally attack humans.

boto (Amazon River dolphin)

piranha in the Amazon

Questions

_____ 1. Which of the following could refer to the Amazon rain forest?

- **a.** The Global Kidney.
- **b.** The Lungs of the Planet.
- **c.** Old Smokey.
- **d.** The Saltwater Highway.

_____ 2. Which of the following statements is probably true?

- **a.** Many global warming foundations focus on saving the Amazon rain forest.
- **b.** The Amazon River is the world's largest source of salt water.
- **c.** The Amazon River is the fastest flowing river in the world.
- **d.** Amazon water is undrinkable for humans because it has too many poison frogs.

_____ 3. Piranhas probably ______.

- **a.** can survive on land
- **b.** are a freshwater fish
- **c.** are always red
- **d.** always hunt alone

_____ 4. Which of the following statements is probably NOT true?

- **a.** The Amazon River is in South America.
- **b.** The Amazon rain forest is known as a cradle for animal life.
- **c.** All species of dolphins live in salt water.
- **d.** The Amazon River is a good source of hydro power.

_____ 5. It is quite likely that Brazil ______.

- **a.** does not allow tourists near the Amazon River
- **b.** has built dams and halted the flow of the Amazon River
- **c.** is home to the top three longest rivers in the world
- **d.** gets most of its drinking water from the Amazon River

Global warming increases the chances of many types of disasters.

hurricane

35 Global Warming

035

There is an environmental crisis that is threatening the planet. It's called "the greenhouse effect" or "global warming." The problem comes from fossil fuels such as natural gas, oil, and coal. When countries burn these fuels for energy, they release carbon dioxide (CO_2) and other dangerous "greenhouse gases" into the atmosphere. These gases prevent heat from escaping into outer space. They're like a blanket that is causing both land and sea temperatures to rise.

Global warming is a lot more serious than a few more days of hot weather every year. As the planet heats up, the balance of nature begins to change. This increases the chances of many types of disasters, such as hurricanes, floods, and drought. It is difficult for plant and animal life to adapt to hotter temperatures, so global warming threatens our crops and the survival of certain species as well.

One of the most dangerous consequences of global warming is the huge amounts of ice in the Arctic and Antarctic regions that have started to melt. The melting of this polar ice causes worldwide sea levels to rise, threatening people who live in low-lying countries like Bangladesh. In fact, some reports predict that countries like the small Pacific island of Tuvalu could be completely underwater by the year 2100.

The good news is that there's something we can do to fight global warming. We must use less fossil fuel.

Governments around the world started focusing on developing renewable energy sources.

Governments around the world have begun to focus on renewable energy sources such as wind, geothermal, water, and solar power. Many individuals have also made positive steps by improving their personal habits. Some have purchased electric cars and others have sold their cars altogether.

However, there is a long way to go before global warming is solved. Unfortunately, many people around the world still don't take the problem very seriously.

Questions

_____ 1. Which of the following statements is probably true?
- a. Support for coal energy has increased a lot over the past 10 years.
- b. The government of Germany is investing in solar energy technology.
- c. All of the ice in the Arctic and Antarctic region has already melted.
- d. Global warming is caused by planting too many trees.

_____ 2. An electric car probably _______.
- a. does not release CO_2
- b. cannot be purchased yet
- c. is very inexpensive
- d. is bad for the environment

_____ 3. Which of the following statements is probably NOT true?
- a. Some ships can now travel through waters in the Canadian Arctic.
- b. Island nations are very worried about global warming.
- c. Flooding has decreased around the world over the past 10 years.
- d. The list of endangered species has grown over the past 10 years.

_____ 4. Global warming has caused which of the following?
- a. Days are longer and nights are shorter around the world.
- b. People use fewer and fewer plastic bags.
- c. Cars have become more expensive.
- d. Polar bears have become a threatened species.

_____ 5. Tuvalu probably _______.
- a. is a very wealthy country
- b. is a very large country
- c. has a diverse culture
- d. is a very low-lying country

1-8 Critical Thinking

Critical thinking means asking questions. When you read, ask yourself "why," "where," "when," and "how." Ask questions about the information you are reading and also about why the author chose to include that information and not something else. Doing this will help you form your own opinions about what you read and help you understand the writing process.

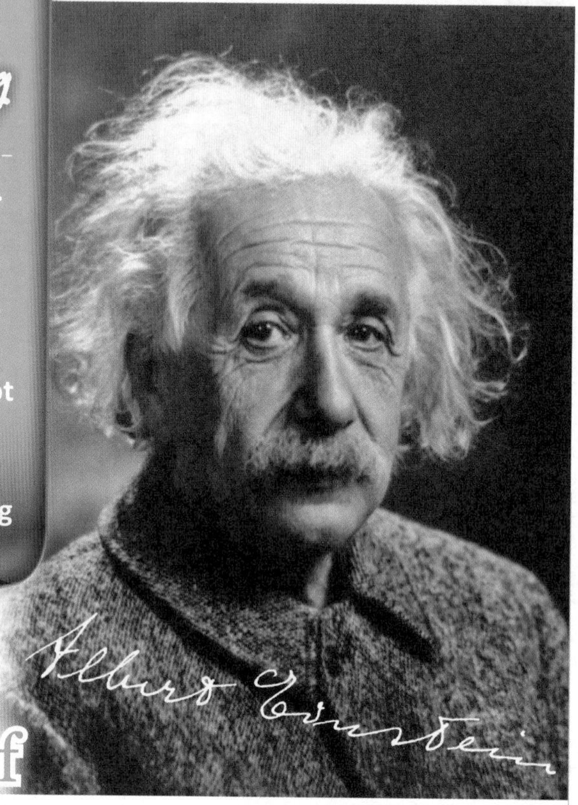

Einstein (1879–1955) in 1947

36 The Genius of Albert Einstein

036

Einstein started to speak when he was three years old. (1882)

You must have heard of the formula $E = mc^2$. This is still the most famous scientific formula ever worked out. It remains an important cornerstone of science, and devising it made the scientist Albert Einstein famous.

Before he published the calculations in 1905 that showed why $E = mc^2$, scientists around the world strongly believed that $E = \frac{1}{2} mc^2$. Today, a high school physics student can do the calculations and understand what Albert Einstein did to become famous.

Albert Einstein was born into a Jewish family in Germany on March 14, 1879. He started to speak when he was three years old. Young Einstein did not do well at school because he didn't work hard in the classes that bored him. As a result, many people thought that he was stupid. Eventually he became interested in science and tried to discover a law of physics that would explain how everything in science works.

In 1922, he received the 1921 Nobel Prize in Physics. Later, he moved to the United States and became a professor at Princeton

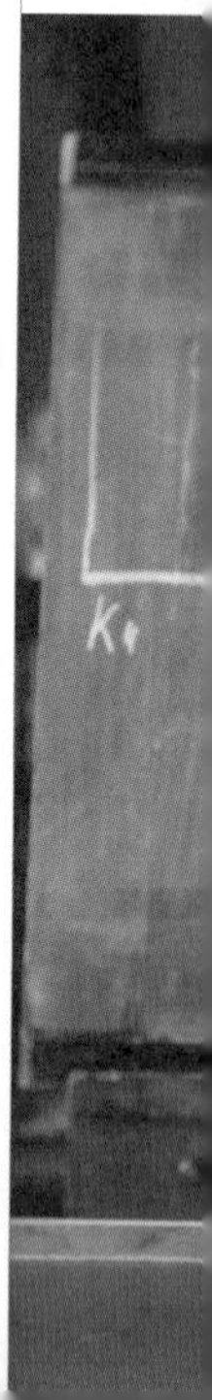

University. In 1939, Einstein, together with Leo Szilard, a Hungarian American physicist, wrote a letter to US President, Franklin D. Roosevelt, saying that America should develop an atomic bomb before the Germans did. This letter resulted in the development of the atomic bombs that would be dropped on the Japanese cities of Hiroshima and Nagasaki in August 1945.

Einstein died in Princeton, New Jersey, on April 18, 1955. In his life, more than 300 scientific works and over 150 nonscientific works of his were published. Most of his ideas are still used by many scientists today. His name, "Einstein," has become synonymous with genius.

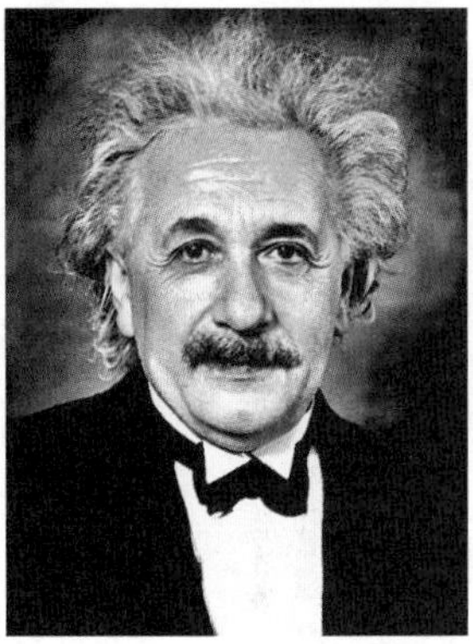

» Einstein in 1935 at Princeton

Questions

_____ 1. Why is Albert Einstein a famous scientist?
- **a.** He devised the most important scientific formula, $E = mc^2$.
- **b.** He was a professor at Princeton University in the United States.
- **c.** He wrote and published many nonscientific works.
- **d.** He wrote an important letter to the US government.

_____ 2. Einstein wrote a letter to the US president because ______.
- **a.** he thought the United States should make an atomic bomb
- **b.** he had won the Nobel Prize
- **c.** he wanted to work at Princeton University
- **d.** he was working on nonscientific writing

» Einstein received the 1921 Nobel Prize in Physics.

_____ 3. What was the reason that Einstein didn't do well at school?
- **a.** He couldn't speak.
- **b.** He wasn't very smart.
- **c.** He was often bored.
- **d.** He didn't want to please his parents.

_____ 4. The passage is mainly about ______.
- **a.** a famous invention
- **b.** a major prize
- **c.** a personal life
- **d.** a professional life

_____ 5. Which of the following opinions would the author agree with?
- **a.** It was a good choice to drop the atomic bomb.
- **b.** Einstein made a major impact on scientific thought.
- **c.** Princeton University is a good place to work.
- **d.** Einstein's family never understood him.

37 Democracy in the Modern World

037

Do you know what "democracy" is about? A democracy has leaders who are elected by the people in a particular area through voting. The government belongs to all the people, not to any king, dictator, or small group. Democracy is based on the idea that citizens have the power and responsibility to select new leaders if the old leaders are not doing a good job. If there is freedom of speech and freedom of the press in a democratic country, each citizen can be informed about the potential leaders and can vote wisely.

Taiwan is a democracy. So are the United States, the United Kingdom, and many other countries in the world. Currently, there are about 123 countries that say they have democratically elected leaders. Unfortunately, some countries that claim to be democratic are not in fact democracies.

Democratic freedoms include the freedom of speech.

Having a democracy does not guarantee that the leaders of the government will do good things. During the years leaders are in power, they may decide to do bad things and the citizens may have a limited ability to stop them. The courts, legislature, or free press can often limit the damage being done by a bad leader. A democracy needs many honest and wise leaders as well as an educated and thoughtful people. A democracy

The establishment of universal male suffrage in France in 1848 was an important milestone in the history of democracy.

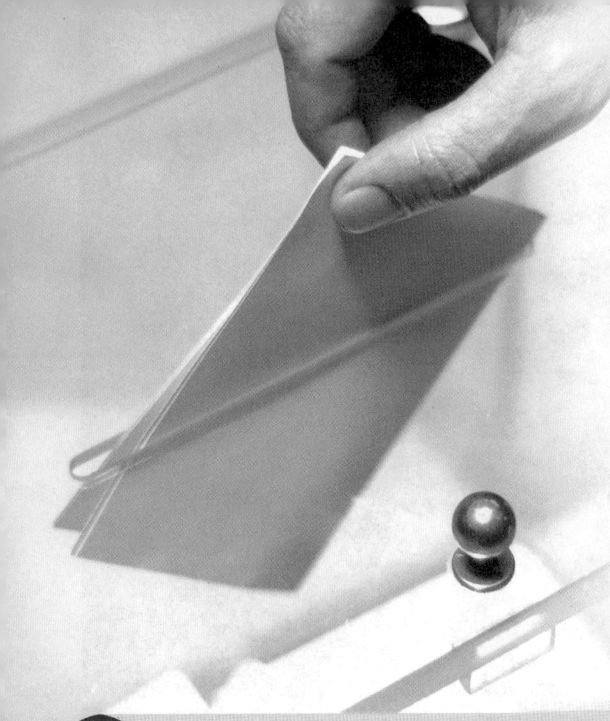

also needs to grow and change in order to improve itself. Examples of mature and strong democracies can be found in Europe, North America, Australia, and New Zealand.

An open and honest democracy is what most of the people in the world desire. Despite lies that may be told by bad leaders, people all over the world will continue to struggle for the healthy democracies that they deserve.

Questions

_____ **1.** Which of these things does NOT belong in a democracy?

a. Citizens who can vote.
b. A powerful king.
c. Temporary leaders
d. Freedom of speech.

_____ **2.** Why doesn't democracy guarantee good government?

a. Because leaders can do bad things while in power.
b. Because the people can't change their leaders.
c. Because leaders are in power for life.
d. Because too much free press stops things from working.

_____ **3.** Why is education important in a democracy?

a. It gives glory to the government and the nation.
b. It helps leaders get the power they need.
c. It promotes freedom of the press around the world.
d. It helps citizens make informed decisions when they vote.

_____ **4.** How can democracies improve themselves?

a. By electing more leaders every year.
b. By using kings as well as presidents.
c. By growing and changing.
d. By hiding bad leaders.

_____ **5.** Who is responsible for leadership in a democracy?

a. The citizens. **b.** The press.
c. The king. **d.** The courts.

^ Arjuna *(left)* and his charioteer, Krishna *(right)*, on the Battlefield in an epic scene from the *Mahabharata* (cc by Infinite Eyes)

38 The Blue Hero of Hinduism

038

Krishna, considered a major god in Hinduism and Vaishnavism, decided to appear on earth probably in 3,228 BCE in Mathura, India. Often represented with blue skin, he is believed to be the original source of the all-powerful god Vishnu. We know his story thanks to three works describing his life: the *Mahabharata*, the *Bhagavad Gita*, and the *Harivamsa*.

Krishna's life was full of mischief, love, and adventure, yet his tale had a very sad beginning: Krishna was born in a prison cell. His mother had been put there by her own brother, King Kamsa. A priest told Kamsa that he would be killed by his nephew, so he decided to have them all killed. Luckily, Krishna survived and escaped the prison. He was raised by a foster mother and lived among the village cowherds. There he would often get into trouble, stealing some milk when no one was looking. But the cowherds still loved him. At a very young age, Krishna was even believed to have killed two monsters named Trinavarta and Putana.

Upon reaching adulthood, Krishna returned to the land of his birth and killed his evil uncle. Afterwards, he became an advisor to the new prince and got drawn into a terrible war. His successes on the battlefield are described in the *Bhagavad-Gita As It Is*.

One of the most memorable stories of Krishna's life is his love of Radha. The two were deeply in love,

Krishna at Sri Mariamman Temple in Singapore (cc by Ms Sarah Welch)

but they never married. Why? There are many theories. One is that Radha believed her status in society was too low to marry Krishna. Another is that Krishna believed in a firm separation between love and marriage. Some people view Radha as a representation of the human soul. For them, the love between Krishna and Radha is the love between god and humanity.

Questions

Krishna adorning Radha at a secluded place (cc by Infinite Eyes)

_____ 1. Who is Krishna believed to be?
- **a.** The god of love.
- **b.** The god of mischief.
- **c.** The original source of a powerful god.
- **d.** The god of cowherds.

_____ 2. Who was King Kamsa?
- **a.** The king of the cowherds.
- **b.** The king whom Krishna fought a war against.
- **c.** Krishna's uncle.
- **d.** Krishna's brother.

_____ 3. What is true about Krishna's relationship with Radha?
- **a.** The two ran away together.
- **b.** The two never had a marital relationship.
- **c.** The two became enemies.
- **d.** The two fought a war together.

_____ 4. Why do so many people connect with the story of Krishna?
- **a.** Because he's a god who lived life like a human.
- **b.** Because he's a god who killed his enemies.
- **c.** Because he's a god with blue skin.
- **d.** Because he's a god who cared about social status.

_____ 5. What is the main purpose of this article?
- **a.** To explain why Hinduism is the best religion.
- **b.** To describe the life of Krishna.
- **c.** To debate the nature of marriage.
- **d.** To prove that King Kamsa was evil.

Krishna with Radha and the eight Gopis (milkmaids of Vrindavan) (cc by Infinite Eyes)

Charles-Édouard Jeanneret (Le Corbusier, 1887–1965) (cc by Susleriel)

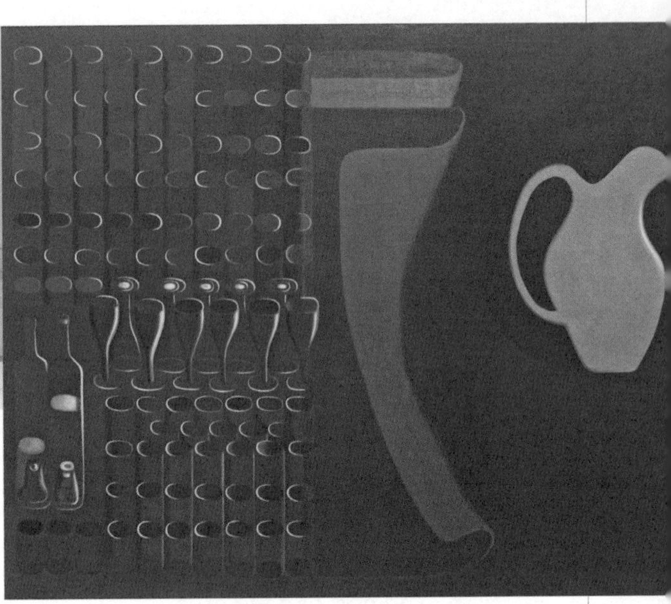

Composition à la Carafe (1926–1930) by Amédée Ozenfant(1986–1966) (cc by Pedro Ribeiro Simões)

39 Organized Art

039

Art often reflects events that happened at the time it was created. Groups of artists who have the same artistic goals, similar styles, and who sometimes work in the same city or region create "art movements." How would an art movement after World War I look? It was the first war using machines and new types of weapons. An estimated 8.5 million soldiers and 13 million people died.

After the violence of World War I, people in Europe were eager to return to their orderly, everyday lives. This desire was reflected in an artistic movement known as Purism. It was started by two French artists, Amédée Ozenfant and Charles-Édouard Jeanneret, who was also an architect. They published a book, *Après le Cubisme* (After Cubism), in 1918 to explain the goal of their art. They believed that people would find joy in an organized world and would feel satisfied by helping to create order for society. Purist paintings used geometric shapes and often focused on machinery, vases, and cups. Colors could be bright but browns and grays were also used.

The Purist movement was small and didn't last long. Fernand Léger was the third artist to join the movement. Poet Paul Dermée also worked with Ozenfant and Jeanneret to publish a review called *L'Esprit Nouveau*,

Centre Le Corbusier (Heidi Weber Museum) in Switzerland, the last building designed by Le Corbusier (cc by Roland zh)

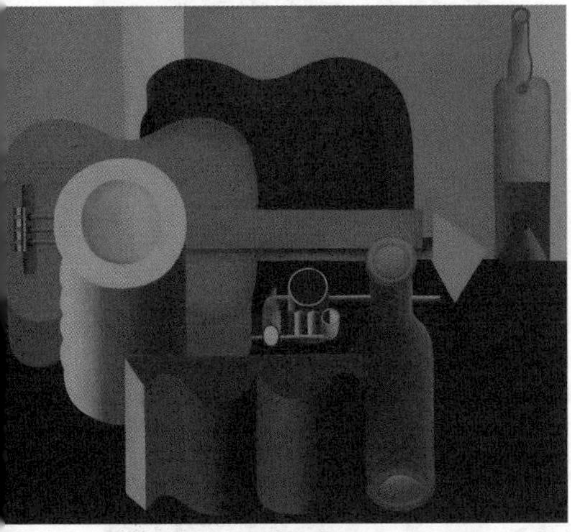

Nature Morte (1920) by Charles-Édouard Jeanneret (cc by Gwen Fran)

which means "the new spirit." One of the most famous creations of Purism was the Pavillon de l'Esprit Nouveau (Pavilion of the New Spirit), built in 1925 for the International Exposition of Decorative and Industrial Arts in Paris. Jeanneret, who called himself "Le Corbusier" when he was working as an architect, designed the building.

Although the Purist movement lasted only seven years, it reflected people's desire to recover from a terrible war and to return to order. It showed the order that artists were able to find in everyday life.

Questions

The City (La Ville) (1919) by Fernand Léger (1881–1955) (cc by Tom Ipri)

_____ 1. How is an art movement created?
- **a.** By Amédée Ozenfant and Charles-Édouard Jeanneret.
- **b.** By artists who share the same goals and work in similar styles.
- **c.** By nobles affected by historical events.
- **d.** By creating paintings which reflect an organized world.

_____ 2. What influenced the creators of Purism the most?
- **a.** The beauty of the French countryside.
- **b.** An art movement.
- **c.** Scientific discoveries.
- **d.** World War I.

_____ 3. Which of the following best explains the goals of Purism?
- **a.** To bring joy to people through beauty.
- **b.** To end war and violence.
- **c.** To start a new type of art.
- **d.** To create joy through order.

_____ 4. What would you likely see in Purist painting?
- **a.** A table with dishes.
- **b.** Trees and flowers.
- **c.** People in a city.
- **d.** Mountains and rivers.

_____ 5. What is the main purpose of this article?
- **a.** To explain how World War I influenced Purism.
- **b.** To tell the history of Purism.
- **c.** To show the connection between Purism and architecture.
- **d.** To explain different art movements in France.

Audi Pop.Up Next with Airbus drone on Turin Auto Show, June 7, 2018

40 Trading Tires for Rockets

040

In the world of science fiction, a flying car typically looks like a conventional car but is actually an aircraft that anybody can fly directly from one place to another without using roads or runways. Science fiction authors have written about flying cars for such a long time that the expression "Where are the flying cars?" has become an indication of a failure of modern technology.

Now flying cars are getting ready to fly out of the sci-fi world and into reality, and the long-cherished dream of science fiction writers will come true.

The first known "sky car" or "roadable aircraft" able to change from a road to an air vehicle was the LaBiche Aerospace FSC-1, also called LaBiche 460sc. It looks like an expensive sports car. You can drive the FSC-1 on the road like a normal car. If you touch a button, however, its wings and propeller fold out and it can take off, fly, and land as an airplane. The owners of this special car can therefore choose if they want to drive or fly. In 2006, founder Mitchell LaBiche finished the FSC-1 prototype for road and

flying car

Moller with his creations: M200M, M200X, and M400

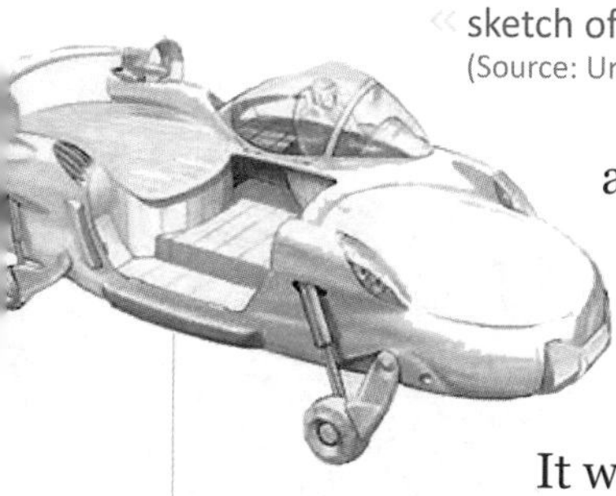

sketch of the Urban Aeronautics X-Hawk
(Source: Urban Aeronautics website: http://www.urbanaero.com/Frame-X-Hawk.htm)

air testing. However, more recent flying car concepts seem to have overtaken LaBiche Aerospace's prototype.

The Urban Aeronautics X-Hawk is another type of sky car. It is a vertical take-off and landing (VTOL) aircraft. It was first flown in 2009. At the 2018 Farnborough Air Show, Aston Martin, a British manufacturer of luxury sports cars, introduced their Volante Vision flying car concept, which might become James Bond's new vehicle of choice. More and more companies are looking at producing VTOL personal aircraft, which focus less on driving on the road and more on being easy to fly and land. Some of these new vehicles are even fully electric or hydrogen-powered.

As with any new technology, flying cars have taken a long time to be developed. Once they are here, we may very well ask ourselves "What did we do before the flying car?"

Questions

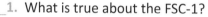

AeroMobil 3.0 on display, July 2, 2016

_____1. What is true about the FSC-1?
- **a.** It looks like a normal car on the road.
- **b.** Its design was based on a science fiction novel.
- **c.** It's the first known sky car.
- **d.** It cannot be driven on roads.

_____2. Where would this article probably appear?
- **a.** A literary magazine.
- **b.** A magazine about technology.
- **c.** A collection of science fiction stories.
- **d.** A magazine produced by airlines.

_____3. Where were flying cars first mentioned?
- **a.** In America.
- **b.** In reality.
- **c.** In science labs.
- **d.** In science fiction novels.

_____4. When someone asks "Where are the flying cars," what does he or she really mean?
- **a.** Technology has not advanced the way we thought it would.
- **b.** Where on earth did I park my flying car?
- **c.** Technology is getting cheaper and easier to create over time.
- **d.** Flying cars and other technology are bad ideas.

_____5. What might be an advantage of VTOL (vertical take-off and landing) cars for drivers?
- **a.** They only need gas power to fly.
- **b.** They are more attractive than normal airplanes.
- **c.** They are easy to learn how to fly.
- **d.** They have fold-out wings and propellers.

1-9 Fact or Opinion

It's always good to ask yourself whether a statement is fact or opinion. A fact is something that can be verified by other sources. With facts, there's a right and a wrong answer. Opinions are how someone feels about something. Thus, you can disagree with opinions but not with facts.

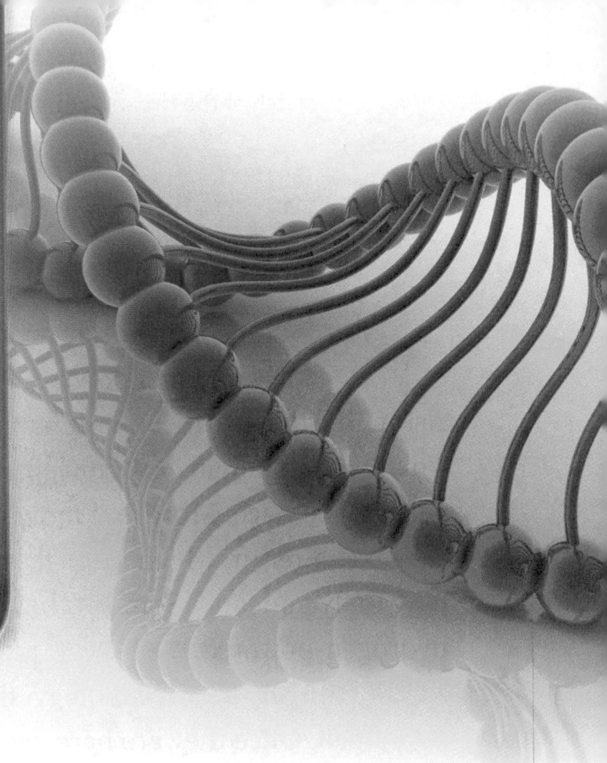

41 The Wonders of DNA

041

DNA helps to make you who you are.

1 DNA (deoxyribonucleic acid) helps to make you who you are. It is like a tiny instruction manual in each of your cells. DNA tells them how they should assemble your body. Your DNA determines what you will look like, and it even has a strong influence on your personality.

2 DNA is very similar from one human to another. In fact, scientists believe that the DNA of all humans is around 99 percent identical. It's that one percent difference that makes us unique individuals. And if that wasn't crazy enough, some studies claim that humans and chimpanzees have DNA that is 96 percent identical. Thus, a difference of one percent can make you bald, but four percent can have you swinging from the trees!

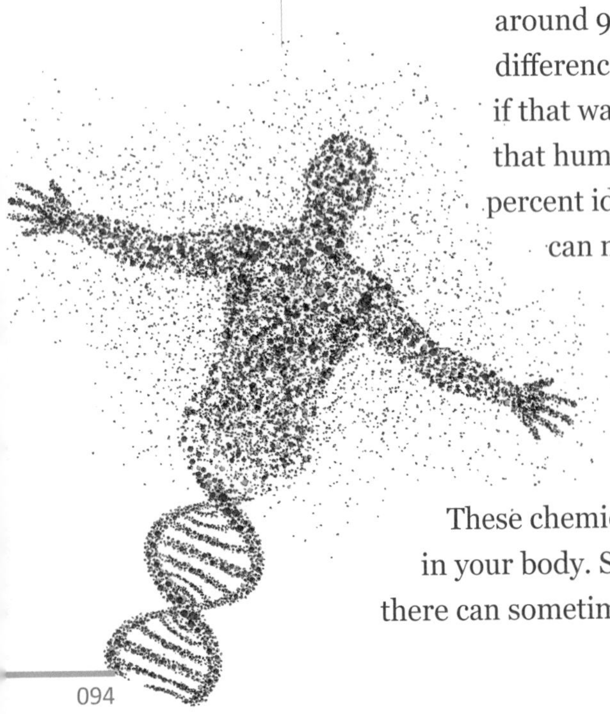

3 A DNA strand is called a "helix," and it looks like a pair of coiled strings. Each helix contains information in the form of chemicals. These chemicals are complicated instructions for the cells in your body. Since the instructions are very complicated, there can sometimes be mistakes when the DNA helix copies

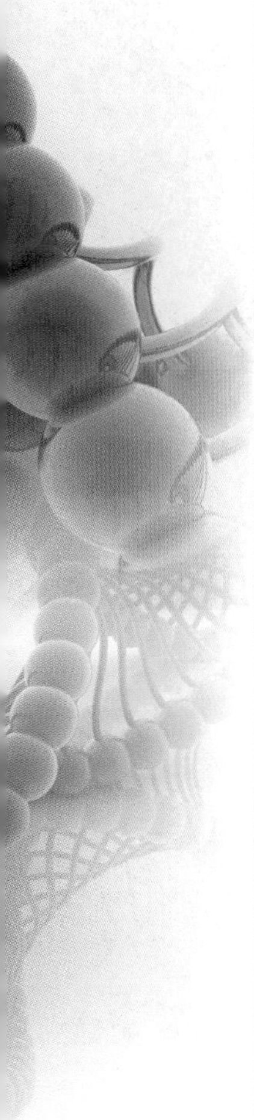

« DNA structure

itself. This is called a "mutation." Mutations are slight changes in someone's DNA, and these changes can be responsible for serious diseases and other problems. Cancer is one such example. DNA mutations can dramatically increase a person's chance of developing cancer later in life.

4 Scientists have only recently been able to map out the entire DNA helix. This has helped them discover new ways to repair problems in people's DNA. However some people believe that continued DNA research could create negative consequences, like human cloning. Therefore, we should always keep this in mind and be cautious in our future DNA research.

Questions

_____ 1. Which of the following is a fact?
- **a.** DNA is the most important topic in science.
- **b.** DNA research should not be pursued.
- **c.** The DNA of humans and chimps is 96 percent identical.
- **d.** Biology is a far more difficult subject than chemistry.

_____ 2. Which of the following is an opinion?
- **a.** A mistake in DNA is called a "mutation."
- **b.** DNA mutations can cause various diseases.
- **c.** DNA can affect a person's personality.
- **d.** A DNA helix looks like a coiled string.

_____ 3. The sentence in the fourth paragraph, "we should always keep this in mind and be cautious in our future DNA research" is a statement of ______.
- **a.** fact **b.** opinion

_____ 4. The sentence in the third paragraph, "a DNA strand is called a helix" is a statement of ______.
- **a.** fact **b.** opinion

_____ 5. Which of the following is a statement of opinion?
- **a.** Humans share 99 percent identical DNA.
- **b.** Continued DNA research is negative.
- **c.** DNA mutations can increase the chance of cancer.
- **d.** Scientists have mapped out the entire DNA helix.

42 *Game of Thrones*: A Fantasy World Inspires Your Imagination

042

1 It seems like the world is now divided into two types of people—those who talk about *Game of Thrones* every chance they get, and those who can't believe others are talking about that silly show *again*. Either way, everyone knows what *Game of Thrones* is. It's a television show that has turned into an important worldwide cultural trend.

2 So what's the secret of its success? For one, the show is based on a series of popular books called *A Song of Ice and Fire*, which has allowed for consistent storytelling. There's less of a risk of the television writers running out of ideas. Another thing that sets *Game of Thrones* apart is the show's high production values. On average, one episode costs around US$6 million to make. That's a full US$4 million more per episode than regular shows on cable television. *Game of Thrones*' higher budget allows for a cast of quality actors and huge battle scenes with advanced special effects.

3 Still not sure about the show's popularity? Well, perhaps it's the fact that *Game of Thrones* has more violence and adult themes than other shows. Or it might be that the line between "good" and "evil" is often not clear in the show. You might like a character in the beginning, only to see them do something horrible that changes your opinion in the end.

Game of Thrones poster (cc by Global Panorama)

scene from "Battle of the Bastards" in *Game of Thrones* (cc by BagoGames)

scene from "No One" in *Game of Thrones* (cc by BagoGames)

scene from "Dark Hedges of Armoy" in *Game of Thrones* (cc by horslips5)

On the other hand, an evil character might perform some unexpected act of mercy. Or maybe your favorite character will just die horribly, without warning. That's another feature of *Game of Thrones*: major characters have very short lifespans.

4 In truth, the show's success probably stems from a combination of these factors. Whatever the case, its audience continues to grow with each passing season. Love it or hate it, *Game of Thrones* isn't going anywhere.

« Klis Fortress, the set of *Game of Thrones*

» *A Song of Ice and Fire* series by George R. R. Martin (cc by Robert)

Questions

_____1. Which of the following is a fact?

a. It seems like the world is divided into two types of people.
b. The show's audience continues to grow with each passing season.
c. The show's success probably stems from a combination of factors.
d. There are those who talk about *Game of Thrones* too much.

_____2. Which of the following is an opinion?

a. One episode of *Game of Thrones* costs US$6 million to make on average.
b. *Game of Thrones* has more violence and adult themes than other shows.
c. The line between "good" and "evil" is not always clear.
d. Several characters in *Game of Thrones* die unexpectedly.

_____3. Which of the following is a fact?

a. *Game of Thrones* has production values that are too high.
b. *Game of Thrones* is based on a popular set of books.
c. *Game of Thrones* might be too violent.
d. *Game of Thrones* is better than regular television shows.

_____4. What is the sentence in the final paragraph: "Love it or hate it, *Game of Thrones* isn't going anywhere"?

a. A fact. **b.** An opinion.

_____5. What is the sentence in the first paragraph: ". . . *Game of Thrones* . . . has turned into an important worldwide cultural trend"?

a. A fact. **b.** An opinion.

Geneva

43 Switzerland

043

1 Switzerland is a beautiful country in the center of Europe. It borders Italy, Austria, Germany, Liechtenstein, and France. Its capital city is Bern, and Zurich is its largest city. About 8.4 million people live in Switzerland. It is a very rich country, and visitors often remark that it is very clean. Zurich and Geneva often rank very highly on lists measuring the quality of life of global cities.

Zurich

2 The best thing about Switzerland is its natural beauty. The scenery is dramatic, with high, snow-capped mountains, green hills, deep valleys, and blue lakes. These high mountains have historically kept invaders out. They also provide plenty of clear water. During the winter, tourists come from all around Europe to go skiing in the Swiss Alps.

Switzerland

3 Switzerland is a neutral country, meaning it doesn't get involved in wars and other conflicts. This is why it is home to so many international institutions, such as the Red Cross and the International Olympic Committee.

4 Switzerland is famous for watches, clocks, and chocolate. For centuries, the Swiss have made some of the finest watches and clocks in the world. Swiss timepieces are now more sought-after than ever.

Although Switzerland is not the only country to make good chocolate, Swiss chocolate is of a very high quality and is very popular. Today you can buy Swiss chocolate all over the world.

5 Switzerland is a very culturally advanced country because it has four official languages. Sixty-three percent of the population speaks German, 23 percent speaks French, and about eight percent speaks Italian. The other official language is Romansh, and it is spoken by less than one percent of the population. While it is not an official language, English is also frequently used as another way for people to communicate with one another in everyday life.

Swiss brand Omega Speedmaster was worn on the moon during the Apollo missions. Switzerland is responsible for half of the world production of watches. (cc by Shane Lin)

Questions

_____ 1. Which of the following is a fact?
   - **a.** Switzerland is the prettiest country in Europe.
   - **b.** Switzerland has four official languages.
   - **c.** The Swiss Alps look like a white fence.
   - **d.** Swiss chocolate tastes better than Belgian chocolate.

_____ 2. Which of the following is an opinion?
   - **a.** English is not an official language of Switzerland.
   - **b.** Switzerland is a neutral country.
   - **c.** Switzerland shares a border with Italy.
   - **d.** Switzerland is the cleanest country in Europe.

Swiss chocolate is of a very high quality and is very popular.

_____ 3. The first sentence of the second paragraph, "The best thing about Switzerland is its natural beauty," is a statement of ______.
   a. fact **b.** opinion

_____ 4. The first sentence in the fifth paragraph, "Switzerland is a very culturally advanced country," is a statement of ______.
   a. opinion **b.** fact

_____ 5. The fourth sentence in the first paragraph, "About 8.4 million people live in Switzerland," is a statement of ______.
   a. fact **b.** opinion

44 Star Signs of the Zodiac

044

March 21–April 20

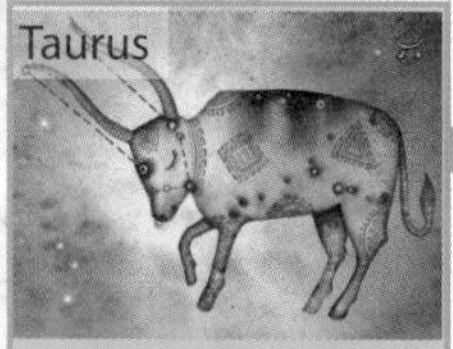

April 21–May 21

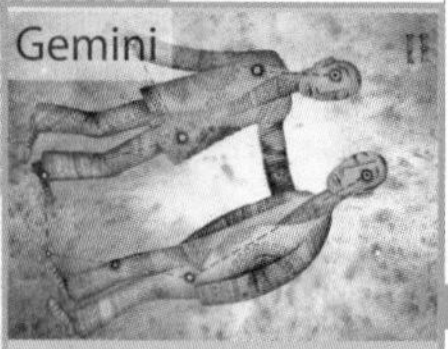

May 22–June 21

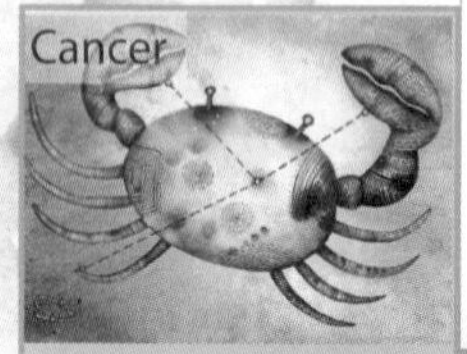

June 22–July 23

1 What is your star sign? Many people believe that the 12 star signs can give us deep insight into our daily lives, talents, special qualities, and future. Knowing your star sign may also help you to overcome some of life's difficulties.

2 The 12 star signs form the zodiac. In ancient Greece, the word "zodiac" meant "circle of little animals." The 12 star signs were named after animals that they resemble. We can see different star signs in the night sky depending on what month of the year it is.

3 Ancient Greek astronomers used the 12 divisions of the zodiac to make the study of stars and planets easier. These 12 equal divisions of the night sky are called the "signs of the zodiac" or "star signs." The 12 star signs are: the ram (Aries), the bull (Taurus), the twins (Gemini), the crab (Cancer), the lion (Leo), the maiden (Virgo), the scales (Libra), the scorpion (Scorpio), the archer (Sagittarius), the goat (Capricorn), the water carrier (Aquarius), and the fish (Pisces).

4 Ancient fortune-tellers believed that the movement of stars and planets affected the lives of normal people. This meant that people born under the same star sign would have similar personality traits. The study of how the zodiac affects people's personalities came to be known as "astrology." In some countries, the use of astrology to predict the future has become a very profitable business.

5 Since it is hard to prove that stars and planets affect human behavior, there are many people who believe that the zodiac is merely an ancient star map with no special powers. But how can they explain why so many Cancers are always moody? It seems that the night sky does affect us, but in ways that will always remain a mystery.

Questions

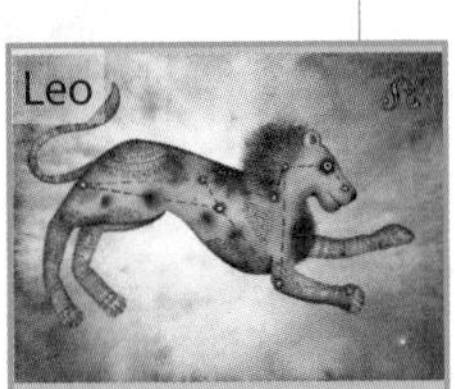

July 24–August 23

August 24–September 23

September 24–October 23

October 24–November 22

_____ 1. The final sentence in the fifth paragraph, "It seems that the night sky does affect us, but in ways that will always remain a mystery," is a statement of ______.
a. fact **b.** opinion

_____ 2. The second statement in the first paragraph, "the 12 star signs can give us deep insight into our daily lives," is a statement of ______.
a. fact **b.** opinion

_____ 3. Which of the following is a fact?
a. The zodiac affects our everyday lives.
b. Astrology is an important field of study.
c. Everyone should know their star sign.
d. The bull star sign is called Taurus.

_____ 4. Which of the following is an opinion?
a. Cancers are always moody.
b. There are 12 star signs in the zodiac.
c. The crab star sign is called Cancer.
d. Astrology is a form of fortune-telling.

_____ 5. The first sentence in the third paragraph, "Ancient Greek astronomers used the 12 divisions of the zodiac to make the study of stars and planets easier," is a statement of ______.
a. fact **b.** opinion

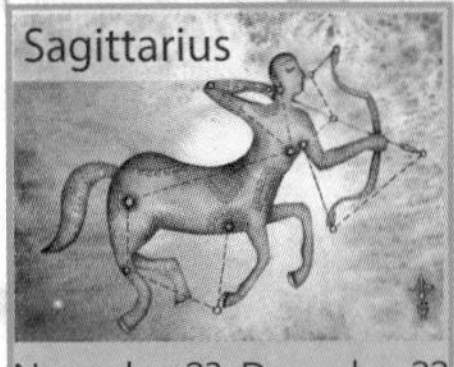

November 23–December 22

December 23–January 20

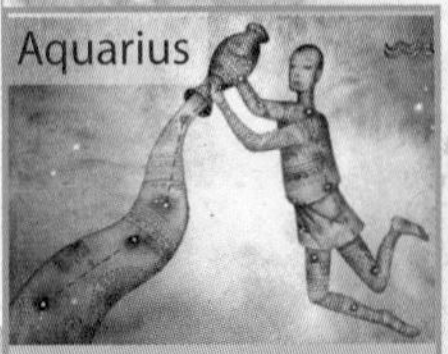

January 21–February 19

February 20–March 20

45 045
Avoiding Cancer

1 Cancer is a terrible disease that occurs when something goes wrong with the cells in a person's body, causing them to attack surrounding tissue. About 25 percent of all human deaths in Western countries are caused by cancer. It is also a serious problem in Asia. Many people believe that cancer is a bigger threat to human health than global warming or dwindling natural resources.

2 Why is it that more and more people are getting cancer? The answer probably has something to do with modern lifestyles. Smoking cigarettes, breathing polluted air, not exercising, living with too much stress, drinking polluted water, drinking too much alcohol, and not eating enough fresh fruit and vegetables can all increase your chances of getting cancer. Recent research has even suggested that the frequent use of a cell phone might also increase cancer risks.

3 It's not always a person's lifestyle or environment that causes cancer. Cancer can also be hereditary. This means people with parents who had cancer have a higher chance of getting it themselves. Therefore, a healthy lifestyle might not be enough if your family has a history of cancer.

4 There are lots of people who survive cancer, but since there is no cure, it can sometimes come back. However, there are things that people can do to reduce their risk. Medical research indicates that if you avoid smoking, alcohol, pollution, and stress, as well as maintain a healthy diet, you can reduce your chances of getting cancer.

5 If everyone were a little healthier, they would feel a lot better about themselves and the cancer rate would go down, too. That means exercising every day, getting about eight hours of sleep every night, drinking clean water, eating healthy foods, and reducing the amount of fat, salt, and sugar in your diet. It's that easy!

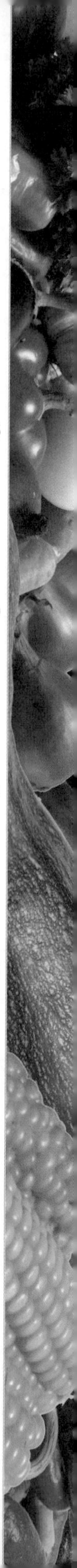

Ways to reduce your risk of cancer

Exercise regularly.

Eat a plant-based diet.

Avoid alcohol.

Do not smoke.

Questions

_____ 1. The statement in the first paragraph, "cancer is a bigger threat to human health than global warming or dwindling natural resources," is a statement of ______.

a. fact b. opinion

_____ 2. The second sentence in the third paragraph, "Cancer can also be hereditary," is a statement of ______.

a. fact b. opinion

_____ 3. Which of the following is a fact?

a. Cancer is the most depressing thing that can happen to someone.
b. The more someone exercises, the happier he or she is.
c. Frequent exercise can reduce a person's cancer risk.
d. Cancer is the most terrible disease in human history.

_____ 4. Which of the following is an opinion?

a. Modern lifestyles are increasing cancer rates.
b. We should change the way we live.
c. Cancer accounts for 25 percent of deaths in the West.
d. Cancer can be hereditary.

_____ 5. The final sentence in the second paragraph, "Recent research has even suggested that the frequent use of a cell phone might also increase cancer risks," is a statement of ______.

a. fact b. opinion

1-10 Review Test

Tyrannosaurus rex was one of the largest land carnivores of all time.

46 Terrible Lizards

046

Dinosaurs were animals that lived more than 65 million years ago. In Greek, the word "dinosaur" means "terrifying lizard." During the Mesozoic Era, dinosaurs were the dominant animals for over 160 million years. But they died out long before the development of the modern large animals we know today. The earliest types of humans, for example, first existed about five or six million years ago.

dinosaur nest model in the Natural History Museum of London
(cc by Drow male)

There were thousands of types of dinosaurs, and we know about only a few of them from the fossils we have found. We know that some dinosaurs were carnivorous (meat-eaters), and some were herbivorous (plant-eaters). Some dinosaurs were gigantic, while others were very small. The heaviest dinosaur was probably *Brachiosaurus*, which could weigh 80 tons. The tallest dinosaur was probably *Sauroposeidon*, whose head was 17 meters off the ground! The longest dinosaur was *Diplodocus hallorum*, which was over 40 meters long. The smallest dinosaurs that we know of were about the size of a chicken.

Some dinosaurs were very fierce. Creatures like *Tyrannosaurus rex* and *Spinosaurus* were larger than elephants, and some could run faster than a human being. Scientists say that some dinosaurs,

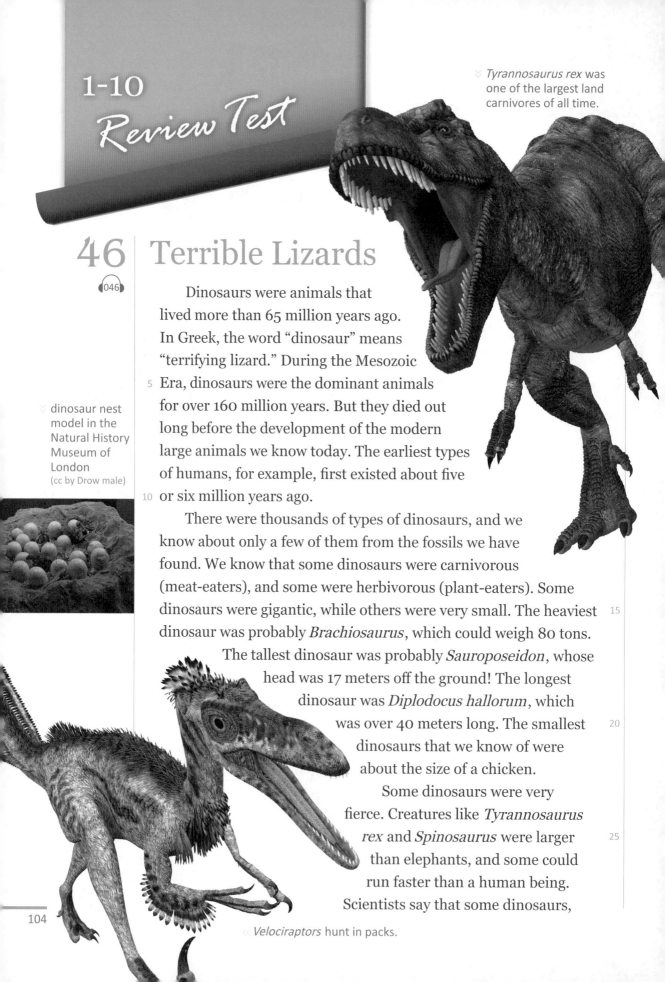

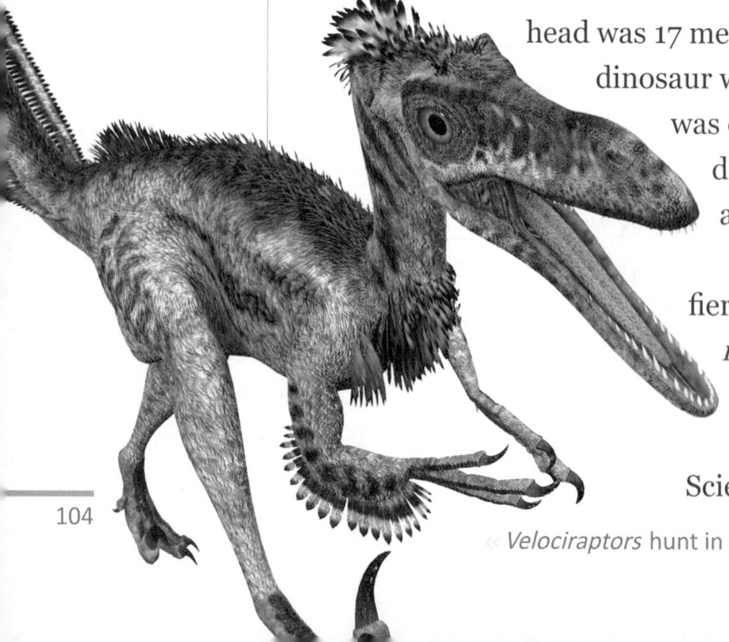

Velociraptors hunt in packs.

Birds may be the surviving relatives of one kind of dinosaur.

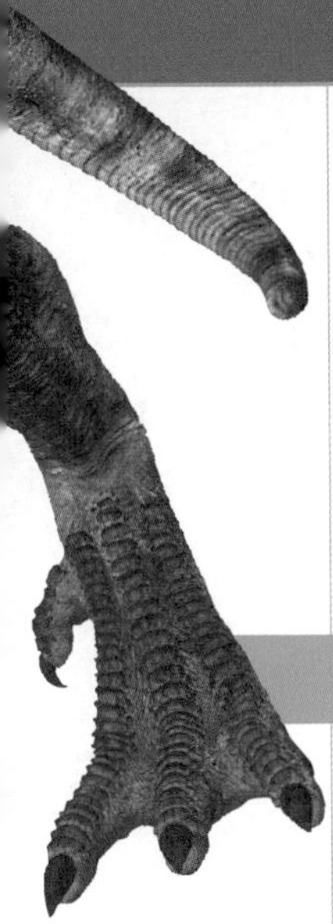

like *velociraptors*, hunted in packs like today's wolves and lions do. But it will take many more decades before scientists know about the many kinds of dinosaurs that existed long ago.

There are no dinosaurs today. It is believed that they completely disappeared about 65 million years ago. The cause of their sudden extinction was probably the impact of a large asteroid in Mexico. Some of the dinosaurs' relatives still live among us, though—birds. Scientists say that *theropod* dinosaurs were most likely the ancestors of today's birds. Next time you hear a bird sing, just think how remarkable its ancestors were.

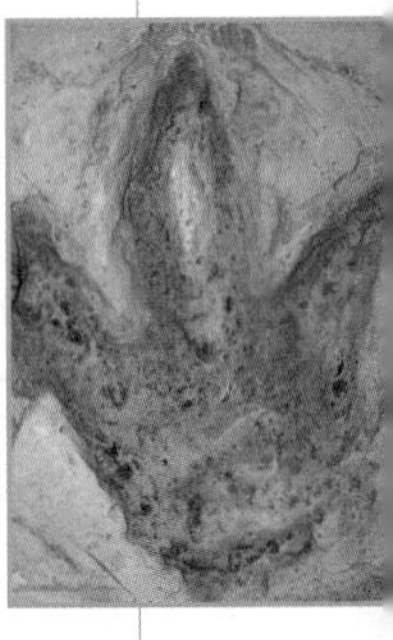

dinosaur footprint

Questions

_____ 1. What is the subject matter of this article?

a. Birds. **b.** Evolution. **c.** Dinosaurs. **d.** Scientists.

_____ 2. What is the main idea of this article?

a. Dinosaurs are related to birds.
b. We don't know how dinosaurs became extinct.
c. Fossils can't tell us much about dinosaurs.
d. There were many types of dinosaurs.

100-million-year-old dinosaur egg on display at the University of Zurich, Switzerland

_____ 3. What can you infer from the article?

a. There might be some dinosaurs that were smaller than chickens.
b. We know about all the dinosaurs that ever lived.
c. Dinosaurs were probably not killed by an asteroid.
d. We probably won't learn much more about dinosaurs.

_____ 4. What happened as a result of an asteroid crashing into Mexico?

a. Dinosaurs became related to birds.
b. Dinosaurs became extinct.
c. Dinosaurs grew taller.
d. Dinosaurs moved to other places.

_____ 5. Which event happened most recently?

a. Human beings existed. **b.** Dinosaurs hunted in packs.
c. Dinosaurs died out. **d.** A large asteroid hit Mexico.

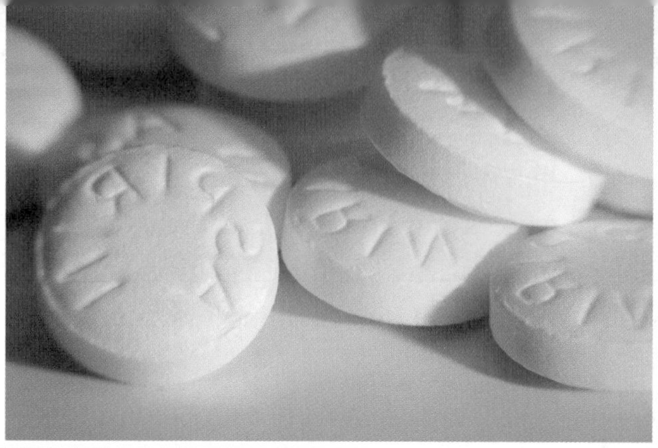

Aspirin can help prevent heart attacks, strokes, blood clot formation, and even cancer.

47 Aspirin

047

1 What do you do when you get a headache, toothache, or fever? Well, if you go to the doctor, there is a good chance that he or she will give you medicine with at least some aspirin in it. Aspirin is a drug that has become more and more popular because it can help people with many ailments. Today, about 40,000 metric tons of aspirin are consumed each year, and it has become one of the most widely used medications in the world.

advertisement for aspirin in 1958

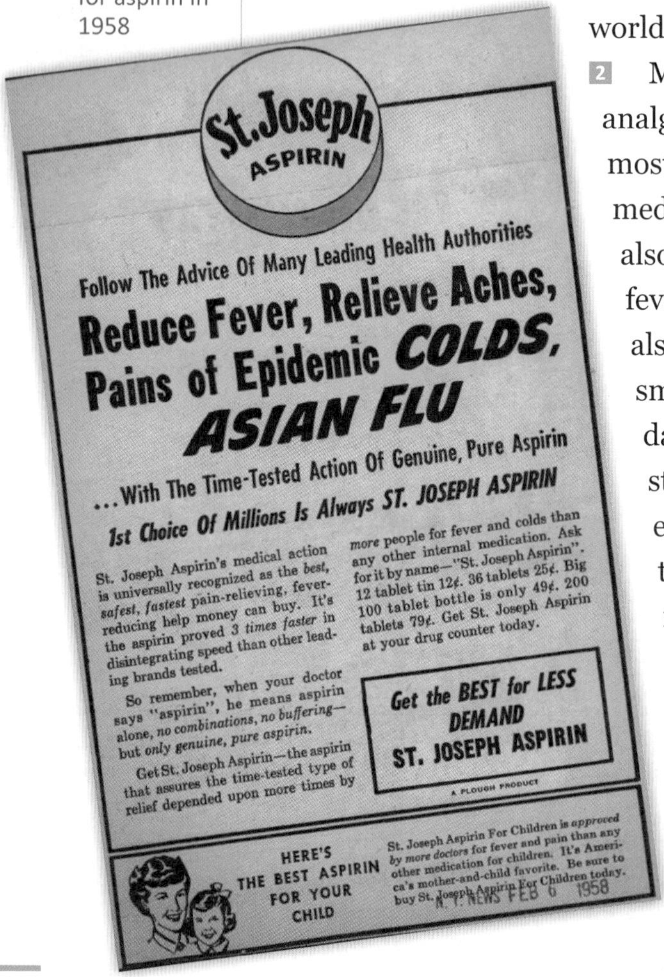

2 Most people use aspirin as an analgesic to stop pain. Therefore, most headache tablets and painkiller medicines have aspirin in them. It is also used as an antipyretic to stop a fever. Many cold and flu medicines also have aspirin in them. Moreover, small amounts of aspirin taken every day can help prevent heart attacks, strokes, blood clot formation, and even cancer. It does this by making the blood thinner, so the blood can move around the body more easily.

3 Is aspirin dangerous? Does aspirin have side effects? Aspirin is a drug, and like any other drug, it can be quite dangerous. Several hundred people die each year from taking too much aspirin. High doses of aspirin

Many people get help for various ailments by taking a tablet that contains aspirin.

may cause stomach ulcers and stomach bleeding and tinnitus. People suffering from gout are advised not to take low-dose aspirin, commonly referred to as baby aspirin (81 mg), because it decreases uric acid excretion. Aspirin has also been removed from children's cold and flu medicines, because sometimes children die from taking aspirin.

4 Overall, aspirin is usually not dangerous for adults if it is taken in small amounts. Many people get help for various ailments by taking a tablet that contains aspirin. It is truly an amazing drug.

Questions

_____ 1. Why was aspirin removed from children's cold medicine?
- **a.** Because it was expensive.
- **b.** Because children had died from taking it.
- **c.** Because it was preventing cancer.
- **d.** Because it's not good for people with gout.

_____ 2. Why has aspirin become more popular?
- **a.** Aspirin can treat many different kinds of illnesses.
- **b.** Aspirin is a drug, and like any drug, it can be very dangerous.
- **c.** People don't like to go to see a doctor.
- **d.** It is very good for children.

_____ 3. The tone of this article is mostly ______.
- **a.** biased **b.** persuasive
- **c.** angry **d.** informative

_____ 4. What is this article about?
- **a.** A drug. **b.** An illness.
- **c.** A hospital. **d.** An event.

_____ 5. What is the main idea of the third paragraph?
- **a.** Aspirin is a new drug. **b.** Aspirin can be dangerous.
- **c.** Aspirin is very safe. **d.** Aspirin is difficult to find.

» stone money on the island of Yap

48 The First Money

048

1 Everyone loves money, but do you know where money originally came from? Do you know who were the first people to use money? Scientists say that over 10,000 years ago, people in Swaziland, Southern Africa, were using red dye as a type of money. The aboriginal people of Australia were also using a similar dye as a type of money around that period of time. Later, people in several other parts of the world used shells and other valuable things as a type of money to buy or trade for things they wanted. This is known as a barter system, a form of trade where some goods are exchanged for other goods.

2 Many things have been used as money, from pigs to spices to salt. For a long time, pepper could be used to pay for things in Europe. On the Micronesian island of Yap, people used very big stone "coins," some of which were up to eight feet wide and weighed more than a small car.

3 **However**, the most convenient forms of money were pieces of valuable metals like gold and silver. Historians think that the Lydians were the first people to introduce the use of gold and silver coins around 650 BC. Gold and silver are still quite valuable today.

» The first coins were made by the Lydians out of an alloy of gold and silver.
(cc by CNG)

4 The first banknotes appeared in China in the seventh century, and the first banknotes in Europe were issued in 1661.

5 Money has changed through the ages, but it has always been important. Whether it's paper or pigs, most people like to have some money.

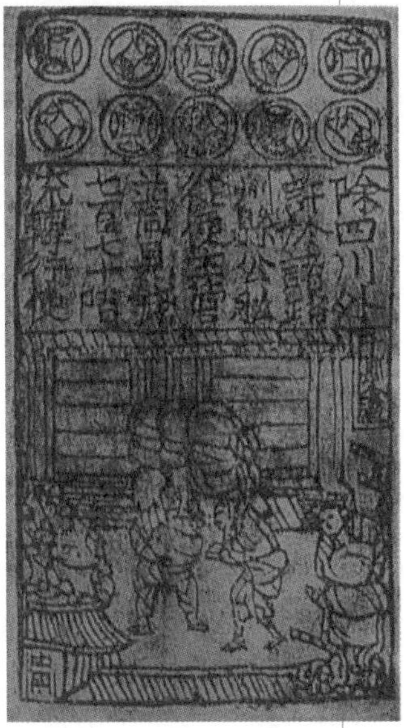

Song Dynasty jiaozi, the world's earliest paper money

Questions

_____ 1. What is the main idea of this article?
- **a.** Money is the key to a happy life.
- **b.** Money is a problem for many people.
- **c.** There have been many kinds of money.
- **d.** Money has a long history in China.

_____ 2. What happened most recently?
- **a.** Banknotes were issued in Europe.
- **b.** Lydians used gold coins.
- **c.** Banknotes appeared in China.
- **d.** Australian aboriginals used dye for money.

_____ 3. In the third paragraph, the author uses **however** to ______.
- **a.** show a contrast
- **b.** make a comparison
- **c.** create interest
- **d.** tell a joke

_____ 4. "Many things have been used as money." Which sentence below supports this sentence?
- **a.** Money is important all over the world.
- **b.** Pepper could be used to pay for things in Europe.
- **c.** The origin of money is very mysterious.
- **d.** Money has changed a lot through the ages.

_____ 5. What would the author probably agree with?
- **a.** Large stone coins were inconvenient.
- **b.** Dye was not the first money to be used.
- **c.** Banknotes are not popular forms of money.
- **d.** Gold and silver aren't valuable.

49 The History of Iraq

049 1 Iraq is located in Western Asia and borders Kuwait and Saudi Arabia to the south, Jordan to the west, Syria to the northwest, Turkey to the north, and Iran to the east.

2 Historians say that human civilization originally comes from Mesopotamia, an ancient country that today is known as Iraq. In the Greek language, Mesopotamia means "between the rivers," referring to the Tigris and Euphrates rivers. It was home to the first **civilization** of the world, the Sumerian culture, which dates back to 6,000 BC. This culture created the first writing, mathematics, science, and laws, and **therefore** is called the "Cradle of Civilization." Even today, we still use the same mathematical system, calendar, and system of time the Sumerians used 7,000 years ago.

Babylonian stone with cuneiform writing

3 Mesopotamia was an empire until the British took control of it in 1918. It was renamed Iraq, and it became an independent country in 1932. In 1979, Saddam Hussein became president. Saddam was a dictator and ruled with an iron fist. During the eight-year Iran-Iraq War, Iraqi forces attacked Iranian soldiers and

Mesopotamian art

Saddam Hussein (1937–2006)

civilians with chemical weapons. Saddam Hussein also ordered soldiers to use poison gas in an attack on Kurdish civilians inside Iraq. This terrible attack is known as the Halabja massacre, which was the largest-scale chemical weapons attack aimed at a civilian-populated area in the history of the world. Saddam Hussein was tried in court for his many crimes, found guilty, and executed in 2006.

4 As the cradle of human civilization, Iraq has a long history. However, this does not mean that it is a peaceful country today. It sometimes has terrorist attacks committed by various religious and political fanatics. But most of the Iraqi people want peace and development. That is the direction the country is moving in.

Kurdish children in Iraq
(cc by jamesdale10)

Questions

____ 1. What does the author suggest will happen in Iraq's future?
- **a.** It will be a peaceful nation.
- **b.** It will be the cradle of civilization.
- **c.** It will have chemical gas attacks.
- **d.** It will be ruled by Saddam Hussein.

____ 2. In the second paragraph, what does the author use **therefore** to do?
- **a.** To show a contrast.
- **b.** To show a result.
- **c.** To show a change in time.
- **d.** To show a biased opinion.

Akkadian ruler (2300–2000 BC)

____ 3. What does the author mean by **civilization**?
- **a.** History and the deep past.
- **b.** A peaceful, calm existence.
- **c.** Math, science, writing, and law.
- **d.** Chemical and biological weapons.

____ 4. What is this article about?
- **a.** A person.
- **b.** A country.
- **c.** A continent.
- **d.** A culture.

____ 5. What happened before Iraq became an independent country?
- **a.** Saddam Hussein became president.
- **b.** There was a war between Iran and Iraq.
- **c.** Saddam Hussein was executed.
- **d.** The British took over the country.

050

50 Leonardo da Vinci

self-portrait of Leonardo da Vinci (1452–1519) in red chalk (c. 1512)

1 Leonardo da Vinci was an Italian scientist, botanist, anatomist, engineer, inventor, mathematician, architect, sculptor, musician, writer, and painter. He is widely regarded as one of the greatest painters of all time and the most talented polymath who ever lived. He was born in 1452 in Vinci, Italy, and died in 1519.

2 As an engineer, da Vinci conceptualized many of our modern inventions such as helicopters, tanks, calculators, and solar power. However, most of his inventions could not be constructed because the science of his time was not advanced enough.

3 As an anatomist, da Vinci cut open human corpses and drew the human skeleton and its parts: muscles and sinews, sex organs, and various internal organs. He recorded his studies of science and engineering in notebooks, leaving 13,000 pages of drawings, scientific diagrams, and ideas about the nature of painting. His studies about anatomy, art, and engineering are brought together in his illustration, *The Vitruvian Man*. This illustration shows a beautifully detailed man moving his arms and legs in a symmetrical, realistic way. Because of his detailed study of human anatomy, da Vinci could create incredibly realistic

The Vitruvian Man (c. 1490)

the *Mona Lisa* (c. 1503–1506)

The Last Supper (1498)

drawings and paintings. His most famous paintings are the *Mona Lisa* and *The Last Supper*.

4 Da Vinci's father was a Florentine notary. His mother was a peasant woman or possibly a slave from the Middle East. When he was 14 years old, he went to work in the studio of a famous painter. It was there that he began to learn the skills he would master so completely.

5 We know very little about da Vinci's life. Luckily, some of his work remains behind to inspire us.

Questions

_____ 1. How does the author develop the main idea?

a. In order of events.
b. Humorously.
c. By showing cause and effect.
d. By themes.

_____ 2. What is the fourth paragraph about?

a. Da Vinci's slaves.
b. Da Vinci's engineering studies.
c. Da Vinci's early life.
d. Da Vinci's paintings.

_____ 3. What is true about most of da Vinci's inventions?

a. They were never built.
b. They do not work.
c. They exist in museums.
d. They were old ideas.

_____ 4. What was a result of da Vinci's study of human anatomy?

a. He made realistic pictures.
b. He became a great surgeon.
c. He created amazing inventions.
d. He studied with a famous painter.

_____ 5. Which is the author's opinion about da Vinci?

a. He was born in Vinci, Italy.
b. We are lucky to have the work he left behind.
c. His father was a notary.
d. He recorded his studies in many notebooks.

Unit 2

Word Study

This unit will help you practice some skills for building your vocabulary and understanding new vocabulary in a text. In this unit, you will practice identifying words that have the same meaning, which will make your writing more colorful and more interesting. You will learn to identify words with opposite meanings as well, which can help you create contrasts.

You will also practice understanding words from their context. Guessing the meaning of new words from their context is one of the most useful language skills you can learn. Mastering context is a great way to be able to build your vocabulary on your own.

2-1 Synonyms

The English language has lots of words. In fact, there are so many of them that sometimes different words can mean the same thing. If you wanted to say that the ice cream you're eating is good, you could just as easily say it's acceptable, excellent, nice, pleasing, super, or amazing.

51 The Life of a Leopard

051

1 The leopard lives in Africa and parts of Asia. It is the smallest of the four roaring cats in the *Panthera* genus, the other three being the tiger, lion, and jaguar. The leopard lives alone, except for the brief period when a mother leopard has her cub. Leopards look similar to cheetahs and jaguars, except that leopards are bigger than cheetahs and smaller than jaguars.

2 A leopard tries to avoid areas where there are wild dogs, spotted hyenas, tigers, and lions, because these animals may steal its food or kill a leopard cub. Leopards are very **fast** and can run 57 kilometers an hour, leap a distance of six meters, and jump three meters in the air. Leopards are also **known** for their skill at climbing trees. Even though leopards are smaller than the other three members of the *Panthera* genus, they are very strong and can pull a dead gazelle into a tree to keep it away from scavengers.

3 During the day, leopards usually hide. Their hiding places can be in some tall grass or high in a tree branch. Leopards are nocturnal, which means they sleep during the day and are **active** at night.

the leopard

the lion

4 Female leopards have one cub each year, and after giving birth, a mother leopard usually goes off to hunt and leaves her cub alone.

5 Leopards are **beautiful** and very difficult to find, but that doesn't mean that they can't be found if you know where to look. Leopards are one of the "big five" that tourists visit Africa to see. The "big five" refer to the five most **popular** animals in Africa: the lion, the African elephant, the African buffalo, the leopard, and the rhinoceros.

the rhinoceros

the African elephant

Questions

_____1. Which of the following words has the same meaning as **fast** in the second paragraph sentence "Leopards are very **fast** and can run 57 kilometers an hour"?

a. Dull. **b.** Slim. **c.** Swift. **d.** Idle.

_____2. Which of the following has the same meaning as the word in capital letters in the phrase "the five most **POPULAR** animals in Africa"?

a. Hated. **b.** Feared. **c.** Well-known. **d.** Unique.

_____3. Which of the following explains the use of **known** in the context of the second paragraph sentence "Leopards are also **known** for their skill at climbing trees"?

a. They are very bad at climbing trees.
b. They are born and live their early lives in trees.
c. Lots of people are aware that leopards can climb trees.
d. Lots of people mistake leopards for being good climbers.

the African buffalo

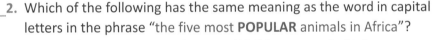

_____4. Which of the following has the same meaning as the word in capital letters in the sentence "Leopards are **BEAUTIFUL** and very difficult to find"?

a. Humorous. **b.** Jealous. **c.** Joyful. **d.** Handsome.

_____5. Which of the following explains the use of **active** in the context of the third paragraph sentence "Leopards sleep during the day and are **active** at night"?

a. They usually sleep during both day and night.
b. The nighttime is when they hunt and travel.
c. They are most dangerous during daytime.
d. They only give birth during nighttime.

52 New Zealand: The Country at the Edge of the World

052

Auckland is the largest city in New Zealand.

1 New Zealand is a country made up of two main islands (North Island and South Island) and many smaller islands. It is located about 2,000 kilometers southeast of Australia. Many people **say** that it is the most remote country in the world. The capital city of New Zealand is Wellington, although Auckland is its largest city. There are over four million people living in New Zealand. The **majority** of the population is of European descent, and other significant minority groups include Maori, Asian, and non-Maori Polynesian.

2 New Zealand was one of the last **major** landmasses on Earth to be settled by humans. Scientists believe that the Maori first arrived on the islands sometime between AD 1250 and 1300. The Maori people call New Zealand "Aotearoa," which means "land of the long white cloud."

3 Because New Zealand is so far away from most other countries, about 80 percent of its plants and many of its birds and animals are endemic, which means they cannot be found anywhere else in the world. Some of New Zealand's unique **native** species include

New Zealand

giant weta
(cc by kiwe Mikex)

the giant weta, an insect that is over 10 cm long, and Maui's dolphins, one of the world's rarest marine dolphins. Sadly, many of New Zealand's distinct birds are now extinct because of the arrival of humans and the mammals that came with them.

4 New Zealand is very beautiful. It was used as a setting for the three *Lord of the Rings* movies and has become a popular place for tourists to visit because of these Hollywood blockbusters. If you need a vacation and are looking for a **unique** place to visit, why not go to New Zealand? You may be surprised at what you find there.

New Zealand is a filming location for the three *Lord of the Rings* movies.

Questions

_____ 1. Which of the following explains the use of **majority** in the context of the first paragraph sentence "The **majority** of the population is of European descent"?
- a. The Europeans were there the longest.
- b. Most of the population has European roots.
- c. The youth of New Zealand are all European.
- d. New Zealand is a country in Europe.

_____ 2. Which of the following has the same meaning as the word in capital letters in the phrase "New Zealand's unique **NATIVE** species"?
- a. Foreign. b. Global. c. Local. d. Threatened.

_____ 3. Which of the following words has the same meaning as **major** in the second paragraph sentence "New Zealand was one of the last **major** landmasses on Earth to be settled by humans"?
- a. Small. b. Island. c. Uninhabited. d. Large.

_____ 4. Which of the following words has the same meaning as **unique** in the fourth paragraph phrase "If you need a vacation and are looking for a **unique** place to visit"?
- a. Special. b. Common. c. Old. d. Interesting.

_____ 5. Which of the following has the same meaning as the word in capital letters in the sentence "Many people **SAY** that it is the most remote country in the world"?
- a. Shout. b. Claim. c. Assume. d. Wish.

facsimile sheet of music of the Requiem Mass in D minor (K. 626) in Mozart's own handwriting

Wolfgang Amadeus Mozart (1756–1791)

53 Amadeus Mozart: The Man and the Mystery

053

1 Amadeus Mozart is one of the most famous and enduringly popular classical composers in history. He was born on January 27, 1756, in Salzburg, Austria. His father, Leopold Mozart, was one of the best music teachers in Europe at the time. In fact, Leopold published a very successful violin textbook the same year that his son Wolfgang Amadeus was born. Under his father's influence and teaching, Mozart began to show a talent for music at a very young age. He started **composing** his own music when he was only five years old. By the time he was six, he could play the piano blindfolded.

2 When he was young, Mozart traveled frequently and **performed** for many of Europe's royal courts. During his travels, he met a great number of famous musicians of the time. According to some historians, Mozart could speak up to 15 languages. By the time of his death, he had written about 600 compositions, and many of them are still well-known today.

Mozart's birthplace at Getreidegasse 9, Salzburg, Austria

3 Mozart had money problems throughout his life. He frequently had to write letters to friends and beg them to lend him some money. This was a little **strange** because Mozart earned a good salary for most of his life. The problem was that he spent more than he earned. Mozart died in late 1791 at the age of 35. Mystery still surrounds the circumstances of Mozart's death. In particular, historians disagree on what sickness caused his death. Some even believe that he was poisoned by Antonio Salieri, another composer who was **jealous** of Mozart's talent.

4 Mozart is considered to be one of the greatest musicians who ever lived, and his **influence** on classical music has been profound. Although more than two centuries have passed since Mozart's death, his talent remains unsurpassed.

>> In his early years, Mozart's father, Leopold Mozart (1719–1787), was his only teacher.

Questions

_____**1.** Which of the following has the same meaning as **compose** in the first paragraph sentence "He started **composing** his own music when he was only five years old"?

a. To listen. **b.** To produce. **c.** To destroy. **d.** To criticize.

_____**2.** Which of the following has the same meaning as **strange** in the third paragraph sentence "This was a little **strange** because Mozart earned a good salary for most of his life"?

a. Common. **b.** Colorful. **c.** Angering. **d.** Peculiar.

_____**3.** Which of the following has the same meaning as the word in capital letters in the phrase "Antonio Salieri, another composer who was **JEALOUS** of Mozart's talent"?

a. Envious. **b.** Appreciative. **c.** Hateful. **d.** Dismissive.

_____**4.** Which of the following explains the use of **perform** in the context of the second paragraph sentence "Mozart traveled frequently and **performed** for many of Europe's royal courts"?

a. He played music in palaces all over Europe.
b. He visited landmarks in every European city.
c. He was part of a traveling music troupe.
d. He did taxes for various European kings.

_____**5.** Which of the following has the same meaning as the word in capital letters in the sentence "His **INFLUENCE** on classical music has been profound"?

a. Knowledge. **b.** Impact. **c.** Distrust. **d.** Gratitude.

54 Amazing Chocolate

054

» chocolate

1 Do you like chocolate? Most people love it. Its sweet, creamy flavor is hard to **resist**. But where did chocolate come from?

2 About 2,600 years ago, the Olmec, who lived in Central and South America made use of chocolate. They used cocoa beans to make a special drink, but this drink wasn't sweet like the chocolate we are used to. It was very bitter. In the years that followed, they started adding other things to their cocoa drink to make it taste better.

» cocoa tree with fruit pods in various stages of ripening

3 Chocolate was very important for the Maya, another group in Central America. Mayans **used** cocoa beans as money, and it is said that 10 beans could buy a rabbit. Cocoa beans were also used in Mayan religion and wedding ceremonies. The Mayans also used cocoa beans to make a chocolate drink, but only rich people could afford to drink it.

4 When the Europeans arrived in South America, they started to bring this popular drink back to their home countries. Milk, cream, and sugar were added, and eventually the chocolate we know was born. In the year 1689, chocolate milk was **developed** in Jamaica.

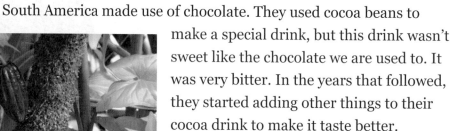

» Chocolate is created from cocoa beans.

5 Chocolate is now one of the most popular flavors in the world. In modern society, we can enjoy chocolate in bars, ice cream, cakes, milkshakes, pies, and many other foods. Some studies have

found that dark chocolate is good for our health because it benefits the circulatory system and has other anticancer **properties**. Thus, small but regular amounts of dark chocolate might be able to reduce the risk of a heart attack.

6 Nothing is perfect, and chocolate is no **exception**. Chocolate can contain a large amount of calories, so people who eat a lot of chocolate risk becoming obese. Perhaps the secret to enjoying chocolate's flavor and not ruining your health is very simple: don't eat too much of it!

Questions

A Mayan chief forbids a person to touch a jar of chocolate.
(cc by Mayan Civilisation)

Mayan writing referring to cocoa
(Wikipedia)

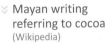

_____ 1. Which of the following has the same meaning as the word in capital letters in the sentence "It benefits the circulatory system and has other anticancer **PROPERTIES**"?

a. Effects. **b.** History.
c. Studies. **d.** Medicine.

_____ 2. Which of the following has the same meaning as the word in capital letters in the sentence "Mayans **USED** cocoa beans as money"?

a. To research. **b.** To employ.
c. To eat. **d.** To grow.

_____ 3. Which of the following has the same meaning as the word in capital letters in the sentence "In the year 1689, chocolate milk was **DEVELOPED** in Jamaica"?

a. Imported. **b.** Exported.
c. Hidden. **d.** Invented.

_____ 4. Which of the following has the same meaning as the word in capital letters in the sentence "Its sweet, creamy flavor is hard to **RESIST**"?

a. To eat. **b.** To taste.
c. To refuse. **d.** To understand.

_____ 5. Which of the following explains the use of **exception** in the context of the sixth paragraph sentence "Nothing is perfect, and chocolate is no **exception**"?

a. Chocolate has faults like everything else.
b. Chocolate tastes better than anything else.
c. Chocolate is healthier than any other food.
d. Chocolate is the only perfect food.

logo of Greenpeace

GREENPEACE

Greenpeace activists marching in the 2018 Toronto Pride Parade

55 Greenpeace: Saving the Environment

055

1 Greenpeace is a global organization that aims to **prevent** companies and governments from harming the environment. While Greenpeace isn't the only international environmental organization, it is the largest and most well-known around the world.

2 Since its founding in 1971 in Vancouver, Canada, Greenpeace has been involved in several high-profile historic events. In 1995, a Greenpeace ship interfered with a French nuclear weapon test, bringing worldwide attention to the issue. The French government signed an international treaty banning nuclear weapon tests soon after the incident. Greenpeace has also repeatedly sent ships to protect whales from Japanese whalers. The organization has also **launched** political campaigns against Japanese and Norwegian whaling companies to prevent them from expanding their whaling operations in the future.

3 Greenpeace activists are **involved** in a wide variety of environmental issues. They are usually fighting against big companies or governments that are harming the environment for personal or corporate profit. Some of these issues include the **destruction** of rain forests, bottom trawling, whaling,

inflatable snowman with the "Stop Global Warming!" slogan at the G8 (2007)
(cc by Stop Global Warming)

global warming, nuclear power, nuclear disarmament, and clean energy. Greenpeace tries to bring public attention to these issues so that regular people will become involved and help protect the environment.

4 Greenpeace activists have occasionally **put** themselves in danger to stand up for what they believe in. They have used small boats to try to stop huge whaling vessels. They have also tied themselves to trees that were about to be chopped down by logging companies.

5 Greenpeace is well supported by people all around the world, but environmental destruction still continues to this day. However, with all of the organization's past success, it looks like the environment would be a lot worse if there had never been a Greenpeace to protect it.

» Greenpeace's second *Rainbow Warrior* ship

Questions

_____ 1. Which of the following has the same meaning as the word in capital letters in the sentence "Greenpeace is a global organization that aims to **PREVENT** companies and governments from harming the environment"?

a. To help. **b.** To investigate. **c.** To stop. **d.** To enable.

_____ 2. Which of the following has the same meaning as the word in capital letters in the sentence "The organization has also **LAUNCHED** political campaigns against Japanese and Norwegian whaling companies"?

a. To end. **b.** To start. **c.** To research. **d.** To criticize.

_____ 3. Which of the following has the same meaning as **involved** in the third paragraph sentence "Greenpeace activists are **involved** in a wide variety of environmental issues"?

a. To learn. **b.** To run. **c.** To engage. **d.** To dismiss.

_____ 4. Which of the following has the same meaning as **destruction** in the third paragraph sentence "Some of these issues include the **destruction** of the rain forests"?

a. Ruin. **b.** Recovery. **c.** Expansion. **d.** Protection.

_____ 5. Which of the following explains the use of **put** in the context of the fourth paragraph sentence "Greenpeace activists have occasionally **put** themselves in danger . . ."?

a. They avoid conflict whenever possible.
b. They sometimes do dangerous things.
c. They have been trained in negotiation.
d. They have been trained to avoid danger.

2-2 Antonyms

The English language has a rich vocabulary and includes many words with opposite meanings to each other. Some opposites, such as *dead* versus *alive*, express one of only two possibilities. Others have variations: *huge*, *giant*, and *big* are all opposites of *small*. Learning more words with opposite meanings will improve your vocabulary and make your writing more interesting.

The Coca-Cola logo was created by Frank Mason Robinson in 1885.

John Pemberton (1831–1888), the inventor of Coca-Cola

056

56 Coca-Cola

1 Coca-Cola is the most **famous** soft drink in the world. You will see Coca-Cola signs on buildings in almost every country. It is sold in stores, restaurants, and vending machines in more than 200 countries. Many people love the sweet, brown, **fizzy** drink that we also call "Coke." However, there are also many people who dislike it and other kinds of pop because of their high sugar content. Nutritionists advise that pop can be **unhealthy** for your body if you drink too much of it.

2 In 1885, John Pemberton invented Coca-Cola at a drugstore in Columbus, Georgia. It was sold as a medicine in Atlanta, Georgia in 1886. It did not become popular as a drink until Asa Candler bought Pemberton's company and set up the Coca-Cola Company in 1888. Asa Candler used many **smart** marketing ideas to make his cola a popular soft drink. In 1894, Coca-Cola was sold in bottles for the first time. It wasn't until 1955 that cans of Coke appeared.

3 During World War II, most Americans were allowed only a small amount of sugar. Coca-Cola, however, was permitted to use as much

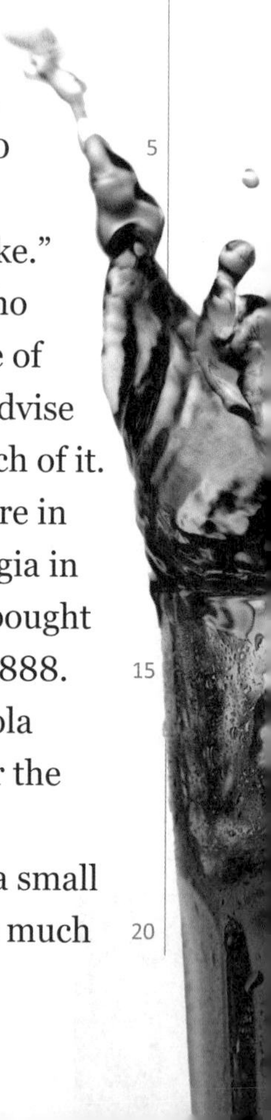

the Las Vegas Strip *World of Coca-Cola* museum in 2003
(cc by MykRevve)

sugar as it wanted. Many people bought Coke for the taste of something sweet. Coke was also given to American soldiers for free. This wartime consumption of Coca-Cola may be another important reason why Coca-Cola has become legendary.

4 After the war, many people continued to drink it. Coca-Cola branched out, creating Cherry Coke, Diet Coke, and other drinks, pushing into other markets. Today, Coke is still everywhere, and it shows no signs of **slowing down**. Who knows? Your grandchildren may drink Coke as a treat.

Questions

_____**1.** Which word means the opposite of **famous**?
a. Fizzy. **b.** Difficult.
c. Popular. **d.** Unknown.

_____**2.** What word means the opposite of **unhealthy** as it is used in the first paragraph?
a. Nutritious. **b.** Sickly.
c. Expensive. **d.** Diet.

_____**3.** Which of the following is the opposite of **slowing down** in the final paragraph?
a. Pushing into.
b. Branching out.
c. Continuing to.
d. Speeding up.

_____**4.** Which word is the opposite of **fizzy**?
a. Sour. **b.** Cold.
c. Flat. **d.** Healthy.

_____**5.** Which word can be the opposite of **smart** in the second paragraph?
a. Invented. **b.** Dull.
c. Bright. **d.** Honest.

Princess Diana (1961–1997) in 1982 (cc by Joe Haupt)

Prince Charles (1948–) in 2015

57 England's Royal Family: A Monarchy in the Modern Age

057

1 The United Kingdom has the most well-known royal family in the world. Right now, the UK (England, Scotland, Wales, and Northern Ireland) has a queen, Queen Elizabeth II. Although the royal family does not hold political power, they represent British culture and history. During Queen Elizabeth's rule, which began in 1952, she has been admired for her **dedication** to her royal duties and to the British people. Her son, Prince Charles, is next in line for the throne.

2 As the future king, Prince Charles has been in the public eye almost as much as the queen. When he married Lady Diana Spencer in 1981, people around the world watched the wedding. Princess Diana, as she became known, was admired for her style and beauty. More **notably**, she brought attention to problems around the world, including landmines, AIDS, and leprosy. Her work to help others led to her nickname, the People's Princess. After her divorce from Prince Charles, she died in a car accident in 1997. People around the world **mourned** the death of the beloved People's Princess.

3 Some British people feel that the royal family is **obsolete**, since its members no longer hold any political power. But there are also those who still **adore** the royals. Diana and Charles's sons, William and Harry, are

Queen Elizabeth II (1926–2022) in 2011 (photo by Julian Calder for Governor-General of New Zealand)

known for having their mother's warmth and humanity. Prince William, the oldest and second in line to the throne, married a woman who is not from a noble family, Kate Middleton. Both William and Kate are known for being hands-on parents to their three children. Their eldest son, Prince George, will be king one day. Prince Harry also married a regular person, an American named Meghan Markle. William and Harry are following in their mother's footsteps to make the royal family relatable to ordinary people.

« Prince William (1982–) and Kate Middleton (1982–) in 2016

» Prince Harry (1984–) and Meghan Markle (1981–) in 2017 (cc by Mark Jones)

Questions

_____**1.** In the first paragraph, which word is the opposite of **dedication**?
a. Appreciation. **b.** Laziness. **c.** Dishonesty. **d.** Effort.

_____**2.** What is the opposite of **notably** as it is used in the second paragraph?
a. Importantly. **b.** Quickly. **c.** Incredibly. **d.** Insignificantly.

_____**3.** Which word is the opposite of **adore** in the third paragraph?
a. Avoided. **b.** Hated. **c.** Loved. **d.** Admired.

_____**4.** Which of the following is the opposite of **mourned** in the second paragraph?
a. Celebrated. **b.** Remembered.
c. Apologized. **d.** Grieved.

_____**5.** Which of the following is the opposite of **obsolete** as it is used in the third paragraph?
a. Old-fashioned. **b.** Expensive. **c.** Interesting. **d.** Modern.

« samurai and retainers with various types of armor and weapons, 1880s

» samurai sculpture

58 The Samurai

058

1 In Europe, some well-trained nobleman warriors were honored by the king or queen and called "knights." In Japan, these warriors were called "samurai." A samurai was an **excellent** swordsman who lived his life according to a special set of rules called the "Bushido," meaning "Way of the Warrior." Bushido was the samurai's moral code and way of life. It told the samurai how to act in war and in peace and how to live his life. The Bushido code contains seven **core** virtues: rectitude, courage, benevolence, respect, honesty, honor, and loyalty.

2 A samurai always owned two swords, one long and one short. The longer sword, called the "katana," was used in fighting. A samurai had to

» traditional Japanese sword cases and the katana *(top)* and the shorter wakizashi *(bottom)*

samurai armor at the Tokyo National Museum

be an expert in the use of the katana. He **depended on** the katana for fighting, and the katana became a part of his soul. The shorter sword was called the "wakizashi," and a samurai would always have it with him. It was often used as a backup sword for close-quarters combat.

3 Honor was the most important thing to a samurai. A samurai had to follow the rules of the Bushido, or he would be dishonored. Dishonor was worse than death for a samurai. Sometimes, a samurai who had done something dishonorable would commit ritual suicide with his wakizashi.

4 Doing one's best was also a **key** part of the samurai culture. A samurai spent most of his time trying to become better at everything he did. This is why he was such a **fierce** warrior.

5 Today, there are no samurai like those from the past, but many people consider the samurai to have been great men who strongly influenced modern Japanese culture.

Questions

_____ 1. When something is **excellent**, it is not ________.
a. failing b. fine
c. extremely good d. top-notch

_____ 2. When you don't **depend on** something, you don't ________.
a. ignore it b. avoid it c. skip it d. rely on it

_____ 3. Which of the following is the opposite of **core**?
a. Center. b. Basis. c. Root. d. Outside.

_____ 4. Which word is the opposite of **key** as it is used in the fourth paragraph?
a. Significant. b. Convenient c. Proud. d. Unimportant.

_____ 5. Which word is the opposite of **fierce** in the fourth paragraph?
a. Timid. b. Slow. c. Stupid. d. Violent.

samurai around the 1860s

⌃ Chengdu Research Base of Giant Panda Breeding

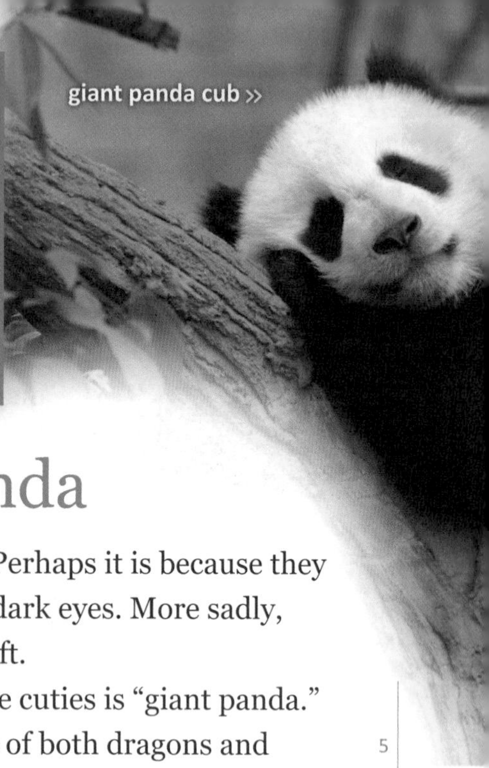
giant panda cub »

59 The Mysterious Panda

059

1 Why do people love pandas so much? Perhaps it is because they look very cute, with their round faces and dark eyes. More sadly, perhaps it is because there are not many left.

2 The real name of those black-and-white cuties is “giant panda.” Giant pandas originated in China. Pictures of both dragons and giant pandas are often regarded as symbolic of China.

3 Many people also call giant pandas “pandas” or “panda bears.” Giant pandas were only **recently** confirmed as bears—for many years, scientists thought they were more closely related to raccoons. Giant pandas look different from other bears, because they are white with black patches around their eyes, over their ears, and across their bodies. Although they look **adorable** and move slowly, they can be as dangerous as any other bear when they are angry. Pandas eat mostly bamboo, but they may also eat other food like eggs, fish, oranges, and bananas.

4 Many people think that giant pandas have **few** babies, and that is one of the reasons that there are not many of them left. But scientists say that a female panda may have about five to eight cubs during her life. The female panda gives birth to one or two panda

« Pandas eat mostly bamboo.

cubs, but she is only able to take care of one cub at a time. As a result, one of her cubs dies soon after birth because of a lack of **intense** care.

5 The giant panda is a **vulnerable** species, and there are only about 2,000 giant pandas left in the world. People have been trying hard to protect giant pandas. It looks like their work is paying off, because the number of giant pandas is increasing.

» At birth, a giant panda cub typically weighs 100 to 200 grams and measures 15 to 17 centimeters long. (cc by Colegota)

Questions

_____ **1.** Which phrase means the opposite of **recently** in the third paragraph?

a. True or valid.
b. Bigger than average.
c. In the distant past.
d. Not long ago.

_____ **2.** Which word is the opposite of **adorable**?

a. Ugly. **b.** Cute.
c. Lovely. **d.** Interesting.

_____ **3.** Which word is the opposite of **vulnerable**?

a. Endangered.
b. Threatened.
c. Safe.
d. Risky.

_____ **4.** Which word is the opposite of **few**?

a. Less. **b.** Some.
c. Half. **d.** Many.

_____ **5.** What of the following is the opposite of **intense**?

a. Great. **b.** Lazy.
c. Sharp. **d.** Powerful.

« The giant panda is a vulnerable species.

logo of the TauTona Mine

TauTona is owned by the global gold mining company AngloGold Ashanti.

60 The Deepest Mine in the World

060

1 We all know that gold and diamonds come from deep in the ground, but how do people get to them? Well, they dig into the earth and build mines. Mines are underground places where people work to find and **remove** valuable minerals.

2 One of the deepest mines in the world is in South Africa. It's called TauTona, which means "great lion" in Setswana, a **local** language. TauTona is 3.9 kilometers deep. It was created to get access to gold that exists deep underground.

About 5,600 miners in TauTona work to find gold.

3 TauTona was originally built in 1957, but at first it was not as deep as it is now. The mine started operation in 1962 and had been in **continuous** operation until 2017. It reached 3.9 kilometers deep in 2008. It can take a **whole** hour to travel from the surface to the bottom of the mine!

4 Today, TauTona has over 800 kilometers of tunnels, where about 5,600 miners worked to find and dug out gold. Because the mine is so deep, temperatures in the mine may **rise** to dangerous levels. With air-conditioning equipment, the temperature can be brought down from 55°C to 28°C.

TauTona is a gold mine west of Johannesburg.

Mines are dangerous places to work.

5 The mine is a dangerous place to work, and about five miners die every year in rock falls and explosions underground. Even so, many people in South Africa don't have other job options, so this dangerous mine seems like a good choice. However, the final blast at TauTona took place on September 15, 2017, and the mine has since been closed. From that day on, AngloGold Ashanti has been looking for gold in new areas.

Questions

_____1. Which of the following is the opposite of **continuous**?
a. Nonstop. **b.** Interrupted. **c.** Lasting. **d.** Stable.

_____2. Which word is the opposite of **local** in the second paragraph?
a. Foreign. **b.** Nearby. **c.** Popular. **d.** Narrow.

_____3. Which of the following doesn't have the same meaning as **remove**?
a. Add. **b.** Lift. **c.** Shift. **d.** Relocate.

_____4. When something is **whole**, it is not _____.
a. intact **b.** complete **c.** partial **d.** entire

_____5. The word **rise** in the fourth paragraph cannot be used in the same way as which of the following?
a. Increase. **b.** Fall. **c.** Climb. **d.** Grow.

2-3 Words in Context

You can stare at a word for days and not figure out what it means. But if you look at the words around it, you'll have the answer in no time. The context of a word can teach you its meaning. Try it out yourself: read this again and try to guess what "context" means.

tsunami

61 Run! It's a Tsunami!

061

1 A tsunami is a series of huge waves that can kill many people and even destroy whole countries. One of the most **terrible** tsunami disasters ever recorded happened on December 26, 2004. On that day, a huge tsunami swept through the Indian Ocean, killing more than 227,000 people and leaving around 1.6 million others homeless.

2 The word "tsunami" comes from the Japanese words meaning "harbor" (tsu) and "wave" (nami). A tsunami can be caused by landslides, volcanic eruptions, and earthquakes that occur in or near water. They can also be caused by a large **asteroid** impact, but it's been a long time since a large object from outer space has hit Earth.

memorial to those who died in the 2004 tsunami at Kanyakumari Beach, India

3 A tsunami usually cannot be seen while it travels through deep water. It can reach speeds of up to 1,000 kilometers per hour. Some **witnesses** of the 2004 tsunami saw the sea suddenly disappear before the huge waves hit. A few of these people knew that water suddenly drawing back **indicated** that a tsunami was coming, so they ran to higher ground. Unfortunately, many still did not survive.

4 Countries around the Indian Ocean established a variety of new safety measures to make sure that the **tragedy** of the 2004 tsunami is never repeated. A region-wide tsunami warning system monitors water movement in the middle of the ocean. If a tsunami is detected, an alert is sent to the governments of countries that are in danger. Japan has its own system that was used on March 11, 2011, to warn

A village near the coast of Sumatra lies in ruin after the 2004 tsunami.

the 2004 tsunami in Thailand

A boat left on land among debris by the 2011 tsunami in Ofunato, Iwate Prefecture, Japan

people 15 minutes before a tsunami hit. Even using the most advanced warning system, the tsunami still killed almost 16,000 people. In addition, it severely damaged Fukushima Daiichi Nuclear Power Plant, causing one of the world's worst nuclear disasters. Clearly, tsunamis continue to be a serious threat to countries in the Pacific Ocean.

Questions

_____1. The word **terrible** in the first paragraph means which of the following?
a. Awful. **b.** Expected. **c.** Homesick. **d.** Preventable.

_____2. The word **asteroid** in the second paragraph means which of the following?
a. A nuclear bomb. **b.** A huge rock in space.
c. A common type of tree. **d.** A sinking ship.

_____3. In the third paragraph, what does the word **witness** mean?
a. Someone who sees something happen.
b. Someone who steals from someone.
c. Someone who is always getting sick.
d. Someone who is scared of water.

_____4. The word **indicated** in the third paragraph means which of the following?
a. Harvested. **b.** Rejected. **c.** Argued. **d.** Signaled.

_____5. The word **tragedy** in the last paragraph means which of the following?
a. Present. **b.** Development.
c. Disaster. **d.** Blessing.

tsunami warning signs and broadcast tower

62 McDonald's

062

McDonald's logo in the late 90s

McDonald's in Bangkok *(top)* and Milan *(bottom)*

1 Have you ever eaten a Big Mac? If you have been to a McDonald's, then the answer is probably yes. McDonald's was the very first fast-food restaurant chain, and it is still one of the largest ones on the planet. A chain is a group of restaurants that do almost everything the same way. They use the same name, serve mostly the same food, and maintain the same level of quality control.

2 Richard and Maurice McDonald founded McDonald's in California in 1940. Around 1948, the brothers started using new techniques to cook their food. These techniques helped to increase speed and **efficiency** in the restaurant. Eventually, they began to call their product "fast food." In 1961, an Illinois businessman named Ray Kroc bought the company from the brothers and began to open several new franchise locations. A franchise is a store, restaurant, or other business that is granted the license by a company to **operate** in a specific territory and use that company's name and business techniques.

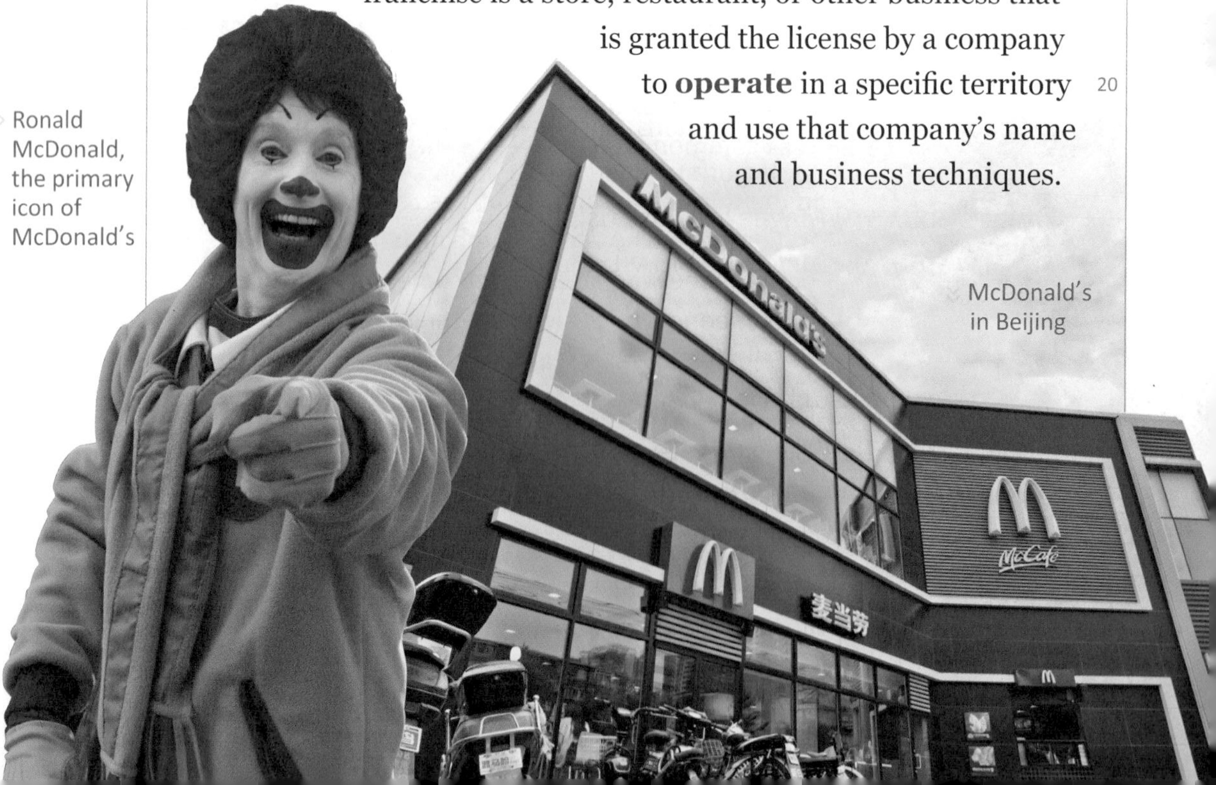

Ronald McDonald, the primary icon of McDonald's

McDonald's in Beijing

3 McDonald's now has over 37,000 franchised restaurants in 120 countries. These franchises employ over 1.9 million people around the world, and they serve almost 69 million customers each day. McDonald's is seen as a symbol of the American lifestyle, and some people believe that the international spread of McDonald's represents a **triumph** of American values.

4 Despite all this success, there are some people who don't like to eat at McDonald's. These **critics** say that eating too much fast food is very unhealthy. Many doctors agree, and studies have found that too much fast food can lead to **obesity**. Maybe that's why more and more people are too large to fit into airplane seats. McDonald's is also aware of this problem. In response, many of their restaurants have begun to introduce healthy choices, like salads.

McDonald's in Jerusalem

Questions

_____ **1.** The word **efficiency** in the second paragraph refers to which of the following?
a. Magic. **b.** Memory. **c.** Productivity. **d.** Strength.

_____ **2.** The word **operate** in the second paragraph means which of the following?
a. Function. **b.** Destroy. **c.** Reject. **d.** Create.

_____ **3.** The word **triumph** in the third paragraph means which of the following?
a. Failure. **b.** Defeat. **c.** Success. **d.** Perfection.

_____ **4.** In the fourth paragraph, **critics** are people who _____.
a. approve of something **b.** always eat fast food
c. disapprove of something **d.** write books

_____ **5.** The word **obesity** in the fourth paragraph means the condition of being which of the following?
a. Very thin. **b.** Very fat. **c.** Frightened. **d.** Excited.

McDonald's in Times Square, New York City

« albatross

» Taking off is one of the main times albatrosses use flapping to fly and is the most energetically demanding part of a journey. (Wikipedia)

63 (063) The Albatross

1 The ostrich is the biggest bird in the world, but it cannot fly. Do you know what the largest flying bird is? It's the albatross. These birds live in the northern and southern Pacific Ocean, and someone might mistake one for a giant **seagull**. Albatrosses can stay in the air for several days because of their large wingspan, or in other words, the distance between their wing tips. An albatross's wingspan can be up to 3.4 meters from tip to tip.

¥ Albatrosses can stay in the air for several days because of their large wingspan.

2 An albatross's **diet consists** of squid, fish, and other small sea animals. It hunts in one of two ways. Sometimes, it will fly low over the sea and grab its food from the water's surface. Other times, it will dive deep into the water and catch unsuspecting fish.

3 A male and female albatross will usually stay together for a few years. Every year, they make a nest and **breed**, laying an egg that will **hatch** a member of the next generation. Usually it's only one egg because female albatrosses tend to lay one egg per year. Some of these albatross pairs will remain together their whole lives. Some scientists even believe that albatross couples perform special dances together in order to make their relationship last longer.

» Some of the albatross couples remain together their whole lives.

4 When they fly, albatrosses use their long wings to glide through air that is rising. These large rising air currents help albatrosses save energy by carrying them high into the sky. That way they don't need to flap their wings very often. With this help from nature, albatrosses are able to find food in far-off places.

5 Albatrosses are currently threatened with extinction because of several factors. They are threatened by natural enemies such as rats and wild cats as well as man-made problems like pollution and overfishing.

Laysan albatross pair with chick

Questions

_____ **1.** The word **seagull** in the first paragraph is which of the following?

a. A type of cat. **b.** A type of mouse.
c. A type of boat. **d.** A type of bird.

_____ **2.** The word **consist** in the second paragraph means which of the following?

a. Include. **b.** Deceive. **c.** Complain. **d.** Digest.

_____ **3.** The word **diet** in the second paragraph means which of the following?

a. What we eat and drink.
b. Where we sleep.
c. Something that lives in the sea.
d. Something that lives on land.

_____ **4.** The word **breed** in the third paragraph means which of the following?

a. Argue. **b.** Have babies. **c.** Store food. **d.** Sleep.

_____ **5.** The word **hatch** in the third paragraph means which of the following?

a. Break. **b.** Disappear. **c.** Produce. **d.** Die.

the actual Apollo 13 lunar landing mission prime crew: *(from left to right)* Commander, James A. Lovell Jr. (1928–); Command Module pilot, John L. Swigert Jr. (1931–1982); and Lunar Module pilot, Fred W. Haise Jr. (1933–) (Wikipedia)

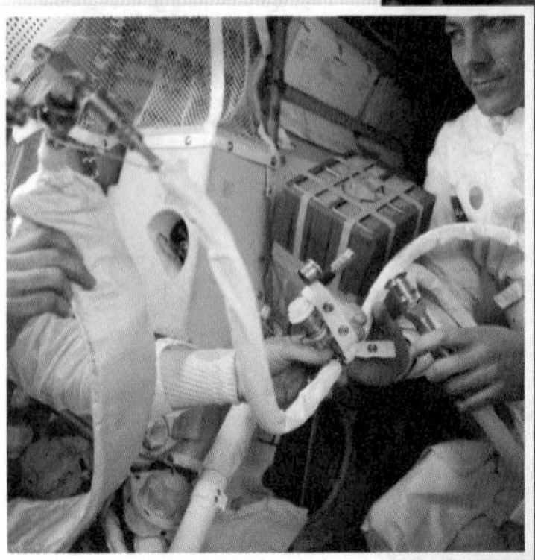

interior view of the Apollo 13 Lunar Module during the journey back to Earth

64 Almost to the Moon: The Story of Apollo 13

064

Apollo 13 launches from Kennedy Space Center, April 11, 1970

1 In July 1969, American Apollo 11 astronauts Neil Armstrong and Buzz Aldrin landed on the moon. They left a message on the lunar surface that said "We came in peace for all mankind." This marked the end of the "space race" between the United States and the former Soviet Union to see who would be first to put a human on the moon. In the end, American technological superiority **triumphed**. But the story doesn't end there. American pride and curiosity about the moon continued long after 1969.

2 Apollo 13 was the name given to the third mission of astronauts that America sent to the moon. This was the most difficult Apollo mission of all. On **route** to the moon, there was an **explosion** in one of their spacecraft's **oxygen** tanks. This accident caused astronauts James Lovell, Fred W. Haise Jr., and John L. Swigert Jr. to lose their primary oxygen supply. Television viewers all over America watched live as the

Apollo 13 LEM capsule displayed at NASA

crisis happened, and many of them thought the crew would die. However, the astronauts reacted quickly and **obtained** a secondary oxygen supply from another part of the ship. Thanks to the training and experience of the astronauts and NASA support team on Earth, the badly damaged spacecraft was able to swing around the moon and get home safely.

3 Four more groups of Americans went to the moon after Apollo 13. Eventually, America decided it was too expensive to send any more astronauts, so they ended the program. People often face danger, whether it is on Earth or in space. The example set by the Apollo 13 crew and NASA can teach us how training, experience, teamwork, and bravery are enough to overcome even the most dangerous situations.

Questions

_____ **1.** The word **triumphed** in the first paragraph means which of the following?
a. Lost. **b.** Won. **c.** Destroyed. **d.** Investigated.

_____ **2.** The word **route** in the second paragraph means which of the following?
a. Victory. **b.** Garden. **c.** Path. **d.** Plan.

_____ **3.** In the second paragraph, an **explosion** is _____.
a. a tool to repair equipment **b.** an oxygen distribution method
c. a sudden burst of flame **d.** tiny pieces of metal in space

_____ **4.** The word **oxygen** in the second paragraph means which of the following?
a. Metal. **b.** Food. **c.** Fire. **d.** Air.

_____ **5.** The word **obtained** in the second paragraph means which of the following?
a. Got. **b.** Lost. **c.** Disconnected. **d.** Arrived.

>> Mission Operations Control Room during Apollo 13's fourth television transmission

» *Fortnite* dock icon (cc by kom-a)

65 Online Gaming—A New Social Network

065

EverQuest

World of Warcraft

1 In 2018, Reuters reported that video games had become the most popular form of entertainment. While other forms of entertainment (TV, music, and film) are showing a decrease in popularity, video gaming's popularity grows yearly by about 10 percent. This growth can be attributed to online gaming's evolution.

2 In the beginning of online gaming, massively multiplayer online role playing games (MMORPGs) dominated. In games like *EverQuest* and *World of Warcraft*, players form teams to complete missions or just simply chat online while checking out each other's avatars, which are the players' physical representation in this online fantasy world. Players are captivated by the social aspect of the game as there are thousands of players online at the same time. However, massively multiplayer online games (MMOs) can be very time consuming. Some missions take hours to complete, and levelling up your character, by gaining abilities and

trailer for *Fortnite* (cc by BagoGames)

Playerunknown's Battlegrounds (PUBG) (cc by BagoGames)

acquiring new and improved costume pieces, can take days or even weeks of constant playing to accomplish.

3 In 2017, with the **advent** of battle royale games, like *Playerunknown's Battlegrounds (PUBG)* and *Fortnite*, the time commitment **issue** has been solved. Players go online and enter a single battle against other players, starting with no gear or equipment. Players then search the map of a life-like island (or islands) for quality weapons and equipment their character can use before the battle even begins. The battle lasts until only one player remains, and the game can be completed in minutes. These games can also be played on any gaming system or on any mobile device, meaning no long-term commitment or computer is required.

4 Gaming producers have created elaborate online worlds that give people the choice to stay for long or short visits, and it has become a main way of maintaining friendships and social interaction for millions of consumers. Because the gaming world continues to **evolve**, its growth will continue.

Questions

_____ 1. In the first paragraph, the phrase "can be attributed to" best means which of the following?

- **a.** Can be named by.
- **b.** Is caused by.
- **c.** Is different than.
- **d.** Can be for other reasons than.

_____ 2. In the second paragraph, the phrase "captivated by the social aspect" in this context best means which of the following?

- **a.** Amazed by the computer screen.
- **b.** Interested in the gameplay.
- **c.** Amazed by the picture quality.
- **d.** Interested in talking to other people.

_____ 3. In the third paragraph, the word **advent** in this context best means which of the following?

- **a.** Ending.
- **b.** Meaning.
- **c.** Beginning.
- **d.** Finding.

_____ 4. In the third paragraph, the word **issue** in this context best means which of the following?

- **a.** Problem.
- **b.** Magazine.
- **c.** Record album.
- **d.** Solution.

_____ 5. In the last paragraph, what phrase is the best synonym for the word **evolve**?

- **a.** Stay the same.
- **b.** Become a new monster.
- **c.** Improve and grow.
- **d.** Become something completely different.

2-4 Review Test

kabuki scene (yakusha-e) by Toyohara Chikanobu (Yōshū Chikanobu, 1838–1912)

66 Kabuki: A Dance That Began With Controversy

066

1 Kabuki, over its 400-year history, has gone from being **banned** by the Japanese government to being a protected part of Japanese culture. Kabuki is a distinct form of theater that is unique to Japan. It uses specialized music, dance, acting techniques, makeup, and costumes to tell the stories of nobility, tradesmen, and common people.

2 Kabuki is performed **exclusively** by men today, but it was invented by a woman. In 1603, a woman named Izumono Okuni began to perform her own dances in Kyoto. The performances, which included her and other dancers, became popular. But the Tokugawa rulers believed that the performances negatively affected the behavior of the public. The female dancers were replaced by boys, but by the mid-17th century, only adult men performed kabuki.

3 Like Shakespeare's plays, kabuki was entertainment for the common people rather than the nobility. Kabuki plays and those of Shakespeare also shared similar topics. Plays could be about historical characters and events (while being careful to avoid criticizing the current rulers) or the daily lives of people and their problems. Although kabuki was originally thought to **corrupt** public morals, plays began to contain the idea of *kanzen-chōaku*—reward the virtuous and punish the wicked.

Izumono Okuni (1572–?)

Kabukiza Theater in Ginza, Tokyo

4 Audiences at today's kabuki performances will see much of the same as audiences from Kabuki's golden age at the end of the 17th century. The **premier** theater is Kabukiza in Tokyo. At a kabuki theater, a bridge extends into the audience, bringing the actors close. Kabuki actors wear a base of white paint with exaggerated expressions painted on top to communicate whether they are a hero or a **villain**. Music adds to the drama of the story. Modern viewers can enjoy kabuki for both its artistic and historical elements.

Questions

In a kabuki theater, a bridge extends into the audience. (cc by urasimaru)

kabuki performance (cc by GanMed64)

_____ 1. Which word has the same meaning as **exclusively** in the second paragraph?
a. Expensively. b. Only. c. Partially. d. Poorly.

_____ 2. What is the opposite of **banned** as it is used in the first paragraph?
a. Loved. b. Allowed. c. Forbidden. d. Created.

_____ 3. What is the meaning of **corrupt** in the third paragraph?
a. Negatively affect. b. Educate.
c. Burn quickly. d. Build carefully.

_____ 4. Which of the following is the opposite of **premier** in the fourth paragraph?
a. Insignificant. b. Important.
c. Respected. d. Exciting.

_____ 5. Which word has the same meaning as **villain** in the fourth paragraph?
a. Main character. b. Minor character.
c. Good character. d. Evil character.

the Bruges City Hall

067

67 The Rise, Fall, and Rebirth of a European City

aerial view of St. Salvator's Cathedral in Bruges, Belgium

interior of the Bruges City Hall
(cc by Tanya Hart)

1 If the streets of Bruges could talk, they'd have quite a story to tell. This city in Belgium has gone from busy trading center to **ghost town**, and back again over its long history.

2 The tale begins in ancient times, when the Romans built **fortifications** in the area to protect against pirates. These fortifications didn't work: in the 9th century, Vikings invaded the area and built a small trading post there. Many believe that the name "Bruges" comes from the Viking word "Brygga," which means "harbor."

3 In the early years, Bruges **thrived** thanks to the Zwin river that connected it to the North Sea. Traders from all around Europe would gather in the city to exchange Flemish cloth and wool. By the year 1500, Bruges was home to over 200,000 people, almost double the population of London. But then the Zwin filled up with dirt and became unusable in the 16th century. Economic activity began to shift toward Antwerp, a nearby city on the North Sea. The

Rozenhoedkaai Canal and the Belfry of Bruges

The Church of Our Lady (cc by kishjar?)

population of Bruges **plummeted** after the merchants disappeared, leaving empty stores and houses behind. For around 400 years, the city was ignored by the world.

4 But that began to change when it was rediscovered by tourists. Bruges is now a **desirable** tourist destination that draws over nine million tourists every year. It has earned the nickname "the Venice of the North" due to its beautiful canals. Unlike nearby cities, Bruges was untouched by the two world wars. Much of its old, medieval architecture is still standing. In fact, UNESCO has listed the historical center of Bruges as a World Heritage Site.

5 It's no secret why Bruges is so popular. A walk down its cobbled streets can transport you to another time, when Bruges was the economic heart of Europe. The history of the city shows that sometimes the harder you fall, the stronger you rise.

Questions

_____1. Which word is closest in meaning to **thrived** in the third paragraph?
a. Prospered. b. Ignored. c. Considered. d. Organized.

_____2. What does **ghost town** mean in the first paragraph?
a. A place that is very religious.
b. A place where no one lives.
c. A place that is unfriendly to strangers.
d. A place that is easy to find.

_____3. Which word is the opposite of **desirable** in the final paragraph?
a. Feared. b. Rare. c. Mysterious. d. Unwanted.

_____4. Which is closest in meaning to **plummeted** in the third paragraph?
a. Recovered. c. Arrived. d. Decreased. e. Benefitted.

_____5. What are **fortifications** in the second paragraph?
a. Walls and castles. b. Marketplaces and harbors.
c. Government buildings. d. Small houses.

The Burg in Bruges (1691–1770) by Jan Baptist van Meunincxhove (1620/25–1703/04)

Theodor Seuss Geisel (Dr. Seuss, 1904–1991)

68 Dr. Seuss and *The Cat in the Hat*

068

1 *The Cat in the Hat* is a rhymed children's book written by American writer Dr. Seuss. The main character in the book is a **mischievous** talking cat, wearing a tall, red-and-white striped hat. The cat appears in six of Dr. Seuss's children's books, but *The Cat in the Hat* was the first. *The Cat in the Hat* has become popular around the world because it is such a fun book for young readers.

The Cat in the Hat book cover

2 "Dr. Seuss" is actually the pen name of Theodor Seuss Geisel. He studied at Lincoln College, Oxford, and tried to earn a PhD in literature. However, he returned to the United States without earning the degree. Theodor Geisel used the title "Dr." with his pen name "Seuss" as an acknowledgment of his father's unfulfilled hope that he would earn a **doctorate**.

3 Theodor Seuss Geisel was not only a writer but also a colorful cartoonist. Before World War II, he wrote children's books. After World War II started, he drew political cartoons opposing the viciousness of Hitler and Mussolini. After the war, he returned to writing children's

movie poster for *The Cat in the Hat*

« Dr. Seuss logo

Dr. Seuss™

Dr. Seuss at work in 1957

books. In 1954, he learned that children were not interested in reading because their books were **boring**. To **encourage** reading, he wrote *The Cat in the Hat*, using only 236 **basic** words. After its success, he went on to write many other children's books, including the all-time favorites *Horton Hears a Who!*, *Green Eggs and Ham, Dr. Seuss's ABC, One Fish Two Fish Red Fish Blue Fish*, and *Hop on Pop*. All of these books have whimsical pictures and rhyming texts, which help children remember words as they read them.

4 Theodor Seuss Geisel's books are now accepted as classics. Dr. Seuss books continue to attract and entertain readers around the world.

Questions

_____ 1. Which word is closest in meaning to **mischievous** in the first paragraph?

a. Sad. **b.** Expensive.
c. Elderly. **d.** Naughty.

_____ 2. Which word is closest in meaning to **doctorate** in the second paragraph?

a. Medicine. **b.** Degree.
c. University. **d.** Lesson.

_____ 3. Which is the correct use of **encourage**?

a. A good teacher encourages her students.
b. It's late; let's encourage home.
c. She's sad because he encouraged her.
d. We should encourage the class to end.

_____ 4. When something is **boring**, you don't find it _____.

a. exciting **b.** flat
c. dull **d.** uninteresting

_____ 5. In the third paragraph, the word **basic** means _____.

a. special **b.** difficult
c. simple **d.** foreign

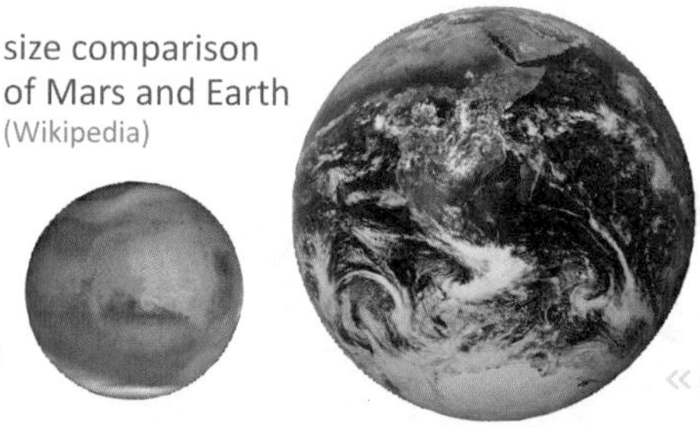

size comparison of Mars and Earth (Wikipedia)

Mars

Earth

69 Mars, the New Focus of Space Exploration

069

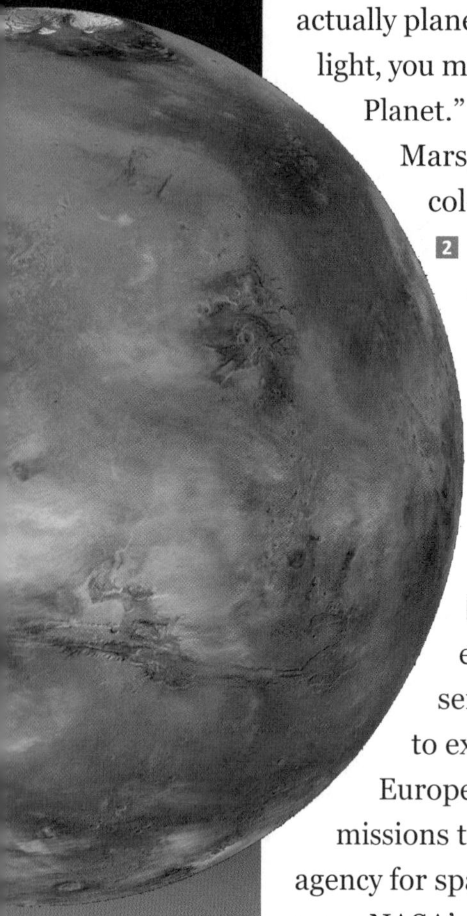

Mars

1 When you look into the night sky, you see not only stars. Some of the bright spots you see are actually planets. If you see a reddish-pink spot of light, you may be looking at Mars, known as the "Red Planet." The ancient Romans called the planet Mars, after their god of war. Its reddish-pink color reminded them of blood.

2 Interest in Mars has only grown since then. In 1609, Galileo was the first person to view Mars through a telescope. As telescopes **improved**, **astronomers** found that the Red Planet is about half as big as Earth. People imagined that Mars was inhabited by strange creatures.

3 During the modern era of space exploration, several countries have sent spacecraft to orbit Mars and rovers to explore its surface. The former USSR, Europe, United States, and India have sent missions to Mars. NASA is the United States' agency for space exploration. From 1965 through 1972, NASA's Mariner series of robot spacecraft took many close-up pictures of Mars. In 1971, the USSR's Mars 3 made the first successful landing on the surface of Mars.

4 Missions to Mars continue today. So far, the missions have discovered that ice covers the Martian polar regions, and buried ice exists in other areas.

launch of the Atlas LV-3 Agena-D carrying the Mariner 4 spacecraft (November 28, 1964)

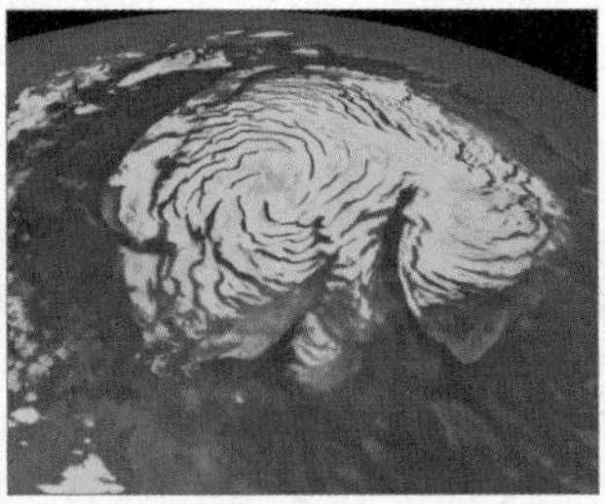

northern ice cap of Mars (May 26, 2010) (cc by NASA/JPL-Caltech/MSSS)

layers of water, ice, and dust on Mars' northern ice cap (cc by European Space Agency)

model of Soviet Mars 3 lander

Mars is mostly a **vast** desert with immense mountains, extremely deep **canyons**, and enormous dust storms. Equatorial regions can get warm, but -63°C is the average Martian temperature.

5 Some scientists believe a global warming gas that is more than 9,500 times more effective than carbon dioxide could be manufactured on Mars. This gas could help to warm the cold Red Planet and make it more like Earth. Changing a planet to create an earthlike environment is called terra-forming. Someday, Mars may have human explorers, colonists, and tourists hiking across its surface.

Questions

_____1. In the second paragraph, what does "inhabited by strange creatures" mean?

a. Strange creatures will sell it.
b. Strange creatures are trying to get away from it.
c. Strange creatures live in it.
d. Strange creatures are afraid of it.

_____2. Which word means the same as **improved** in the second paragraph?

a. Damaged. **b.** Advanced. **c.** Harmed. **d.** Weakened.

_____3. Which of the following is the opposite of **vast** as it is used in the fourth paragraph?

a. Small. **b.** Broad. **c.** Large. **d.** Endless.

_____4. Based on the second paragraph, what is an **astronomer**?

a. A person who studies planets.
b. A person who studies gods.
c. A person who makes telescopes.
d. A person who names things.

_____5. Which word is the opposite of **canyon**?

a. Lake. **b.** Mountain. **c.** Valley. **d.** Cave.

duck-billed platypus swimming

duck-billed platypus
(cc by TwoWings)

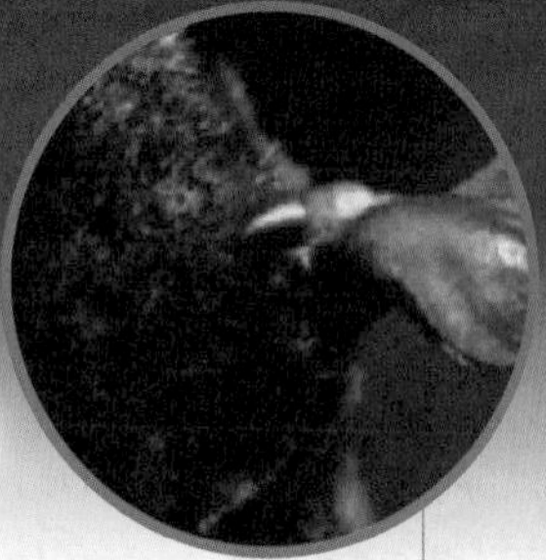

The calcaneus spur found on the male's hind limb is used to deliver venom.
(Wikipedia)

70 Nature's Joke: The Duck-Billed Platypus

070

1 Which animal is one of the few mammals that lays eggs? Which creature has fur and a beak? It sounds like something out of a science fiction or fantasy movie, but it is real. This animal is called the duck-billed platypus.

2 Platypuses live in eastern Australia. They are small, about the size of a house cat. The male platypus has spurs on its hind feet that can be filled with poison. It uses the spurs to defend itself from animals that might try to kill it. Although the platypus's venom is very powerful and able to kill smaller animals, it isn't **strong** enough to kill humans. Nevertheless, the pain caused by the venom can be terrible.

3 Platypuses have webbed feet and swim in streams and rivers. They use their duck-like beak to catch crayfish and other small animals living in the muddy riverbeds. Their **bills** look hard,

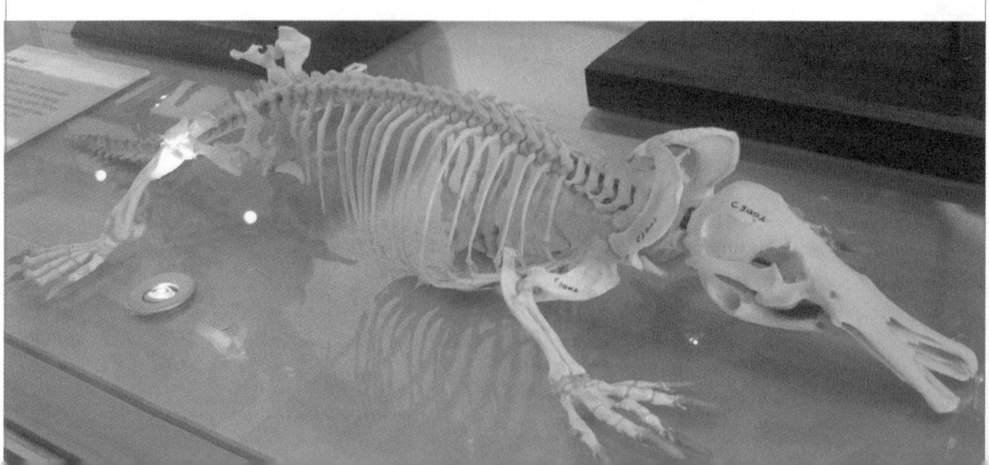

duck-billed platypus skeleton
(cc by Peter Halasz)

but they are actually very **sensitive**. They even have nostrils on their beaks that they can open and close. When they find something to eat in the muddy water, their beaks allow them to strain the water out while keeping their prey trapped inside. The body and tail of the platypus are covered with **dense** brown fur that keeps the animals dry and warm.

4 Many scientists say that platypuses are the strangest animals in the world. This is mainly because they lay eggs and have venom, even though they are warm-blooded mammals. Only one other kind of mammal lays eggs.

5 Some people consider this egg-laying, venomous, duck-billed, otter-footed mammal "one of nature's jokes" or "an **elaborate** fraud." Platypuses may be funny looking, but they certainly are interesting. The world would be a less interesting place without them.

» big duck-billed platypus at the Australian Axeman's Hall of Fame (Wikipedia)

Questions

_____ **1.** Which word means the same as **dense** in the third paragraph?
a. Open. **b.** Beautiful.
c. Sharp. **d.** Thick.

_____ **2.** Which word means the opposite of **sensitive** in the third paragraph?
a. Perceptive. **b.** Smart.
c. Dull. **d.** Canny.

_____ **3.** The word **elaborate** in the final paragraph means _____.
a. mean-spirited **b.** complex
c. unwanted **d.** expensive

_____ **4.** If you know **strong** is the opposite of **infirm**, you know **infirm** means _____.
a. active **b.** powerful
c. firm **d.** weak

_____ **5.** The word **bills** in the third paragraph probably means the same thing as _____.
a. feathers **b.** beaks
c. feet **d.** tails

Unit

3

Study Strategies

This unit will help you understand and use different parts of a text to gather information. Visual material like charts and graphs, and reference sources, like indexes and dictionaries, all provide important information. However, they don't present ideas in long pieces of text. Instead, they use pictures, numbered lists, alphabetical lists, and other methods to show information.

Reference sources will often help you find your way through books. Charts, tables, and graphs will help you understand complicated information more quickly than reading. Learning to use all these different parts of a text will help you fully comprehend the ideas you are reading about.

3-1 *Visual Material*

Tables, graphs, charts, and maps show complex information, like relationships and patterns, more easily than words can. To understand visual material, first read the titles carefully and check for legends. Then, read the headings of table columns and rows and read the axes on graphs. Once you understand the layout, you can read and understand the information itself.

71 (071)

Map: The World of Narnia

Maps are graphical representations of places. They show us towns, cities, roads, parks, and even imaginary worlds. For instance, have you read *The Lion, the Witch, and the Wardrobe*? It's a masterpiece of fantasy writing for young people, and the first of a series of books about the mythical land of Narnia.

C. S. Lewis wrote *The Lion, the Witch, and the Wardrobe* and created the world of Narnia, a complex landscape of places, events, and characters. Children have been getting lost in this magical world ever since, just like the main character, Lucy, first got lost in Narnia herself after hiding in a wardrobe.

With the help of a map, however, we can find information about where we are, where we want to go, and how to get there in Narnia. Below is a map of the world of Narnia. Use the map to help answer the questions about areas in Narnia.

Questions

_____**1.** Which island is furthest east?

a. Dragon Island. **b.** Deathwater.
c. Dark Island. **d.** Terebinthia.

_____**2.** Where are the Tombs of the Ancient Kings?

a. In the Downs. **b.** In the Eastern Ocean.
c. On Deathwater Island. **d.** In the desert.

_____**3.** Which place is in Calormen?

a. Ettinsmoor. **b.** The Western Wild.
c. Calavar. **d.** The Seven Isles.

_____**4.** Where is the Silver Sea?

a. Far to the east. **b.** Slightly north of Calavar.
c. Far to the west. **d.** Slightly southeast.

_____**5.** Cair Paravel is ______.

a. North of the City Ruinous
b. South of Harfang
c. East of the Silver Sea
d. South of the Seven Isles

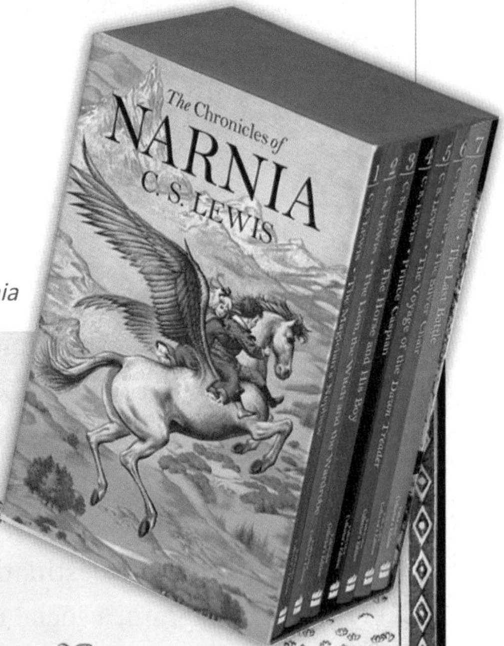

» *The Chronicles of Narnia*

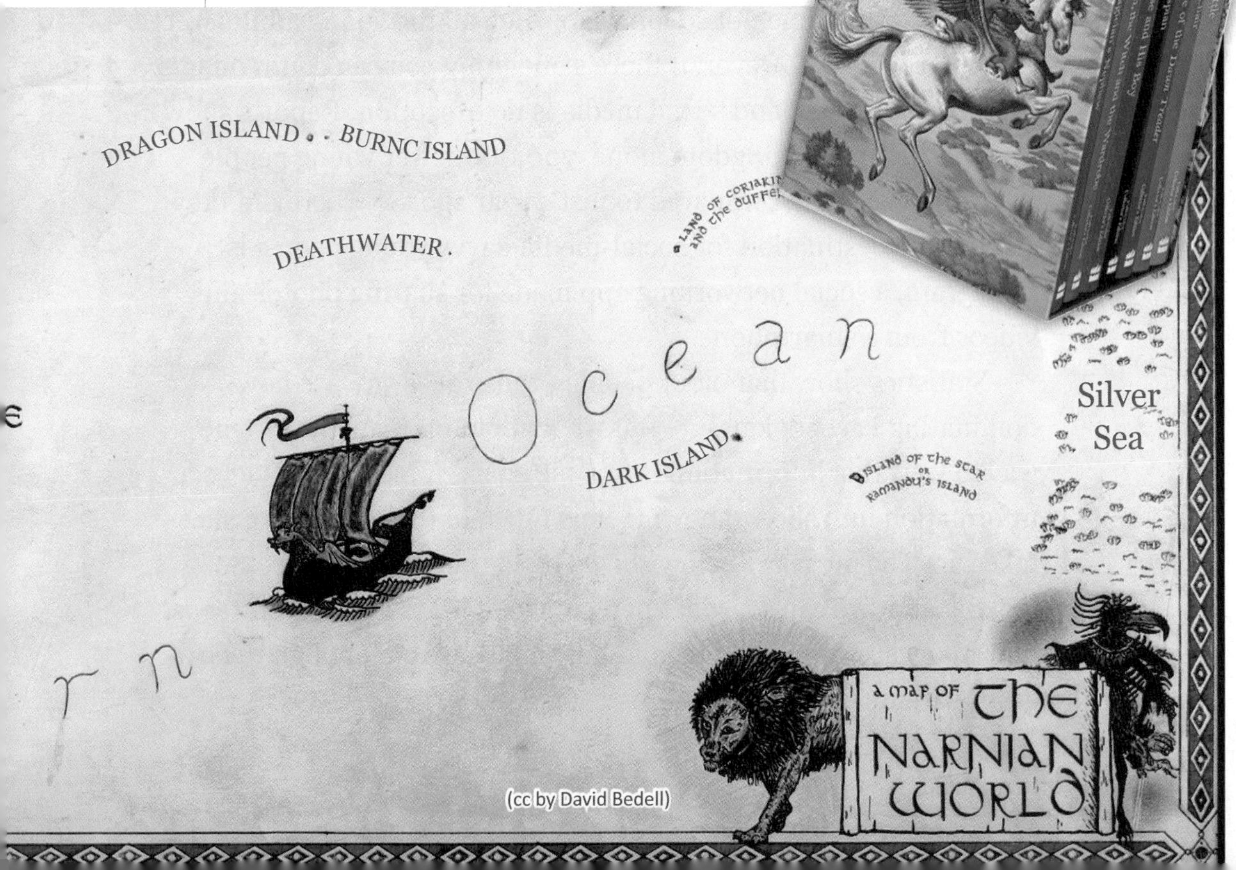

(cc by David Bedell)

« Instagram app on an iPhone screen

» Instagram log-in page

^ Instagram icon

72 Pie Chart: Who Uses Instagram?

072

There was a time not so long ago when all the young adults were using Facebook. However, if there's one thing you can count on, it's that trends change, and social media is no exception. Reports show that, in the United Kingdom alone, 700,000 fewer young people are using Facebook compared to just a year ago. So where did they all go? One destination for social-media-savvy young people is Instagram, a social networking app made for sharing photos and videos from a smartphone.

Statistics show that older people—those over 55—are now dominating Facebook usage. But what about on Instagram? One way to view this information is in a pie chart. A pie chart divides information into slices, showing how much of the whole each slice takes up. The pie chart below shows Instagram users by age. So by looking at, it we can see what percentage of users are in their teens, how many are young adults, and how many are old enough to be grandparents.

Instagram Users by Age (2018)

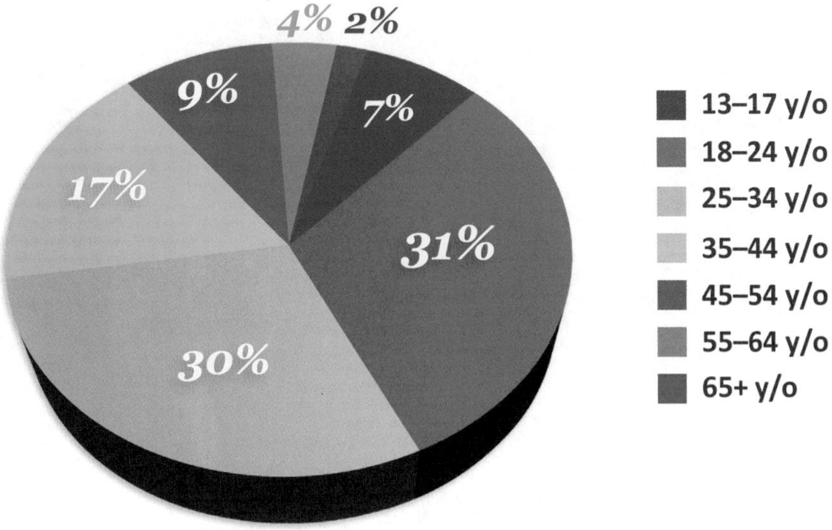

Questions

_____1. What does the pie chart show?

a. The number of Instagram users by country.

b. The favorite social media sites of people aged 55 and older.

c. How old Instagram users are.

d. The popularity of several social media sites.

_____2. What percentage of Instagram users are aged 65 and over?

a. 30% b. 4% c. 17% d. 2%

_____3. What does the yellow pie slice represent?

a. Half of Instagram's users.

b. All of Instagram's users.

c. Instagram users who also use Facebook.

d. Instagram users aged between 35 and 44.

_____4. Which age group makes up the largest percentage of Instagram users?

a. Twenty-five to thirty-four year olds.

b. Eighteen to twenty-four year olds.

c. Fifty-five to sixty-four year olds.

d. Forty-five to fifty-four year olds.

_____5. Together, users aged between 18 and 34 make up how much of Instagram's total users?

a. Three-quarters. b. Ninety-nine percent.

c. Less than ten percent. d. More than half.

73 Line Graph: My Reading Habits

073

Line graphs show information in an easy-to-read way. They show how things have changed instead of how things are. So, if we want to show how something has increased or decreased, we will use this kind of graph.

Here is an example of how we could use a line graph to organize data. Read the following paragraphs and look at the chart to see how the weather affects the author's reading habits.

I really like to read, but I also like to run, do yoga, swim, play badminton, go hiking, and just spend as much time outside as possible. Sometimes I don't know when I can find the time to read for fun.

That's where the rainy season steps in to help me. I live in a country with a well-defined rainy season. During the rainy season, I miss playing outside, but I love having so much time to read. I decided to track how many books I read over the course of the year.

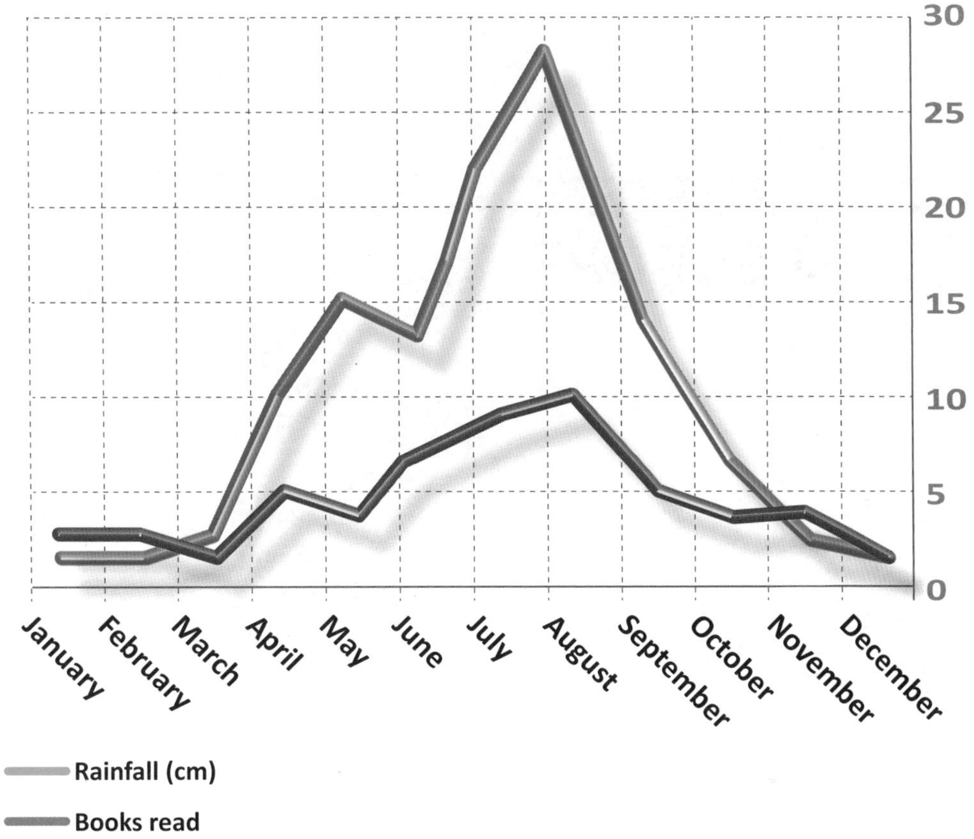

Questions

_____1. What does the blue line represent?

a. The author's favorite books.

b. Rainfall in centimeters.

c. Number of books read.

d. Temperatures by season.

_____2. Which month has the highest rainfall?

a. April. **b.** December. **c.** August. **d.** September.

_____3. Which month has the highest number of books read?

a. August. **b.** May. **c.** July. **d.** February.

_____4. In what month did the author read five books?

a. November. **b.** April. **c.** January. **d.** June.

_____5. In what month was there 15 centimeters of rain?

a. December. **b.** October. **c.** April. **d.** May.

74 Table: A Continent Divided

Tables are diagrams in which information is arranged into rows (running left to right) and columns (running up and down). Each column has a title and it tells what kinds of facts are in the column.

Here is an example showing how to use a table for demographical information. Read the following paragraph. Then, study the table on the next page and answer the questions.

There is a cultural and economic divide between Western Europe and Eastern Europe, and its origins go all the way back to the end of World War II. After the Soviet Union invaded Germany and ended the war, the government in Moscow decided to leave soldiers in various countries in Eastern Europe. These countries came to be known as the Eastern Bloc. This period of history impacts Europe to this day.

Country	Population (2018)	Capital City / Largest City
Belarus	9,452,113	Minsk
Bulgaria	7,036,848	Sofia
Czech Republic	10,625,250	Prague
Hungary	9,688,847	Budapest
Moldova	4,041,065	Chişinău
Poland	38,104,832	Warsaw
Romania	19,580,634	Bucharest
Russian Federation	143,964,709	Moscow
Slovakia	5,449,816	Bratislava
Ukraine	44,009,214	Kiev

(Source: http://www.worldometers.info/world-population/eastern-europe-population/)

Questions

_____ 1. Which is the capital city of Ukraine?
- **a.** Bratislava. **b.** Bucharest.
- **c.** Kiev. **d.** Warsaw.

_____ 2. Which is the Eastern European country with the highest population?
- **a.** Belarus. **b.** Ukraine.
- **c.** Poland. **d.** Russian Federation.

_____ 3. Which is the Eastern European country with the lowest population?
- **a.** Romania. **b.** Slovakia.
- **c.** Moldova. **d.** Bulgaria.

_____ 4. Bucharest is the capital city of which Eastern European country?
- **a.** Romania. **b.** Russian Federation.
- **c.** Bulgaria. **d.** Moldova.

_____ 5. Sofia is the capital city of which Eastern European country?
- **a.** Hungary. **b.** Czech Republic.
- **c.** Poland. **d.** Bulgaria.

75 Bar Graph: Nutrition in the United States

075

A bar graph lets you quickly see and understand information. Instead of using numbers, as we do in a table, we use "bars." Each bar represents a number or value. It is easy to see which number is the largest because the "bar" that represents it is the longest.

junk food

Bar graphs do not usually give you complicated or difficult information. They give basic, statistical information so that you can easily read the graph and make comparisons. Next, you'll find an example of how we use bar graphs to represent statistical information.

It's no secret that Americans—and much of the rest of the world—have been getting fatter for some time now. In recent decades, talk has shifted from how to get enough to eat to how to lose weight. Sometimes people act like there must be some kind of "magic bullet" to help get fit and healthy, but really, being healthy is about making good choices every day. The bar graph shows us the percentages of what Americans eat every day.

sugary drinks

fruit

green leafy vegetable

What Americans Eat Every Day

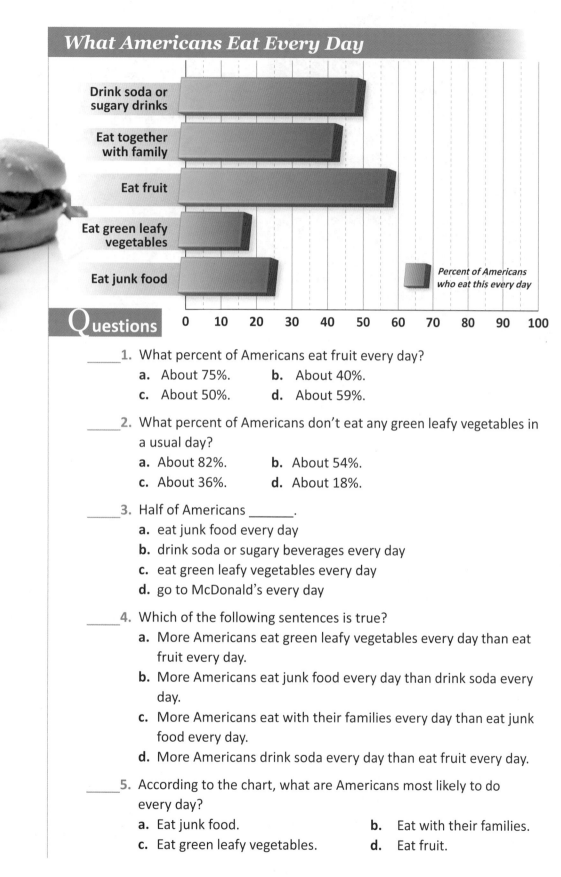

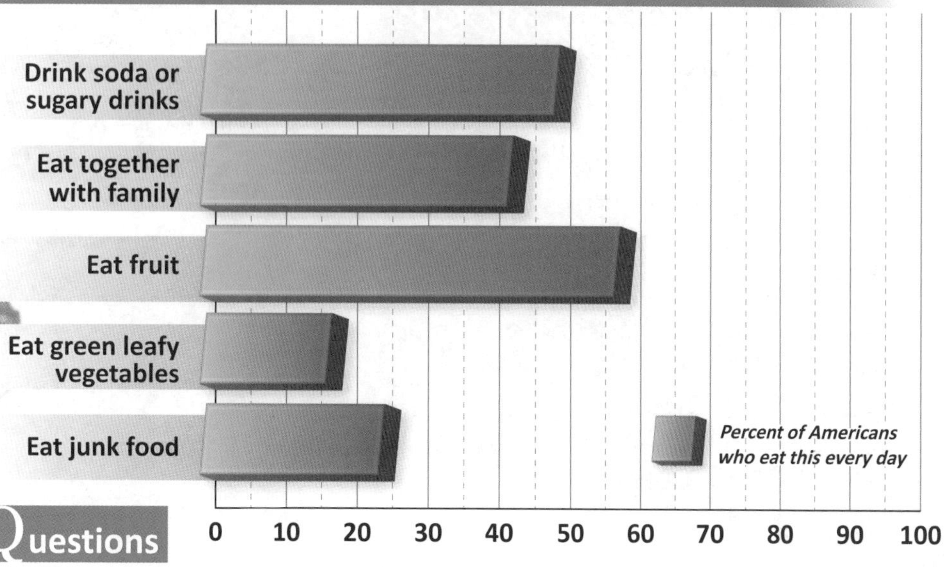

Questions

_____1. What percent of Americans eat fruit every day?

a. About 75%. **b.** About 40%.
c. About 50%. **d.** About 59%.

_____2. What percent of Americans don't eat any green leafy vegetables in a usual day?

a. About 82%. **b.** About 54%.
c. About 36%. **d.** About 18%.

_____3. Half of Americans ______.

a. eat junk food every day
b. drink soda or sugary beverages every day
c. eat green leafy vegetables every day
d. go to McDonald's every day

_____4. Which of the following sentences is true?

a. More Americans eat green leafy vegetables every day than eat fruit every day.
b. More Americans eat junk food every day than drink soda every day.
c. More Americans eat with their families every day than eat junk food every day.
d. More Americans drink soda every day than eat fruit every day.

_____5. According to the chart, what are Americans most likely to do every day?

a. Eat junk food. **b.** Eat with their families.
c. Eat green leafy vegetables. **d.** Eat fruit.

3-2 Reference Sources

In the Internet Age, information is everywhere and anyone can access it. There's so much information that finding something specific can be hard. At times like this, reference sources like dictionaries, encyclopedias, and atlases can be a big help. That means you should learn how to use these important tools.

76 Dictionary: The Human Imagination

076

While it is true that humans share a lot in common with chimpanzees, these animals are missing an important part of what makes humans special. What is it that makes humans so unique in the animal kingdom? Maybe it's our power to **imagine** places that don't exist and events that haven't happened. We use these **imaginary** concepts to tell stories that can teach us about what it is to be human. Our **imaginations** can also be used to picture new ways to improve society and technology. Clocks, the steam engine, computers, and countless other inventions all came from someone **imagining** a more efficient way of doing things.

What is "imagination," anyways? You might be wondering what it means and how to use it in a sentence. Looking the word up in a dictionary is a good way to find out. Dictionary entries contain a lot of different information about words, and they will always be listed in alphabetical order. A dictionary entry will tell you the word's definition, the amount of syllables, its pronunciation, and its part of speech. Sometimes, the dictionary will even tell you what language the word originally came from.

i-mag-i-na-ble (i-maj′i-na-bl), *a.* Capable of being imagined or conceived: as, "He ran into all the extravagancies *imaginable*" (Steele, in "Spectator," 82).—**i-mag′i-na-ble-ness,** *n.*—**i-mag′i-na-bly,** *adv.*
i-mag-i-nal (i-maj′i-nal), *a.* In *entom.*, of or pertaining to, or in the form of, an imago.
i-mag-i-na-ry (i-maj′i-nā-ri), *a.* [L. *imaginarius,* < *imago*: see *image.*] Existing only in the imagination or fancy (as, "Besides real diseases, we are subject to many that are only *imaginary*": Swift's "Gulliver's Travels," iv. 6); not real; fancied; also, imaginative† (as, "My soul's *imaginary* sight Presents thy shadow to my sightless view": Shakspere's "Sonnets," xxvii.); in *math.*, noting or pertaining to a quantity or expression involving the square root of a negative quantity, and thus having no real existence.—**i-mag′i-na-ri-ly,** *adv.*—**i-mag′i-na-ri-ness,** *n.*
i-mag-i-na-tion (i-maj-i-nā′shon), *n.* [OF. F. *imagination,* < L. *imaginatio(n-),* < *imaginari*: see *imagine.*] The action of imagining, or of forming mental images or concepts of what is not actually present to the senses; also, the faculty of forming such images or concepts; the power of the mind of reproducing images or concepts stored in the memory under the suggestion of associated images ('reproductive imagination'), or of recombining former experiences in the creation of new images different from any known by experience ('productive imagination' or 'creative imagination'); specif., the faculty of producing ideal creations consistent with reality, as in poetical or literary composition (distinguished from *fancy*); also, the product of imagining; a conception or mental creation, often a baseless or fanciful one; also, the act of planning or scheming, or a plan, scheme, or plot (archaic: as, "Thou hast seen all their vengeance and all their *imaginations* against me," Lam. iii. 60); also, mind, or thinking or thought (now rare).—**i-mag-i-na′tion-al,** *a.*
i-mag-i-na-tive (i-maj′i-nā-tiv), *a.* [OF. F. *imaginatif,* < LL. *imaginativus.*] Given to imagining, as persons; having exceptional powers of imagination; sometimes, fanciful; also, pertaining to or concerned with imagination (as, the *imaginative* faculty); also, characterized by or bearing evidence of imagination (as, "the *imaginative* tale of Sintram and his companions, by Mons. Le Baron de la Motte Fouqué": Scott's "Guy Mannering," Introd.).—**i-mag′i-na-tive-ly,** *adv.*—**i-mag′i-na-tive-ness,** *n.*
i-mag-i-na-tor (i-maj′i-nā-tor), *n.* One who imagines.
i-mag-ine (i-maj′in), *v.*; *-ined, -ining.* [OF. F. *imaginer,* < L. *imaginari,* picture to one's self, fancy, imagine, < *imago*: see *image.*] **I.** *tr.* To form a mental image of (something not actually present to the senses: as, "And far beyond, *Imagined* more than seen, the skirts of France," Tennyson's "Princess," Conclusion, 48); represent to one's self in imagination; conceive; hence, to assume or suppose (as, for the sake of argument *imagine* this to be the case); conjecture or guess (as, I cannot *imagine* whom you mean); think, believe, or fancy (as, "I doubt not of the facts which you relate, but *imagine* that you impute them to mistaken motives": Johnson's "Rasselas," ix.); also, to plan, scheme, or plot (archaic: as, "How long will ye *imagine* mischief against a man?" Ps. lxii. 3). **II.** *intr.* To form mental images of things not present to the senses; exercise the imagination.—**i-mag′in-er,** *n.*

Questions

_____1. Where would the word imitate appear in this dictionary?
- a. Before imaginable.
- b. Before imaginative.
- c. After imitation.
- d. After imagine.

_____2. How many syllables are there in the word imaginary?
- a. Two.
- b. Three.
- c. Five.
- d. Six.

_____3. What part of speech is the word imaginator?
- a. Verb.
- b. Adverb.
- c. Adjective.
- d. Noun.

_____4. Which is true of the word imaginary?
- a. It has a special definition in math.
- b. It has a special definition in physics.
- c. Its part of speech is a noun.
- d. It comes from the Spanish language.

_____5. What part of speech is the word imaginary?
- a. Verb.
- b. Adverb.
- c. Adjective.
- d. Noun.

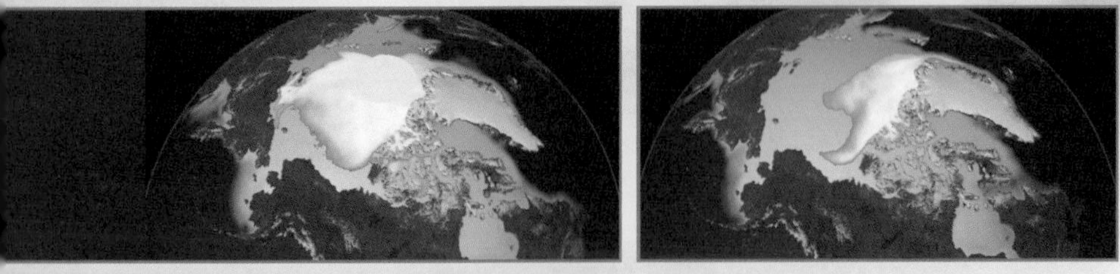

Arctic ice coverage in 1980 *(left)* and 2012 *(right)*
(Wikipedia)

77 Table of Contents: The Big Melt

077

A table of contents appears at the beginning of almost every book, and it helps you find your way through the book. It usually gives a list of chapters or article titles and page numbers on which each chapter or article can be found.

Here is a paragraph on global warming. Read the paragraph and then study the table of contents to answer the questions.

> Global warming has gone from science fiction to science fact in only 20 short years. Now, climate scientists are becoming very worried about warm weather melting Arctic ice. If the Arctic ice melts completely, it will add lots of water to the world's oceans. The additional volume will cause water levels to rise all around the world. Melting Arctic ice will also change how goods are transported worldwide. The ice in northern Canada is melting earlier every year, and ships are starting to take advantage of a quicker route between the Atlantic and Pacific Oceans. This new Arctic shipping route is called the Northwest Passage.

Now, let's take a look at the following table of contents to answer the questions.

melting ice »

08 TEMPERATURE

The global temperature record is an important indicator of global climate change, and as a result is a major focus of attention for climate skeptics.

10 ARCTIC SEA ICE

The Arctic contains a thin, vulnerable layer of sea ice which reaches a minimum every September, providing a regular opportunity to highlight the impacts of climate change.

12 DROUGHT

Already one of the most widespread and damaging natural disasters, drought is likely to affect more people more severely as temperatures increase.

14 El Niño

The El Niño–Southern Oscillation (ENSO) involves abnormal warming (and cooling) of the central and eastern Pacific Ocean. It has impact around the global.

16 FLOODING

Climate change is likely to increase flooding, and given physical limits to flood adaptation, emissions reductions are needed to prevent unmanageable flooding in the future.

18 HEATWAVES

As average global temperatures increase, we are likely to see more record highs, and fewer record lows. This would make heatwaves longer, more frequent and more intense.

20 SNOW & COLD

Cold and snowy weather attracts media attention and can have an impact on public opinion and concern about a warming world, but it does not disprove climate change.

22 SPECIES EXTINCTION

Climate change will likely make a bad situation worse for many species, and could become the main cause of species extinction in the future.

24 THE SEASONS

A warming world shifts the seasonal activities of plants and animals, with uncertain consequences.

26 WILDFIRES

Wildfires are important to most ecosystems, but higher temperatures can alter natural fire regimes, permanently releasing greenhouse gases and amplifying climate change.

Questions

_____1. On what page would you find information about Arctic ice?

a. Eight. b. Ten. c. Twelve. d. Fourteen.

_____2. If you were interested in the warming of the central and eastern Pacific Ocean, what unit would you refer to?

a. Temperature. b. El Niño.
c. Species Extinction. d. Wildfires.

_____3. If you were interested in how the weather affects public opinion, what unit would you refer to?

a. Snow & Cold. b. El Niño.
c. Drought. d. Arctic Sea Ice.

_____4. Which of the following would the Heatwaves unit likely NOT include?

a. How to cope with hotter summers.
b. Global air-conditioning usage rates.
c. A map of the Northwest Passage.
d. A map of rising average temperatures in Europe.

_____5. Which of the following would the Wildfires unit likely include?

a. A list of the most severe droughts since 2000.
b. Public opinion polls on global warming.
c. A list of species that have disappeared since 1990.
d. A map of areas at high risk of forest fires.

78 Index: Caligula—The Mad Emperor

078

The index of a book is usually found at the back. An index lists the important words or topics that are contained in the articles or chapters in the book. The words are listed in alphabetical order. Next to each word, you will see one or more numbers. These numbers are the page numbers where you will find the information you need.

Take Caligula for example. In an encyclopedia, you might find an article about Caligula, one of the most well-known Roman emperors. Once Caligula became emperor in AD 37, he started acting in a strange and often brutal manner. He believed that he was a god and

The Vatican Obelisk was first brought from Egypt to Rome by Caligula. It was the centerpiece of a large racetrack he built. (Wikipedia)

Caligula (AD 12–AD 41)

ordered that statues of himself be built in temples and other places of worship. He was also very fond of his racehorse Incitatus. He was known to give this horse precious stones and expensive fabrics as gifts, and some historians believe that he even considered granting it an official political position.

To find more information about Caligula, all you have to do is look up "Caligula" in the index. Now, let's take a look at the index to answer the following questions.

>> Roman coin depicting Caligula

Questions

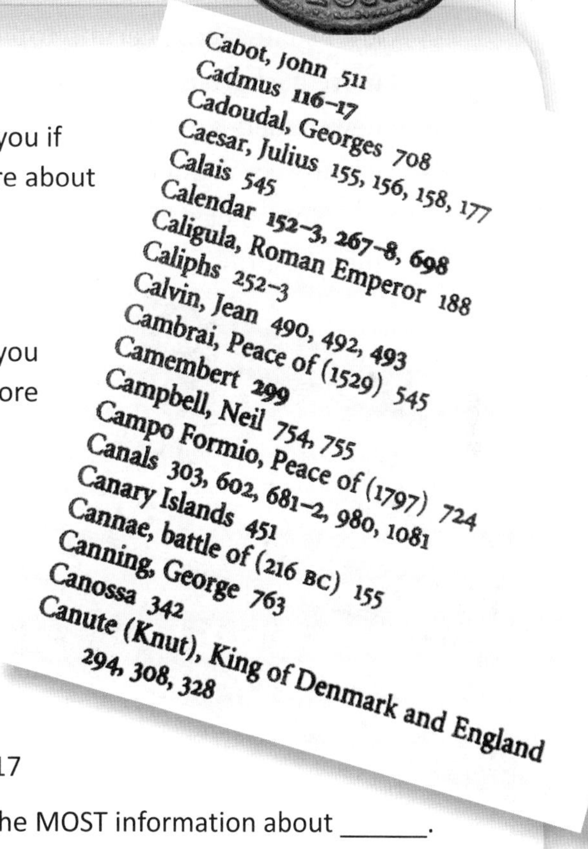
Cabot, John 511
Cadmus 116–17
Cadoudal, Georges 708
Caesar, Julius 155, 156, 158, 177
Calais 545
Calendar 152–3, 267–8, 698
Caligula, Roman Emperor 188
Caliphs 252–3
Calvin, Jean 490, 492, 493
Cambrai, Peace of (1529) 545
Camembert 299
Campbell, Neil 754, 755
Campo Formio, Peace of (1797) 724
Canals 303, 602, 681–2, 980, 1081
Canary Islands 451
Cannae, battle of (216 BC) 155
Canning, George 763
Canossa 342
Canute (Knut), King of Denmark and England 294, 308, 328

_____ **1.** Which page would help you if you wanted to learn more about Caligula?

a. 200 **b.** 289
c. 188 **d.** 90

_____ **2.** Which page would help you if you wanted to learn more about Calais?

a. 545 **b.** 823
c. 715 **d.** 200

_____ **3.** Which page would help you if you wanted to learn more about Cadmus?

a. 177 **b.** 511
c. 708 **d.** 116–17

_____ **4.** This book probably has the MOST information about ______.

a. Calais
b. Cadmus
c. Canals
d. the Canary Islands

_____ **5.** This book probably has the LEAST information about ______.

a. Caliphs **b.** Canute (Knut)
c. Caesar, Julius **d.** Calendar

79 Magazine vs. Newspaper: Tests Got You Stressed?

Everyone gets stressed out sometimes, whether it's at work, school, or home. The following are two articles that discuss stress. One is taken from a newspaper, and the other is from a magazine. Can you tell the difference between them?

Here's a hint: newspaper articles are about current events. They usually give the reader basic facts about what is happening in the world. Magazine articles on the other hand are usually about certain topics, and they often give the reader more background information than newspaper articles. Also, newspapers are usually printed every day, and magazines usually come out on a monthly basis.

Now, please read the two articles about stress and answer the questions.

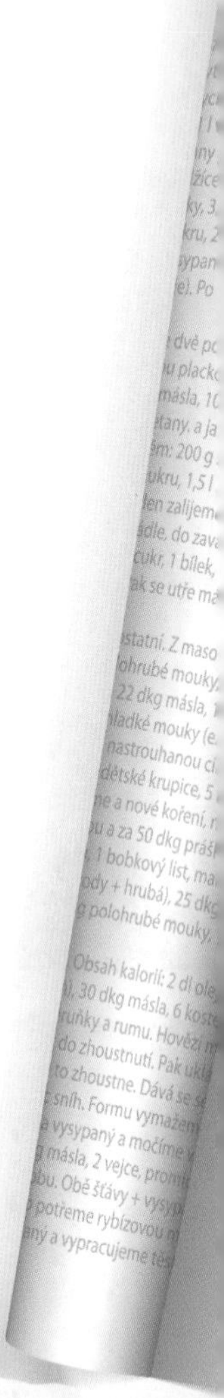

Newspaper Report

Local Resident Works Himself to Death

A local resident named John Smith died of a heart attack at his office today. He had worked for a small paper company for the past 20 years. According to his coworkers, John had become extremely stressed after being given an important assignment by his boss. When his body was discovered, he was face-down at his desk, still holding on to a cup of coffee. Witnesses confirmed that it was his eighth cup of coffee that day.

John Smith

Stress: Can Worrying Be Deadly?

Magazine Article

The same scene is happening all over the world. A patient visits his doctor and complains of headaches, dizziness, and an upset stomach. He wants some medicine, but the doctor already knows that pills won't help. This patient is suffering from too much stress. However, as soon as the doctor says that stress is the problem, the patient will start to deny it or make excuses. It's always the same story. People don't know that stress can cause real health problems like high blood pressure, heart attacks, and arthritis.

Questions

_____1. Which of the following stories appears in this newspaper article?

a. The history of the Roman Empire.
b. A detailed map of Central Europe.
c. A report on someone dying on the job.
d. An analysis of the last US presidential election.

_____2. This magazine article suggests ______.

a. baseball and other North American sports are becoming popular
b. people often don't realize they're suffering from stress
c. Japanese elections will be held by the end of this year
d. drinking too much coffee can kill you

_____3. Which of the following statements is NOT true about the articles?

a. The newspaper article describes an event.
b. The magazine article describes a problem.
c. Both articles involve the topic of stress.
d. The newspaper article is about a paper company.

_____4. If you wanted to know about a robbery in your city, where would you look?

a. A newspaper. **b.** A magazine.
c. An atlas. **d.** An encyclopedia.

_____5. If you wanted to know about tomorrow's weather report, where would you look?

a. A newspaper. **b.** A magazine.
c. An atlas. **d.** An encyclopedia.

80 Encyclopedia: Albert Camus

080

An encyclopedia is usually a set of books that provides facts about people, places, and things. The entries are arranged alphabetically.

When looking for information about a famous person in an encyclopedia, you should note that people are listed by their surnames, not their first names. So, you will find "George Washington" under "W," not "G." The subject will be written as "Washington, George." Subjects beginning with "The" will be found under the first letter of the word directly after "The." The same is true with article titles beginning with "A." For example, you will find *A Midsummer Night's Dream* written as *Midsummer Night's Dream, A*.

Here is a short biography of Albert Camus that might be found in an encyclopedia's volumes. Read the paragraph and answer the following questions.

Albert Camus, born in 1913, was a French Algeria—born writer who won the Nobel Prize in Literature in 1957. He was an author, a journalist, and also a philosopher. His literary works were praised as having a "clear-sighted earnestness" that "illuminates the problems of the human conscience in our times."

Albert Camus
(1913–1960)

Albert Camus's gravestone (cc by Walter Popp)

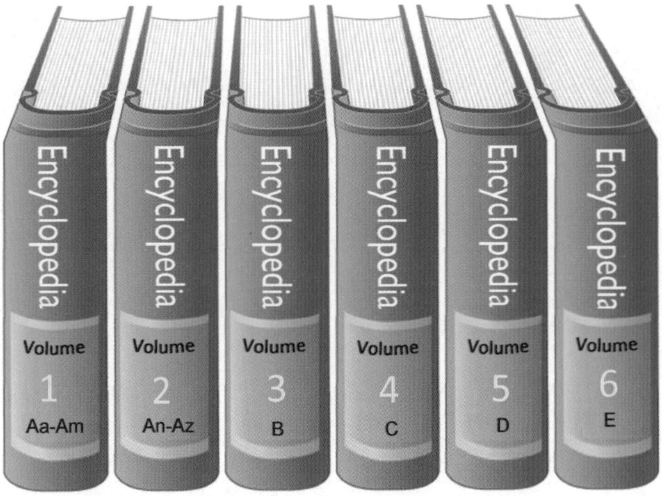

Questions

_____1. If you wanted to know more about Sir Winston Churchill, the winner of the 1953 Nobel Prize in Literature, which volume should you consult?

a. Volume 2. **b.** Volume 3.
c. Volume 4. **d.** Volume 6.

_____2. Camus's works are considered to be a contribution to the philosophy of absurdism. In which volume would you find information about absurdism?

a. Volume 1. **b.** Volume 2.
c. Volume 3. **d.** Volume 4.

_____3. If you wanted to find the article about Albert Camus, you should look in ______.

a. Volume 1, under "Albert Camus"
b. Volume 4, under "Camus, Albert"
c. Volume 1, under "Algerian"
d. Volume 2, under "Articles"

_____4. In which volume would you find information about "conscience"?

a. Volume 1. **b.** Volume 4.
c. Volume 5. **d.** Volume 6.

_____5. People often connect Camus with existentialism. If you would like to find out what existentialism is, which volume should you look in?

a. Volume 3. **b.** Volume 4.
c. Volume 5. **d.** Volume 6.

Unit

4

Final Reviews

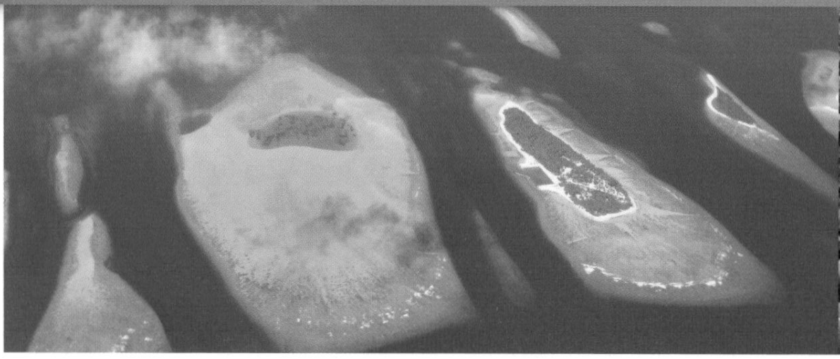

4-1 Final Review (1)

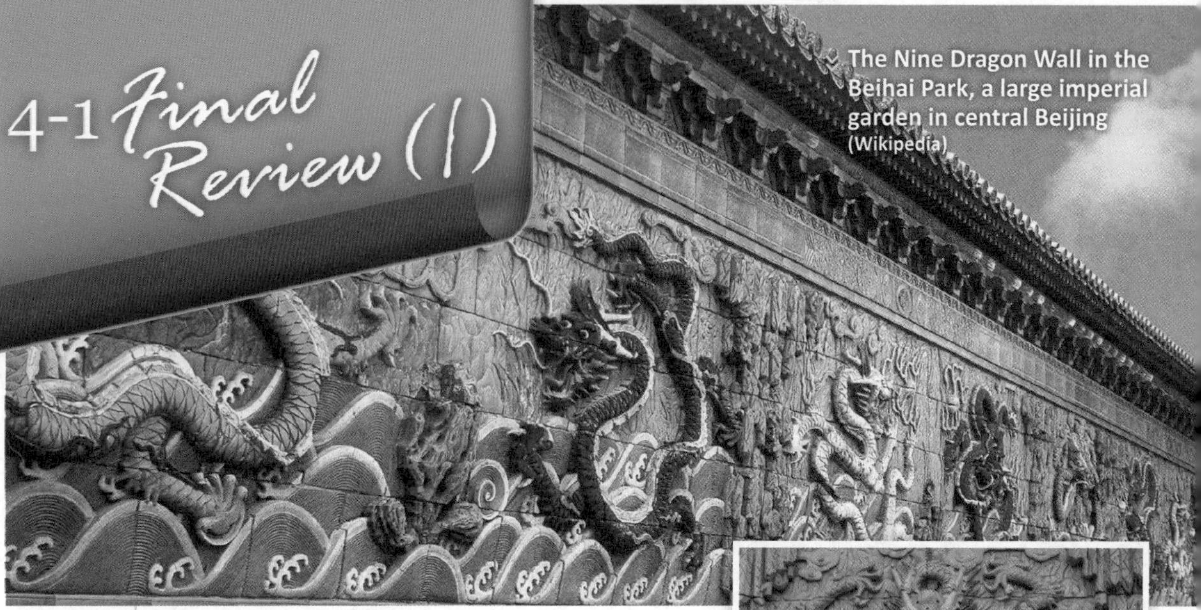

The Nine Dragon Wall in the Beihai Park, a large imperial garden in central Beijing (Wikipedia)

81 Dragons

081

Many cultures in the world tell stories about dragons. In some cultures they are good, and in some they are bad. Whether they are good or bad, in stories dragons are always strong and have supernatural powers. Some people say that there used to be real dragons, but most agree that they are imaginary creatures.

In China and other Asian countries, dragons are usually considered to be kind. People say that they bring strength, harmony, good luck, and health. In ancient China, dragons were symbols of the Chinese emperors. Some Chinese people believe that dragons live underwater most of the time. Unlike European dragons, they do not have wings. Instead, they fly using magic. The Chinese dragon, sometimes called the Oriental dragon, looks like a long snake with four claws. In the Chinese zodiac, people born in the Year of the Dragon are said to be lucky, brave, ambitious, healthy, energetic, excitable, short-tempered, and stubborn. A "dragon person" can achieve great things in life if he or she knows how to make the best use of his or her tremendous energy, intelligence, and talent.

Dragon robe of ancient Chinese emperor. In ancient China, dragons were symbols of the Chinese emperors.

In European legends, on the other hand, dragons are usually seen as greedy, **cruel** winged monsters. They were strong and smart, but not kind. They usually guarded

The Chinese dragon looks like a long snake with four claws.

« *Saint George and the Dragon* (1889–90) by Gustave Moreau (1826–1898)

things, like treasure. Many European stories describe brave knights fighting terrible dragons. Any knight who killed a dragon was able to get not only its treasure but also its wisdom. In Christianity, the devil is sometimes shown as a dragon.

People might not believe in dragons anymore, but these magical creatures live on in storybooks. Modern fantasy writers still write books about heroes fighting dragons.

In European legend, dragons are usually seen as monsters.

Questions

_____ 1. What can you infer about the devil from this article?

- **a.** The devil is wise.
- **b.** The devil is bad.
- **c.** The devil died out with dragons.
- **d.** The devil ate dragons.

_____ 2. Why might a knight kill a dragon?

- **a.** For good luck.
- **b.** To sell the dragon meat.
- **c.** To gain a place in the zodiac.
- **d.** To get the dragon's treasure.

_____ 3. Why do people remember dragons?

- **a.** Because they fly using magic.
- **b.** Because they are cruel.
- **c.** Because people tell stories about them.
- **d.** Because they guard treasure.

_____ 4. Which of the following opinions would the author agree with?

- **a.** Dragon stories will remain popular for a long time.
- **b.** People born in the year of the dragon are smart.
- **c.** Dragons were real animals at one time.
- **d.** Dragons were a poor choice of symbol for emperors.

_____ 5. Which word is closest in meaning to **cruel**?

a. Generous. **b.** Mean. **c.** Lucky. **d.** Ugly.

» *Alice's Adventures in Wonderland* (1865)

» *Through the Looking-Glass* (1872)

» Lewis Carroll (1832–1898)

82 Lewis Carroll

082

1 Have you ever read *Alice's Adventures in Wonderland*? It was written by Lewis Carroll. He was an English writer, poet, scientist, photographer, and deacon. His real name was Charles Lutwidge Dodgson. Lewis Carroll was his **pen name**. He was born in 1832 and died in 1898.

2 He is most famous for writing two children's fantasy books about a young girl named Alice. The first one was called *Alice's Adventures in Wonderland* (1865). Its sequel is *Through the Looking-Glass* (1872). In the books, Alice falls into a hole and enters a strange, magical world. Many of the vivid characters and scenes from these stories are referenced by other writers in other stories. The smoking caterpillar and the Cheshire Cat are common images nowadays.

3 Later, Carroll wrote a famous poem, "The Hunting of the Snark," published in 1876. This poem is important and interesting for the many new words Carroll made up to use in it. He was an expert at wordplay and used words in many different ways. Carroll

88

"The Queen of Hearts she made some tarts
All on a summer day:
The Knave of Hearts he stole those tarts,
And took them quite away!"

"Now for the evidence," said the King, "and then the sentence."

"No!" said the Queen, "first the sentence, and then the evidence!"

"Nonsense!" cried Alice, so loudly that everybody jumped, "the idea of having the sentence first!"

"Hold your tongue!" said the Queen.

"I won't!" said Alice, "you're nothing but a pack of cards! Who cares for you!"

At this the whole pack rose up into the air, and came flying down upon her: she gave a little scream of fright, and tried to beat them off, and found herself lying on the bank, with her head in the lap of her sister, who was gently brushing away some leaves that had fluttered down from the trees on to her face.

︾ page from the original manuscript copy of *Alice's Adventures Under Ground*, 1864

» the smoking caterpillar

wrote a lot of this kind of "nonsense" **verse**. Another famous poem of his, "The Jabberwocky," is in *Through the Looking-Glass*. Some of these ways of using words were quite new. His wordplay influenced many other writers in his time and now. Many people still study his work and his life today.

4 Although they seem to have been written for children, Lewis Carroll's books and poems are enjoyed by people of all ages. If you have not read *Alice's Adventures in Wonderland*, which is also referred to by the short title *Alice in Wonderland*, you should read it soon. No matter how old you are, you will find it exciting and enjoyable.

the Cheshire Cat in Tim Burton's 2010 film *Alice in Wonderland*

Jessie Willcox Smith's illustration of Alice surrounded by the characters of Wonderland (1923) (Wikipedia)

Questions

_____ 1. Which of the following can be inferred about **pen name**?
- **a.** It's a name used for writing.
- **b.** It's a name used by a criminal.
- **c.** It's a childhood nickname.
- **d.** It's a person's family name.

_____ 2. What happened after Lewis Carroll published *Through the Looking-Glass*?
- **a.** He became well-known by people.
- **b.** He wrote "The Hunting of the Snark."
- **c.** He started to write plays.
- **d.** He wrote "The Jabberwocky."

_____ 3. What is probably the author's opinion of *Alice in Wonderland*?
- **a.** It's a boring book for children.
- **b.** It's a good book that people should read.
- **c.** It's a good book for children, but not adults.
- **d.** It's not as good as "The Jabberwocky."

_____ 4. What made Lewis Carroll's writing new and unique?
- **a.** The fact that he wrote books for children.
- **b.** That he wrote books as well as poems.
- **c.** That he created many characters.
- **d.** The wordplay and language that he used.

_____ 5. Which of the following words has a similar meaning as **verse** in the third paragraph?

a. Painting. **b.** Book. **c.** Poetry. **d.** Writer.

Maldives

sunset in the Maldives

83 The Maldives

083

islands in the Maldives

Most people dream of traveling to remote islands where they can relax and enjoy scenic natural beauty. There are many islands, like the Maldives, which have unspoiled beaches and azure seas. Yet the island nation of the Maldives is one of the most popular destinations for beach lovers.

It may be so popular because its location is so convenient. The Maldives is close to India and Eastern Asia, and it is also one of the closest island chains to Europe.

Perhaps it's popular because the Maldives does not have too many hotels. In 2017, there were only 12 hotels on its 1,192 islands. Tourists who come can be sure that they will be able to enjoy their privacy as well as the natural beauty.

Sadly, it's getting more well-known now because people are worried that the Maldives will soon disappear. It is recorded as the lowest country in the world. Most of its islands (the larger ones are called "atolls") are only about two meters above sea level. With sea levels rising every year, the Maldives will have to fight hard for survival and may even disappear underwater in a few decades. Already, its leaders are making plans for what to do when the waters begin to close over their homes.

Whatever the reason for its popularity, the Maldives is a great place to visit. Tourism plays a **vital** role in the Maldives' economy. In 2017, about 1,389,500 tourists visited the islands of the Maldives. Now, there are over 124 tourist resorts in operation. So, if you want to see the Maldives, you'd better not wait too long.

Malé, the capital of the Maldives

Questions

_____ 1. What might people who live in the Maldives have to do soon?

- **a.** Open new hotels.
- **b.** Build more islands.
- **c.** Move to another place.
- **d.** Encourage tourists from India.

_____ 2. What happened most recently?

- **a.** There are over 105 tourist resorts in the Maldives.
- **b.** There are 67 hotels in the Maldives.
- **c.** There are 1,192 islands within the Maldives.
- **d.** Many islands are only two meters above sea level.

_____ 3. Which word means the opposite of **vital** in the final paragraph?

- **a.** Large. **b.** Unattractive.
- **c.** Expensive. **d.** Unimportant.

_____ 4. Which of the following can you infer from the article?

- **a.** The Maldives gets many tourists from Europe.
- **b.** People don't like to go to the Maldives.
- **c.** The Maldives has excellent food.
- **d.** The Maldives is very crowded with tourists.

_____ 5. Which of the following statements is an opinion?

- **a.** The Maldives is the nearest island chain to Europe.
- **b.** The Maldives has the best beaches in its region.
- **c.** The Maldives is made up of many islands.
- **d.** Tourism is important to the Maldives' economy.

Oriental sweetlips *(Plectorhinchus vittatus)* in the Maldives' waters

Many people like to keep parrots as pets.

84 (084)
Can Parrots Talk?

1 Parrots are amazing birds. They are mostly green, but some of them have many **bright** colors. They are very pretty, but their most amazing trait is that they can talk. However, many scientists say that they do not actually speak; instead, they just **repeat** what they hear. Lately, some scientists disagree.

2 A scientist named Irene Pepperberg did years of experiments that proved that parrots are very intelligent and can actually understand what people are saying. Irene bought an African grey parrot from a pet shop when the bird was about one year old. She named the bird Alex (an acronym of Avian Learning Experiment). After many experiments, Irene reported that Alex did not merely repeat what he heard. In fact, she said, the bird could use words creatively and answer 80 percent of the simple questions she asked him. Moreover, Alex could even understand what he himself said. Other scientists do not believe Alex's achievements. They insist that Alex was just repeating the answers as he was taught to do. In other words, Alex just performed by memorizing rather than using language.

Some parrots have many bright colors.

3 Whatever scientists say, many people like to keep parrots because they can "talk." It is **fun** to say something and have a parrot repeat it. Unfortunately, many parrots are being taken from the jungles of Asia and South America to be sold as pets. As a result, the number of wild parrots is **declining** every year. If the **wild** parrot **population** continues to drop, they could become extinct.

4 Parrots are smart and beautiful birds. They are great to have as pets, but they are better left in the wild, where their homes really are.

Questions

_____1. Which of the following words means the opposite of **bright** in the first paragraph?

a. Dull. b. Shiny.
c. Loud. d. Original.

_____2. Which of the following means the same as **fun** in the third paragraph?

a. Boring. b. Exciting.
c. Frightening. d. Difficult.

_____3. What does **declining** mean in the third paragraph?

a. Growing in size. b. Getting fewer in number.
c. Shrinking in area. d. Getting taller.

_____4. Which of the following means the same as **repeat**, in the context of the first paragraph?

a. Think of. b. Create.
c. Lower. d. Mimic.

_____5. In the context of this article, **wild population** means the opposite of ______.

a. free population b. large population
c. pet population d. parrot population

Tooth Fairy

Little boy with missing tooth receives money from the Tooth Fairy.

Children know that once a tooth falls out, the Tooth Fairy will visit. (cc by John Anes)

85 A Modern Fairy Tale

085

1 In the United States, children make money off their teeth. Who buys them? The Tooth Fairy. When children first feel that a baby tooth is loose, they likely feel a mixture of nervousness and **anticipation**. A loose tooth can cause **discomfort**, but children know that once it falls out, the Tooth Fairy will visit. Once the tooth falls out, it is washed and carefully put under the pillow at bedtime. The next morning, the tooth is gone. In its place is money, brought by the Tooth Fairy.

2 The invention of the Tooth Fairy, who brings money in exchange for teeth, is surprisingly recent. While many cultures have had **rituals** connected to baby teeth, the idea of the Tooth Fairy began to spread in post-World War II United States. First, this was a time of **prosperity** and economic growth, meaning parents now had money to spend on children. It was also a time when parents began to focus more on their children. Lastly, Walt Disney himself helped popularize fairies through movies such as *Cinderella*.

3 While the Tooth Fairy is an enchanting idea for children, this fantasy figure, played by parents, has several significant responsibilities. Removing a tooth from under the pillow of a sleeping child can be a challenge. Children also know the Tooth Fairy would

never miss a visit, so parents can't make the mistake of forgetting to take the tooth on the scheduled night. And now Tooth Fairies face another **tough** decision. How much money should they leave? Considering that children lose 20 baby teeth, the cost of being the Tooth Fairy can be high!

4 Belief in the Tooth Fairy has now spread to children in other countries. It helps children feel excitement about the uncomfortable experience of losing teeth and lets parents add a little magic to childhood.

» little girl dressed as the Tooth Fairy

Questions

_____ 1. In the first paragraph, what is the meaning of **anticipation**?
 a. Eagerness. **b.** Growth. **c.** Boredom. **d.** Disinterest.

_____ 2. What is the opposite of **discomfort** as it is used in the first paragraph?
 a. Embarrassment. **b.** Pain. **c.** Relief. **d.** Help.

_____ 3. Which word has the same meaning as **ritual** in the second paragraph?
 a. Custom. **b.** Role. **c.** Rule. **d.** Use.

_____ 4. Which of the following is the opposite of **prosperity** in the second paragraph?
 a. Wealth. **b.** Peace. **c.** Confusion. **d.** Poverty.

_____ 5. What is the meaning of **tough** as it is used in the third paragraph?
 a. Strong. **b.** Difficult. **c.** Surprising. **d.** Scary.

» Dolphins are playful animals.

86 Dolphins

086

1 Many people like dolphins because they appear **friendly** and are playful and **smart**. In fact, scientists say that dolphins are the most intelligent animals in the world, after human beings. Dolphins are related to whales and porpoises. Like whales and porpoises, dolphins originally lived on land. Then, about 50 million years ago, dolphins **entered** the water and became marine mammals.

2 There are about 40 types of dolphins. The smallest dolphins are about 1.2 meters long, and the largest are about 9.5 meters long. All dolphins eat mostly fish. Dolphin experts now know that dolphins make very loud noises to **stun** fish and make them easier to catch. Some say that dolphins also make sounds to "talk" to one another.

3 Like people, dolphins have warm blood, breathe air, and have offspring that feed on milk from their mothers. Most dolphins have very good eyesight, and their sense of hearing is even better than that of humans. Dolphins live in families called "pods," which can include around 12 dolphins. However, where there is a lot of food, pods can come together to form "superpods" of more than 1,000 dolphins.

4 Dolphins are playful animals. They play with seaweed, other dolphins, and sometimes even with human swimmers. Their friendly appearance, their unusual intelligence, and their playful characteristics make them very popular with humans. Movies and books about dolphins and

dolphin performances in many water parks around the world have greatly increased their popularity.

5 Unfortunately, many dolphin species are **threatened** with extinction. It is believed that the Yangtze River dolphin has now become extinct because of pollution and increasing ship traffic on the Yangtze River.

6 Dolphins have been important in human culture for a long time. It would be a shame if we did not do all we could to save them.

Questions

_____ 1. Which of the following means the same as **smart** as it is used in the first paragraph?
a. Playful. **b.** Marine. **c.** Friendly. **d.** Intelligent.

_____ 2. What does the word **threatened** mean in the fifth paragraph?
a. Protected from. **b.** Put in danger of.
c. Eaten by. **d.** Not used to.

_____ 3. From the passage in the second paragraph, what does **stun** probably mean?
a. Paralyze. **b.** Energize. **c.** Feed. **d.** Hide from.

_____ 4. Which word has the closest meaning to **friendly** in the first paragraph?
a. Outgoing. **b.** Cheerful. **c.** Mean. **d.** Fearful.

_____ 5. Which of the following phrases means the opposite of **entered** in the first paragraph?
a. Got out of. **b.** Got into. **c.** Dove in. **d.** Remained.

87 Bar Graph: Top World Cup Players

087

Soccer is the world's most popular sport, with an estimated 3.5 billion fans worldwide. Every four years, soccer fans tune in to watch the FIFA World Cup, an international competition between 32 national teams. For the players, performing well in the World Cup is perhaps one of the most important goals of their soccer careers. With the whole world watching, those who perform well are guaranteed to go down in the history books as some of the best players of all time.

The bar graph below shows some of these exceptional players. Information includes how many World Cup matches they have played and how many goals they scored over the course of those matches. Use the graph below to answer the following questions about history's top World Cup players.

« Miroslav Klose (1978–) (cc by Sven Mandel)

Top World Cup Players

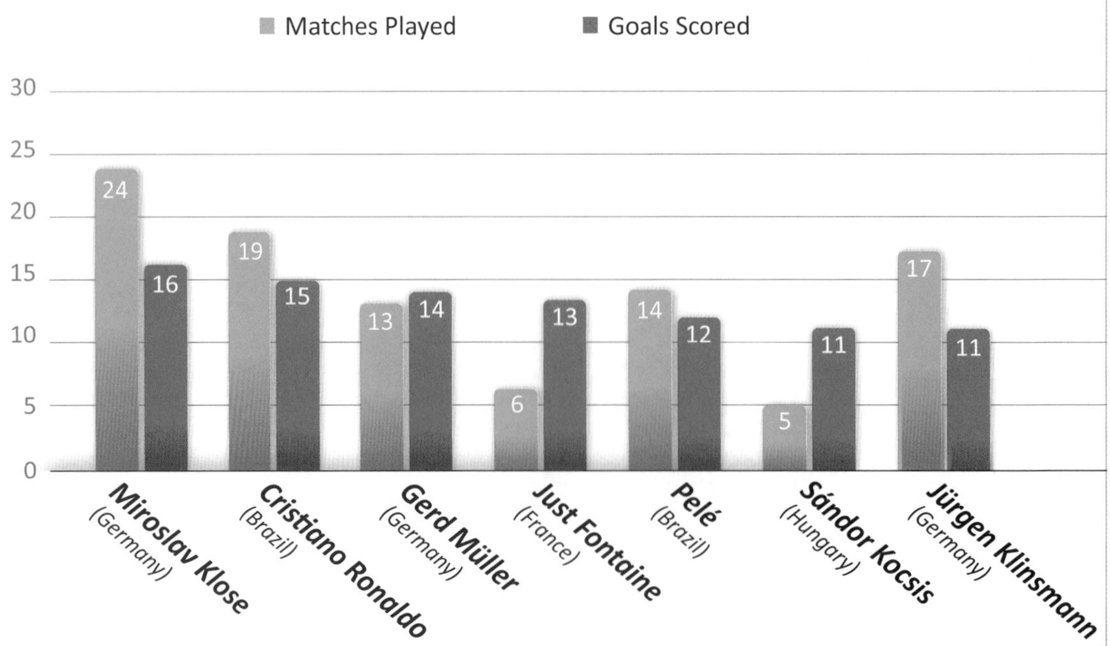

Questions

_____1. Which player has participated in the most World Cup matches?
- a. Gerd Müller.
- b. Ronaldo.
- c. Just Fontaine.
- d. Miroslav Klose.

_____2. How many World Cup goals has the Hungarian player scored?
- a. Eleven.
- b. Sixteen.
- c. Five.
- d. Seventeen.

_____3. Who has scored the most goals in World Cup games?
- a. Miroslav Klose.
- b. Jürgen Klinsmann.
- c. Cristiano Ronaldo.
- d. Just Fontaine.

_____4. Which player on the list has played the fewest number of World Cup matches?
- a. Just Fontaine.
- b. Sándor Kocsis.
- c. Pelé.
- d. Jürgen Klinsmann.

_____5. Which of the following is true about Just Fontaine?
- a. He has scored the same number of World Cup goals as Gerd Müller.
- b. He has played in more World Cup matches than Ronaldo.
- c. He has scored more World Cup goals than Pelé.
- d. He has played in the same number of World Cup matches as Sándor Kocsis.

Pelé (1940–) (cc by Marcello Casal Jr. ABr)

Gerd Müller (1945–) (cc by Cristophe95)

Jürgen Klinsmann (1964–)

Cristiano Ronaldo (1985–)

88 Table: Clean Governments

088

No, "clean" doesn't mean that the floors are shining and the bathrooms smell like roses. "Clean," when it comes to governments, means "not corrupt." It means that government officials won't act dishonestly or break the rules in return for money or favors.

Corruption is a worldwide problem. Some places have a problem with small-scale corruption: for example, paying a police officer a small amount of money to ignore a traffic violation. Other places have large-scale corruption: for example, a corporation paying a huge amount of money to have a regulation rewritten or ignored so that the company can dump toxic waste illegally. There are many examples of corruption, large- and small-scale.

Sometimes, corruption seems convenient. It seems simple to be able to pay to have a parking ticket disappear or to change the date on a document. But when corruption becomes widespread, it means that the rules don't matter. No one can count on protection from the law if the law depends on only money. It is easy to think that small-scale corruption doesn't matter, but corruption seems to spread like a disease. It's better to stop it before it can take hold, like the countries in the table on the next page have done.

Parliament of Norway, Oslo, Norway

CORRUPTION PERCEPTIONS INDEX 2017

SEARCH TABLE

Enter a country or score to search the grid

RANK	COUNTRY	SCORE
1	New Zealand	89
2	Denmark	88
3	Finland	85
3	Norway	85
3	Switzerland	85
6	Singapore	84
6	Sweden	84
8	Canada	82
8	Luxembourg	82
8	Netherlands	82
8	United Kingdom	82
12	Germany	81
13	Australia	77
13	Hong Kong	77
13	Iceland	77
16	Austria	75
16	Belgium	75
16	United States	75

(Source: https://www.transparency.org/news/feature/corruption_perceptions_index_2017#table)

*The CPI ranks countries on a scale from 100 (very clean) to 0 (highly corrupt).

Questions

_____ 1. When was this information collected?
a. 2007 **b.** 2012 **c.** 2017 **d.** 2015

_____ 2. What country got a CPI score of 81?
a. Canada. **b.** Germany. **c.** New Zealand. **d.** Iceland.

_____ 3. According to the table, which of the following countries is perceived as being the least corrupt?
a. Spain. **b.** Japan. **c.** Sweden. **d.** France.

_____ 4. According to the table, which of the following countries has the lowest CPI score?
a. Austria. **b.** Denmark. **c.** Hong Kong. **d.** Luxembourg.

_____ 5. Which two countries have the same CPI score?
a. Canada and Germany. **b.** Belgium and Finland.
c. Norway and Australia. **d.** Netherlands and United Kingdom.

89 Using a Thesaurus

089

A thesaurus is a resource that gives you synonyms and antonyms of a particular word. Unlike a dictionary, not every thesaurus will give you the definition of a word. A thesaurus is a very useful resource for poets and creative writers or any writer who wants to avoid being repetitive.

As a student, you must talk and think a lot about **learning**, so much so that you might get tired of saying the word "learn" over and over. Well, stop. There are dozens of other terms you can use: ascertain, drink in, **soak up**, pore over, discover, and many more.

English is a language rich in synonyms. There's no need to ever get stuck on one word when you have so many to choose from.

Here is an example of a thesaurus. Take a look at the example and answer the following questions.

Main Entry: **learn**

Part of Speech: *verb*

Definition: acquire information

Synonyms: apprentice, attain, be taught, be trained, become able, become versed, brush up on, burn midnight oil, commit to memory, con, crack the books, cram, determine, drink in, enroll, gain, get, get down pat, get the hang of, get the knack of, grasp, grind, imbibe, improve mind, lucubrate, major in, master, matriculate, memorize, minor in, peruse, pick up*, pore over, prepare, read, receive, review, soak up, specialize in, study, take course, take in, train in, wade through

Notes: **Learn** means to acquire or gain skills, knowledge or comprehension; **teach** means to impart skill, knowledge or comprehension to

Antonyms: teach

* = informal/nonformal usage

(Source: http://thesaurus.com/browse/learn?s=t)

Questions

_____1. What is the definition of **learn** according to this thesaurus?

a. Teach. b. Acquire information.
c. Peruse. d. Determine.

_____2. The word **learn** is ______.

a. a verb b. a noun
c. an adjective d. an adverb

_____3. According to the information on the previous page, which of the following is an antonym for **soak up**?

a. Cram. b. Learn.
c. Check out. d. Teach.

_____4. Which is a synonym for **be taught**?

a. Impart knowledge. b. Tell how.
c. Learn. d. Teach.

_____5. Which is not a definition of **learn**?

a. Acquire comprehension. b. Gain knowledge.
c. Impart skill. d. Acquire information.

Permaculture is a branch of environmental design and ecological design and engineering.

90 Index: Permaculture

Permaculture is a system of designing things like homes, farms, and indoor and outdoor environments so that they are good for both humans and the environment. Permaculture is strongly influenced by nature. Its designs are often based on natural systems and are intended to improve rather than harm the environment. Permaculture systems focus on growing one's own food, using natural energy sources, reducing consumption, reusing, recycling, supporting communities, and other practices.

Bill Mollison and David Holmgren first designed an agricultural system they called "permaculture" in the late 1970s. Since the 1970s, the idea of permaculture has been spreading. There are now permaculture systems operating around the world.

The following index is about permaculture. Use the index to answer the questions.

Bill Mollison (1928–2016) in 2008

herb spiral, an element of permaculture

INDEX

The capitalized listings refer to headings in the text.	
aboriginal statement of life, *3*	barrier dams, *159*
acid rain, *172–5, 210–23*	Bee Range, 427–8
acids, *196*	Benching, *235–6*
Active Involvement in Investment, *553*	berry crops, *412*
aerobic waters, *175, 465*	biocides, *170, 185*
age of systems, *33*	Biological Indicators, (8.15)
agricultural disease, *185, 410*	Birch, Six Principles, *5*
agriculture, modern, *412*	black frost, *149*
Aid and Assistance (14, 15), *557–8*	blackberry control, *422, 465*
albedo, *115*	boreal forests, *425*
alkalies, *196*	boulders, *248*
alphabet and number, *98*	boundaries, *76–8*
Animal Barriers, *276–7*	box canyons, *316*
Animal Stocking, Fixed, *439*	Building a Soil, *216–7*
Barrier Plants, *273–6*	burning, *203*
barrier dams, low, *167*	

Questions

_____ 1. Which topic is a heading in the book?
- **a.** Barrier dams.
- **b.** Animal Barriers.
- **c.** Boreal forests.
- **d.** Berry crops.

_____ 2. Where will you find information about controlling blackberries?
- **a.** On pages 422 and 465.
- **b.** On page 149.
- **c.** On pages 76–8.
- **d.** On page 412.

_____ 3. Which topic probably contains the most information?
- **a.** Burning.
- **b.** Acid rain.
- **c.** Barrier plants.
- **d.** Boulders.

_____ 4. What topic is discussed on page 425?
- **a.** Acid rain.
- **b.** Barrier dams.
- **c.** Benching.
- **d.** Boreal forests.

_____ 5. Which topic would you not find on this page of the index?
- **a.** Waterfalls.
- **b.** Acids.
- **c.** Boulders.
- **d.** Box canyons.

Afternoon tea is a small meal typically eaten between 2:00 to 5:00 p.m.

91 Where Elegant Meets Delicious

091

finger sandwiches

Afternoon tea refers to a small meal that used to be eaten sometime between 2:00 to 5:00 p.m. in Britain and other Commonwealth countries. It consists of a delicious spread of tiny sandwiches, scones, rolls, meats, and of course tea. People don't "eat" afternoon tea; they "take" it. However, it has been a long time since afternoon tea was widely popular. In modern society, it's hard to take afternoon tea at 2:00 p.m. when you're working a full-time job.

Even though people have stopped taking afternoon tea every day, the custom survives in some parts of the world. Many people view afternoon tea as an elegant meal that only aristocrats and other very rich people used to enjoy. Therefore, it's not rare for a group of friends to go to a fancy restaurant and take afternoon tea on a rainy Sunday afternoon as a special treat.

Hundreds of years ago, it wasn't just rich people who took afternoon tea. Poor people who worked all day took it as well. So why do we think of afternoon tea as such an elegant tradition? The answer may have to do with the origins of the custom.

cup of tea

According to legend, afternoon tea was invented by the Duchess of Bedford, one of Queen Victoria's ladies-in-waiting. It seems like the Duchess didn't usually eat lunch, so she would always suffer from "a sinking feeling" of hunger around four o'clock. In the beginning, the Duchess would send for her servants and ask them to bring her tea and snacks. Later, she began sending out invitations to her friends so she wouldn't have to eat her snacks alone. Some of the guests liked these informal gatherings so much that they started organizing their own afternoon tea parties. And just like that, the tradition of afternoon tea was born.

cupcakes

Questions

_____ 1. What would you say is the main topic of this article?
- **a.** The origin of a well-known British tradition.
- **b.** The dining habits of Queen Victoria.
- **c.** The lifestyles of the rich and famous in ancient Britain.
- **d.** A history of the conflict between Britain and France.

_____ 2. This article is about ______.
- **a.** Queen Victoria
- **b.** the Duchess of Bedford
- **c.** afternoon tea
- **d.** rich people

_____ 3. Which of the following is probably true about the Duchess of Bedford?
- **a.** She was weak and sick her whole life.
- **b.** She secretly hated Queen Victoria.
- **c.** She was originally from Spain.
- **d.** She was a rich aristocrat.

_____ 4. Why do people believe that afternoon tea is very elegant nowadays?
- **a.** Because the teacups always used to be made of gold.
- **b.** Because the custom was started by a Victorian lady-in-waiting.
- **c.** Because afternoon tea is always very expensive at restaurants.
- **d.** Because the custom was started by a French king.

scones

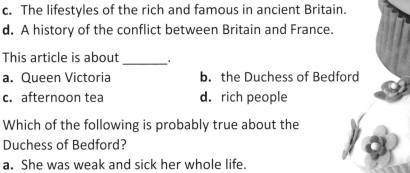

_____ 5. This article can best be described as a(n) ______.
- **a.** narrative essay
- **b.** biography
- **c.** informative essay
- **d.** myth

92 Li Shizhen: A Medical Legend

092

Li Shizhen (1518–1593)

Chinese history is full of famous rulers, generals, monks, and advisers. There are several well-known doctors as well. Li Shizhen is one of these doctors. Some people call him "the father of Chinese herbal medicine."

Li Shizhen was born in Hubei in 1518 during the Ming Dynasty. In his early life, he was always sick and never studied enough to pass the state examinations that would have given him a secure position in the local government. Instead, he spent his time studying medical textbooks and observing his father at work. His father taught him a lot about how to treat patients.

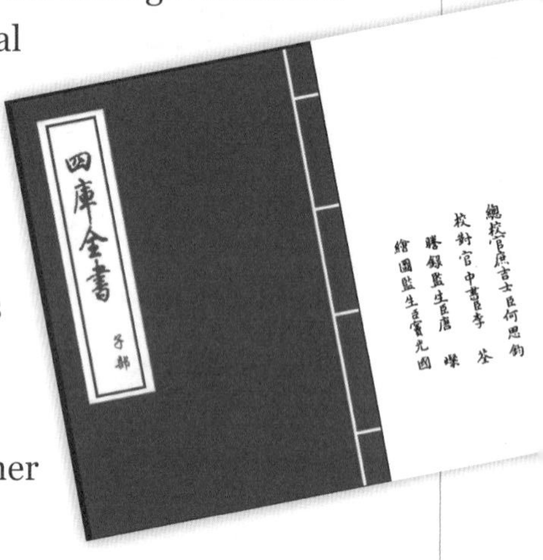

Bencao Gangmu (Compendium of Materia Medica) Siku Quanshu edition (Wikipedia)

When it came to medicine, Li was a quick learner. It wasn't long before he was granted a medical position in the capital. While he was there, he read rare medical books and exchanged views with many other influential scholars.

illustration from a copy of *Bencao Gangmu* (1800) (Wikipedia)

Li didn't stay in one place for long. He began a massive project called the *Bencao Gangmu* and traveled throughout the region looking for strange plants and new ways to cure diseases. *Bencao Gangmu* is an encyclopedia of medical herbs. It combines information from more than 800 other books and contains detailed descriptions of 1,892 substances. He spent almost 30 years writing this enormous book, but unfortunately he didn't get to see the book

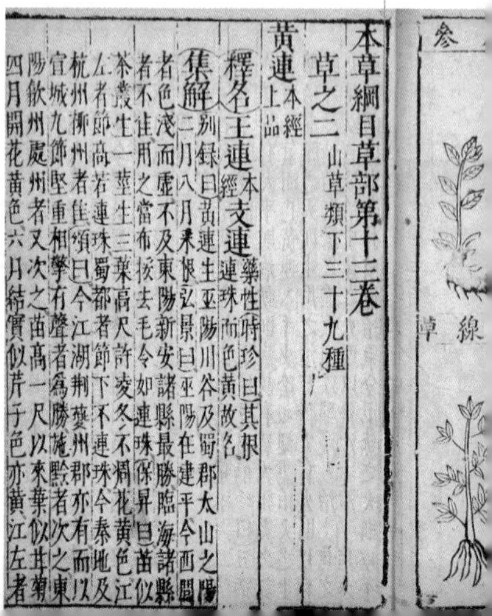
本草綱目草部第十三卷
草之二 山草類下三十九種
黃連 本經上品

Bencao Gangmu recorded information about many kinds of traditional Chinese medicine in detail.

published before his death in 1593. During his writing process, he relied on his sons and grandsons, who helped with the transcripts, illustrations, and editing. If it weren't for their hard work, one of the most important books in Chinese medicine may never have been published.

While *Bencao Gangmu* might have been Li Shizhen's biggest accomplishment, it certainly wasn't the only one. He is also credited as being one of the first doctors to discover gallstones and use ice as a treatment for fever and steam as a treatment for infection.

» Li Shizhen is one of the first doctors to discover gallstones. (cc by haitham alfalah)

Questions

_____ 1. Which of the following happened first?
- **a.** Li Shizhen's sons and grandsons edited his book.
- **b.** Li Shizhen studied medicine under his father.
- **c.** Li Shizhen moved to the capital.
- **d.** Li Shizhen began to travel and research for his book.

_____ 2. Which of the following statements about Li Shizhen is NOT true?
- **a.** He was born in Hubei Province during the Ming Dynasty.
- **b.** He never passed the state examinations.
- **c.** He spent a period of time working in the capital.
- **d.** He was the first doctor to cure cancer.

_____ 3. It's probably true that _______.
- **a.** Li Shizhen was the first doctor to study medicinal herbs
- **b.** Li Shizhen's grandsons all passed the state examinations
- **c.** Li Shizhen's father was a doctor
- **d.** Li Shizhen briefly worked as a lawyer

_____ 4. This article can best be described as a _______.
- **a.** narrative essay
- **b.** biography
- **c.** timeline
- **d.** joke

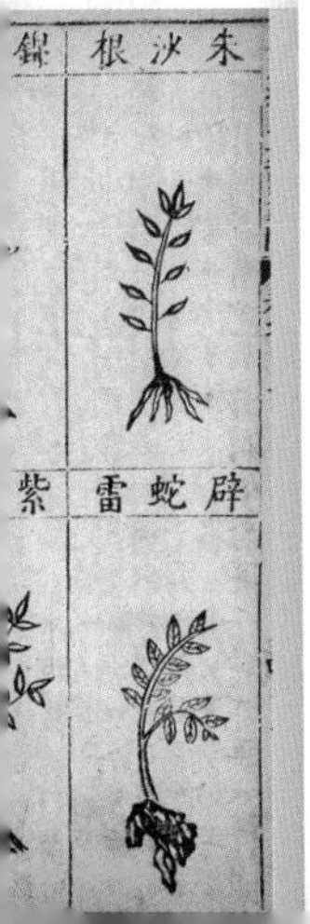

_____ 5. Which of the following is a fact?
- **a.** Li Shizhen is one of the most important doctors in Chinese history.
- **b.** *Bencao Gangmu* was Li Shizhen's greatest accomplishment.
- **c.** Li Shizhen would have been more successful if he had stayed in the capital.
- **d.** *Bencao Gangmu* contains descriptions of 1,892 substances.

» the Giant Crystal Cave in Naica
(cc by Alexander Van Driessche)

93 Exploring the Giant Crystal Cave

093

Imagine finding yourself in a secret cave deep beneath the earth's surface. You blink to try to adjust your eyes to the darkness, but it's no use. You can't see a thing. The air around you is extremely humid and you feel a bit uncomfortable. All of a sudden, you remember that you brought a flashlight. You turn it on and can't believe your eyes. There are giant crystals everywhere. Some are clear, others are light blue, and all of them tower above you. You could explore the cave for hours.

Although this sounds like a place that can exist only in the human imagination, it's as real as Mount Everest or Ha Long Bay in Vietnam. This is the Giant Crystal Cave in Naica, Mexico. The cave is nearly 300 meters beneath the earth's surface. It's full of giant crystals that are made out of selenite. Some of these crystals are as large as 12 meters in length. The crystals are so big because of their unique environment. They have been in very hot water for over 500,000 years.

Before you book a plane ticket to Mexico, there's one thing you should know. Unfortunately, the cave is not open to the public. The atmosphere inside the cave is hot enough to kill you. Temperatures can be as high as 58 degrees Celsius. Thus, anyone exploring the cave needs to wear special protective equipment.

water-clear selenite crystal "floater" from the Naica Mine. Size: 18×14×13 cm, weight 2.6 kg
(cc by Rob Lavinsky)

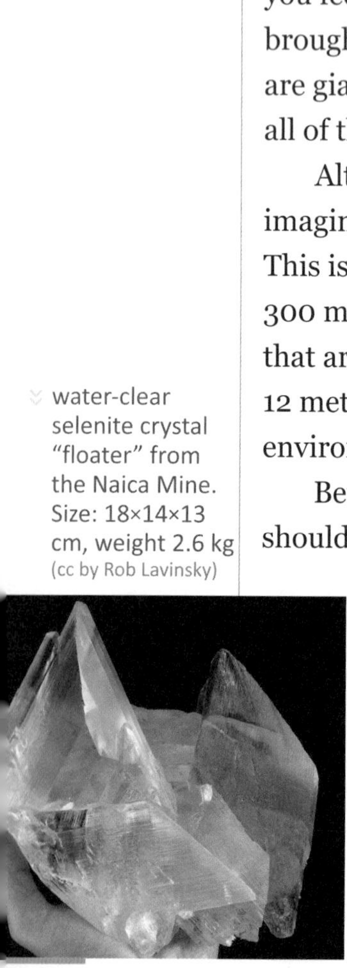

Even the professionals with protective gear won't be able to enjoy the cave for long. Exposure to air has a damaging effect on the giant crystals. Therefore, the organization that is responsible for the cave plans to flood it with water after enough photos and videos have been taken.

Questions

green fluorite framed by white calcite, Naica Mine, mined in the 1980s. Size: 5.5×5.1×4.4 cm
(cc by Rob Lavinsky)

selenite "sword" from the Naica Mine. Size: 22.6×2.6×1.6 cm
(cc by Rob Lavinsky)

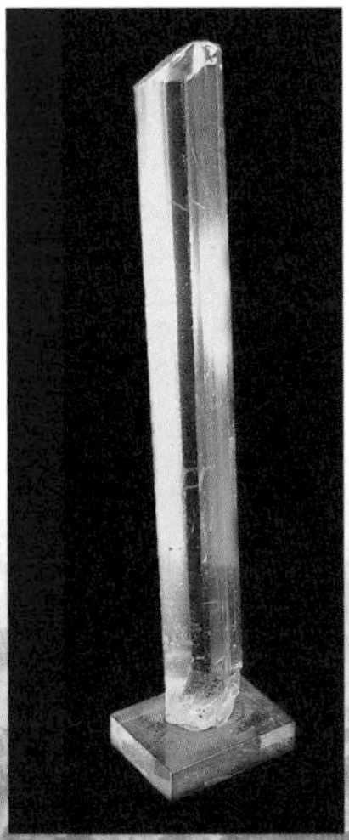

_____1. Which of the following statements is NOT a fact?
- **a.** The inside of the cave is hot enough to kill a human.
- **b.** It took over 500,000 years for the crystals to form.
- **c.** The cave is about 1,000 feet below the earth's surface.
- **d.** The cave is the most beautiful landmark in North America.

_____2. Which of the following statements about the Giant Crystal Cave is NOT true?
- **a.** The cave is located in Morocco.
- **b.** The cave is around 1,000 feet underground.
- **c.** The atmosphere is extremely hot.
- **d.** The cave is not open to the public.

_____3. Why will the cave be flooded with water?
- **a.** Because it's full of dangerous gas.
- **b.** To boost local fish populations.
- **c.** Because open air harms the crystals.
- **d.** To destroy the crystals and allow for mining.

_____4. How does the author capture readers' attention in the first paragraph of this article?
- **a.** A personal narrative. **b.** A fact.
- **c.** A comparison. **d.** A myth.

_____5. This article is about ______.
- **a.** tourist spots in Mexico **b.** diamonds
- **c.** mining **d.** a natural landmark

» feral dogs
(cc by Andrey)

94 The Feral Dog Epidemic

094

1 Over the past 50 years, owning a pet has become very popular all over the world. In the United States alone, dog ownership has tripled since the 1960s. One **negative** consequence of this trend has been a dramatic increase in the number of feral dogs. According to some **estimates**, there are about 100 million feral dogs and cats living in the streets of America today.

2 Unfortunately, the biggest factor behind the growing number of feral dogs is irresponsible owners. Some people buy a puppy because they can't resist how cute it is. Eventually, the dog grows up and everything changes. Now it's less about heart-melting cuteness and more about going out for walks every day, picking up poop, and paying for dog food and **veterinarian** bills when the dog gets sick. How do some owners deal with these responsibilities? They don't. Instead, they choose to abandon their pet on the street.

3 Another factor contributing to the problem is the trend of shrinking animal control budgets. Now that cities have less money to spend, they are less willing to fund programs that can help control feral pet populations. For example, one program that has been very effective in the past is the TNR approach.

veterinarian

This stands for "trap, neuter, and release." TNR programs help ensure that abandoned pets don't breed. With no TNR programs, feral pet populations will continue to **grow** at an uncontrollable rate.

4 Most **urban** residents don't feel that feral dogs are a problem, but this is exactly what feral dogs want them to think. Feral dog packs aren't stupid, and they know that the less they're seen, the safer they are. Thus, they tend to stay out of sight until very early in the morning. In total, they only spend about 10 percent of their time in places where humans can see them.

» Some people buy a puppy simply because they can't resist how cute it is.

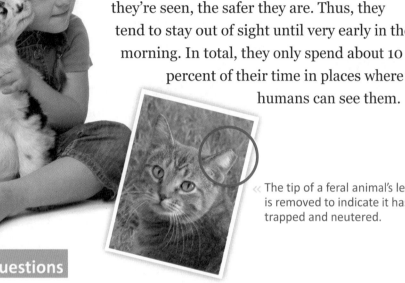

« The tip of a feral animal's left ear is removed to indicate it has been trapped and neutered.

Questions

_____1. In the second paragraph, a **veterinarian** is a(n) ______.
a. type of engineer b. type of lawyer
c. government worker d. animal doctor

_____2. Which of the following has the same meaning as the word in capital letters in the sentence "One **NEGATIVE** consequence of this trend has been a dramatic increase in the number of feral dogs"?
a. Bad. b. Good.
c. Crazy. d. Lazy.

_____3. In the third paragraph, what means the opposite of **grow**?
a. Combine. b. Shrink.
c. Appreciate. d. Small.

_____4. **Estimates** in the first paragraph means which of the following?
a. Guesses. b. Times.
c. Songs. d. Breeds.

_____5. In the fourth paragraph, what means the opposite of **urban**?
a. Angry. b. Metro.
c. Rural. d. Province.

Stop the Violence Inc. is a nonprofit organization dedicated to assisting victims of domestic violence.

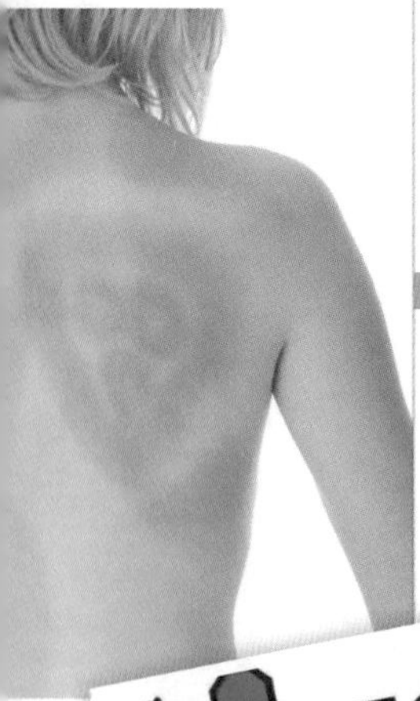

Stop the Violence logo

95 (095)

Borrowing From a Living Library

1 The world is full of different people who have lived very different lives. Some are rich, and others are poor. Some have conquered violence and hatred; others have never known fear. We all have our own story, but what's the best way to tell this story to another person? You could write it down in a book, or better yet, go and tell them face-to-face. This is the idea behind the Human Library.

2 The story of the Human Library began at the Roskilde music festival in Denmark in 2000. That's where a nongovernment youth organization called Stop the Violence set up a small tent in order to **spread** their antiviolence message. They believed that people could better understand strangers with different backgrounds if they had a face-to-face discussion about their experiences in life. At the time, there were over 75 "books" available, including policemen, politicians, graffiti artists, feminists, and soccer fans. The crowd's response at the festival was so **positive** that Stop the Violence decided to expand the program overseas.

At the time, there were over 75 "books" available in the Human Library.

LIVING-library.org
Take out your prejudice

Human Library logo

3 Now there are over 45 Human Libraries all over the world and they are all organized by the Human Library Organization in Denmark. These libraries are **run** by Human Library organizers who are responsible for collecting books and lending them out to the public.

4 A **typical** book catalog will include general characteristics about the person, or "book," that's being offered. For example, there might be a book called "Muslim" that lists the following characteristics:

extremist, fundamentalist, **aggressive** terrorist. These are all popular prejudices toward Muslims. In other words, they're characteristics that people wrongly believe that every Muslim has. By listing these prejudices and giving people an opportunity to meet a real Muslim, the Human Library is trying to challenge the way people see other groups in society.

The Human Library is trying to challenge the way people see other groups in society.

Questions

_____ 1. **Aggressive** in the fourth paragraph means which of the following?
a. Weak. b. Timid. c. Powerless. d. Dangerous.

_____ 2. According to the fourth paragraph sentence "A **typical** book catalog will include general characteristics about the person . . . that's being offered," which of the following words has the same meaning as **typical**?
a. Rare. b. Expensive. c. Usual. d. Complex.

_____ 3. Which of the following has the same meaning as the word in capital letters in the sentence "These libraries are **RUN** by Human Library organizers"?
a. Stolen. b. Written. c. Stored. d. Managed.

_____ 4. In the second paragraph, what means the opposite of **positive**?
a. Beneficial. b. Negative. c. Sensitive. d. Dismissive.

_____ 5. **Spread** in the second paragraph means which of the following?
a. Expand. b. Destroy. c. Invent. d. Agree.

The common basilisk is bright green.

96 The Holiest of Lizards

096

1 There is a strange type of lizard that lives in Latin America called the common basilisk. Why is it strange you ask? Well, it's not this creature's diet that makes it unique. The common basilisk is an omnivore, which means it eats both plants and meat. It's also not the creature's appearance that is so strange. The common basilisk is **bright** green and can grow up to three feet in length. Rather, it's a **special** ability that sets it apart from other lizards. This amazing creature can actually walk on water, a characteristic that has earned it the nickname "Jesus Christ lizard."

The common basilisk eats both plants and meat.

2 According to Christian religious beliefs, Jesus Christ walked on water in front of his followers. If the story is true, Jesus was able to do this because he was the son of God.

3 With the Jesus Christ lizard on the other hand, God has nothing to do with its ability to walk on water. It relies on long toes with webbed skin to keep it from falling in. These webbed toes increase the surface area of the lizard's footprint, making it less likely that its foot will break the surface of the water. The webbing on its toes is also retractable, which means that it can fold up and then unfold again whenever the Jesus lizard needs to walk on water.

The common basilisk can grow up to three feet in length.

4 To be truthful, the Jesus Christ lizard doesn't walk on water. After all, no matter how webbed its toes are, if it took a leisurely **stroll** on top of a lake, it would **definitely** fall in. The Jesus Christ lizard **runs** on water, and it maintains a very quick **pace** of 1.5 meters per second. It can usually stay on the surface for about 4.5 meters before falling in. It is also a very good swimmer and can hold its breath for up to half an hour.

» The common basilisk can walk on water.

Questions

____ 1. **Stroll** in the fourth paragraph means which of the following?

a. Swim. **b.** Camp.
c. Walk. **d.** Talk.

____ 2. **Pace** in the fourth paragraph means which of the following?

a. Shoes. **b.** Interaction.
c. Speed. **d.** Warning.

____ 3. In the first paragraph, what means the opposite of **bright**?

a. Colorful. **b.** Yellow.
c. Dust. **d.** Dark.

____ 4. Which of the following has the same meaning as the word in capital letters in the sentence "If it took a leisurely stroll on top of a lake, it would **DEFINITELY** fall in"?

a. Certainly. **b.** Quickly.
c. Slowly. **d.** Completely.

____ 5. Which of the following has the same meaning as the word in capital letters in the sentence "Rather, it's a **SPECIAL** ability that sets it apart from other lizards"?

a. Uncommon. **b.** Common.
c. Weak. **d.** Medical.

97 Pie Chart: Better Sundays Through Efficiency

097

People often assume that all kids are very disorganized, but that is not true. Take me for example. I work hard all week going to school, doing homework, practicing the piano, and doing chores around the house. I even walk our dog, Crispy, twice a day. My parents are aware of how hard I work from Monday to Saturday, so they let me do whatever I want for seven hours and 15 minutes every Sunday.

That's a whole lot of free time for one kid to handle. A lot of other kids would waste most of it trying to decide what to do next. Should I climb a tree or go hunt for beetles? I'm not one of those kids. I've drafted a strict schedule for how to spend my Sunday afternoons. Once the time is up for one activity, an alarm on my watch will go off, and I'll move on to the next one on the list. If you don't believe me, I've made a chart that shows how I like to spend my time on Sundays.

People often assume that all kids are very disorganized, but that is not true.

Free Time

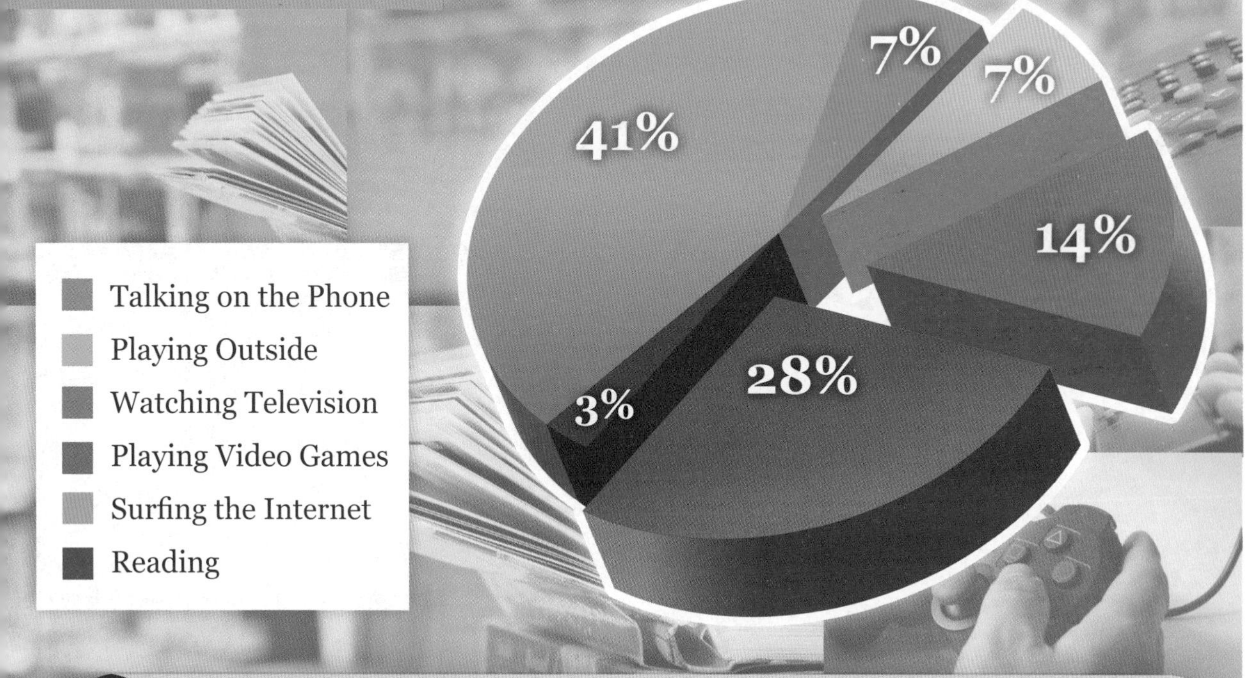

Questions

_____1. What does the author spend the most time on according to the chart?

a. Talking on the Phone. b. Playing Video Games.
c. Watching Television. d. Surfing the Internet.

_____2. What percentage of the author's time is spent on playing video games?

a. 28% b. 41%
c. 7% d. 3%

_____3. Which does the author spend the least time on according to the chart?

a. Playing Video Games. b. Surfing the Internet.
c. Reading. d. Watching Television.

_____4. Which color represents the author's time spent on watching television?

a. Blue. b. Yellow.
c. Dark green. d. Red.

_____5. Which color represents the author's time spent on the Internet?

a. Blue. b. Light green.
c. Yellow. d. Red.

98 Bar Graph: Taiwan—Beware of Typhoons

098

If you're going to visit Taiwan, be sure to bring a pair of shorts, a T-shirt, and an umbrella. Actually, maybe it's better if you bring two umbrellas. It's always possible that the first one will be destroyed by a powerful burst of wind during a typhoon.

Taiwan has a typhoon season that generally lasts from July to September. These large tropical storms can be very dangerous. They often bring damaging winds and very heavy rain to this area. Everyone stays indoors whenever a typhoon passes over the island.

For more detailed information on rainfall in Taiwan, refer to the bar graph. A bar graph represents data using a series of bars, making it easy to compare different values. Use the bar graph to answer the following questions.

» The weather in Taiwan is usually hot and humid with a lot of rainfall.

Average Rainfall in Tainan, Taiwan

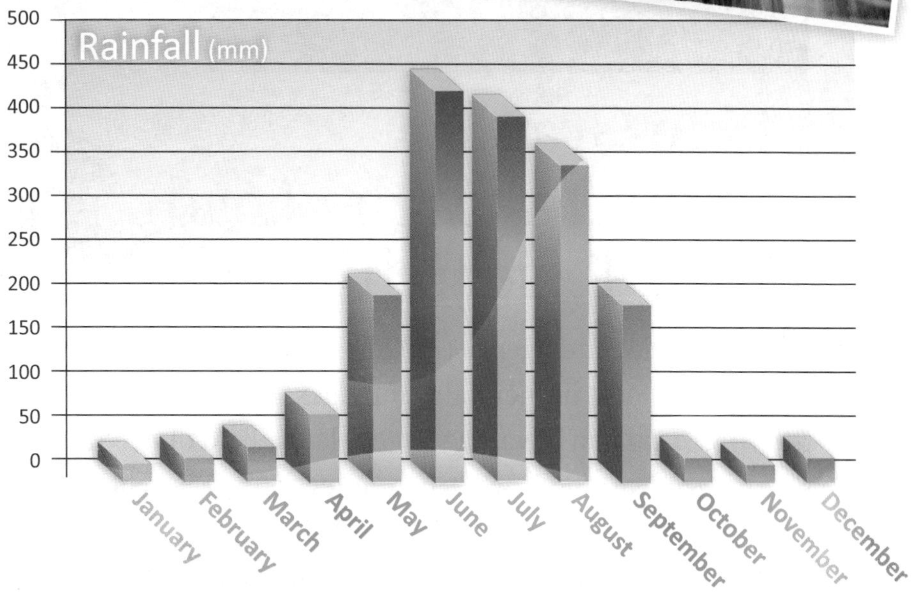

Questions

_____1. What month has the highest average rainfall?

a. June. **b.** July.
c. August. **d.** January.

_____2. Which month has the least average rainfall?

a. September. **b.** March.
c. November. **d.** July.

_____3. In which month was there over 350 mm of rainfall?

a. January. **b.** February.
c. April. **d.** August.

_____4. In which month was there less than 100 mm of rainfall?

a. January. **b.** July.
c. June. **d.** September.

_____5. Around how much average rainfall is there in the month of May?

a. 600 **b.** 350
c. 400 **d.** 200

>> China is developing the technology of deep learning.

>> artificial intelligence

99 Line Graph: China Takes the Lead in AI Research Race

099

Artificial intelligence (AI) has been the primary focus for some of today's most influential companies. Now different businesses are trying to gain an advantage in the latest field of AI—deep learning.

Deep learning is when computer software is able to recognize and analyze patterns. In other words, it's computers analyzing a set of data and drawing their own conclusions. Increasingly, the deep learning process doesn't need to be supervised by humans.

It remains to be seen whether China or the United States will win the race to develop deep learning. The United States started strong, but now it's China's time to win. The winner will receive a valuable prize. They'll be able to write the rules for the new technology, just like the United States did when US researchers invented the Internet. These rules will play a big part in how deep learning impacts society.

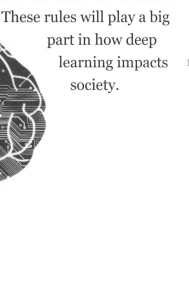

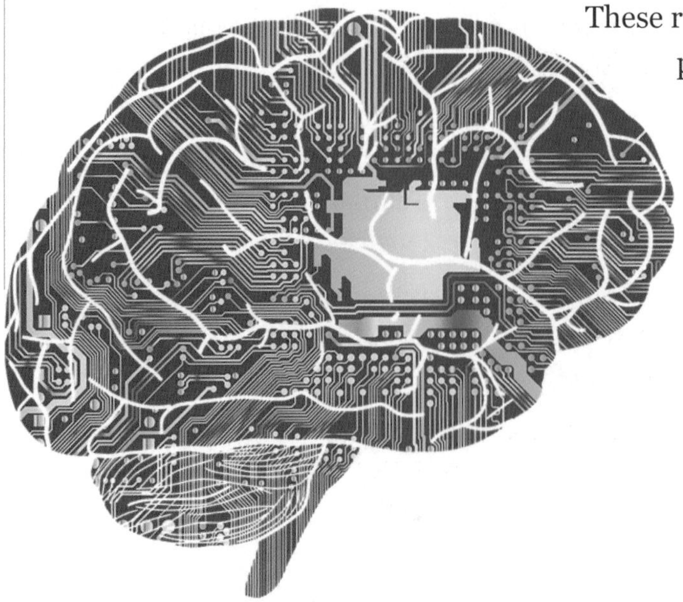

>> deep learning

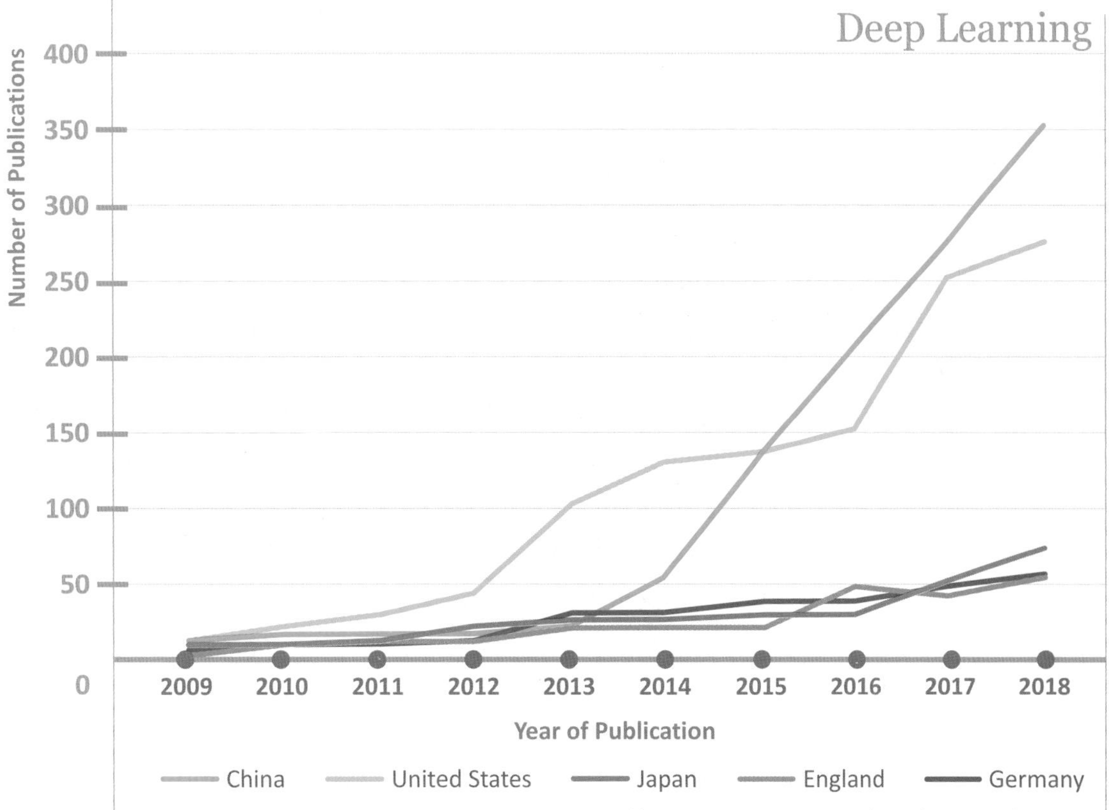

(Source: https://www.washingtonpost.com/news/the-switch/wp/2016/10/13/china-has-now-eclipsed-us-in-ai-research/)

Questions

_____ **1.** What does the graph show?

a. Where major experts on deep learning were born.
b. Different kinds of publications about deep learning.
c. The number of publications on deep learning around the world.
d. The cost of different deep learning programs in major universities.

_____ **2.** When did China's number of publications reach 350?

a. 2018 **b.** 2014 **c.** 2009 **d.** 2012

_____ **3.** Overall, how would you describe the number of publications in China and the United States?

a. They're rising sharply. **b.** They're rising slowly.
c. They're decreasing sharply. **d.** They're decreasing slowly.

_____ **4.** According to the graph, which country is in third place behind China and the United States?

a. England. **b.** France. **c.** Germany. **d.** Japan.

_____ **5.** How many publications did the United States publish in 2017?

a. 140 **b.** 175 **c.** 250 **d.** 25

100

100

Table of Contents: Home Remedy

When most people get sick, the first reaction is to go to the doctor and get medicine. However, a growing number of people are deciding not to go to the doctor immediately. Instead, they try a home remedy first.

"Home remedy" is a very broad classification. It represents any kind of medicine that isn't sold by large pharmaceutical companies. Therefore, it can include herbal remedies from ancient cultures in different parts of the world. In other words, a home remedy used in the United States to cure a headache might have originated in ancient China.

Home remedies can sometimes be preventative. For example, if you are suffering from an upset stomach, a book of home remedies may tell you that your diet is the problem. From the table of contents in the beginning of a book on home remedies, you can easily find out which page you should turn to for the appropriate information. Take a look at the following table of contents of a home remedy book. Then, answer the following questions.

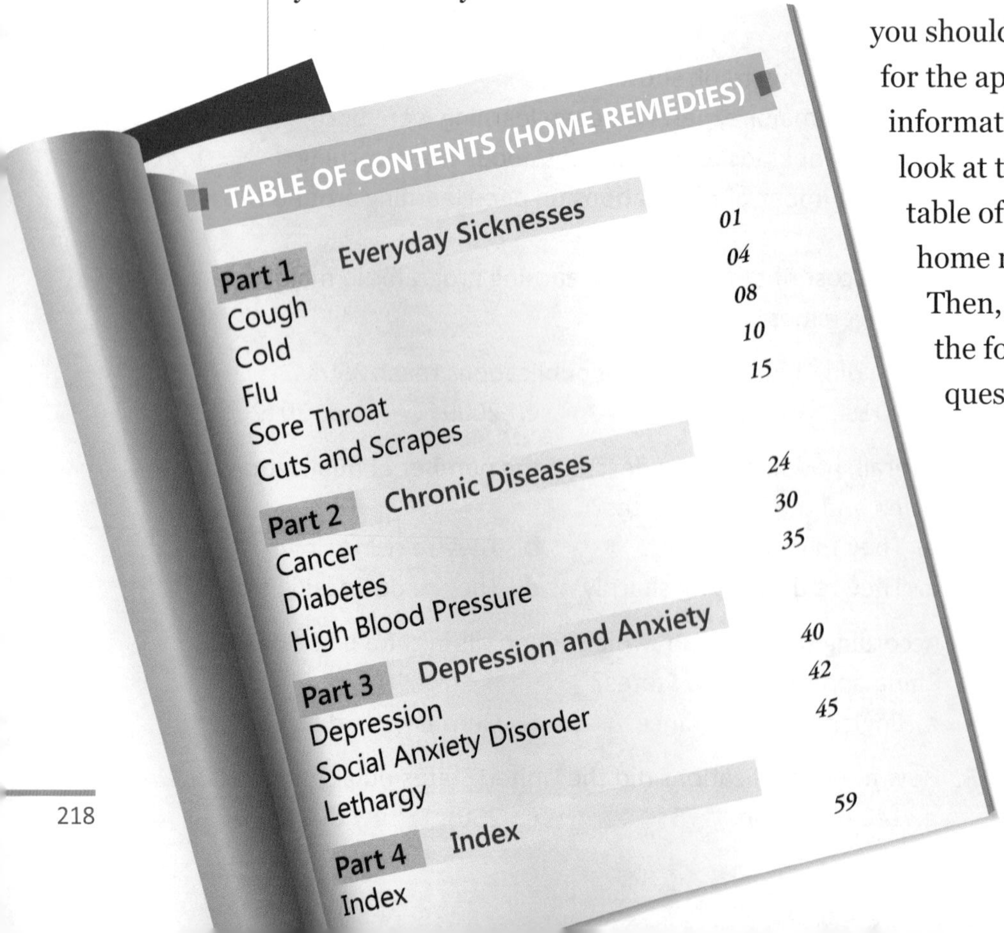

TABLE OF CONTENTS (HOME REMEDIES)

Home remedies include herbal remedies from ancient cultures.

Questions

_____ 1. If you're feeling blue, in which part of the book should you look for home remedies?

- a. Part 1.
- b. Part 2.
- c. Part 3.
- d. Part 4.

_____ 2. What page would you turn to for information on home remedies for Cancer?

- a. 59
- b. 30
- c. 24
- d. 10

_____ 3. What page would you turn to for the index?

- a. 59
- b. 30
- c. 24
- d. 10

_____ 4. **High Blood Pressure** belongs to what category?

- a. Index.
- b. Depression and Anxiety.
- c. Chronic Diseases.
- d. Everyday Sicknesses.

_____ 5. If you accidentally cut yourself while cooking, in which part should you look for home remedies?

- a. Part 1.
- b. Part 2.
- c. Part 3.
- d. Part 4.

Unit 1 閱讀技巧

本單元將幫助你練習瞭解文章整體結構的技巧。單元內容包括明辨主題、歸納要旨、找出支持性細節、情節排序、理解因果關係、釐清寫作技巧、進行推論、批判性思考，以及分辨事實與意見。

章節裡所討論的技巧，能幫助你了解文章欲傳達的訊息、事件發生的時間，以及發生的原因。你也能學會依據文章線索，推論未提及的資訊和作者對文章的感想，並且練習用事實來佐證看法，用文章細節來佐證文章主旨。

1-1 明辨主題

文章主題是文章內容的最概括要點。我們閱讀的時候，會先掌握「大方向」，再繼續深究特定的「小細節」。而「主題」即為含有這些細節的大方向。了解文章的整體概念，便可幫助你理解上下文中的細節。

1. 黃石公園之旅 P. 014

走一趟黃石公園之旅，就好像重返過去的時光。黃石公園是全世界最古老的國家公園，創立於 1872 年。美國原住民住在黃石公園地區內，已有至少一萬一千年之久。這座公園主要座落在美國懷俄明州境內，占地廣大，涵蓋的範圍將近 9,000 平方公里，擁有廣大的森林、明媚的湖泊、峽谷、河流和高山峻嶺。而它之所以稱為「黃石」，是因為「黃石河」貫穿其中。

一趟黃石之旅，可以體驗到美國在未有人跡前的樣貌。你可以在公園裡看到一大群野牛和麋鹿，不過並非所有園中野生動物都是溫馴沒有攻擊性。你可得小心，黃石公園是野生灰熊和狼的棲息地，而熊有瞬間致人於死的能力，必須盡量避開。狼群攻擊人的傳聞也時有所聞，千萬不可以餵食熊或狼，因為這樣會讓牠們變得不怕人類，攻擊你或其他人的可能性也會相對提高。

如果你去參觀黃石公園，一定要拜訪園中最令人嘆為觀止的老忠實噴泉（Old Faithful）。老忠實噴泉是一座錐形的間歇性噴泉，在園內超過 1 萬座天然泉和間歇泉當中，它並非最高或最大的，卻是最富盛名的。這個壯觀的噴泉大約每一個半小時就會向空中噴出平均 44 公尺高的滾燙泉水。想像一下那番情景吧！

這個著名的間歇噴泉因為規律且反覆地噴出泉水，在 1870 年，華士本探險隊的成員便將之命名為「老忠實」。雖然它間歇性的平均噴發時間已逐年延長，但老忠實仍如一世紀前那樣美麗壯觀，如期噴出泉水。

2. 令人驚奇的蝴蝶 P. 016

我的麥特叔叔過去常收集蝴蝶，他會把捕捉到的蝴蝶陳列在書房的玻璃箱中。這些美麗的有翅昆蟲常令我嘆為觀止。如今我的其中一個嗜好，就是在野外看著蝴蝶自由地飛翔，欣賞牠們多采多姿的翅膀，和優美的飛行所構成的不同圖案。

麥特叔叔告訴我許多關於蝴蝶的趣事。舉例來說，他告訴我蝴蝶有四隻翅膀，而不是兩隻；牠們拍動翅膀的速度比很多其他昆蟲還慢，但這也表示牠們能夠飛得比較遠。夏天時，蝴蝶可以一天連飛 24 個小時，飛越日不落的北極圈。許多蝴蝶會進行長距離的遷移，例如，帝王斑蝶能在一年內飛行 4,000 到 4,800 公里，從墨西哥飛到美國北方。

成蝶不會再長大，也不能咀嚼食物，因為牠們沒有嘴巴，只有一根長長、像細吸管一樣的虹吸管，蝴蝶用這個長「吸管」從潮濕的地面啜飲水分，並且主要以花蜜為食。有些蝴蝶會從花粉、樹汁、腐爛的水果、糞肥和濕土裡已分解的礦物中獲取養分。蝴蝶也很嬌弱，在暴風雨來襲時，牠們必須在樹林或灌木叢中躲雨，否則可能會喪命。

今日，全世界共有超過一萬五千種蝴蝶。可惜這個數量正在逐漸減少當中。汙染與棲息地的流失，使得蝴蝶的數量越來越少。

3. 中途島之戰 P. 018

1941 年 12 月 7 日珍珠港突襲轟炸事件，迫使美國加入第二次世界大戰。當時裕仁天皇所領導的日本銳不可當，先是控制了大部分中國，還有可能攻擊西太平洋的任何地區。

1942 年的 5 月初，美國在珊瑚海之役中極力反攻。日本損失兩艘航空母艦、兩艘驅逐艦、一百架左右的飛機，大約 3,500 名士兵殉難。而美國則損失了一艘航空母艦、一艘驅逐艦、一架油輪、65 架飛機和 540 人。

然而，日本仍控制了大部分的太平洋地區。當時的海軍上將山本負責指揮日本海軍，他認為美國海軍已遭重創，便計畫引誘美國少數剩下的航空母艦進入圈套，加以擊沉之後占領中途島。

1942 年 6 月 4 日，中途島之戰開打。鬥志堅強的美國船員，擊沉了四艘日本航空母艦、兩艘巡洋艦和三艘驅逐艦，並擊落了兩百名經驗豐富的海軍飛行員。美方則損失一艘航空母艦和一艘驅逐艦。

這場戰役是抗日之戰的轉捩點。在中途島戰爭後，整個太平洋勢力的平衡轉為對美國有利。在那之後不久，美國強大的科學、技術和經濟實力，都展現更佳的備戰狀態，而日本卻無力在航空母艦、戰艦、巡洋艦、驅逐艦、潛水艇、補給艦、飛機、魚雷和炸彈的建造上，與美國一較高下。

1945 年 8 月，一顆原子彈摧毀了廣島，另一顆則破壞了長崎，但日本仍然不投降。最後，在美國杜魯門總統允許無須廢除裕仁天皇之後，日本才投降。

你也許對杜魯門總統投下原子彈，和保護裕仁天皇免負戰爭罪責的決定有所異議，但不管這些決定的功過如何，1942 年 6 月的中途島之戰，確實為日本控制整個太平洋的計畫，劃下了句點。

4. 哈佛大學 P. 020

根據《新聞週刊》的報導，全世界最好的大學是哈佛大學。你可能聽過哈佛大學，但你對這個學校了解多少？你知道什麼樣的嗜好可以幫助你進入哈佛嗎？

哈佛大學是位於麻州劍橋的一所私立大學，也是美國最古老的高等學府。哈佛成立於 1636 年，一開始它被稱為新學院，1639 年時，以約翰．哈佛這位年輕的牧師為名，改名為哈佛學院。直到 1780 年才改制為大學。

在 1869 年到 1909 年間，查爾斯．威廉．艾略特擔任哈佛校長。他建立選修課程、小班制，和一律以入學考試來錄取學生的制度，使哈佛煥然一新，成為第一所現代化的美國大學。

現在，哈佛擁有約 2,400 位教授，6,700 位大學生，以及 15,250 名研究生。要進入哈佛比進入美國的其他大學來得困難。2018 年，哈佛大學的錄取率僅 4.59%，為其史上新低錄取率。

哈佛大學的圖書館系統一共有約 80 所獨立的圖書館，擁有超過 1,800 萬冊的藏書。哈佛的圖書館是全美最大的學術圖書館，也是全世界第四大的圖書館。

大型的圖書館是非常有益的，因為廣泛的閱讀是你能大量增進字彙與改善寫作技巧的方法。大量閱讀是哈佛教育的重要一環。成為具有優異閱讀技巧的讀者，是在知識時代成功的關鍵。如果你想進入哈佛或其他名校，你的主要嗜好就必須是「閱讀」。

157 位諾貝爾獎得主與哈佛大學密切合作。從 20 世紀初，共有 124 位諾貝爾獎得主與 43 名普立茲獎得主，陸續在哈佛擔任教職。哈佛大學研究生畢業的名人，包括美國總統約翰．甘迺迪、喬治．布希和歐巴馬，另外還有作家麥克．克萊頓以及詩人艾略特。

5. 被蛇咬傷 P. 022

羅伯·庫勒特在南非當野生動物公園管理員。他對非洲動物、昆蟲和爬蟲類瞭解甚深，也正因如此而失之大意了。

一天晚上，羅伯一個人在外露營。在他伸手撿拾一塊大木材時，感覺手臂被什麼東西碰了一下。當時他不以為意，不一會兒，手臂竟開始疼痛。他靠近一看，手臂皮膚上有兩個齒痕，他明白自己被毒蛇咬了，他的脈搏開始加快。

羅伯的思緒不斷湧出，想著該做些什麼才能保命。他知道自己必須保持冷靜，不能亂動，讓被咬的手臂保持低於心臟的位置，而且不能吃也不能喝，尤其是含酒精的飲料。他也知道，切開傷口將毒液吸出並不是個好方法。

他利用無線電對講機求救。等待救援時，他以肥皂和清水清洗傷口。為了減緩毒液的擴散，他在傷口上方兩吋的地方綁上繃帶，但不能綁太緊，必須留下一根手指頭可以插入的空隙，避免血液不流通。大約半個小時後，他的朋友麥克趕到了。麥克帶羅伯到當地醫院注射抗蛇毒血清——一種對抗蛇毒液的解毒劑。

羅伯還是很喜歡露營，只不過現在他會非常、非常小心，不會再打草驚蛇了。

1-2 歸納要旨

文章（不管是短文或段落）的要旨，是它所要表達的關鍵訊息，這訊息有可能是一種看法或一個事實。一篇談論貓的文章，也許會傳達不同的意旨，可能是「貓是好寵物」或「貓很神秘」。文章要旨通常會用主題論述的方式來呈現。

6. 機器戰士：遊戲開始！ P. 024

你知道什麼是 Boxbot、Flipper、Thwackbot 嗎？它們是專門在電視上對打的機器人。「機器戰士」（BattleBots）是一家主辦這些機器人大戰的美國公司，同時也是一個機器人大戰的電視節目名稱。像《機器戰士》和《機器人大戰》這樣的機器人戰鬥節目，已在全世界廣為流行，觀賞節目的影迷已有好幾百萬。

工程師團隊設計打造出價值可高達五萬美金的機器人，送去參加電視比賽。他們會為自己的機器人取一些駭人或無厘頭的名字，像是「弗拉德穿心魔」、「法官」和「麥片盒剋星」。在機器人大戰的比賽中，參賽者帶來可以遙控、配有武器的裝甲機器人，將它們放入比賽場中，盡全力摧毀對方。機器人在比賽中的手段可說是無所不用其極。

機器人一場比賽要對打三分鐘。如果其中一個機器人因為被毀壞或被困住，30 秒內動彈不得，另一個機器人就獲勝。如果雙方在比賽中都未陣亡，將由三位裁判選出獲勝者。裁判們將根據三個項目的高分者來決定勝方，依序為：侵略性（機器人勇敢奮戰的程度）、策略（機器人如何攻擊對方的弱點、保護自己，和處理危機），以及攻擊力（機器人如何攻擊，同時自己毫髮無傷）。如果我方機器人快要被摧毀了，參賽者可以喊出「投降」，那麼他們將輸掉比賽，但是可以保住機器人免於解體。

雖然機器人大戰在美國受歡迎的程度已大不如前，但在世界其他國家仍有其支持群眾。

7. 白噪音？ P. 026

你是否曾注意到，在下著雨的夜裡，四周彷彿鴉雀無聲？雨聲淹沒了一切。而且，即使雨下了一整夜不停歇，也不會讓你徹夜難眠。雨聲就是一種「白噪音」，意即穩定、不變、低調的聲音。

「白噪音」是以人耳可聽見的各種音頻所構成，只是每一種頻率的強度皆相同。之所以稱為「白噪音」，其實是和白光的原理一樣，白光也是由肉眼可見的所有波長光線組成。你可能會以為所有的音頻加起來應該很吵才對，其實恰恰相反。原因在於白噪音能掩蓋其他聲音。想像一下雨聲，如果是一滴水，例如水龍頭漏水的聲音，會非常明顯而惱人，兩滴水也是一樣，甚至連續滴落的三滴水，我們都能聽得很清楚。但若是五滴、十滴或一千滴，你已經聽不出每一滴水聲。所有的水聲融合成一種低鳴或輕悄的隆隆聲，說不定還能助眠。

白噪音的鎮靜特性，已開始被用於治療各種問題。白噪音對容易焦躁者有助眠作用，也能讓偏頭痛患者一覺好眠。對於注意力不集中的人亦十分有用，這些人很容易被周遭的聲音影響，因此白噪音有助於他們專心。診療師或其他希望保護隱私的人，會運用白噪音來掩蓋個別的談話內容。誰能想到，聲音的大雜燴反而帶來平和與寧靜呢？

8. 笑話 P. 028

「笑話」是我們說來讓人發笑的東西。有些笑話只是短短的一句話，有些是需要花點時間講述的故事。以下是兩則簡單的笑話：

問：鳥為什麼往南飛？

答：因為太遠了走不到。

問：為什麼蜂鳥只會嗡嗡叫？

答：因為牠們不認識字啊。

多數人都愛笑，很會說笑話的人通常很受歡迎。不過笑話可不是只有文字好笑而已，說笑話的方式也很重要。說笑話就是要製造懸疑。很多笑話的幽默來自於讓人驚訝的元素，所以說笑話的人一定要很會演。有些人天生就是說笑話的好手，有些人則不是。

不過，有些笑話不是你很會說就好笑。如果一個笑話不好笑或很愚蠢，我們就會說它是「老梗」。以下就是一個老掉牙的笑話：

問：雞為什麼要過馬路？

答：為了到另一邊啊。

（當然，有些人就像我，還滿愛這些老梗呢！）

每一種語言和文化都有自己的笑話，很多笑話被翻譯成另一種語言，或放到另一種文化脈絡下，就失去幽默的成分了。有些笑話靠的是挖苦或諷刺來達到好笑的目的，但是，這些笑話往往會很不禮貌、羞辱到別人。

有時笑話和某個種族或宗教有關，這種「種族笑話」或「宗教笑話」也是很羞辱人的。笑話如果牽涉到性別上的假設性特質，常被認為是「性別歧視語言」。讓別人不舒服其實一點都不好笑。逗人笑的方法千千百百種，你最近有聽過好笑的笑話嗎？

9. 臨陣脫逃 P. 030

走上紅毯前那一刻想落跑的新娘、斥資參加跳傘之旅卻腳軟無法跳出機門的人、到卡拉 OK 點歌又不敢上台獻唱的人，這些人的共同點就是所謂的「臨陣脫逃」（cold feet）。

英文裡說的「cold feet」，是指一個人原本計劃好要做某件事，卻突然緊張而想臨陣脫逃的情況。這個片語描述一個人不敢做他原本期待的事。這種恐懼通常是莫名的，往往內心的渴望必須大於恐懼感才能克服這種 cold feet。

「cold feet」一詞是個俚語，不過是否有事實根據呢？研究顯示真有其事。美國電視節目《流言終結者》讓三個人處於自己所懼怕的環境裡，並且測量他們足部的溫度。一位搭乘驚險刺激的特技飛機，一位讓蜘蛛爬滿全身，另一位則吃昆蟲。其中兩人開始害怕的時候，足部的溫度也驟降。

研究人員認為，這跟所謂的「對抗或逃避」反應有關。我們害怕的時候，身體會做好要對抗還是逃跑的準備。這時更多血液進入肌肉，以應萬變。而皮膚與其他器官裡的血管則會收縮，以減少萬一受傷的出血量。當對抗或逃避反應啟動，腳部的小肌肉所獲供血量減少。表示說，我們害怕的時候，足部真的會降溫！

那麼當我們覺得會緊張的時候，是不是應該穿上厚襪子呢？大可不必。咬牙克服自己的恐懼，冰腳丫也就沒事了。

10. 莎士比亞的一生與作品 P. 032

威廉・莎士比亞被公認為是最富盛名的英語創作作家與詩人，也是舉世卓越的劇作家。莎士比亞在 1564 年生於英國，卒於 1616 年。他所遺留的作品包括 38 部戲劇、154 首十四行詩（一種必須要有十四行，並遵循特定格律的詩）、兩首長敘事詩和許多其他詩作。

莎士比亞最著名的是他的戲劇，幾乎主要的現存語言中都已經有這些戲劇的譯作，演出次數更是冠於其他劇作家的作品。一些名劇包括有《仲夏夜之夢》、《威尼斯商人》、《哈姆雷特》、《羅密歐與茱麗葉》、《李爾王》、《馬克白》和《暴風雨》。許多喜愛閱讀古典英文的人熱愛他的作品。主修英文的大學生通常至少必須研讀一部莎士比亞的戲劇。

莎士比亞在 18 歲時便與一名 26 歲的女子結婚。在 1585 年到 1592 年間，他以演員、劇作家和張伯倫勳爵劇團（The Lord Chamberlain's Men）合夥人的身分，在倫敦展開他的事業。他的劇本多半就是在倫敦所寫的。儘管他在當時便已頗富盛名、小有所成，但還不及今日的聲譽。

威廉・莎士比亞去世後聲名仍漸長，直到他成為當時最優秀的詩人與作家。而這個地位至今仍屹立不墜。

1-3 找出支持性細節

「支持性細節」是作者用來支持文章主題句的細節內容，例如事實、直喻、說明、敘述、比較、舉例等，或是任何能佐證主題的資訊。閱讀文章時，別只執著於一種細節，因為細節通常不止一個。

11. 連接兩大洋的運河 P. 034

你是否想過，船舶是怎麼從大西洋航行到太平洋的呢？在 1914 年之前，船舶必須航行至南美洲南端，繞過德雷克海峽與合恩角才辦得到。這樣一趟漫長的航程，會經歷強風大浪、洶湧洋流、甚至是冰山。對船舶而言，這條航線可說是危機四伏。

為了縮短航程、讓往返的船舶更安全，開闢一條連接大西洋與太平洋的運河，就是最合理的解決之道。巴拿馬是美洲最狹窄的國家，因而雀屏中選。法國人率先於 1881 年建造運河卻未果。施工期間，約有兩萬兩千人死於疾病和意外事故。1904 年，美國接手運河的修建工程。他們以船閘系統，解決了在不同海平面地區修建運河的問題。巴拿馬運河於 1914 年正式啟用。儘管施工期間的總死亡人數約為 27,600 人，這條全長 82 公里（51 英里）的運河讓航運更加安全。1977 年，美國將運河管理權移交給巴拿馬。當時，巴拿馬運河早已成為來往世界各地海運的必要航線。

20 世紀以來，用來運輸貨物的船舶越來越龐大。因此，巴拿馬決定拓寬運河，好讓更大型的貨運船得以通過。斥資 52 億又 5000 萬美金後，拓寬工程終於在 2016 年竣工，不僅拓寬了運河的寬度，也加深了運河的深度，讓體積更龐大的新型貨運船得以暢行無阻。

巴拿馬運河這項考驗膽識的工程，力求提高旅行和貨運的安全性與效率，更成為全球海運航線的要角。從開鑿到竣工，再到後續的拓寬，堪稱現代工程奇蹟的巴拿馬運河，已就此改變航海模式。

12. 好萊塢傳奇：華特・迪士尼 P. 036

每個人都聽過米老鼠、唐老鴨和布魯托，它們都是華特・迪士尼的創作。華特・迪士尼是一位有才幹的編劇家、導演兼製片人、配音員、動畫師和企業家。

華特・伊利亞斯・迪士尼在 1901 年生於芝加哥。他一生中創造了不少影史最著名的角色。而迪士尼樂園和位於美國、日本、法國以及中國的迪士尼渡假主題樂園，都以他的名字命名。

迪士尼在堪薩斯市開創他的事業，製作了幾部卡通影片，但不久後公司就破產了。隨後，他決定在電影工業的首都——加州的好萊塢，成立一間電影製片廠。

雖然迪士尼的第一部電影並沒有大賣，但他不輕言放棄。1928 年，他創造了米老鼠，一個明星從此誕生了。米老鼠的首部有聲電影是《蒸汽船威利》，結果大受歡迎，也因此華特・迪士尼決定在他後續所有的卡通影片及電影中配上聲音。直到 1947 年為止，他都親自為米老鼠配音。

華特・迪士尼的動畫公司接著創造出許多經典傑作，像是《白雪公主》，還有《小鹿斑比》。1932 年，華特・迪士尼因為創造了米老鼠而獲得奧斯卡特別獎。他一生中獲得 59 次奧斯卡提名，贏得了 26 座獎。許多人懷疑是否還會有其他的電影製作人，可以像華特・迪士尼那樣具有影響力。

在佛羅里達州的迪士尼世界開幕前幾年，華特・迪士尼於 1966 年 12 月 15 日死於肺癌。

如今，他所創辦的華特迪士尼公司，每年的收益超過 550 億美金，成為全世界最有名、獲利最豐的電影公司。

很少有人沒看過迪士尼電影和卡通。他的創意與努力，為各地的小孩和大人帶來了許多的愉悅、歡樂與笑聲。

13. 橄欖球賽制！ P. 038

一名球員帶著橢圓形的大球，被敵隊一位球員擒抱摔倒，有時甚至是整個球隊的阻截，而且雙方都沒有穿戴護具。這就是「橄欖球」賽，1871 年在英格蘭發明的一項運動，而「橄欖球」一詞其實是指「聯盟式橄欖球」（Rugby League）與「聯會式橄欖球」（Rugby Union）這兩種相似的運動賽事。

這兩種賽制贏得球賽的方式，均以比賽 80 分鐘後得分數最高的一隊為獲勝隊伍。球員得分的方式有兩種，一是將橄欖球帶至 100 公尺長方形賽場盡頭的達陣區觸地得分，二是將球踢進兩根球門柱中間的球門範圍。不過，在緊湊又時而粗暴的橄欖球賽事中，想要得分並非易事。

不易得分的原因在於，若想讓球向前移動，球員不能就這麼把球向前拋，而是只能往後扔給隊友；該隊友則是一邊向前衝刺，一邊避開想要阻截不讓他進球的對手。

球員遭擒抱摔倒後的處理方式，則是這兩種橄欖球賽制的主要差異。「聯盟式橄欖球」的球員被擒抱摔倒後，只要站起來，用腳傳球給後面的隊友，即可繼續進行比賽。可是一旦被擒抱六次後，就必須攻守交換，將控球權交給另一隊。而「聯會式橄欖球」則有兩種處理方式。如果球員被一人以上的敵隊球員擒抱，就必須以「冒爾」（maul）或「勒克」（ruck）的規則處置。無論是哪一種情況，雙方均需派出最孔武有力的球員來試圖推擠逼退對方。推擠成功的一方即獲得控球權。

橄欖球賽進行期間，幾乎沒有休息時間。球員在整場賽事中不是在衝刺，就是傳球、擒抱或推擠。搶分的困難程度以及緊湊的比賽節奏，就是令觀眾目不轉睛的最大亮點。

14. 擴增實境：運用科技提升生活品質

P. 040

擴增實境是未來人們會越來越耳熟能詳的科技。「augment」有「擴充、加大」的意思。因此，擴充實境（簡稱 AR）就是以更豐富的方式來讓大家欣賞真實世界的科技。

想想智慧型手機，它能錄音錄影，還能即時加入電腦影像或音效。簡而言之，這種將真實世界與虛擬世界融合在一起的方式就是 AR。AR 也會出現在電視轉播體育賽事以及一些電玩遊戲中，像是 2016 年流行的「精靈寶可夢 GO」等。科技公司紛紛運用 AR 來協助人們將網路世界與真實世界相結合，也因為這種不同世界之間的聯繫，使得 AR 的普及率正逐年迅速攀升中。

某些令人引頸期盼的 AR 科技仍處於開發階段。其中一個例子就是「Magic Leap One AR 系統」。配備包括一支遙控器、一台小型主機，以及一副特殊眼鏡。Magic Leap One 的使用者可藉此系統看見週遭真實環境裡的 AR 影像。使用者可在家中查看產品、進行虛擬會議，或是在房間裡投影電玩畫面。透過這項科技，使用者就能突破智慧型手機的侷限，把 AR 帶進全新的疆界。

不過，AR 不僅是便於打電玩或購物的利器，將來還可能協助拯救生命。醫師可運用 AR 來練習艱難的手術，而不需擔心會傷及真正的病患。汽車擋風玻璃上會出現平視顯示幕，讓駕駛人在讀取重要資訊的同時，也不忘注意前方路況。AR 還可以幫我們做些什麼呢？擁有 AR 這類的科技，就擁有無窮的可能性。

15. 馬塞族 P. 042

肯亞與坦尚尼亞北部的馬塞族，是非洲最有名的部落之一。他們特殊的部落文化和打扮方式幾世紀來都未曾改變。許多馬塞人過著一種半遊牧的生活方式。他們使用一種叫做 Maa 的語言，但很多馬塞人也會說肯亞和坦尚尼亞的官方語言斯華西里語和英文。

對馬塞人來說，牛非常重要。他們把牛當成錢來使用，也就是說，他們用牛隻而非貨幣來購買自己所需物品。牛也是馬塞人主要的一種食物來源。由於牛在馬塞社會非常重要，牠們也常被用來衡量一個人的經濟狀況。

馬塞人相信他們的神祇恩克艾（Enkai）賜給他們世界上所有的牛。因此，如果有個非馬塞族的人擁有一些牛，馬塞人會認為他一定是從某個族人那裡偷來的。也因為這樣，他們相信從其他部落偷牛是理所當然的事，因為他們只是拿回屬於自己的東西而已。

馬塞族的男人會跳一種「跳躍舞」來展現自己的威風。傳統馬塞文化中，年輕人在結婚前必須先殺一頭獅子。女性在馬塞文化中幾乎沒有任何權利，她們只負責煮飯、養育孩子，為家人建造居住的小屋。

約有 90 萬馬塞人住在肯亞和坦尚尼亞。有些馬塞人已經不再住在農村地區了，和其他部落的人一樣，他們也搬進城鎮或都市中，過著像世上許多現代人一樣的生活。然而，還有許多馬塞人仍然努力維持傳統文化。

1-4 情節排序

瞭解文章內容的事件順序十分重要。想像一下，如果先綁鞋帶再穿鞋會是什麼感覺？當你試著了解資訊順序時，記得找尋 before（之前）、after（之後）、next（接下來）、then（然後）、later（待會兒）、previously（以前）等語詞或其他時間標記。

16. 沙漠之舟：駱駝 P. 044

駱駝被稱為「沙漠之舟」。為什麼？嗯，就像船隻載運貨物和人橫渡海洋一樣，駱駝也載運貨物和人橫越沙漠。對沙漠民族來說，駱駝十分重要。

駱駝一直不斷在進化，最早的駱駝出現在 4,000 或 4,500 萬年前的北美。約 500 萬年以前，駱駝橫跨路橋進入亞洲，並且不再返回，駱駝自此在北美絕跡。駱駝有兩種：只有一個駝峰的單峰駱駝，或稱為阿拉伯駱駝，以及有兩個駝峰的雙峰駱駝，牠們最後全都變得非常適應沙漠生活。駱駝的腳進化成適合在炎熱的沙漠沙地上行走，而身體也可以在不喝水的狀況下存活數星期；牠們的毛短而厚，可以保護牠們免於日曬，對抗沙暴；牠們長長的眼睫毛，則能夠防止沙子進到眼睛中。

這種實用的生物後來被人類飼養，作為嚴酷氣候中的駝獸，人類很快地就發現到牠們的便利之處。駱駝早在西元前 4000 年，就被中東和中國的人們所利用；大約在西元前 2000 年，則在中亞和非洲被使用。人們飼養駱駝的另一個原因，是為了牠們的乳汁和肉。據說，駱駝奶比牛奶含有更豐富的脂肪和蛋白質。駱駝肉則已在下列地區食用了好幾世紀，如索馬利亞、沙烏地阿拉伯、埃及、利比亞、蘇丹、哈薩克和一些乾燥地區。在部分地區，駱駝血也被視為是鐵質、維他命 D、鹽分和礦物質的重要來源。

駱駝以牠們的壞脾氣聞名，牠們常以發出響亮的咕噥聲來表達情緒。但是駱駝是如此地重要，因此飼主並不介意牠們的壞脾氣。駱駝站在沙漠中生存與死亡的交界，誰還會在意牠們的壞脾氣呢？

17. 美國音樂之都：納許維爾 P. 046

詹姆斯．羅伯特森於 1779 年在康柏蘭河畔建立村莊時，嘴裡一定哼著鄉村小調。畢竟這可是將來世界知名的音樂發源地呢。

1806 年，羅伯特森的村莊正式晉升為「都市」，並以美國獨立戰爭的知名將軍弗朗西斯．納許為命名靈感，將此都市稱為「納許維爾」。不久後，這座新興都市儼然發展為製造業重鎮與鐵路中心。1843 年，納許維爾成為田納西州的首府。雖然田納西州目睹了美國南北戰爭的慘烈戰況，但音樂卻始終縈繞在州民的心中。在內戰最黑暗的時期，黑人靈歌費克斯清唱樂團就此成立；這個舉世聞名的音樂團體還曾受邀為英國維多莉亞女王獻唱。

不過，1920 年代廣播電台的盛行才真正讓納許維爾這座音樂殿堂聲名大噪。1925 年，納許維爾成立第一家全功率的廣播電台 WSM，而 1926 年成立的另一家廣播電台 WLAC，也很快就加入這個行列。在這兩家廣播電台聯袂推廣下，吸引了全國各地的人才前來朝聖。無論你是鋼琴家、歌手還是吉他手，如果想讓自己的音樂曝光，就會去納許維爾。

到了 1930 年代的經濟大蕭條時期，納許維爾開始發展出獨有的音樂風格，也就是現今耳熟能詳的「鄉村音樂」。1947 年，弗朗西斯．克雷格於此地錄製發行的唱片《靠近你》，是納許維爾出品的第一張擁有百萬銷售量的專輯。1956 年，艾維斯．普里斯萊錄製了〈傷心旅館〉，迅速替他拿下暢銷單曲排行榜的冠軍。普里斯萊一炮而紅，就此成為鄉村音樂的指標性人物，直至今日仍為家喻戶曉的「貓王」。到了 1958 年，全美上下的話題均圍繞著「納許維爾之聲」。如今，仍有數不盡的暢銷鄉村音樂與納許維爾息息相關；就連鄉村歌星麥莉．希拉也在納許維爾出生長大，且不時在當地舉辦演唱會。

音樂貫穿了納許維爾的歷史，納許維爾擁有「美國音樂之都」的美稱，可謂名副其實。

18. 肥胖症 P. 048

醫生說肥胖症是 21 世紀的大患。但什麼是肥胖症？

如果一個人「肥胖」，就表示他的體重太重了。這個過重的問題是由於脂肪的過度累積所造成的。研究顯示，肥胖與各種疾病密切相關，像是心血管疾病、睡眠窒息、特定類型的癌症、痛風和骨關節炎。此外，肥胖也會縮短人的壽命。

一個人的 BMI（身體質量指數）可以顯示他是否過胖。BMI 計算方式是將體重（以公斤計）除以身高（以公尺計）的平方。所以，如果有一個人體重是 80 公斤，身高 1.6 公尺的話，BMI 就是 31.25。BMI 介於 18.5 和 24 之間的人，可說是健康的；而 BMI 如果高於 30，就代表可能過胖。

在過去，肥胖被認為是美麗的，因為那代表你擁有足夠的食物。如今，肥胖已經變成一個嚴重的大眾健康問題。1980 年代到今日，美國肥胖的人數遽增，這是人類歷史上首次體重超重的人口竟多於挨餓的人口。體重超重的人比健康的人更需要醫療照護，所以肥胖問題對社會而言，是很沉重的經濟負擔。

但為什麼有這麼多人過胖？有許多原因，大致上來說，就是我們吃得太多，運動量太少。我們的飲食型態也有很大關係，含糖食物和加工食品帶給我們便利，卻無法提供太多的養分。這些食物也會令人上癮。食用垃圾食物無法提供我們需要的能量，反而使我們體力不振，也讓人很難打起精神運動。

但我們可以設法控制，作為個人和社會一份子，我們應該仔細檢視自身選擇，並做出一些改變。

19. 格林兄弟 P. 050

你一定聽過《韓賽爾和葛麗特》、《長髮公主》和《灰姑娘》。雖然這些故事現在廣受兒童歡迎，但一開始它們卻是格林兩兄弟雅各．格林和威廉．格林，為大人所創作的故事。

格林兄弟對童話和民間故事非常感興趣，他們藉由和農夫、村民聊天，收集了數百則故事。1812 年，他們將自己首次收集成冊的 86 篇德國童話故事，以「獻給孩子和家庭的童話故事」為名出版；1815 年，他們的第二本內含 70 篇的童話故事也出版了。1816 年到 1818 年間，他們出版了兩本名為《德國傳說》的書籍，裡面共收集了 585 篇德國民間故事。

雅各．格林和威廉．格林對民間故事的態度並非僅止於個人興趣而已，他們也是認真研究此主題的大學教授。所謂的「民間傳說」或「民間故事」是一種在某地區平民百姓間，藉由口耳相傳而流傳下來的故事、童話或傳說。民間故事通常是非常久遠的故事，而且帶有教化的寓意。舉例來說，「韓賽爾和葛麗特」教導我們不可太貪心；「長髮公主」告訴我們，如果一開始沒有成功，就再試一次；而「灰姑娘」則是使我們體認到：仁慈是會有回報的，而殘忍是會被懲罰的。

格林兄弟或許是第一個出版那麼多民間故事，也是第一個寫出如此多故事的人。即便這些故事已被書寫下來，但隨著時間過去，卻還是不斷被小幅改編。有些人認為原始的故事情節對兒童而言，過於嚇人或暴力，因此之後的版本被改編得較為平易近人。今日我們在書上或電影中所見的故事版本，已不再是原本的黑色童話。

多虧了格林兄弟，這些（不同版本的）故事才得以被用來在全世界娛樂和教導大眾。

20. 語言的重要性 P. 052

語言不只是用來說話而已，它是我們最重要的溝通工具。透過語言，我們可以告訴其他人我們的想法、感覺，還有需要。文明本身就是靠著人類的溝通能力所建立。

沒有人知道人類到底是何時首度使用語言的。一些科學家認為，人類在大約 200 萬年前開始與其他人說話，而有些則認為人類語言的使用僅於 5 萬年前才開始。

語言會留存、成長、消失、遷移，並且隨著時間改變。有些語言非常古老；有些則是新出現的。現今，全世界大約有七千種不同的語言仍在使用中（雖然語言種類有許多不同算法），也有超過數千種語言已經絕跡。這些語言或許聽來各異，但一般認為它們都來自單種古代的語言。舉例而言，英語最初是由古日耳曼語演變而來。日耳曼語系分為三支系：西日耳曼語、東日耳曼語和北日耳曼語。西日耳曼語進化為古英語，隨時間推移，變成今日的英語。

今日，語言不僅用於對話，也運用在圖書館和書店裡的雜誌、書籍和電影中。人類表達長篇故事的能力，讓我們與類人猿有所區隔。

綜觀整個歷史，有許多語言曾被用來當成「通用語」，也就是一種能夠拿來當作不同文化間橋梁的語言。現今，英語在全世界扮演主要通用語角色。有超過 20 億人會說英語，其中大多數的人還曾將英語當成是第二或第三語言來學習。

英語幫助人們相互合作、分享知識與感情，並建造現代化的社會。人類文明中多種語言的發展歷程，也正是幫助人類邁向文明的重要過程。

1-5 理解因果關係

為了完全瞭解事件始末，清楚事件發生原因及最終結果是很重要的。事件發生的原因稱為「因」，最終結果稱為「果」。because of（因為）和 as a result of（由於）等片語用於說明「原因」；as a result（因此，不加 of）、resulting in（導致）和 so（所以）等片語則說明「結果」。

21. 披頭熱 P. 054

披頭四是一個在 1960 年成立的樂團，成員來自英國利物浦。披頭四對 1960 年代音樂和文化上的改變貢獻良多。甚至到了今日，他們的音樂仍然激勵著全世界的年輕人。

這個樂團由四個年輕人所組成：約翰 ‧ 藍儂、保羅 ‧ 麥卡錫、喬治 ‧ 哈里遜和林哥 ‧ 史達。他們引領了 1960 年代中期樂壇的「英倫入侵（美國）」。披頭四演唱搖滾樂和流行樂，並且在英美兩地發行了許多唱片，其數量超過 20 世紀其他歌手或樂團。約翰 ‧ 藍儂、保羅 ‧ 麥卡錫、喬治 ‧ 哈里遜和林哥 ‧ 史達於是成為 1960 年代和 1970 年代最著名的人士，在全世界擁有數百萬的樂迷。

在披頭四的演唱會和巡迴世界各大城的演出中，他們的樂迷總是發出強烈的歇斯底里尖叫聲。往往在一場演唱會中，樂迷尖叫聲可以大到將樂隊音樂完全壓過。報紙和雜誌注意到了披頭四樂迷的狂熱，「披頭熱」一詞於是誕生。

披頭四不僅透過他們的音樂影響人們，他們也在服裝、髮型、行為和語言上引領時尚。

1960 年代全球交通與通訊的進步發展，使披頭四能夠接觸到來自世界各地的樂迷。他們極富創造力的影響，在那十年中也擴展到文化與政治上，造成巨大的改變。許多人甚至認為，披頭四幫助推動英語成為全世界最受歡迎的外國語言。

雖然這個樂團在 1970 年解散了，但披頭四對流行文化的影響仍然非常明顯，且仍有許多人是死忠的披頭四迷。眾多披頭四迷深信，披頭熱將會一直持續到永遠。

22. 美國總統甘迺迪 P. 056

約翰 ‧ 費茲捷勒 ‧ 甘迺迪在 1961 年成為美國第 35 任總統，1963 年遭到暗殺。儘管他擔任總統不到三年時間，但美國人仍將他視為最偉大的總統之一。

約翰 ‧ 甘迺迪是一位自由主義的總統，他認為所有美國人一律平等，且種族主義和宗教都不該是拿來當成否定個人擁有其政治權利的藉口。

約翰 ‧ 甘迺迪也主張用戰爭捍衛民主。在第二次世界大戰期間，他在海軍服役，並因拯救同袍性命，獲得海軍及陸戰隊勛章。甘迺迪總統希望美國能成為歐洲（若非亞洲）自由和民主的守護者。甘迺迪總統最有名的一句話就是：「親愛的美國同胞，不要問你的國家為你做了什麼，先問你為你的國家做了什麼。」

約翰 ‧ 甘迺迪希望美國人和其他國家為共同敵人而戰，共同敵人指的是：暴政、貧窮、疾病和戰爭本身。為了達成此目標，他建立了著名的和平部隊，鼓勵美國志願者提供開發中國家人民在教育、農業和健康照護方面所需的協助。

1961 年，前蘇聯是美國最大的威脅，「太空競賽」也成為美蘇兩國競爭角力之一。甘迺迪總統為美國設下了一個目標：在 1960 年代結束前，必須讓人類登陸月球。這對前蘇聯來說，同樣是一項科技上的挑戰。人類登月所費不貲，但此舉能讓成功做到的國家獲得聲望。甘迺迪認為美國應該登陸月球，並且完成其他的事，「不是因為它們輕而易舉，而是因為它們困難重重」。在甘迺迪死後約 6 年，1969 年 7 月 20 日，他的登月目標實現了。

23. 亞洲的戈壁沙漠 P. 058

戈壁沙漠是亞洲最大的沙漠，也是全世界第四大沙漠。其形成是由於喜馬拉雅山阻擋了雨水抵達戈壁地區。戈壁沙漠覆蓋了中國北部和西北部，還有蒙古南部。整個沙漠在最寬處約有 1,600 公里，約為台灣 36 倍大。和很多沙漠不同的是，覆蓋戈壁沙漠大多數地區的不是「沙」，而是岩石。

戈壁沙漠歷史悠久，某些地區因當地發現的化石和古器具聞名。戈壁沙漠是蒙古人的居住地，他們曾在約八百年前建立了橫跨中國的蒙古帝國。連接中國與西方著名的絲路，即穿越了戈壁沙漠。在西元 1271 年，馬可．波羅旅經絲路來到中國，他極力推崇中國的城市與文化。當時他還拜見了蒙古帝國的大可汗，也就是成吉思汗的孫子忽必烈。

戈壁沙漠的溫度變化劇烈。夜間溫度甚至可以比白天低上攝氏 35 度。在冬天可以降到攝氏零下 45 度；而夏季卻可高達攝氏 45 度。除此之外，還有一些暴風雪和沙暴。這些都讓在戈壁沙漠中的生活更加困難。儘管環境惡劣，戈壁仍是許多沙漠動物的棲息地，包括棕熊和狼。

儘管幅員已如此遼闊，戈壁沙漠面積卻越來越大，並以駭人的速率擴增。「沙漠化」指的就是沙漠擴增、取代綠地的過程。戈壁沙漠生態變化相當快速，其嚴酷的景觀也愈加廣闊。

24. 神秘的羅姆人 P. 060

歐洲、巴爾幹半島、中東、北非與美洲都有羅姆民族的足跡。雖然許多人稱他們為「吉普賽人」，但他們亦被稱為「羅姆人」。「吉普賽」一詞是由歐洲人所發明，因為當初他們誤以為羅姆人來自埃及。

上百年來，羅姆人因為文化與信仰的緣故，遭受不平待遇和歧視。很多人認為他們是女巫，以巫術為非作歹。還有人認為他們是燒殺擄掠的罪犯。之所以有這些對羅姆人的錯誤印象，只是因為多數人對羅姆人少有了解。長期以來，羅姆人沒有留下書寫歷史，了解他們的唯一辦法就是透過言語交談。

據說羅姆人源自印度次大陸的北邊。大約一千年前，他們開始經由伊朗高原遷徙。行經中東與歐洲時，即與當地人通婚。現在歐盟國的羅姆人約有 600 萬，全球的羅姆人則至少有 1,000–1,200 百萬。

許多羅姆人仍以小家庭的型式，遠離城鎮與都會區群居，並且會定期四處遷徙。部分羅姆人已放棄舊有的流浪生活型態，轉而定居市鎮。

數世紀以來，羅姆人因為迥異的民族特性而受到嚴重迫害。然而，世人已逐漸接納，因為大家願意花時間深入了解他們。

25. 911 浩劫 P. 062

2001 年 9 月 11 日，在全球歷史上已成為一個非常重要的日子。那天早上，19 名伊斯蘭教恐怖分子劫持了四架民航客機。他們刻意將其中兩架衝撞世貿中心的兩座高樓（稱為「雙子星大樓」），造成雙子星大樓倒塌；第三架飛機撞上了美國的軍事總部「五角大廈」；而改向飛往華盛頓特區的第四架飛機，則是在幾位乘客和飛航機組員奮勇抵抗下，從恐怖分子手中奪回飛機時，墜毀在賓州的田野上。

2001 年 9 月 11 日，總共有 2,974 名無辜民眾，在這場蓋達自殺攻擊中喪生。包括四架飛機中的 246 人，在雙子星大廈內和路上的 2,603 人，以及五角大廈的 125 人，且還有 24 名人士仍列失蹤名單。罹難者大多是平民，包括來自超過 90 個不同國家的人士。死亡名單還包括了進入世貿中心救援的警察和消防隊員。

此外，雙子星大廈解體後所產生的上千噸有毒殘骸，也使參與救援和復原工作的人員出現不適症狀。

這場恐怖攻擊對美國和全球股市產生了非常重大的經濟影響，即便到了今日，恐怖攻擊的負面效應仍然影響著全球航空業。

為了回應這些攻擊事件，美國展開了「反恐怖主義戰爭」。美國和英國為了避免恐怖攻擊再度發生，遂聯手入侵阿富汗，將那些必須為 911 事件負責的恐怖分子制伏或消滅。不幸的是，跟隨而來的這些戰爭，反而造成更多無辜的百姓死傷。

1-6 釐清寫作技巧

釐清寫作技巧包括理解字彙和片語的應用，以及分辨作者用來讓文章大意與支持性細節更加清楚、更引人入勝的寫作方式。有時候，最重要的釐清技巧就是要能分辨文章類型和作者意圖。

26. 好萊塢諧星泰斗：羅賓．威廉斯 P. 064

在他超過 36 載的成功演藝生涯中，他扮演過的角色包括外星人、老嫗、教師、甚至是美國總統。但到頭來他證明了，最難克服的角色是做自己。

上述說的這位演員就是才華洋溢的羅賓．威廉斯，他可說是好萊塢最亮眼的巨星。年輕一代的觀眾對他的印象應該是《博物館驚魂夜》裡的羅斯福總統，或是《快樂腳》裡的拉蒙。有些人對他在《窈窕奶爸》裡飾演為了接近孩子而扮成女人的角色記憶猶新。長青觀眾則可能想起更久以前的《默克與明蒂》這部在 1978 年開播，讓威廉斯一戰成名的電視劇。

羅賓．威廉斯是少數幾個廣受大家喜愛的演員。他以獨角喜劇起家，即興演出的天賦眾所皆知。無論是什麼樣的場景劇情，威廉斯都能信手拈來，引得觀眾捧腹大笑。不過，倘若單靠他的喜劇才華，無法達到今日的泰斗地位；主要還是他充滿真誠特質的演技引人入勝。他願意藉由大螢幕上的角色，顯現出自己脆弱的一面。這種呈現弱點的演繹方式，因十分貼近我們日常生活中時而產生的感受，而讓觀眾對他產生共鳴。

威廉斯或許是從自己煎熬的私生活中擷取表演靈感。他一生中不斷在憂鬱症、藥物、酒精等問題中苦苦掙扎。他在世的最後幾年更罹患了腦疾，造成視力減弱與睡眠障礙等生理問題。2014 年，威廉斯在加州自宅結束自己的生命。雖然他這麼早就離開人世，令大家悲慟萬分，但他身後留下流傳於世的影視作品，已然賦予這個世界燦爛的火花。

27. 吉薩大金字塔 P. 066

在埃及開羅西南方約 25 公里處，吉薩高原上座落著三座巨大的金字塔。這片古代遺跡由古夫金字塔（又名大金字塔或奇歐普斯金字塔）、卡夫拉金字塔，和曼卡拉金字塔所組成。在這三座金字塔當中，又以大金字塔最為古老雄偉，也是世界七大奇景中唯一現存的古蹟。

古埃及建造了許多金字塔，用來當作法老王最後的陵寢（法老王指的就是埃及的國王）。雖然很難判斷這些金字塔是何時建造，但很多專家認為，最古老的金字塔約是在 4,700 年前所建。

過去，埃及人相信法老是神祇。每一座金字塔被建來保存一位死去的法老，以及他的黃金、食物、動物甚至僕役。據信所有與法老陪葬的物品都將隨著他到下一世。這也讓人很難不為其僕役感到難過，這些僕役服侍法老多年，不但沒有加官晉爵，反而得與法老屍體長眠。

如今，金字塔已不若以往雄偉。隨著時間流逝，太陽與風沙損毀了金字塔的外觀。盜墓者也會闖入金字塔內，偷走許多與死去法老置放在一起的貴重寶藏。

金字塔對許多歷史學家和科學家來說，還是很有趣又帶點神祕。這並不令人訝異，畢竟，金字塔是史上最宏偉的地標！

28. 新墨西哥州羅斯威爾的幽浮墜毀事件 P. 068

1947 年的夏天，在一場劇烈的暴風雨中，一架幽浮（UFO，不明飛行物體）墜毀在新墨西哥州羅斯威爾的農田上——至少人們是這樣認為的。當然，美國政府在事件過後並無發表任何聲明，只是一概否認有任何不尋常的事件發生過。

宣稱是目擊者的人說，此事件確實有怪異之處。他們所形容的飛行器並不像飛機。有些人甚至堅持自己看到裡頭有幾個死掉的外星人，眼睛像黑色碟子般圓睜。不論這架奇特的飛船是什麼，它並沒有在農田裡久留。墜毀後不久，那架飛船的所有碎片就被帶到羅斯威爾陸軍航空基地了。之後，據報飛船由一台鐵路平板車，運送到俄亥俄州的萊特派特森空軍基地接受檢驗。美國政府宣稱，那不是幽浮，而是一個氣象探測氣球。

但是許多美國人認為，政府只是試圖掩蓋真相。他們提出了兩個尚待澄清的疑問：第一，如果那只是個氣象探測氣球，為什麼必須留置在秘密的軍事基地，並由空軍來進行檢驗？第二，到底是誰建造了那麼大又貴重的氣象探測氣球，使得它必須在武裝戒護下，以鐵路平板車來運送？

如果你今天造訪羅斯威爾，你會發現人們仍在議論著：在 1947 年，到底是什麼東西墜毀在農田？你也可以參觀鎮上的幽浮博物館，因為有它，使得這個故事持續存在著。

29. 來揮棒吧！ P. 070

只要是努力爭取得來的事物，就會格外珍惜。下次舉辦派對時，不妨將平常放在碗裡任人取食的糖果，裝進皮納塔紙偶裡吧！超夯的兒童派對好物「皮納塔」（piñata）是用薄紙製成的裝飾容器，可以做成卡通人物或足球等不同造型。從皮納塔取出糖果的過程就是好玩又刺激的遊戲。孩子們輪流用棍子或球棒來敲打懸掛在樹上或天花板的皮納塔。若要讓比賽更有挑戰性，參賽者還要先戴上眼罩、轉個幾圈才能揮棒。孩童看到朋友猛揮棒卻落空的模樣，皆哄堂大笑。幾次重擊後，皮納塔開始破裂，裡面的糖果就會掉出來。此時，小孩便會一擁而上，爭先恐後地撿拾掉落的糖果。皮納塔到最後還會整個爆開！

雖然「皮納塔」一字源自西班牙文，但世界各地均有此傳統。大名鼎鼎的威尼斯商人馬可．波羅曾於 13 世紀末遊歷至中國，他是第一個描述皮納塔的人。他親眼目睹中國人製作彩色紙偶，並在裡面放滿了種籽。以棍棒揮打時，紙偶破裂，種籽也隨之撒了出來。馬可．波羅將這個點子帶回義大利。皮納塔最後成為基督宗教慶典的元素之一。

同一時期，阿茲提克人也有類似的傳統，但他們使用的容器材質是盆罐，而非紙偶。經過裝飾的輕薄陶盆，裝滿小型供品後，即擺放在神像前，再以棍棒打破，將供品留在神像處。

皮納塔原為世界各地涉及宗教儀式的用品，如今色彩鮮艷的皮納塔則是趣味與歡頌節日的象徵。

30. 攀登 K2（喬戈里峰） P.072

大部分人都聽說過聖母峰，也就是全世界第一高峰，但卻鮮少人談論第二高峰。這座第二高峰就是 K2 峰，其海拔高度為 8,611 公尺，座落在中國和巴基斯坦間的喜馬拉雅山脈。

K2 峰有個不為人知的秘密：那就是死於攀登 K2 峰的人數，遠高於攀登聖母峰的人數。雖然聖母峰的頂峰高於 K2 峰，但 K2 峰惡劣的氣候環境，使得攀登更加困難和危險。無法預測、惡劣的氣候模式，使得 K2 峰被譽為世界上最難攀登的山峰。

雖然人們從 1902 年就開始嘗試攀登 K2 峰，但是一直到 1954 年，才有首批遠征隊登上峰頂。他們是一群由阿迪托．迪塞奧所領導的義大利登山客。自此，有超過 300 人成功攻頂，約 80 人死於攀登途中。也就是說每 4 人登頂，就約有 1 人死亡。

K2 峰對女性登山者特別不友善。1986 年，汪達．盧琪薇姿是第一位登上 K2 的女性。直至 2017 年，成功攀登的女性登山者增加到 12 人。不過，其中有 3 人命喪下山途中，另 2 人則於之後的攀登旅程中遇難。有些人甚至認為，這些死亡是 K2 峰對女性登山者的詛咒。

總之，莫怪乎 K2 峰被暱稱為「野蠻之峰」（Savage Mountain）。

1-7 進行推論

「推論」意指運用已知的資訊，來猜測未知的情況。每當你仰望空中烏雲，準備拿傘的時候，就是在推論等一下會下雨。讀者也會如此，而作者通常會透露訊息，讓讀者能自行推論文意。

31. 維基百科：線上萬事通 P. 074

網路上最棒的資料搜尋去處就是維基百科。此線上百科全書是由世界各地無數網民共同編寫而成。任何人均可針對感興趣的主題貢獻一己心力。同樣地，文句不通順或資料不正確的主題也可以修改。因此，毋須具備大學教授的身分，也能成為維基百科的作者。

維基百科是由哲學家賴瑞·桑格與商人吉米·威爾斯於 2001 年所創。他們希望設立一個不含廣告、人人均可編輯的線上英文百科全書。不過，維基百科設立的初衷，是希望拉高「Nupedia」（這是另一個由專家執筆的網路百科全書）的流量。「Nupedia」網站於 2003 年 9 月關閉，其內容文章全數移轉至維基百科。

截至 2017 年 12 月，維基百科上已有五百多萬篇英文文章。此外，還有 4,000 萬篇文章是以 301 種不同語言（網路百科全書上的語言版本）編寫的。維基百科因而成為最具國際知名度的網站。許多人將維基百科視為消息來源，原因在於百科內容經常更新。

耐人尋味的是，研究人員發現氣候不佳的國家其維基百科頁數，比陽光充足的國家還多。這也許是因為居住溫暖氣候地區的人，坐在電腦桌前的時間較少。

不過，維基百科也有隱憂。許多人投訴維基百科上的資訊不正確，甚至連一些重要的議題都未含括在內，從而造成撰文者之間的紛爭。據悉，2014 年 1 月的維基百科點擊率比去年同期少了 20 億次。

管理維基百科的工作人員均虛心受教與回應投訴。他們表示，網站內容的準確度一直以來均持續提升。維基百科能成為網路上第五大熱門的網站，必然有其經營之道。

32. 深入了解文森·梵谷 P. 076

有些人說他是瘋子，有些人說他是奇才。無論人們怎麼評論文森·梵谷，無庸置疑的是他偉大畫家的身份。梵谷的畫作售價可達上百萬美元，全球數一數二的藝廊均展示他的作品。但是在這些名氣的背後，卻是一個擁有困頓生活的藝術家。

文森·梵谷於 1853 年生於荷蘭。成年後早期，曾任藝術品經銷商、教師和傳教士等各種工作。1880 年，他首執畫筆。以畫家維生的日子裡，他周遊了比利時與法國。在成為畫家的頭 10 年，梵谷創作了將近 860 幅油畫和 1,300 幅繪畫作品。

梵谷在世時，畫作一直乏人問津，因此很難維持生計。在他的一生中，一直有弟弟西奧的扶持，西奧總是會設法讓梵谷得以溫飽。

懷才不遇的困境使梵谷變得憂鬱且焦慮。1888 年，他與另一位畫家爭執過後，做出了後人皆知的割耳舉動。這件事後，他還待在精神醫院一陣子。不幸的是，他最後無法承受憂鬱的情緒，在 1890 年舉槍自盡。

梵谷寫給弟弟的最後一封信提及，他的畫作是他的心血結晶。而這些作品很快地就受到全世界的注意。梵谷過世後，成為史上最知名的畫家之一。他最廣為人知的畫作包括《十二朵向日葵》以及《星夜》。

33. 馬達加斯加的狐猴 P. 078

狐猴是很可愛的動物，棲息在全世界第四大島馬達加斯加島上。牠有大大的眼睛，長長的鼻子和一條長尾巴（光面狐猴除外），住在馬達加斯加森林裡的樹上高處。狐猴相當聰明，是猴子的表親，而且看起來也很相似。跟猴子一樣，牠們也會在樹林間穿梭擺盪，並且以家庭的型態生活在一起。

狐猴有許多不同種類。有些狐猴（如光面狐猴）會發出像鯨魚一樣的叫聲；而有些（如跳狐猴）則會像芭蕾舞者一樣滑步而行。有些狐猴很小，如只有 25 公克重的侏儒狐猴；有些像光面狐猴，則可以重達 10 公斤。有些狐猴屬於夜行性，晚上清醒，白天睡覺；有些則屬於日行性，日行性動物就像人類一樣，都是白天清醒。一般來說，較小型的狐猴多屬於夜行性，而較大型的則在日間活動。每種種類的狐猴都屬於馬達加斯加所特有。

不幸的是，馬達加斯加島民破壞了狐猴棲息的森林，來建造新農場或房子。一些當地人也獵補狐猴為食。還有些人認為牠們會招致惡運而加以獵殺。種種行為使得許多種狐猴幾世紀以來已經絕種，剩餘的狐猴也瀕臨絕種。若我們不趕快採取行動，牠們也將消失殆盡。

目前仍有一百多種狐猴存活著，許多專家擔心這個數字將迅速減少。如果我們再不採取積極行動來保護馬達加斯加島的僅存狐猴，未來將沒有狐猴存在了。

34. 亞馬遜：世界上最大的河 P. 080

亞馬遜河起源於秘魯的安地斯山脈，穿越巴西北部，流至大西洋。它被認為是僅次於非洲尼羅河的世界第二長河。若以流量來論，亞馬遜河也是全世界最大的河流。由於流域及流量廣大，亞馬遜河因此被稱為「河海」。在亞馬遜河匯流大西洋處，河口約有 330 公里寬，這個數字幾乎和英國的泰晤士河總長度（346 公里）一樣寬。除此之外，亞馬遜河所攜帶的水量，比全世界其他河流都還大，整條河的總流量，甚至大於排名在它之後的十大河流，所注入大海的總流量。

亞馬遜河有超過 1,100 條支流，這些是從主流分支出來的小河流，有 17 條支流超過 1,500 公里長。

亞馬遜河對全人類非常重要，因為它可以使世上最大的雨林——亞馬遜雨林將水排放出來。全世界有將近三分之一的物種棲身在亞馬遜雨林中，這座雨林幫助我們吸收大氣中的二氧化碳，這也是為什麼亞馬遜雨林被視為是對抗全球暖化的重要堡壘。

亞馬遜河擁有全世界五分之一的淡水，以及約莫 5,600 種的魚類，包括「波頭豚」（boto），一種亞馬遜河豚，還有多種會捕食家畜，偶爾會攻擊人類的食人魚。

35. 全球暖化 P. 082

現今地球面臨了環境危機的威脅，也就是所謂的「溫室效應」或「全球暖化」。問題來自於天然氣、石油與煤炭等石化燃料。當各國以燃燒此類燃料做為能源時，就會將二氧化碳和其他危險的「溫室氣體」釋放到大氣層。此類氣體會阻擋熱氣散發至外太空，就像一條毯子般，使陸地與海洋溫度升高。

全球暖化的問題，比每年氣候炎熱天數與日俱增還要嚴重。隨著地球溫度升高，大自然的平衡狀態也會開始改變，亦增加了許多天災發生的機會，例如颶風、水災和旱災。動植物都難以適應更高的溫度，因此全球暖化問題會威脅農作物以及特定物種的存活率。

最危險的全球暖化後果之一，就是北極和南極冰層開始大量融化。極圈冰層融化會使全球海平面上升，威脅居住在孟加拉等地勢低窪國家的人民。事實上，有些報告預測，到了 2100 年，諸如圖瓦魯之類的小型太平洋島國可能會完全淹沒於海平面下。

好消息是，我們還是能採取一些措施來抵禦全球暖化的問題，那就是必須減少石化燃料的用量。各國政府已開始著重於風力、地熱與水力發電，以及太陽能等可再生能源。也有許多人以改善個人習慣的方式，盡一己之力。有些人會購買電動車，有些人則乾脆把車賣了。

不過，要想解決全球暖化問題，還有很長的一段路要走。不幸的是，全世界還是有很多人尚未嚴正以待此問題。

1-8 批判性思考

批判性思考指的是「提問問題」。閱讀的時候，一定要在心裡質疑「為什麼？」（why）、「何地？」（where）、「何時？」（when）以及「如何做？」（how）這幾個問題。針對你所閱讀的資訊，和作者為何選擇透露該資訊而提問，能幫助你建構對文章的看法，以及了解寫作過程。

36. 天才愛因斯坦 P. 084

你應該聽過 $E=mc^2$ 這個方程式，這是科學方程式中最著名的一個，也一直是科學的重要基礎。而科學家亞伯特．愛因斯坦也因為發明了這個方程式而成名。

1904 年，在愛因斯坦發表為何用 $E=mc^2$ 來演算前，全世界的科學家都堅信 $E=1/2\ mc^2$。如今，隨便一個高中物理科學生都可以做出這個演算，並了解亞伯特．愛因斯坦到底做了什麼而聞名於世。

亞伯特．愛因斯坦在 1879 年的 3 月 14 日出生於德國的猶太家庭。他一直到三歲時才開始講話。年輕時的愛因斯坦在學校表現並不好，因為他對不感興趣的課並不用心。也因此，很多人認為他笨。最後，他開始對科學感興趣，並且試圖找出一種物理定律，可以用來解釋自然科學中所有事物運行方式。

1922 年時，他榮獲了 1921 年的諾貝爾物理學獎。之後他搬到美國，成為普林斯頓大學的教授。1939 年，愛因斯坦和一位匈牙利裔的美國物理學家利奧．西拉德（Leo Szilard），一同寫信給當時的美國總統羅斯福，表示美國應該要搶先德國發展出原子彈。這封信導致美國在 1945 年 8 月，於日本廣島和長崎投下原子彈。

愛因斯坦在 1955 年的 4 月 18 日逝世於紐澤西的普林斯頓。他一生共發表超過 300 篇科學著作，及超過 150 篇的非科學作品。他的大多數見解，直至今日仍被許多科學家所運用，而他的名字「愛因斯坦」也成為天才的同義詞。

37. 現代世界的民主 P. 086

你知道「民主」是什麼嗎？民主政體的領導人是經由人民透過投票所選出。政府是屬於所有人民，而非國王、獨裁者或任何小型集團。民主的概念是建立在，如果舊領導人沒辦法把事情做好，那麼人民就有權力和責任選出新的領導者。如果一個民主國家裡有言論與新聞自由，每個人民就可以充分了解每位候選領導人，並且明智地投票。

台灣是一個民主國家，美國、英國和世界上大多數的國家也是。目前約有 123 個國家自認擁有經民主制度所選出的領導人。但不幸的是，許多宣稱民主的國家，事實上並不民主。

擁有民主政體並不保證政府領導人就會做好事。在領導人執政期間，他們也可能決定做壞事，但人民在阻止這樣的事情上卻能力有限，只有法院、立法機關、院（議）長和新聞媒體能夠限制不好的領導人所造成的傷害。一個民主國家需要誠實、明智的領導人，以及受過良好教育和考慮周延的人民。為了有所進步，民主國家本身也必須成長並有所改變。我們可以在歐洲、北美、澳洲和紐西蘭看到一些成熟、強盛的民主國家典範。

一個開放誠信的民主國家是全球大多數人的渴望。儘管一些不好的領導人可能編織謊言來欺騙人民，但全世界的人們仍會繼續為他們應得的健全民主國家而奮戰不懈。

38. 印度教的藍膚英雄 P. 088

克里希納是印度教和毗濕奴教派的主要神祇，約於西元前 3228 年降世於印度馬圖拉。克里希納常見的形象就是一身的藍皮膚，據說他是萬能守護神毗濕奴的化身。我們之所以知道他的故事，要歸功於《摩訶波羅多》、《博伽梵歌》、《哈瑞梵沙》這三部闡述他生平事蹟的經典著作。

雖然克里希納的人生離不開調皮搗蛋、愛情與冒險元素，但他的故事卻有個非常悲慘的開端：克里希納生於監牢，因為他的母親被親哥哥卡姆薩國王監禁。祭司告訴卡姆薩，他的生命將會斷送在外甥手上，所以他決定斬草除根。幸好克里希納活了下來，並逃出監獄。他由養母撫養長大，住在村裡的牧牛人家。他常趁大家不注意時偷牛奶而闖禍，但牧牛人家仍然很愛他。據說克里希納甚至在很小的時候，就殺死了名為崔拿瓦塔和普妲娜的怪物。

克里希納長大成人後回到出生地，殺死了他的壞舅舅。爾後，他成了新王的宰相，並捲入一場可怕的戰事。《博伽梵歌原意》中描述了他戰場大捷的事蹟。

克里希納的生平事蹟中最令人難忘的其中一個故事，就是他和羅陀的愛情故事。他們深愛對方，卻從未結褵。為何？原因眾說紛紜。有人說，羅陀認為自己的社會地位太低，不配嫁給克里希納。另一則說法是，克里希納深信愛情與婚姻是兩回事。有些人視羅陀為凡人的代表。對他們來說，克里希納和羅陀之間的愛情就是神人之愛。

39. 井然有序的藝術 P. 090

藝術在創始之初，通常會反映出時事。一群有著相同藝術目標、相似風格、甚至有時在同一座城市或地區工作的藝術家，會自然而然組成「藝術運動」。那麼第一次世界大戰之後的藝術運動是什麼模樣呢？這是史上第一場使用軍事機器與新式武器的戰爭，估計約有 850 萬名軍人和 1,300 萬人民喪生。

歷經第一次世界大戰的摧殘後，歐洲人民迫切希望回到原本井然有序的日常生活。這樣的心境反映在名為「純粹主義」的藝術運動上。此運動是由阿米迪．歐贊凡與查爾斯．愛德華．詹努勒這兩位藝術家所帶動（詹努勒亦身兼建築師）。他們在 1918 年出版了《立體主義之後》一書來說明其藝術目標。他們相信，人們能在有條不紊的世界裡重拾歡顏，也能在創建社會秩序之際感到滿足。純粹主義畫作採用幾何圖形來表達機械、花瓶與杯具等主題。其色彩鮮明，亦夾帶棕色與灰色兩種色調。

純粹主義運動的規模不大，也沒持續多久。費爾南德．雷捷是第三位加入此運動的藝術家。而詩人保羅．戴牧亦與歐贊凡和詹努勒合作出版了意喻「新精神」的評論型刊物 L'Esprit Nouveau。純粹主義最享譽盛名的代表作，就是詹努勒於 1925 年在巴黎國際裝飾工業藝術博覽會建造的「新精神館」。自稱「柯比意」的詹努勒以建築師身分設計了這棟建築。

雖然純粹主義運動僅為期短短七年，卻反映出人民亟欲擺脫可怕戰事、重回生活正軌的心願，也展現了藝術家在日常生活中所找出的秩序。

40. 從馳騁平地到呼嘯升空 P. 092

在科幻小說的世界裡，飛行車通常看起來像一般的汽車，但其實是一種飛行器。任何人都能駕駛飛行車，不需借助公路或跑道，直接從一地飛往另一地。長久以來，科幻小說一直都有飛行車的元素，卻尚未成真。因此，「飛行車到底在哪裡？」此說法衍生出暗指現代科技失敗的意思。

如今，飛行車已蓄勢待發，即將從科幻世界飛進現實生活中。科幻小說作家夢寐以求的飛行車終將成真。

可從陸地交通工具轉變為航空交通工具的第一部「飛行車」或稱「空中飛車」，就是「拉畢希飛航器 FSC-1」（亦稱為「拉畢希 460sc」）。FSC-1 擁有昂貴跑車的外表，能像一般汽車在路上行駛。不過，只要一個按鈕，就能展開機翼和推進器，和飛機一樣起飛、航行與著陸。故此特殊車款的車主可自行選擇開車或飛行。2006 年，發明人米契爾．拉畢希完成了 FSC-1 原型的試駕與試飛程序。不過，近年的飛行車概念似乎已凌駕於拉畢希飛航器的原型之上。

「都會飛航器 X- 飛鷹」是另一款可以垂直升降的飛行車，於 2009 年首度亮相試飛。2018 年在英國法恩堡舉辦的國際航空展上，英國豪華跑車製造商奧斯頓．馬丁發布「航空視野」飛行車概念，而且很有可能現身於下一部 007 電影中。越來越多公司往生產垂直升降私人飛行器的方向努力，更注重可輕鬆飛行與降落的部分，路駕部分的著墨較少。這類新式交通工具甚至有全電動或氫動力的選擇。

飛行車與任何新科技一樣，均經過漫長的研發時間。一旦問世後，我們也許會捫心自問：「飛行車出現之前，我們都在忙什麼？」

1-9 分辨事實與意見

判斷某種說法是「事實」或「意見」，是很好的思考方式。「事實」可經由其他資訊來源來驗證。只要是事實，就有對錯之分。而「意見」是某人對某事物的感覺。因此，你可以不認同他人的「意見」，卻無法否認「事實」。

41. DNA 之謎 P. 094

DNA（去氧核糖核酸）形塑出你的性格樣貌，它就像是深藏在細胞內的微小操作指南一樣。DNA 會告訴細胞要如何打造你的軀體，你的 DNA 決定了你的樣貌，甚至影響了你的性格。

每個人類個體的 DNA 都十分相似。事實上，科學家認為所有人類的 DNA 約 99% 雷同。而那 1% 的細微差異，就足以讓你成為一個獨特的個體。更驚人的是，有些研究宣稱人類和黑猩猩的 DNA 有 96% 相同。也就是說，1% 造成你禿頭與否，而 4% 的差異則會影響你是否能在樹間擺盪！

DNA 鏈看起來就像兩股纏繞的繩子，稱為「雙螺旋」結構。每條 DNA 螺旋上布滿資訊，以化學成分的型態顯示。這些化學成分是給身體細胞的複雜指令。由於這些化學元素太過精密複雜，當 DNA 在自我複製時，它們可能會出現問題，這時「突變」就產生了。突變是 DNA 的變異，這些變異有時會造成嚴重的疾病和其他問題。癌症即為一例，DNA 突變會大幅增加晚年罹癌的機率。

近來，科學家已經能夠排列出整個 DNA 序列。DNA 排序的目的是為了修復人類 DNA 中的問題。然而有些人認為，持續研究 DNA 可能會帶來負面影響，如複製人的問題。在未來的 DNA 研究裡，我們應該更加小心謹慎。

42.《冰與火之歌：權力遊戲》：奇幻世界激發想像力 P. 096

全球觀眾似乎一分為二： 一方是只要逮到機會，就以《冰與火之歌：權力遊戲》這部影集為話題而聊個不停；另一方則是無法置信竟然還有人在聊這部愚蠢的影集。無論如何，《冰與火之歌：權力遊戲》可說是家喻戶曉。這部電視影集儼然成為重要的全球文化指標。

那麼這部影集成功的秘訣為何？第一，這部影集改編自小說《冰與火之歌》系列暢銷書，劇情連貫，電視編劇較不用擔心靈感斷炊。第二，讓《冰與火之歌：權力遊戲》與眾不同的是該劇龐大的製作經費。平均起來，一集影集的製作成本約為 600 萬美金，相當於每集的製作費比有線電視台一般的影集還要多出足足 400 萬美金。《冰與火之歌：權力遊戲》的鉅額預算裨益這部影集聘請優質的演員陣容，運用先進特效建構出磅礴的戰爭場面。

還是對此影集擁有高人氣感到不解嗎？好吧，或許是因為《冰與火之歌：權力遊戲》比其他電視影集出現更多暴力和成人鏡頭，又或者是正邪之間的界線在劇中並不明顯。你可能剛開始很喜歡某個角色，最後卻因其暴行而改變主意。另一方面，陰險的角色也許會有出乎意料的慈悲行為。抑或是你喜愛的角色會在無預警的情況下慘死。這就是《冰與火之歌：權力遊戲》的另一特點：主角的生命如曇花一現。

事實上，這部影集的成功大概綜合了上述所有因素。無論是什麼原因，每一季結束後，影迷均有增無減。不管大家接受與否，《冰與火之歌：權力遊戲》仍屹立不搖。

43. 瑞士 P. 098

瑞士是一個位於歐洲中部的優美國家。鄰近義大利、奧地利、德國、列支敦斯登和法國。首都為伯恩，蘇黎世是最大的城市。瑞士人口約有 840 萬人，國家經濟富庶，遊客對瑞士的評價則是環境非常整潔。在全球都市生活品質排行榜裡，蘇黎世和日內瓦經常名列前茅。

瑞士最令人讚賞的特點就是其自然美景。瑞士不但風景如畫，還有白雪皚皚的高聳山脈、青綠山坡、深幽山谷，以及蔚藍湖泊。自古以來，綿延高山不但形成抵禦外人入侵的屏障，亦為清淨水質的源頭。冬季時節，來自歐洲各地的觀光客都會到瑞士阿爾卑斯山滑雪。

瑞士屬於中立國家，意指它不介入任何戰事與其他衝突。這就是為何許多國際機構會在此成立總部的原因，例如紅十字會和國際奧林匹克委員會。

瑞士以鐘錶與巧克力產業聞名。數世紀以來，瑞士製作出世界上最為精美的鐘錶。如今越來越多人風靡瑞士時計產品。雖然瑞士不是出產優質巧克力的唯一國家，但瑞士巧克力的品質頂級，且廣受歡迎。如今世界各地都買得到瑞士巧克力。

瑞士是一個文化發展十分進步的國家，原因在於其擁有四種官方語言。63% 的人口講德文，23% 講法文，約有 8% 講義大利文。另一種官方語言為羅曼語，使用人口僅佔不到 1%。雖然英文非官方語言，但仍是日常生活裡大家互相溝通的常用語言。

44. 星座 P. 100

你是什麼星座？許多人相信十二星座可以讓你深入了解你的日常生活、才能、特質和未來。了解你的星座也能夠幫助你克服生活上的一些困難。

十二星座形成黃道帶。在古希臘，「黃道帶」這個字原意為「動物圈（獸帶）」，故十二星座即以相似的小動物來命名。每年在不同月分，我們都可以見到不同星座高掛於夜空中。

古希臘天文學家利用黃道帶的十二個部分，來讓星體和行星的研究變得更簡單。夜空中十二均等的部分就稱為「黃道十二宮」或「星座」，這十二個星座分別為公羊（白羊座）、公牛（金牛座）、雙胞胎（雙子座）、螃蟹（巨蟹座）、獅子（獅子座）、處女（處女座）、天平（天秤座）、蠍子（天蠍座）、弓箭手（射手座）、山羊（摩羯座）、裝水的容器（水瓶座），以及魚（雙魚座）。

古代算命師認為星星和行星的移動，會對凡人的生活造成影響。出生於相同星座的人，也會有著相似的性格。研究黃道帶如何影響人類性格的研究稱為「占星學」。在一些國家中，利用占星學來預測未來，已經成為一種小型的營利事業。

由於很難去證明星星和行星會對人類行為產生影響，許多人因此認為，黃道帶只是一種無特殊力量的古代夜空地圖。但是他們要如何解釋為什麼正好有許多巨蟹座的人總是多愁善感？夜空似乎真的對我們有影響，但影響的方式將永遠是個謎團。

45. 遠離癌症 P. 102

癌症是一種可怕的疾病，起因於人體細胞變異，進而攻擊周遭組織所致。西方國家有 25% 的人口死於癌症。亞洲也同樣面臨此嚴重問題。許多人相信，癌症對人類健康產生的威脅，大於全球暖化或天然資源縮減。

但是，為什麼罹癌人數越來越多？原因可能與現代人的生活習慣有關。抽菸、呼吸汙染的空氣、缺乏運動、生活壓力過大、飲用汙染水源、飲酒過量，以及新鮮蔬果攝取不足，都會增加罹癌機率。近期研究結果顯示，經常使用手機也可能提高罹癌風險。

但不一定是個人生活習慣或環境造就癌症，也有可能是遺傳的緣故。這表示父母若患有癌症，子女罹癌的機率就會偏高。因此，如果有癌症方面的家族病史，即便有健康的生活習慣，仍可能不夠。

雖然有很多人戰勝癌症，但由於尚無解藥，因此有時仍會復發。不過，我們還是能實行許多方法來降低罹癌風險。醫學研究結果指出，若能避免抽菸、飲酒、汙染和壓力，並且維持健康的飲食習慣，即可減少罹癌機率。

如果每個人都能變得更健康一點，心情就會更愉快，罹癌率也可能下降。只要每天運動、每晚睡飽八小時、飲用乾淨的水、攝取健康的食物，少油、少鹽與少糖即可，就是這麼簡單！

1-10 實力檢測

46. 恐龍 P. 104

恐龍是一種存活在超過 6,500 萬年前的動物。在希臘文中，dinosaur（恐龍）這個字意指「恐怖的蜥蜴」。在中生代時期，有長達 1 億 6,000 萬年的時間，恐龍是最主要的動物群。但牠們在人們所認識的現代動物出現前，就逐漸消失了。而最早的人類首次出現在 5、6 百萬年前左右。

恐龍的種類有上千種，我們只能靠挖掘到的化石發現少數幾種。有些恐龍是肉食性（肉食動物）；有些則是草食性（草食動物）。有些恐龍非常巨大，但也有部分屬於小型。最重的恐龍可能是腕龍，體重達 80 公噸；最高的恐龍可能是波塞東龍，其頭部距地面高達 17 公尺！最長的恐龍是梁龍，身長超過 40 公尺。目前我們所知道的最小的恐龍，則大約和雞一樣大小。

有些恐龍非常兇猛，而像暴龍和棘龍這類恐龍則比大象還大，有些恐龍則是跑得比人類還快。科學家認為，一些像迅猛龍這類的恐龍，是採群體方式狩獵，如同現代的狼和獅子一般。科學家要發現更多存在許久之前的恐龍，需要花上好幾十年的時間。

現在已經沒有恐龍的存在了，據信牠們已經在 6,500 萬年前完全消失。造成牠們突然絕種的原因，可能是來自於發生在墨西哥一次劇烈的隕石撞擊事件。有些恐龍的親戚至今仍然存在，也就是現今的鳥類。科學家指出，那種前肢短小的食肉恐龍，最有可能就是鳥類的祖先。下次你聽到鳥鳴時，想想牠們的祖先曾是多麼了不起吧！

47. 阿斯匹靈 P. 106

當你頭痛、牙痛或發燒時，你會怎麼辦？如果你去看醫生，那麼他極有可能給你一些含有阿斯匹靈的藥物。阿斯匹靈是一種越來越普遍的藥物，因為它可以治療很多病痛。現今每年所消耗的阿斯匹靈約有四萬公噸，而它也成為全世界最廣泛使用的藥物之一。

大部分的人將阿斯匹靈當作止痛劑來治療疼痛，因此許多頭痛藥和止痛藥都含有阿斯匹靈的成分；另外，它也被當成退熱劑來治療發燒，所以很多感冒藥也含有阿斯匹靈。除此之外，每天服用少量的阿斯匹靈有助於防止心臟病、中風、血栓的形成，甚至是癌症。阿斯匹靈的其中一個作用，是可以使血液變得稀薄，所以血液可以更容易地在體內循環。

阿斯匹靈具有危險性嗎？阿斯匹靈有任何副作用嗎？阿斯匹靈是一種藥物，和其他的藥物一樣，它也可能相當危險。每年有好幾百人因為服用太多阿斯匹靈而死亡。高劑量的阿斯匹靈可能會造成胃潰瘍、胃出血和耳鳴。罹患痛風的人，通常會建議連一般被認為是「小孩的阿斯匹靈」（81 毫克）的低劑量阿斯匹靈都不可服用，因為它會減少尿酸的排泄。現在阿斯匹靈也從兒童的感冒藥中被排除，因為過去曾發生孩童因服用阿斯匹靈而死亡的事件。

大體上來說，如果在少量服用的狀況下，阿斯匹靈對成人並不具危險性。很多人因為服用含有阿斯匹靈的藥物，而改善了各種的病痛。它真的是一種令人稱奇的藥物。

48. 貨幣的歷史 P. 108

人人都愛錢，但是你知道錢的起源嗎？你知道最先使用錢的民族嗎？科學家指出，在一萬多年前，南非史瓦濟蘭的人民就使用紅色的染料來當做貨幣。同一時期左右，澳洲原住民亦使用相似的染料做為貨幣。隨後，世界上一些其他地方的民族，使用貝殼和其他珍貴物品當成貨幣，用來購物或交換物品，這就是所謂的易貨制度，也就是一種以物易物的商業形式。

許多物品都曾被當做貨幣，從豬隻到香料、鹽巴等等。過去有很長一段時間，胡椒是歐洲盛行的付款工具。密克羅尼西亞的雅浦島人民，則使用碩大的「石幣」，有些石幣甚至寬達八英呎，重量超過一部小汽車。

不過，最便利的貨幣形式，莫過於黃金和白銀等貴金屬。歷史學家認為，大約西元前 650 年，利底亞人是最先使用金幣和銀幣的民族。直至今日，黃金與白銀仍為相當貴重的物品。

鈔票的首次使用，則出現在西元 7 世紀的中國，歐洲則是到了 1661 年才發行第一批鈔票。

雖然經過歲月更迭，貨幣也隨之演變，但其重要程度依然不減。無論是紙鈔或豬隻，大多數人還是喜歡身上有錢的感覺。

49. 伊拉克的歷史 P. 110

伊拉克位於西亞，南邊接壤科威特及沙烏地阿拉伯，西鄰約旦，東北有敘利亞，北邊是土耳其，東邊則與伊朗相接。

歷史學家表示，人類文明起源於美索不達米亞一個古老的國家，也就是現今的伊拉克。希臘文裡的「美索不達米亞」意指「兩河之間」，也就是底格里斯河與幼發拉底河。兩河流域孕育出第一個世界文明：西元前六千年的蘇美文化。蘇美文化首創書寫系統、數學、科學和法律制度，因此美索不達米亞被稱為是「人類文明的搖籃」。即使到了今日，我們仍沿用蘇美人七千年前所採用的相同數學系統、曆法和計時方式。

在英國於 1918 年接管之前，美索不達米亞一直維持著帝國的型態。它於 1932 年獨立，並更名為「伊拉克」。1979 年，海珊就任總統，並以獨裁的鐵腕手段統治伊拉克。在長達八年的兩伊戰爭期間，伊拉克軍方以化學武器攻擊伊朗士兵與平民。海珊還下令使用毒氣攻擊伊拉克境內的庫德族人，此殘酷攻擊史稱「哈萊卜傑大屠殺」（Halabja massacre），是全世界有史以來，針對人口密集地區所發生過最大規模的化學武器攻擊事件。海珊因諸多罪狀於法庭受審，最後罪名成立，並於 2006 年處死。

身為人類文明搖籃的伊拉克，雖然擁有悠久歷史，卻不代表該國現今處於和平狀態。有時仍有各種宗教與政治狂熱份子進行恐怖攻擊。但多數的伊拉克人民希望安居樂業，現在伊拉克已往此方向努力。

50. 李奧納多．達文西 P. 112

李奧納多．達文西是義大利的科學家、植物學家、解剖學家、工程師、發明家、數學家、建築師、雕刻師、音樂家、作家與畫家。達文西被公認為世上最偉大的畫家之一，以及最才華洋溢的博學家。他於 1452 年生於義大利芬奇，卒於 1519 年。

達文西擔任工程師時，構思出許多現代發明的概念，例如直升機、坦克車、計算機和太陽能。但由於當時的科技不夠先進，導致他的多數發明均無疾而終。

而身為一位解剖學家，達文西曾解剖人類大體，以及描繪人類骨骼與其構造，包括肌肉與肌腱、性器與各種臟器。他將科學與工程方面的研究，都記錄在筆記本中，其中包含了一萬三千頁的素描、科學圖表以及對繪畫的理念。他的插圖作品《維特魯威人》集結了他對解剖學、藝術與工程學的研究。此插圖描繪一名栩栩如生的男子，以真實的對稱方式移動手腳。由於達文西對人類解剖學的研究十分詳盡，因此他能夠創造出不可思議的寫實素描與畫作。最家喻戶曉的作品就是《蒙娜麗莎的微笑》和《最後的晚餐》。

達文西的父親是佛羅倫斯的法院公證員，母親出身農家，也有一說可能是來自中東的奴隸。達文西十四歲時，到一位知名畫家的畫坊學藝，因而習得讓他運用自如的繪畫技巧。

雖然達文西的生平事蹟鮮為人知，但幸好他遺留下了啟迪人心的作品。

Unit 2 字彙學習

本單元將幫助你練習累積字彙與理解生字的技巧。在本單元中，你將練習辨識同義字，讓寫作的文采更加豐富生動；你也會學到有助建立對比結構的反義字。

此外，你還可練習從文章上下文來理解字彙。依上下文猜測生字的字義，是最為實用的語言學習技巧。掌握此理解能力，對於累積字彙量將大有助益。

2-1 同義字

英文的詞語十分豐富。事實上，許多看似不同的詞語，其實意義都相同。如果你想表達正在享用的冰淇淋很好吃，你可以輕鬆地運用 acceptable（可接受）、excellent（很棒）、nice（很不錯）、pleasing（令人心曠神怡）、super（超讚）或 amazing（好吃得不得了）等用語。

51. 美洲豹的生活 P. 116

美洲豹主要居住在非洲和部分亞洲地區。牠是豹屬動物中，四種會吼叫的大貓裡體型最小的。另外三種是老虎、獅子與美洲虎。美洲豹總是單獨行動，只有母豹會與幼豹短暫生活一陣子。美洲豹體型比印度豹稍大，比美洲虎稍小，但除此之外，三者看來非常相似。

美洲豹會避開有野狗、斑點鬣狗、老虎，和獅子的地方，因為這些動物可能會竊取食物或獵殺幼豹。美洲豹的動作非常敏捷，跑起來時速可達 57 公里，能跳 6 公尺遠，垂直彈跳也有 3 公尺高。美洲豹也以善於爬樹聞名。雖然美洲豹體型比另外三種豹屬動物小，但是牠們非常強壯，可以將一頭死亡的瞪羚拉到樹上，避免其他食腐動物的掠食。

美洲豹白天通常會藏匿於高大的草叢中或樹上高處。牠們是夜行性動物，白天睡覺，晚上才會出來活動。

母豹每年會產下一隻幼豹，生產後，母豹會留下豹寶寶出外覓食。

美洲豹這種美麗生物很難被發現，但只要找對方向，便能尋到蹤跡。牠們是觀光客到非洲必看的「五大動物」之一。這五大動物是指非洲五種最受歡迎的動物：獅子、非洲象、非洲水牛、美洲豹和犀牛。

52. 邊境之域：紐西蘭 P. 118

紐西蘭由兩個主島（北島與南島），和許多小島所組成，位於澳洲東南方約 2,000 公里處，許多人都說紐西蘭是世界上最偏遠的國家。它的首都是威靈頓，但奧克蘭才是紐西蘭最大的城市。紐西蘭只有四百多萬居民，主要人口是歐洲後裔，還有一些族群也不在少數，包括毛利族、亞洲人，與非毛利族的玻里尼西亞人。

紐西蘭是地球上最後一塊被發現的主要陸地之一。科學家認為毛利人是在西元前 1250 到 1300 年間率先抵達此島。毛利人稱紐西蘭為 Aotearoa，意思是「綿綿白雲之鄉」。

由於紐西蘭離多數國家非常遙遠，所以 80% 植物和多數鳥類，皆是當地特有，意即在世界其他地方找不到這些植物與鳥類。紐西蘭當地的特殊物種包括「巨沙螽」，一種身長超過 10 公分的昆蟲，以及全世界最稀有的海豚「毛依（Maui）海豚」。然而，歸因於人類與其攜入的哺乳動物，當地許多特有鳥類正面臨絕種危機。

紐西蘭風景優美，電影《魔戒三部曲》曾在當地取景拍攝，也因為這部系列電影，當地已成為觀光勝地。如果你需要度假，也正在尋找奇特的參觀景點，何不去紐西蘭呢？當地的景緻可能會令你感到驚奇。

53. 莫札特：謎樣的音樂家 P. 120

阿瑪迪斯．莫札特是歷史上最知名，且光環最歷久彌新的古典作曲家之一。他於 1756 年 1 月 27 日出生於奧地利的薩爾茨堡。父親李奧波德．

莫札特是歐洲最頂尖的音樂老師之一。在沃夫岡．阿瑪迪斯出生那年，其父出版了一本相當成功的小提琴教科書。在父親的薰陶與教導下，小莫札特年幼時便顯露音樂天分，年僅五歲就開始作曲，六歲時便可矇眼彈奏鋼琴。

年幼的莫札特經常旅行，在各家王公貴族的宮廷裡表演。旅途中，他遇見當時許多著名的音樂家。有些歷史學家指出，莫札特會說的語言高達 15 種。莫札特一生創作約 600 首曲子，而其中許多曲子至今仍相當知名。

莫札特終其一生都為錢所困。他常需要寫信向朋友尋求金援。這點非常令人匪夷所思，因為莫札特的大半生其實賺進不少錢，或許問題就出在他總是入不敷出。1791 年末，莫札特撒手人寰，享年 35 歲。他的死因是個謎，沒有人知道死於何種疾病。尤其歷史學家對造成他死亡的疾病亦意見分歧。有些人甚至認為他是被另一位作曲家安東尼奧．薩列里，因妒忌其才華而毒殺。

莫札特被視為歷史上最偉大的音樂家之一，影響古典音樂極深。雖然莫札特已辭世逾兩世紀，但其天分仍無人可及。

54. 美妙的巧克力 P. 122

你喜歡巧克力嗎？大多數人都愛不釋手。香甜滑順的口感真的令人難以抗拒。但是巧克力的由來為何呢？

約莫兩千六百年前，居住於中南美洲的奧爾梅克人將巧克力加以應用。他們利用可可豆調製特殊飲品，但這種飲料沒有我們熟悉的巧克力甜味，而是苦到極點。之後，他們開始在可可飲品裡添加其他成分，使其風味更佳。

巧克力對於中美洲的馬雅人來說十分重要。馬雅人將可可豆做為貨幣，據說十顆可可豆可以買到一隻兔子。馬雅人亦將可可豆用於宗教儀式與婚禮。雖然馬雅人同樣會以可可豆製作飲品，但是只有富人才喝得起。

歐洲人抵達南美時，開始將此熱門飲品帶回祖國。相繼添加牛奶、鮮奶油與糖，最後形成了我們所知道的巧克力。1689 年時，在牙買加出現了巧克力牛奶飲品。

如今，巧克力是全世界最受歡迎的口味之一。在現代社會裡，我們可從巧克力棒、冰淇淋、蛋糕、奶昔、派餅和許多食物品嚐巧克力的風味。部分研究顯示，黑巧克力有益健康，對於心血管系統很有幫助，亦有其他抗癌效用。因此，定期攝取少量黑巧克力，可能可以降低罹患心臟病的機率。

但是，沒有任何事物是十全十美的，巧克力也不例外。巧克力屬於高熱量食品，所以大量食用巧克力的人，會有變胖的風險。其實，想要享用巧克力的滋味，又不想危害健康的祕訣非常簡單：就是「適可而止」！

55. 綠色和平：拯救世界 P. 124

綠色和平（Greenpeace）是一全球組織，其宗旨在於防止企業公司和政府機關危害環境。雖然綠色和平並非唯一的國際環保組織，但其規模卻最大，且遠近馳名。

綠色和平自從於 1971 年創建於加拿大溫哥華起，即參與多項備受矚目的歷史事件。1995 年，一艘綠色和平船艇干擾了法國核武測試，因此引起全世界對此議題的注意。此事件不久後，法國政府即簽訂一份禁止核武測試的國際條約。綠色和平亦不斷派遣船艇保護鯨魚，以免受到日本捕鯨船的獵殺。綠色和平組織亦發起抵禦日本和挪威捕鯨公司的政治運動，以防止其將來擴大捕鯨規模。

綠色和平倡導人士積極參與各種環境議題。他們通常會對抗因個人或團體利益，而傷害環境的大公司或政府機關。他們參與的議題包括雨林破壞、底拖網捕撈法、捕鯨問題、全球暖化、核能議題、裁減核武，以及能源清潔問題。綠色和平試圖引起大眾對此類議題的注意力，讓市井小民都能盡一己之力，共同保護環境。

綠色和平倡導人士有時會不顧自身安危，為自己的信念挺身而出。他們曾以小型船隻嘗試制止龐大的捕鯨船艦；也曾將自己綑綁於即將被伐木公司砍伐的樹木上。

雖然綠色和平組織廣受全球民眾支持，但政府單位摧毀環境的行為，至今仍未停息。不過，有鑑於綠色和平組織過去奮戰成功的紀錄，假使沒有他們大力保護環境的作為，我們的環境可能會比現況，更加不堪設想。

2-2 反義字

英文的字彙十分豐富，並有許多語詞的意義恰好相反。有些反義字表達出兩種可能性的其一意義，例如 dead（死亡）和 alive（活著）；也有其他不同變化的詞彙，例如 huge（龐大）、giant（巨大）、big（大）等詞，都是 small（小）的反義字。學會越多反義字，你的字彙量就越能有所增進，也能讓寫作內容更加生動有趣。

56. 可口可樂 P. 126

可口可樂是世界上最知名的無酒精飲料。幾乎在每個國家裡，你都可以看見掛在大樓上的可口可樂標誌。你可以在超過 200 個國家的商店、餐廳，與自動販賣機買到可口可樂。許多人喜愛這種又名「可樂」、味甜色黑、有氣泡的飲料。但也有很多人不喜歡可樂和其他汽水，因為這類飲料含糖量高。營養學家指出，喝太多汽水有害健康。

1885 年，約翰．潘柏特在喬治亞州哥倫比亞市裡的一家藥局，發明了可口可樂。1886 年時，可口可樂在喬治亞州的亞特蘭大，被當成藥物來販售。直到阿薩．肯德勒於 1888 年買下了潘柏特的公司，並創立了可口可樂公司後，可樂才開始暢銷。阿薩．肯德勒運用許多聰明的行銷概念，讓可樂成為一種受歡迎的飲料。在 1894 年時，可口可樂首次以瓶裝的方式販售。直到 1955 年，罐裝可樂才終於問世。

第二次世界大戰中，大部分的美國人只能配給到少量的糖，但是可口可樂對於糖分的使用，卻未受到限制。許多人為了想吃點甜的而購買可樂，而可口可樂也讓美國士兵以免費的方式飲用。戰爭期間所喝掉的可口可樂，或許也是它成為傳奇的重要原因。

大戰過後，飲用可口可樂的人未見減少。可口可樂也擴展其營業版圖，發明了櫻桃可樂、健怡可樂，和其他種類的飲料，將其觸角伸向其他市場。如今，可口可樂依舊隨處可見，毫無衰退跡象。天曉得，或許你的孫兒仍會把飲用可樂視為一大樂事呢。

57. 英國皇室——留存至今的君主制 P. 128

英國擁有全球聞名遐邇的皇室家族。現今，英國（由英格蘭、蘇格蘭、威爾斯和北愛爾蘭組成）的君主是伊莉莎白二世女王。雖然皇室家族並不握有實質政權，但他們代表了英倫文化與歷史。伊莉莎白女王自 1952 年開始執政後，她對自己皇室職責與英國人民的奉獻，一向令人敬佩。而她的兒子查爾斯王子是下一個王位繼承人。

身為未來國王的查爾斯王子，受到萬眾矚目的程度不亞於女王。1981 年他與黛安娜．史賓瑟女爵結縭時，全球都在觀看這場世紀婚禮。黛安娜王妃，或大家熟知的黛妃，因其處事作風與美貌而令人仰慕，尤其是她讓大家注意到世界各地的問題，包括地雷、愛滋病與痲瘋病等。黛妃援助他人所做的奉獻讓她擁有「全民王妃」的別稱。黛妃與查爾斯王子離婚後，於 1997 年的一場車禍中香消玉殞。全世界均哀悼這位備受愛戴的全民王妃之逝世。

有些英國人認為皇室家族沒有存在的必要，因為皇室成員不再掌有任何政權；但也有人民仍然崇敬皇室。威廉和哈利是黛安娜與查爾斯之子，均以繼承母親和藹親民的性格聞名。身兼長子與第二順位繼承人身分的威廉王子，迎娶了非貴族出身的凱特．米道頓。威廉和凱特在教養三個孩子方面均親力親為。他們的長子喬治王子，有朝一日也會繼承王位。哈利王子的妻子亦為平民，也就是來自美國的梅根．馬克爾。威廉王子和哈利王子都追隨其母的腳步，態度親民，引起一般民眾對皇室的認同感。

58. 日本武士 P. 130

在歐洲一些訓練有素的貴族戰士，被國王或皇后授予榮譽，稱為「騎士」。在日本，他的名字則叫「武士」（samurai）。武士指的是劍術優秀的劍士，他們遵循一套名叫「武士道」（Bushido）的特殊規範過活，而這特殊的規範指的就是「武士之道」。武士道是武士的道德規範與生活方式，它教導武士在戰爭與承平時期，如何行事與生活。武士規範包含七種主要美德：正直、勇氣、仁慈、尊重、誠實、榮譽與忠誠。

武士通常配有長短兩把刀。長的叫做 katana（武士刀），用於打鬥。武士是使用 katana 的行家，在打鬥中完全仰賴 katana，所以 katana 便成為他靈魂一部分；而短的刀叫做 wakizashi（腰刀；切腹刀），武士會隨身攜帶。wakizashi 一般當作近身戰鬥的備用武器。

對武士來說，榮譽是最重要的事。武士必須遵循武士道的規則，否則會被視為不名譽之人。對武士來說，不名譽比死還嚴重。有時武士如果做了不榮譽的事，會以自己的 wakizashi 自裁。

「盡己所能」是武士文化的核心。武士將大部分的時間用在精益求精上，這也是造就他成為一個勇猛武士的原因。

如今已經沒有像過去那樣的武士了。但許多人認為，武士是一群優秀之人，並且對現今的日本文化有著深遠的影響。

59. 神秘的貓熊 P. 132

為什麼大家這麼喜愛貓熊？或許是因為牠們長相可愛，也有可能是因為牠們所剩無幾了。

這些黑白相間的可愛毛球，原本學名叫大貓熊（giant panda），源自中國。龍與大貓熊的圖形，都被視為是代表中國的象徵。

有些人也稱大貓熊為熊貓（panda）或貓熊（panda bear）。大貓熊近來才被證實為熊類（多年來，科學家總認為牠們更接近於浣熊）。貓熊和其他的熊長得不一樣，因為牠們在眼睛周圍、耳朵與身上都有黑色的紋路。雖然牠們看起來很可愛，動作又緩慢，但是當牠們生氣時，卻和其他熊一樣危險。貓熊以竹子為主食，但是牠們也吃其他的食物，如蛋、魚、柳丁和香蕉。

許多人認為大貓熊的幼仔不多，而這也是牠們現存數量不多的原因之一。但是科學家說，雌性貓熊在一生中可產下五至八隻幼仔。一胎可以生下一至兩隻幼仔，但牠卻只有能力照顧其中一隻。因此，另外一隻在出生後，由於缺乏密集的照顧，很快就會死亡。

貓熊是易危物種，世界上僅有約兩千隻的貓熊存活。人們一直努力做好大貓熊的保育，而看來他們的努力已經得到了回饋，因為貓熊的數量正逐漸增加中。

60. 世界上最深的礦坑 P. 134

我們都知道黃金與鑽石來自深層的地底。但人們是怎麼挖掘到的呢？他們向地底深掘以建造礦坑。礦坑是地底下人們尋找並挖掘有價礦物的地方。

世界上其中一個最深的礦坑是位於南非的陶托那（TauTona）金礦，TauTona 這個名字在當地的塞茨瓦語裡，意思是「大獅子」。這個礦坑有 3.9 公里深，被用來挖掘深置地底的黃金。

陶托那礦坑於 1957 年建立，剛開始的規模並不像現在這麼深。它於 1962 年開始運作，直到 2017 年。2008 年時，其深度達到 3.9 公里深，要從地面到礦坑的底部，需花上一整個小時的時間。

如今陶托那的隧道超過 800 公里，約有 5,600 百名礦工曾在那挖掘黃金。由於礦坑十分縱深，裡頭的溫度可能會升高至危險的程度。藉著冷氣設備，溫度可以從攝氏 55 度降到攝氏 28 度。

礦坑是個危險的工作環境，每年約有 5 名工人，會因落石與地底爆炸而死亡。然而，在南非許多人並沒有太多工作的選項，因此即便是危險的礦坑，也似乎是不錯的選擇。不過，2017 年 9 月 15 日，陶托那礦坑最後一次爆炸，礦坑從此封閉，不再開採。從那天起，安革金公司持續至新地點另覓金礦。

2-3 依上下文猜測字義

再怎麼跟生字大眼瞪小眼，也無法猜透它的意思。但是如果你瀏覽上下文，就能很快意會這詞彙的意思。詞彙的上下文能讓你理解其意義。試著再閱讀一次此段文字，猜猜看「context」這個字是什麼意思。

61. 快逃！海嘯來了！ P. 136

海嘯意指足以淹沒眾多人口、甚至催毀整個國家的一連串強大海浪。史上最可怕的海嘯災難發生於 2004 年 12 月 26 日。那天從印度洋席捲而來的一場大海嘯，造成 22 萬 7 千多人罹難，約 160 萬人無家可歸。

「tsunami」一字源自日文，意思是「海港」（tsu）和「海浪」（nami）。在水裡或水域附近發生山崩、火山爆發和地震，都會引起海嘯。巨型小行星撞擊地球也會造成海嘯，不過已經很久沒有大型的外太空天體撞擊地球了。

我們通常無法察覺發生在深海的海嘯。海嘯時速可高達 1,000 公里。2004 年海嘯的目擊者在大浪襲擊之前驚見海洋突然消失。有些人知道，當海水突然退潮，就表示海嘯即將來襲，於是他們跑到地勢較高的地方避難。不幸的是，仍有許多人喪生。

印度洋沿岸國家紛紛制定各種新的安全措施，以確保 2004 年海嘯的悲劇不再重演。區域性的海嘯警示系統可監測海洋中的水流。一旦偵測到海嘯的動靜，就會向高風險群的國家政府傳送警報。日本有自己的警示系統，在 2011 年 3 月 11 日海嘯襲擊前 15 分鐘就向人民發布了海嘯警報。即使是採用最為先進的警示系統，日本海嘯仍帶走近一萬六千人的生命。此外，更重創了福島第一核電廠，造成世界上最嚴重的核災之一。顯然，對太平洋沿岸各國而言，海嘯仍是極具殺傷力的威脅。

62. 麥當勞 P. 138

你吃過「大麥克堡」嗎？如果你曾去過麥當勞，你可能有機會享用到。麥當勞是第一家速食連鎖餐廳，目前也仍是全球規模最大的連鎖餐廳。連鎖餐廳指的是以同一種形態開設的餐廳，使用同一個名字，販賣幾乎相同的食物，並且維持同等的品質管制。

麥當勞是於 1940 年，由理查與莫里斯．麥當勞兩兄弟在加州所創立。大約 1948 年時，兩兄弟開始以既快速又經濟的新技術來製作食物。他們最後稱呼所製造出來的美味食物為「速食」。1961 年，伊利諾州的雷．克洛克買下麥當勞兄弟的公司產權，並且開始開設有經銷權的新餐廳，經銷權指的是商店、餐廳或其他企業擁有公司所授與的許可證，經營特定的領域，並使用公司的名稱和技術。

現今，麥當勞在 120 個國家裡，擁有超過 37,000 家的連鎖店，這些連鎖店在全球雇用的員工超過 190 萬人，每天服務超過 6,900 萬人。麥當勞已經變成一個美式生活的代表，有些人認為麥當勞的全球化普及現象，也正代表著美式價值觀的勝利。

即便麥當勞是如此地成功，還是有許多人並不愛吃麥當勞的食物。這些批評者說，吃太多速食是非常不健康的。許多醫生也同意速食過量會引起過度肥胖。或許這就是為什麼越來越多人無法將自己塞進飛機座位裡的原因吧。而麥當勞也發現了此問題，因此許多麥當勞餐廳現在也開始推出像沙拉這類健康的餐點。

63. 信天翁 P. 140

鴕鳥是世界上體型最大的鳥，但是牠不會飛。你知道體型最大而且會飛的鳥是什麼嗎？就是「信天翁」。這種海鳥居住在北太平洋與南太平洋。有的人可能會誤把信天翁認為是大型海鷗。信天翁因為展翼幅度（也就是兩支翅膀尖端間的距離）大，可以在空中飛翔數天，其兩個翅膀尖端的距離可長達 3.4 公尺。

信天翁以烏賊、魚等小型的海中生物為食。牠們有兩種捕食方式，有時牠們會飛近海面，從水面叼起食物；其他時候，牠們會潛到很深的水裡去捕魚。

雄性與雌性的信天翁通常會在一起生活數年。每年牠們都會一起築巢，孵育牠們的下一代。而信天翁通常也只會產一枚卵，因為母信天翁每年只會下一顆蛋。有些信天翁終其一生都會和牠們的配偶結伴生活。科學家甚至認為牠們是用一種特別的舞蹈來維持長久的關係。

信天翁飛行時，牠們會利用長長的翅膀在空中滑翔向上。往上的氣流可以節省力氣，因為牠們不需要不時拍打翅膀，便可以藉著氣流的帶引而上升。有了大自然的協助，信天翁就可以長途跋涉去尋找食物。

由於幾種因素，信天翁目前正遭受絕種的困境。牠們不但被老鼠和野貓這些天敵威脅，還受到汙染及過度捕魚等種種人為因素影響而滅絕。

64. 阿波羅 13 號 P. 142

在 1969 年 7 月，美國阿波羅 11 號太空人尼爾．阿姆斯壯和巴茲．奧爾德林登陸月球。他們在月球表面留下了一段話：「我們為了人類的和平而來」。這也象徵了美國與前蘇聯的「太空競賽」之終結。美國與前蘇聯曾經比賽看誰先將人類送上月球，最後美國憑著優良的技術獲得勝利。但故事並未就此結束，美國對於月球的自豪和好奇心，即便過了 1969 年仍不斷持續。

「阿波羅 13 號」即是美國第三次登月的任務，也是阿波羅系列任務中最艱難的一次。在前往月球途中，其中一個船艙的氧氣罐爆炸，導致太空人詹姆斯．羅威爾、弗萊德．海斯，和約翰．斯威格特失去了主要的氧氣供給。這場危機透過電視實況轉播給美國各地的觀眾，許多觀眾都認為這些太空人應該活不了多久，然而他們很快反應過來，並從另一船艙取得了備用氧氣。藉著太空人的訓練與經驗，以及地球上 NASA 的支援，損害嚴重的阿波羅 13 號得以繞著月球，平安地返回地球。

繼阿波羅 13 號之後，又有四組美國太空人登陸月球。美國最後還是認為將太空人送上月球耗費太大，於是終止了登月計畫。不論在地球或在太空中，人們時常都得面對危險。但是阿波羅 13 號的組員與 NASA 團隊所立下的典範告訴我們，訓練、經驗、團隊合作與勇氣，可以克服艱難的考驗。

65. 線上遊戲——新型態的社群網路 P. 144

2018 年，路透社的報導指出，電玩遊戲已是時下最夯的娛樂方式。儘管電視、音樂與電影等其他娛樂的人氣呈現走下坡的趨勢，電玩遊戲的熱門程度卻每年增加約 10%。這樣的成長率可歸功於線上遊戲的發展。

線上遊戲剛問世時，是由大型多人線上角色扮演遊戲（簡稱 MMORPG）獨占鰲頭。在《無盡的任務》與《魔獸世界》等遊戲中，玩家需組隊完成任務，或在品頭論足彼此的遊戲角色之際，順便在線聊天，而所謂的遊戲角色，就是玩家在這個虛擬網路奇幻世界裡的化身。此類遊戲的社交層面才是令玩家著迷的原因，因為同時有上千名玩家上網玩遊戲。不過，大型多人線上遊戲（簡稱 MMO）十分耗時。有些任務需要數小時才有辦法完成；藉由獲取各種技能以及新穎與改良的配件寶物，進而讓角色升等，有時需要好幾天、甚至是好幾個星期不斷練功才能達成目標。

2017 年，隨著《絕地求生》（簡稱 PUBG）和《要塞英雄》等大逃殺類型的遊戲竄紅，耗時的問題迎刃而解。玩家上線後，以手無寸鐵的狀態進入對抗其他玩家的單場逃殺遊戲。每個玩家必須在一座（或多座）逼真的島嶼環境，趁格鬥尚未開始前，依據地圖找出自己遊戲角色可用的優良武器和設備。戰鬥到僅存一名玩家時，逃殺遊戲就結束。大約幾分鐘時間就能結束一場遊戲，而任何電玩系統或行動裝置均可執行此類遊戲，意即玩家再也不需要長時間投入遊戲或坐在電腦前了。

電玩公司精心設計的線上世界，能讓玩家自由選擇留置遊戲的時間長短。對上百萬名消費者而言，亦成為了維持友誼與社群互動的主要方式。由於電玩世界不斷進化，受歡迎的程度也將日益增長。

2-4 實力檢測

66. 起於爭議的舞蹈：歌舞伎 P. 146

擁有超過四百年歷史的歌舞伎，原本遭到日本幕府禁止，爾後卻成為備受保存的日本文化。歌舞伎是一種獨特的戲劇形式，目前僅存於日本。透過自成一格的音樂、舞步、演技、妝容與戲服，訴說發生在貴族、商人與老百姓身上的故事。

雖然現今的歌舞伎僅由男性演出，但創始人卻是一位女性。1603 年，名為出雲阿國的女性，開始在京都表演自創舞蹈，她和其他舞者的演出大受歡迎。但是德川幕府認為此類表演違反善良風俗，因此由男孩替代女性舞者。不過，到了 17 世紀中葉，則只有成年男性才能演出歌舞伎。

與莎士比亞劇碼的性質相等，歌舞伎算是老百姓的娛樂，而非貴族文化。歌舞伎戲劇和莎士比亞戲劇的主題亦有多處雷同，例如與歷史人物及事件有關（但會謹慎避免批評當政者），或是市井小民的日常生活與煩惱。雖然歌舞伎起初給人的刻板印象是傷風敗德，後來劇情卻開始逐漸納入賞善罰惡的概念。

在現今的歌舞伎表演中，觀眾欣賞到的，和 17 世紀末歌舞伎黃金年代的觀眾所看到的演出大同小異。主要劇院是東京的歌舞伎座。歌舞伎劇院裡，設有延伸至觀眾席的橋樑，能拉近與演員的距離。歌舞伎演員的妝容以白色油彩為底妝，再畫上誇張的表情，角色是英雄還是壞人，觀眾都能一目瞭然。音樂則讓劇情更有張力。現今觀眾可同時欣賞到歌舞伎的藝術與歷史元素。

67. 一座歐洲城市的崛起、殞落與重生 P. 148

布魯日的街道如果能說話，肯定能娓娓道來許多精彩的故事。這座位於比利時的城市，從繁華的貿易中心沒落為鬼城後，經過漫長的歷史沈澱，如今又再現風華。

故事要從古代說起。當時羅馬人在此地修建防禦工事以抵禦海盜，但效果不彰。西元 9 世紀時，維京人入侵並築起一座小型的貿易站。許多人認為布魯日的原文「Bruges」來自維京語的「Brygga」，意思是「港口」。

起初幾年，由於茲溫河能夠通往北海，布魯日因而蓬勃發展。來自歐洲各地的商人會集中到這座城市，來交換佛萊明布料與羊毛。到了西元 1500 年，布魯日的人口超過 20 萬人，幾乎是倫敦人口的兩倍。但是 16 世紀時，茲溫河的泥沙淤積問題嚴重，已無法繼續使用。經濟活動開始轉向另一座鄰近北海的城市——安特衛普。商人外移後，布魯日的人口驟減，徒留空蕩蕩的商店與住宅。將近四百年的時間裡，這座城市遭世人遺忘。

但遊客再度湧入，讓此城市重見天日。布魯日現已成為令人嚮往的旅遊勝地，每年吸引超過 900 萬名遊客前來。優美的運河讓布魯日擁有「北歐威尼斯」的別稱。與鄰近城市不同的是，布魯日並未受到兩次世界大戰的摧殘。因此，許多古老的中世紀建築仍屹立不倒。事實上，聯合國教科文組織已將布魯日極具歷史的貿易中心列為世界遺產。

布魯日為何如此吸引遊客的原因眾所周知。在佈滿鵝卵石的街道漫步，彷彿能帶你回到布魯日當年身為歐洲經濟重鎮的風華年代。此座城市的歷史告訴我們，有時跌得越重，反而後勢看漲。

68. 蘇斯博士與《戴帽子的貓》 P. 150

《戴帽子的貓》是由美國作家蘇斯博士所撰寫的一本兒童韻文書。書中的主角是一隻淘氣、會說話的貓，還戴著一頂紅白條紋的高帽子。這隻貓出現在蘇斯博士所寫的六本童書中，而第一次就是出現在《戴帽子的貓》。《戴帽子的貓》在全球相當受歡迎，因為對年輕的讀者來說，這是一本頗具娛樂性又有趣的書。

蘇斯博士是特奧多爾．蘇斯．蓋澤爾的筆名。他曾就讀於牛津大學的林肯學院，並攻讀文學博士學位。但最後他並未獲得任何學位就回到美國了。他在筆名中用了「博士」這個頭銜，作為對他父親期望他拿到博士學位，卻希望落空的回報。

特奧多爾．蘇斯．蓋澤爾不只是個作家，也是個生動有趣的漫畫家。在第二次世界大戰之前，他曾寫過兒童書籍；而在第二次世界大戰開始之後，他畫了政治漫畫來反抗希特勒與墨索里尼的惡行。二次大戰後，他又回頭繼續撰寫兒童書籍。在 1954 年時，他知道兒童對於閱讀之所以不感興趣，是因為他們的書都很無趣。為了鼓勵閱讀，他用了僅僅 236 個基礎字彙寫出了《戴帽子的貓》這本書。在這本暢銷書之後，他又寫了許多兒童書籍，包括一些經典的賣座書，像是：*Horton Hears a Who*、*Green Eggs and Ham*、*Dr. Seuss's ABC*、*One Fish Two Fish Red Fish Blue Fish* 與 *Hop on Pop*。這些書中都有天馬行空的圖片和押韻的文字，以幫助孩童在閱讀時能記住字彙。

特奧多爾．蘇斯．蓋澤爾的書被大眾視為經典書籍。許多有趣的「蘇斯博士」故事書，將繼續吸引並娛樂全世界的讀者。

69. 太空探索的新焦點：火星 P. 152

當你仰望夜空，映入眼簾的不只是恆星，有些亮點其實是行星。如果你發現一顆偏紅的粉色光點，很有可能就是號稱「紅色星球」的火星。火星的原文「Mars」，是古羅馬人以其信仰的戰神為名，因為偏紅的粉紅色澤讓他們聯想到血的顏色。

自從人類發現火星後，對火星的研究興趣即有增無減。1609 年，伽利略是透過望遠鏡觀察火星的第一人。隨著望遠鏡不斷改良，天文學家發現這顆紅色星球的體積約為地球的一半。人們想像有奇特的生物棲息於火星。

到了太空探索的現代時期，若干國家紛紛發射太空船環繞火星運行，並以探測車探索火星表面。前蘇聯、歐洲、美國與印度均曾執行火星任務。美國太空總署（簡稱 NASA）是美國負責探索外太空的政府機關。從 1965 年到 1972 年，美國太空總署的水手號系列無人太空船，近距離拍下許多火星的照片。1971 年，前蘇聯發射的火星 3 號則首次成功登陸火星表面。

火星任務仍延續至今。到目前為止，集結各任務的發現結果顯示，冰帽覆蓋了火星的兩極地區，其他地區還有深埋於地表下的冰層。火星大部分是一片一望無際的沙漠，伴隨著宏偉的高山、深不見底的峽谷以及規模龐大的沙塵暴。赤道地區雖然會比較溫暖，但火星的平均氣溫是攝氏零下 63 度。

部分科學家認為，我們能夠在火星上製造出一種比二氧化碳效力高出 9,500 倍以上的全球暖化氣體。此氣體有助於暖化嚴寒的火星，使其氣候環境更趨近地球。而改變行星環境以創造出類似地球環境的現象就稱為「地球化」（terraforming）。有朝一日，火星也許會充斥人類探險家、殖民地居民以及在火星表面健行的遊客。

70. 大自然的玩笑：鴨嘴獸 P. 154

唯一卵生的哺乳類是什麼動物？哪一種生物同時擁有毛皮與喙嘴？雖然聽起來像是科幻或奇異電影裡的角色，卻是真實存在的物種。此動物就是「鴨嘴獸」。

鴨嘴獸居住於澳洲東部，體型嬌小，約與家貓一般大。雄鴨嘴獸的後肢有尖刺，會分泌毒液，這是牠避免其他動物掠食自己的防身武器。雖然鴨嘴獸毒液的毒性強烈且足以讓小動物致命，對人類而言卻還不到致死的程度。然而，毒液卻會造成可怕的劇痛。

鴨嘴獸四肢有蹼，可於河流小溪裡游泳。牠們會以鴨嘴般的喙嘴捕食淡水螯蝦和其他居住於泥濘河床的小動物。喙嘴看似堅硬，其實非常敏感。喙嘴上甚至還有可開闔的鼻孔。當鴨嘴獸在泥漿裡覓食，喙嘴能將水排出，同時把獵物困於嘴裡。鴨嘴獸的軀幹和尾部均佈滿茂密的棕色毛皮，能讓鴨嘴獸保持乾燥保暖的狀態。

許多科學家表示，鴨嘴獸是世界上最光怪陸離的動物。主要原因在於溫血哺乳類動物的鴨嘴獸，竟然會產卵且具有毒液的構造。而目前除了鴨嘴獸外，只剩另一種卵生哺乳類動物。

有些人認為會產卵、分泌毒液、具有鴨嘴和水獺足部構造的此哺乳類動物，彷彿是「大自然的一個玩笑」或「刻意拼湊的缺陷」。鴨嘴獸雖然外表逗趣，卻是耐人尋味的生物。如果這世上沒有鴨嘴獸，肯定會少了些趣味。

Unit 3 學習策略

本單元教導你如何理解文意，並運用文章中不同素材來蒐集資訊。表格與圖片等視覺素材，以及索引和字典等參考來源，均能提供重要資訊。不過，這些工具不會直接呈現出文章的含意，而是以圖片、編號清單、依字母順序編列的清單，和其他方法來展示資訊。

參考來源通常能幫助你在書中找到所要的資料。圖表、表格和圖片，可協助你快速理解複雜的訊息，比直接閱讀內文快上許多。學習活用文章中不同的素材，有助於全面地瞭解文章大意。

3-1 影像圖表

表格、圖片、圖表和地圖，比文字更能呈現繁複的資訊，例如事物的關聯性與其模式風格。要理解這類的素材，必須先仔細閱讀標題、查看圖說，然後閱讀表格行列的表頭，以及圖表上的座標軸說明。瞭解影像圖表的版面陳列後，即可解讀所含的資訊。

71. 地圖：納尼亞王國 P. 158

地圖是地方區域的圖片，它能將城鎮、都市、道路、公園，甚至是假想的世界呈現出來。舉例來說，你是否讀過《納尼亞傳奇：獅子、女巫、魔衣櫥》這部小說？這是一本專為青少年所著的奇幻文學作品，亦為神祕納尼亞國度系列套書的首部曲。

C. S. 路易斯是一手打造《納尼亞傳奇：獅子、女巫、魔衣櫥》小說世界的作者，他創造了一個充滿各種場景、事件和人物的國度。無數孩童自此沉迷於這個奇幻世界，如同主角露西因為玩捉迷藏躲進魔衣櫥後，迷失於納尼亞一樣。

然而，只要有了地圖的輔助，我們就能在納尼亞王國裡知道自己身在何處，該往哪兒走，以及如何抵達目的地。下方是納尼亞王國的地圖，利用這份地圖，來回答以下關於納尼亞國境各地的問題。

72. 圓餅圖：誰在玩 Instagram ？ P. 160

才不久之前，年輕人全都在一窩蜂使用臉書。不過，若有什麼事是可以肯定的，那就是瞬息萬變的潮流，而社群媒體也無法倖免。研究報告指出，光是在英國，現在的臉書年輕用戶就比一年前減少了 70 萬人。那麼人潮都往哪裡流動？狂熱社群媒體的年輕人會前往的一個去處就是 Instagram，一款可從智慧型手機分享照片和影片的社群網路應用程式。

統計數據顯示，超過 55 歲的長青族群是臉書目前的主要用戶。那麼 Instagram 的用戶年齡層呢？我們可透過圓餅圖來了解此資訊。圓餅圖能將資訊分為幾塊扇形圖，可一目瞭然每一塊扇形圖所佔的總體比例。以下圓餅圖顯示出 Instagram 用戶的年齡層。因此，透過觀察此圓餅圖，我們就能得知青少年用戶的百分比、青壯年與銀髮族的比例為何。

73. 折線圖：我的閱讀習慣 P. 162

折線圖以一種簡單易讀的方式來呈現資料，它能夠將事物的變化趨勢表現出來，而不是只顯示事物的狀態。因此，如果我們想要表現某事物增加或減少的軌跡，就可利用這類型的圖表來表達。

以下是使用折線圖來組織資訊的範例。閱讀下列短文，並看圖表來觀察氣候對作者的讀書習慣有何影響。

我真的很喜歡閱讀，但我也喜歡跑步、做瑜珈、游泳、打羽毛球、爬山，以及盡量從事戶外活動。有時候，我不曉得何時才能好好享受閱讀的樂趣。

雨季就是一個大好時機。我所居住國家的乾雨季分明。每當雨季來臨時，我都會很想念出外遊玩的時光，但也很開心能擁有充裕的時間閱讀。我決定來記錄一下，自己一年下來可讀多少本書。

74. 表格：分裂的歐洲大陸 P. 164

表格是一種將資料以列（由左到右）和欄（由上到下）的形式所編排的圖表。每欄都有一個標題欄位，告訴你關於這欄的內容。

以下範例教你如何使用表格來呈現人口統計資料。閱讀下列短文，然後查看右頁的表格來回答問題。

在文化與經濟方面，西歐與東歐均有所區隔，其起源須追溯至第二次世界大戰結束的時候。蘇聯攻入德國而結束戰爭後，莫斯科政府決定在東歐各國佈署軍隊，此類附庸國被稱為「東歐國家」。這時期的歷史影響歐洲直至今日。

75. 長條圖：美國人的營養攝取 P. 166

長條圖可以讓你很快地看到並了解所有的資訊。在表格裡，我們會使用數字來呈現資訊，但在長條圖中，我們利用「條柱」來呈現資料。每一根條柱都代表了一個數字或數值。在長條圖中，很容易可以看出哪一個是最大的數值，因為代表它的條柱一定是最長的。

長條圖很少提供複雜或難以處理的資料，它們通常提供基本的、統計化的資訊。這樣一來，你就可以輕鬆地閱讀，並做出比較了。以下是使用長條圖來呈現統計資料的範例。

美國人以及許多其他國家的人民，體重數字日益飆高已是公開祕密。近數十年來，大家討論的話題已從「如何吃得飽」轉變為「如何減重」。有時候，大家似乎認為，一定有什麼「特效藥」能打造窈窕健康體態。其實，維持健康的不二法門，在於每天吃對的食物。以下長條圖顯示了美國人每天所吃的食物百分比。

3-2 參考資料

在現今的網路時代裡，到處充斥著各種資訊，且任何人皆可取得。資訊量如此龐大，想要搜尋特定資料反而困難。因此，字典、百科全書和地圖冊這些參考資料即可派上用場。也就是說，你應該學會如何使用這些重要工具。

76. 字典：人類的想像力 P. 168

雖然人類確實與黑猩猩有很多共同點，但黑猩猩卻缺乏了那種使我們人類與眾不同的重要特徵。那麼，使人類有別於其他動物的特徵是什麼呢？或許就是我們杜撰事物的「想像力」吧。人類能用想像的概念，傳達做人處事的道理。想像力也能被用來描繪改善社會和科技的藍圖。時鐘、蒸氣引擎、電腦，以及各種無數發明，都是靠著「想像如何提升效率」所創。

到底什麼是「想像力」呢？你可能會想知道這個詞是什麼意思，以及如何在句子裡使用它。「查閱字典」是很好的方式。字典會列出許多關於字彙的資訊，裡頭的字詞都是依字母順序來編排。字典裡的條目也會告訴你該字彙的定義、音節數目、發音，以及詞性。有時候，字典甚至會說明該字詞的字源。

77. 目錄：冰融危機 P. 170

目錄幾乎都放在每本書的起始處，幫助你找到書中你所需要的資料。目錄通常會列出章節或文章的標題，以及可以找到每個章節或文章的頁碼。

以下是一篇關於全球暖化的短文。閱讀短文，然後研讀它的目錄來回答問題。

短短二十年的時間，全球暖化現象已從科幻電影情節，成為真實上演的科學事實。如今，氣候專家越來越擔心天氣暖化問題會使北極冰層融化。假如北極冰層完全融化，就會增加全球海洋的水量，進而造成全球海平面上升的問題。北極融冰問題也會改變全球貨物運輸的方式。加拿大北部的冰層每年均提早融化，因此船隻開始利用大西洋與太平洋之間更快的航道。這條嶄新的北極貨運路線稱為「西北航道」。

現在，看看下列的目錄並回答問題。

78. 索引：暴君卡利古拉 P. 172

一本書的索引通常列在書本的最後。它將書中所有文章或章節裡的重要單字或標題編列出來，而這些字也以字母的順序排列。在每個字彙旁，你會看到一個或多個數字，這些數字就是你可以找到這些單字的頁數。

以「卡利古拉」為例，在百科全書裡，你也許會找到一篇關於卡利古拉的文章。卡利古拉是羅馬帝王中最著名的人物之一。他於西元 37 年登基羅馬帝王後，就開始產生怪異且殘暴的行為。卡利古拉深信自己是天神，下令在神廟與其他拜神祈禱的地方建造自己的雕像。他非常喜愛自己的賽馬「英西塔士斯」，經常贈與愛馬許多珍貴寶石和昂貴布匹。有些歷史學家認為，他甚至曾考慮過加冕愛馬一個爵位。

假使想獲知更多關於卡利古拉的事蹟，只要在索引中找到「卡利古拉」這個詞就行了。現在讓我們看著索引來回答以下問題。

79. 雜誌與報紙：考試讓你備感壓力嗎？ P. 174

無論是工作、學業或處理家務，每個人都有壓力爆表的時候。以下兩篇文章都是在討論「壓力」，其中一篇節錄自報紙，另一篇來自雜誌。你能分辨這兩者的差異嗎？

來給大家一個小提示：報紙的文章以時事為主，通常會告訴讀者世界上正在發生的事情；雜誌的文章則通常是以專題的形式，比報紙更能深入提供背景資訊。此外，報紙通常每天發行，雜誌則是每月出版。

報紙新聞

當地居民過勞死

一名名為約翰 · 史密斯的本地居民，今天於公司心臟病發不治。過去二十年間，他都在一家小型紙業公司服務。據他的同事所述，自從老闆分派給約翰一份重要的任務後，他就處於極度緊繃的狀態。當約翰的遺體被發現時，他的面部朝下，趴在辦公桌上，手裡仍握著一杯咖啡。目擊者證實，這是約翰當天所喝的第八杯咖啡。

雜誌文章

壓力是種病：煩惱會致命嗎？

以下現象在世界各地屢見不鮮：患者就診抱怨頭痛、暈眩和肚子不適。患者想拿藥，但醫師已知道吃藥無濟於事，因為問題出在「壓力過大」。不過，當醫師表明病因是來自「壓力」時，患者就會開始否認或找尋藉口，這種狀況總是千篇一律。大家都不曉得，壓力其實會造成高血壓、心臟病與關節炎等健康問題。

80. 百科全書：艾伯特 · 卡謬 P. 176

百科全書通常屬於套書，網羅五花八門的人事物資訊，並且依照字母順序編排每筆資料。

在百科全書查找名人相關訊息時，應留意人物資料均以其姓氏列於目錄，而非名字。也就是說，如果你想查詢「George Washington」（喬治 · 華盛頓），就必須查找「W」字母，而非「G」字母。因此，該筆資料會以「Washington, George」的方式呈現於目錄。而「The」開頭的資料，則會列於接在「The」後方那個名詞的首字母目錄。而標題開頭為「A」的文章亦同理可證。舉例來說，如需查找 *A Midsummer Night's Dream*，你會發現目錄中的呈現方式為 *Midsummer Night's Dream, A*。

我們列出可於套裝百科全書找到的艾伯特 · 卡謬生平簡介。請閱讀此段文字，並回答以下問題。

艾伯特 · 卡謬生於 1913 年，出生地為法屬阿爾及利亞，並於 1957 年贏得諾貝爾文學獎。他兼任作家、記者以及攝影師的身份。他的文學著作獲得激賞，世人對他的評價為「其真知灼見突顯了大時代下的人心問題」。

Unit 4 綜合練習

4-1 綜合練習（I）

81. 龍 P. 180

世界上許多文化都有關於龍的傳說。在某些文化中，龍是良善的；但在另一些文化中，龍卻是邪惡的。不管好或壞，在故事裡龍永遠強而有力，且擁有超自然力量。有些人認為，過去真的有龍存在，但大多數人都認為，龍只是虛構的生物。

在中國和亞洲其他國家，龍常被認為是仁慈的。人們說牠會帶來力量、祥和、好運和健康。在古代中國，龍是帝王的象徵。有些中國人相信，龍大部分時間住在水底。和歐洲的龍不同的是，中國的龍沒有翅膀，牠們利用魔法來飛行。中國的龍有時也被稱為「東方龍」，看起來像是一條長有四隻爪子的長蛇。在中國的生肖中，出生在龍年的人被認為是幸運、勇敢、具企圖心、健康、有活力、容易激動、脾氣暴躁和固執的。屬龍的人如果知道如何將自己驚人的幹勁、智慧和潛能做最好的運用，那他一定能有所作為。

在歐洲的傳說中，龍通常被視為是貪心、殘暴的有翅怪獸。牠們強壯、聰明，但卻不親切，通常守護如寶藏之類的物品。很多歐洲故事都有勇敢騎士對抗邪惡的龍的情節，所有殺害龍的騎士不但可以得到其財富，還可以擁有牠的智慧。在基督教裡，惡靈有時也會化身為龍出現。

人們或許不再相信龍的存在，但龍依舊活躍於故事書中。現代的奇幻小說家仍持續創作英雄對抗飛龍的故事。

82. 路易斯 · 卡羅 P. 182

你是否讀過《愛麗絲夢遊仙境》？這本書的作者是路易斯 · 卡羅，他是一位英國作家、詩人、科學家、攝影師和牧師。路易斯 · 卡羅的本名是查爾斯 · 路特維奇 · 道奇森，路易斯 · 卡羅是其筆名。他生於 1832 年，卒於 1898 年。

路易斯 · 卡羅最廣為人知的著作，就是以小女孩「愛麗絲」為主角的兩本兒童奇幻文學。第一本書名為《愛麗絲夢遊仙境》（1865 年），它的續集是《愛麗絲鏡中奇緣》（1872 年）。書中敘述愛麗絲掉入兔子洞，而進入一個奇幻世界的故事。其他作者也經常在故事裡，提及愛麗絲故事中的活潑人物角色和生動場景。例如愛抽菸的藍毛蟲以及柴郡貓，都是現今家喻戶曉的人物。

路易斯 · 卡羅後來寫了一首名詩《獵殺蛇鯊》，並於 1876 年出版。這首詩耐人尋味的特點在於他所杜撰的新詞。路易斯 · 卡羅是一個懂得玩弄文字遊戲、變化不同文字運用手法的高手。他撰寫許多這類令人「摸不著頭緒」的詩句。另一首名詩則是《愛麗絲鏡中奇緣》的《傑伯瓦奇》。他的用字十分新穎，這種文字玩趣精神亦影響了當代與現今時下的許多作家。至今仍有很多人鑽研他的作品與生平事蹟。

雖然路易斯・卡羅的著作看似兒童文學，但所有年齡層的讀者同樣讀得津津有味。如果你還沒讀過《愛麗絲夢遊仙境》（原文全名為《Alice's Adventures in Wonderland》，亦可簡寫為《Alice in Wonderland》），一定要盡快拜讀。無論你幾歲，都會覺得這本書妙趣橫生。

83. 馬爾地夫 P. 184

多數人都夢想著能到美麗的島嶼旅行。在那裡，他們能夠放鬆，享受秀麗的景色。許多島嶼，如馬爾地夫，都擁有未受破壞的沙灘和蔚藍的大海，但馬爾地夫這個島國卻是最受海灘愛好者青睞的島嶼之一。

馬爾地夫會如此受歡迎，也許是因為地理位置上的便利。它靠近印度和東亞，而且還是最接近歐洲的群島之一。

受歡迎的原因也或許是馬爾地夫沒有太多的飯店。在 2017 年時，馬爾地夫群島的 1,192 座島上，只有 12 家飯店。因此，遊客相信他們能夠在此享受絕對的隱私和自然的美景。

遺憾的是，馬爾地夫之所以越來越受到矚目，是因為人們擔心它快要消失了。根據記載，它是目前全世界地勢最低的國家。馬爾地夫多數島嶼（那些比較大型者稱為「環狀珊瑚島」）只高於海平面 2 公尺。隨著海平面的年年上升，馬爾地夫未來須面臨艱辛的生存奮戰。再過幾十年，甚至終將沉沒於海底。在海水開始逼近家門之時，它的領導當局也已擬定計畫展開行動。

不管馬爾地夫廣受歡迎原因為何，它是個值得一遊的好去處。觀光業也在馬爾地夫的經濟上扮演著不可或缺的角色。在 2017 年，總計約有 1,389,500 名觀光客走訪馬爾地夫群島，而現在營運中的渡假村便有 124 家。所以如果你想去看看馬爾地夫，最好別再等下去了。

84. 鸚鵡會說話嗎？ P. 186

鸚鵡是一種令人驚奇的動物。牠們大多是綠色，但也有些鸚鵡身上充滿眾多亮麗的色彩。鸚鵡非常美麗，而牠們最讓人稱奇的特點就是「會說話」。然而，很多科學家認為牠們並不是真的在說話，只是重覆自己聽到的聲音而已。近來有些科學家並不認同這種說法。

有位名為艾琳・佩珀伯格的科學家做了數年的實驗，證實鸚鵡非常地聰明，而且真的能夠了解人類說的話。艾琳從寵物店買了一隻年約一歲的非洲灰鸚鵡，她將這隻鸚鵡取名為艾力克斯（Alex，也是「鳥類學習實驗，Avian Learning Experiment」中首字母的縮略字）。在許多實驗之後，艾琳發表報告，宣稱艾力克斯不僅是重覆牠所聽到的東西。事實上，這隻鳥還能夠具創意地使用單字，並且回答出八成她所提出的簡單問題。除此之外，艾力克斯甚至還能夠理解牠自己所說的話。其他科學家並不相信艾力克斯所做到的事，他們堅持艾力克斯只是重覆那些牠被教導的答案。換句話說，牠所表現出來的東西只是憑著牠的記憶，而不是真正地使用語言。

不管科學家怎麼說，還是有很多人喜歡養鸚鵡，因為牠們會「說話」。鸚鵡會重覆你所講的話是件有趣的事。不幸的是，許多從亞洲和南非叢林抓來的鸚鵡被當成寵物販賣，也因此，野生鸚鵡的數量年年減少。如果野生鸚鵡的數量繼續減少，牠們就有可能絕種。

鸚鵡是聰明又美麗的鳥類，擁有牠們當寵物的確很棒，但是讓牠們繼續留在野外會更好，畢竟那裡才是牠們真正的家。

85. 現代童話故事 P. 188

美國小朋友會靠牙齒賺零用錢。那麼由誰買單呢？當然是牙仙子。當小朋友發現乳牙開始鬆動，就會既緊張又期待。雖然牙齒鬆動會讓人不太舒服，但小朋友都知道，只要乳牙掉了，牙仙子就會來訪。乳牙掉下後，需清洗乾淨，在睡前小心放在枕頭底下。隔天早上，牙齒不見了，取而代之的就是牙仙子放的零用錢。

以錢易牙的「牙仙子」習俗，其典故竟然發生於近代。雖然許多文化都有與乳牙相關的儀式，但牙仙子習俗是從第二次世界大戰後的美國開始傳播。首先，這是一個繁榮與經濟成長的時期，意指父母終於有錢花在孩子身上。也是從這個時期開始，父母更加關注他們的孩子。最後一點，華特・迪士尼本人也透過了《灰姑娘》等動畫電影，讓仙女相關的童話發揚光大。

雖然牙仙子習俗十分吸引孩子，但這個由父母扮演的奇幻角色，卻身負許多重責大任。要從熟睡孩子的枕頭底下抽出牙齒，是一件充滿挑戰的任務。孩子也知道牙仙子從來不會失約，因此，父母絕對不能忘記在約定好的那個晚上拿走牙齒。如今，牙仙子又需面臨另一個難題。到底應該留下多少零用錢呢？仔細想想，孩子總共會掉20 顆乳牙，看來當牙仙子的代價可不低呢！

牙仙子習俗現已傳播至其他國家的兒童身上。這樣的習俗，能讓小朋友對不適的掉牙經驗感到興奮，父母也可以為孩子的童年增添一點魔法色彩。

86. 海豚 P. 190

很多人都喜歡海豚，因為牠們看起來友善，而且愛玩又聰明。科學家說，海豚是僅次於人類最聰明的動物。海豚和鯨魚與鼠海豚有親戚關係，而和鯨魚與鼠海豚一樣，海豚原本也居住在陸地上，大約 5,000 萬年前，海豚才進入水中，成為海洋哺乳動物。

海豚的種類約有 40 種。最小的海豚大約 1.2 公尺長，而最大的約 9.5 公尺。牠們以魚為主食。研究海豚的專家目前發現，海豚會製造出很大的聲音來震嚇魚群，使牠們更容易去捕食。也有人說海豚會利用聲音來和彼此溝通。

和人類一樣，海豚擁有恆溫的血液、呼吸空氣，並且以母海豚的乳汁來餵養幼仔。絕大多數的海豚擁有極佳的視力，而牠們的聽覺也比人類靈敏。海豚以家庭聚落的方式住在一起，我們稱其聚落為「pod」。一個聚落大約包含了 12 隻海豚，但在食物匯聚的區域，聚落會聚集在一起，形成一個「超級聚落」（superpod），其海豚數量還可高達一千隻。

海豚是一種愛玩的動物，牠們和海草、其他的海豚，甚至和人類的游泳者嬉戲。牠們友善的外表、獨特的智慧，以及愛玩的性格，使牠們受到人類的歡迎。許多有關海豚的電影和書籍，加上世界各地海洋公園裡的海豚表演，大大地增加牠們受歡迎的程度。

不幸的是，許多品種的海豚都面臨了絕種的威脅。一般認為，由於汙染和揚子江（長江）上漸增的航運，白鰭豚現在已經絕種了。

長久以來，海豚在人類文化中占有非常重要的地位，如果我們無法盡所能拯救牠們，那將會是一個莫大的遺憾。

87. 長條圖：頂尖世界盃足球員 P. 192

足球是世上人氣最高的運動，估計全球粉絲約有 35 億人。球迷無不引頸期盼觀看四年一度的國際足總世界盃（FIFA World Cup）足球賽。此國際賽事是由 32 支國家隊角逐名次。對球員而言，足球生涯最重要的目標之一，就是在世界盃踢出亮眼表現。在全球眾目睽睽下，球技出色的球員絕對能獲得最佳球員的殊榮而名留青史。

以下長條圖顯示某些傑出球員的資訊，包括他們參加了幾場世界盃足球賽，在這些比賽中進了多少球。請由下圖回答以下與史上頂尖世界盃球員有關的問題。

88. 清廉的政府 P. 194

不，這裡的原文「clean」並非指「地板乾淨得發亮」或「廁所散發清新玫瑰香」的意思。當我們以「clean」來形容政府的時候，意指「不貪腐」。也就是政府官員不會為了錢財或好處而行事不正或違反紀律。

全世界都有貪汙腐敗的問題。有些地方是小規模的貪腐問題，例如，用點小錢賄賂警察來忽視交通違規。其他地方則是大規模的貪腐問題，舉凡企業以鉅額買通相關單位，重新制定法規，或讓自己擁有逍遙法外的特權，以便非法傾倒有毒廢料。還有各種大大小小的貪腐例子，族繁不及備載。

有時貪汙似乎能帶給人方便。以賄賂的方式取消違規停車罰單，或更改文件日期，看似小事一樁，但當貪汙問題蔓延擴大，民眾就會目無法紀。如果法律制度是看錢辦事，那麼就沒人能倚靠法律所帶來的保障。人們常覺得小貪無妨，但貪腐就像傳染病。最好是效法下頁表格中的國家，在問題根深柢固之前就加以制止。

89. 使用辭海 P. 196

辭海會列出特定字彙的同義字和反義字。與字典不同的是，並非每一本辭海都會列出字的定義。辭海對於想要避免重複詞藻的詩人、創意作家或是任何寫作之人而言，都相當實用。

身為學生的你，一定常常談論和思考「學習」（learning）這件事，次數可能多到讓你對於重複「學習」（learn）這個詞感到疲憊。既然如此，就停止這麼做吧。還有許多其他名詞可使用，例如探知（ascertain）、汲取（drink in）、吸收（soak up）、鑽研（pore over）、探究（discover）等等。

英文的同義字非常豐富，有這麼多語詞可選擇時，就沒有必要老是使用同一個語詞。

以下為一辭海範例，請看此範例回答下列問題。

90. 索引：樸門永續設計 P. 198

「樸門永續設計」是一種設計居家生活、農地、室內外環境的系統制度，使其有益於人類與環境。樸門永續設計的理念受到大自然的強烈影響，且通常以自然系統為基礎，用意在於改善而非破壞環境。樸門永續設計著重於自行栽種食物、使用天然能源、減少消耗量、重複利用、回收利用、社群支援以及其他應用實務。

比爾．莫里森與大衛．荷姆格蘭於 1970 年代晚期首創所謂的「樸門永續設計」農耕系統。1970 年代至今，樸門永續設計的概念逐漸擴散開來。現在世界各地都有人運作樸門永續設計系統制度。

以下為一有關「樸門永續設計」的索引。利用這份索引來回答下列問題。

4-2 綜合練習（II）

91. 優雅與美味的邂逅 P. 200

「下午茶」意指英國與其他共和國家，於下午兩點至五點間所食用的少量餐點。下午茶裡有可口的迷你三明治、司康、麵包捲、肉類，當然還有茶飲。人們不講「吃」下午茶，而講「享用」下午茶。長久以來，下午茶已是廣受歡迎的一種生活習慣。不過在現代社會裡，如果有全職工作在身，就很難在下午兩點的時候享用下午茶。

即使人們已不再天天享用下午茶，這樣的傳統仍留存於某些國家。許多人視下午茶為優雅餐點，一種過去僅有貴族與金字塔頂端的人得以享用的茶點。因此，一群三五好友在下著雨的週日午後，前往時尚餐廳享用下午茶的景象十分常見。

數百年前，並非只有權貴會享用下午茶，工作一整天的窮人也有此習慣。那麼為什麼我們會認為下午茶是一種優雅的傳統呢？答案或許與此習俗的起源有關。

根據傳言，下午茶是由維多莉亞女王的侍女貝德福女爵所發明的。女爵不喜歡豐盛的午餐，因為她到了下午約四點時，還是會有一種「無底洞」似的飢餓感。女爵剛開始會派僕人準備茶飲和點心。後來她開始邀請朋友共襄盛舉，就可以不用獨自一人享用點心。有些賓客很喜歡這樣的非正式聚會，於是也開始籌備他們自己的下午茶派對。就這樣，下午茶的傳統便誕生了。

92. 醫界傳奇：李時珍 P. 202

中國歷史上有許多知名統治者、將帥、僧侶和軍師，也有若干名醫，李時珍即是其中之一。有些人稱他為「中國藥學之父」。

李時珍生於 1518 年明朝的湖北。早年的李時珍總是身體微恙，因此始終無法通過科舉考試，在當地政府謀得一官半職。但他反而將時間花在鑽研醫書上，觀察父親的行醫方式，李時珍的父親亦教導他許多治病良方。

李時珍在藥學方面的學習能力堪稱神速。不久後，他就在首都獲得大夫的職位。當時的他飽讀罕見醫書，並與許多其他具有影響力的學者交流看法。

由於李時珍力求精益求精，他開始編寫工程浩大的《本草綱目》，並周遊國內尋覓能夠治病的奇特草本植物，與新穎醫療方法。《本草綱目》是一本草藥學百科全書，集結超過八百本書籍的資訊，並且詳細記載 1,892 種草藥。他花了將近 30 年撰寫此鉅作，不幸的是，他沒能在 1593 年辭世前親眼見證此書的出版。在編撰過程中，他的兒孫協助記錄、繪圖與編寫。如果少了他們的努力，這部中藥學上最重要的書籍之一，可能永遠無法問世。

《本草綱目》或許是李時珍最具代表性的著作，但他的成就並不僅止於此。他也是第一位發現膽結石病、利用冰敷退燒，以及運用蒸氣治療感染症狀的醫師。

93. 探索巨型水晶洞 P. 204

想像一下，倘若你發現自己置身在地底深處一座隱密的洞窟裡，會是什麼感覺？你試著眨眼，讓雙眼適應漆黑的環境，但卻於事無補，完全伸手不見五指。周遭空氣極為潮濕，讓人有點不適。突然間，你想起自己有把手電筒。點亮手電筒後，眼前景象令你瞠目結舌——到處都是巨型水晶，有些水晶清澈透明，有些水晶呈現淡藍色，所有水晶高聳過人。你甚至可以在此洞穴裡探索數小時之久。

雖然這聽起來像是幻想出來的世界，但卻如聖母峰或越南下龍灣一樣真實，這裡就是墨西哥奈卡的「巨型水晶洞」。此水晶洞距離地表將近 300 公尺深，遍布著亞硒酸鹽所構成的巨型水晶。有些水晶的長度可達 12 公尺。地底洞窟的獨特環境，以及超過 50 萬年來浸沒於高溫熱水中，即是如此碩大水晶結構的成因。

不過，在你預訂飛往墨西哥的機票前，一定得弄清楚，此水晶洞並未對外開放。洞室裡的環境悶熱到足以致命的地步，且溫度高達攝氏 58 度。因此，探勘洞窟的人員，均需穿戴特殊的防護設備。

即使是全副武裝的專業人員，也無法在此久留。由於巨型水晶洞暴露於空氣中會受損，因此負責洞窟勘查的組織，打算先拍攝足夠的照片和影片後，再灌淹水晶洞。

94. 流浪狗悲歌 P. 206

過去 50 年來，飼養寵物已是全球普遍現象。光以美國為例，現今狗飼主的人數已是 1960 年代的三倍。但是這項趨勢的負面效應，就是流浪狗的數量與日俱增。根據一些數據，現在美國約有 1 億隻流浪貓狗露宿街頭。

不幸的是，流浪狗數量不斷增加的主因，就是沒有責任感的飼主。有些人買下幼犬的原因，純粹只是無法抵擋牠可愛的模樣。一旦狗兒長大，一切就都變了——狗兒少了能融化人心的稚氣，飼主多了必須每天外出溜狗、處理排泄物、購買狗食與醫藥費等責任。有些飼主無法妥善打理這些責任，轉而選擇棄養寵物，讓牠們流落街頭。

流浪動物問題的另一起因，則在於動物管制預算縮減。各城市預算緊繃，因此資助流浪寵物數量控管計劃的意願不高。舉例而言，過去曾有一項非常有效的「TNR 計畫」，意指捕捉後再絕育、回放動物。TNR 計劃能確保受到棄養的寵物不會再繁殖。如果沒有 TNR 計劃，流浪寵物數量將持續以不受控的速率成長下去。

多數的都會居民對於流浪狗問題無感，但這就是流浪狗的目的。成群結隊的流浪狗並不傻，牠們知道只要越少現身，就越能確保自身安全。因此，牠們會躲得無影無蹤，直到清晨才會出現。牠們總共只花 10% 的時間待在會撞見人類的地方。

95. 借閱真人圖書館 P. 208

這世界充滿不同生活歷練、形形色色的人。有富裕名門，也有貧苦之人。有的人戰勝暴力與仇恨，有的人則從來不知恐懼為何物。我們都有自己的故事，但是什麼樣的方法最能好好地向他人訴說故事呢？你可以寫進一本書，或是更佳的選擇——親自當面告訴他人。這就是「真人圖書館」的概念。

「真人圖書館」的概念發想於 2000 年丹麥舉辦的羅斯基勒音樂祭。由年輕人組成的非政府組織「停止暴力」（Stop the Violence），在音樂祭場地搭起小型帳棚攤位，以宣達反對暴力的信念。他們認為，如果人們能當面討論彼此生活經歷，就能對不同背景的陌生人更加熟悉。當時有超過 75 本「真人書」可供借閱，包括警察、政客、塗鴉藝術家、女權運動者，以及足球迷。音樂祭的群眾反應熱烈，因此「停止暴力」組織決定將此計劃往海外拓展。

如今，全世界有超過 45 個「真人圖書館」，並由位於丹麥的真人圖書館基金會管理。真人圖書館基金會負責圖書館的營運，包括收集館藏以及開放大眾借閱事宜。

最典型的館藏類別包括「族群一般特性」（也就是所謂可供外借的「真人書」）。舉例而言，「回教徒」這本「書」可能會列出以下特性：「極端分子」、「基本教義派」、「激進恐佈分子」。這些都是大眾對回教徒的偏見。換句話說，它們是大家所誤信的回教徒特徵。而真人圖書館藉由列出偏見，並讓大家有機會認識真正的回教徒，來嘗試挑戰大眾對其他社會族群的觀感。

96.「神聖」的蜥蜴：雙冠蜥 P. 210

有一種居住於拉丁美洲的奇特蜥蜴，稱為雙冠蜥。你可能會納悶牠有何奇特之處，其實讓雙冠蜥獨一無二的原因，不在於牠的飲食習慣，牠是雜食性動物（意指葷素不忌）；也不在於長相怪異，雙冠蜥呈亮綠色，可生長至 3 英呎長。讓雙冠蜥有別於其他蜥蜴的原因，就在於雙冠蜥擁有某種特殊能力——這種驚人的生物能在水上行走。這樣的特性讓牠獲得「耶穌基督蜥蜴」的別稱。

根據基督教的信仰，耶穌基督曾在信徒面前行走於水面上。假使此故事為真，耶穌之所以擁有此能力，是因為他是上帝之子。

不過，耶穌基督蜥蜴水上輕功的能力，與上帝的神蹟無關，而是因為帶蹼的長腳趾能防止牠掉入水中。蹼狀腳趾增加了腳的面積，利用表面張力原理減少掉入水中的機率。而且腳趾上的蹼還可伸縮自如，趾蹼可摺攏，並在耶穌基督蜥蜴需要行走於水面時展開。

坦白說，耶穌基督蜥蜴並非行走於水面。畢竟，無論指蹼面積多大，假使牠悠閒地漫步於湖面上，絕對會掉入水中。耶穌基督蜥蜴彷彿水上飛一般，維持 1.5 公尺的秒速快跑於水面上。牠通常可以在水面奔馳大約 4.5 公尺的距離，才會掉入水中。耶穌基督蜥蜴亦為游泳健將，屏住呼吸的時間可長達半小時。

97. 圓餅圖：有效率的週日假期 P. 212

很多人都以為小孩缺乏條理，其實不是這樣子。以我為例吧，我整個禮拜都認真上學、寫作業、練鋼琴和做家事，甚至每天帶狗狗「脆皮」出門遛兩次。我爸媽知道我週一至週六有多麼勤奮，所以他們每個星期天都讓我自由運用 7 小時又 15 分鐘的時間。

這樣的自由時間對一個小孩而言十分可觀。很多小孩會浪費多數時間來思考該做什麼。例如是要去爬樹呢？還是抓甲蟲？我不是這樣的小孩。我已經擬定週日下午的嚴格時間表。一旦某項活動的時間快結束了，我的手錶鬧鈴就會響起，然後我會進行清單上的下一項活動。如果你不相信，請來看看我做的圖表，這樣就能清楚了解我是怎麼度過週日時光了。

98. 長條圖：台灣——小心颱風 P. 214

如果你打算到台灣觀光，一定要記得帶一件短褲、一件 T 恤，和一把傘。或者最好攜帶兩把傘，因為第一把很有可能在颱風來襲時，被強風摧毀。

每年七月到九月是台灣颱風旺季。這種大型熱帶暴風雨足以釀成災害，且通常會為此地區帶來強風豪雨。一旦有颱風經過台灣，人人都足不出戶。

欲知更多台灣雨量詳情，請參照下方的長條圖。長條圖利用不同長短的「條柱」來呈現資料，使相異的數值易於做出比較。試著用以下長條圖來回答下列問題。

99. 折線圖：中國在人工智能研究領域拔得頭籌 P. 216

現今一些最具影響力的公司均以人工智能（簡稱 AI）為主要重心。不同領域的企業目前都試圖在「深度學習」此最新 AI 領域取得優勢。

「深度學習」意指電腦軟體能夠辨別和分析模式。換句話說，電腦分析一組數據資料後，可自行得出結論。深度學習過程亦逐漸不再需要人類的監督。

到底是中國還是美國會贏得開發深度學習領域的這場比賽，仍有待觀察。美國雖然起步強勁，但現在中國很有可能拔得頭籌。贏家的獎勵豐厚——可為這項新科技制訂規則；就像美國研究人員當初發明網路後，網路規則都由美國說了算一樣。而這些規則將在「深度學習」影響社會的程度上發揮很大的作用。

100. 目錄：居家療法 P. 218

多數人生病時的第一反應，就是看醫生拿藥。不過，越來越多人決定生病不用立即看醫生，而是先嘗試居家療法。

「居家療法」的涵蓋範圍非常廣。只要非製藥大廠所販售的藥品，均可列為居家療法，包括全世界古文明所流傳下來的草本療法。換句話說，在美國被用來治療頭痛的居家療法，即有可能源自古中國。

居家療法的概念有時是預防性的。舉例來說，如果你一直有腸胃不適的毛病，居家療法書籍可能會說是你的飲食出了問題。藉由放在書前的目錄，你可以輕易找到所需資訊的頁碼。參看以下居家療法書籍目錄，然後回答下列問題。

ANSWERS

Unit 1 Reading Skills

1-1 Subject Matter					
1	1. c	2. a	3. d	4. b	5. b
2	1. c	2. b	3. a	4. d	5. b
3	1. b	2. a	3. c	4. d	5. c
4	1. b	2. d	3. a	4. c	5. d
5	1. c	2. a	3. c	4. b	5. a
1-2 Main Idea					
6	1. c	2. a	3. b	4. b	5. d
7	1. a	2. b	3. d	4. a	5. a
8	1. c	2. b	3. a	4. d	5. c
9	1. a	2. c	3. d	4. c	5. a
10	1. a	2. c	3. b	4. c	5. d
1-3 Supporting Details					
11	1. c	2. b	3. d	4. b	5. c
12	1. a	2. d	3. c	4. b	5. a
13	1. a	2. c	3. b	4. d	5. b
14	1. c	2. c	3. a	4. d	5. b
15	1. a	2. d	3. c	4. b	5. b
1-4 Sequencing					
16	1. c	2. d	3. a	4. a	5. d
17	1. c	2. b	3. c	4. b	5. d
18	1. b	2. c	3. c	4. a	5. d
19	1. a	2. b	3. d	4. c	5. a
20	1. c	2. d	3. c	4. b	5. c
1-5 Cause and Effect					
21	1. c	2. b	3. d	4. a	5. b
22	1. c	2. d	3. b	4. a	5. b
23	1. d	2. a	3. b	4. a	5. d
24	1. d	2. a	3. c	4. d	5. b
25	1. b	2. a	3. b	4. a	5. b

1-6 Clarifying Devices					
26	1. b	2. b	3. a	4. d	5. c
27	1. c	2. d	3. a	4. d	5. b
28	1. b	2. a	3. d	4. a	5. a
29	1. a	2. b	3. b	4. c	5. c
30	1. b	2. d	3. b	4. c	5. d
1-7 Making Inferences					
31	1. a	2. a	3. d	4. a	5. c
32	1. b	2. c	3. c	4. b	5. a
33	1. b	2. b	3. c	4. b	5. b
34	1. b	2. a	3. b	4. c	5. d
35	1. b	2. a	3. c	4. d	5. d
1-8 Critical Thinking					
36	1. a	2. a	3. c	4. c	5. b
37	1. b	2. a	3. d	4. c	5. a
38	1. c	2. c	3. b	4. a	5. b
39	1. b	2. d	3. d	4. a	5. b
40	1. c	2. b	3. d	4. a	5. c
1-9 Fact or Opinion					
41	1. c	2. d	3. b	4. a	5. b
42	1. b	2. c	3. b	4. b	5. b
43	1. b	2. d	3. b	4. a	5. a
44	1. b	2. b	3. d	4. a	5. a
45	1. b	2. a	3. c	4. b	5. a
1-10 Review Test					
46	1. c	2. d	3. a	4. b	5. a
47	1. b	2. a	3. d	4. a	5. b
48	1. c	2. a	3. a	4. b	5. a
49	1. a	2. b	3. c	4. b	5. d
50	1. d	2. c	3. a	4. a	5. b

Unit 2 Word Study

2-1 Synonyms

51	1. c	2. c	3. c	4. d	5. b
52	1. b	2. c	3. d	4. a	5. b
53	1. b	2. d	3. a	4. a	5. b
54	1. a	2. b	3. d	4. c	5. a
55	1. c	2. b	3. c	4. a	5. b

2-2 Antonyms

56	1. d	2. a	3. d	4. c	5. b
57	1. b	2. d	3. b	4. a	5. d
58	1. a	2. d	3. d	4. d	5. a
59	1. c	2. a	3. c	4. d	5. b
60	1. b	2. a	3. a	4. c	5. b

2-3 Words in Context

61	1. a	2. b	3. a	4. d	5. c
62	1. c	2. a	3. c	4. c	5. b
63	1. d	2. a	3. a	4. b	5. c
64	1. b	2. c	3. c	4. d	5. a
65	1. b	2. d	3. c	4. a	5. c

2-4 Review Test

66	1. b	2. b	3. a	4. a	5. d
67	1. a	2. b	3. d	4. c	5. a
68	1. d	2. b	3. a	4. a	5. c
69	1. c	2. b	3. a	4. a	5. b
70	1. d	2. c	3. b	4. d	5. b

Unit 3 Study Strategies

3-1 Visual Material

71	1. c	2. d	3. c	4. a	5. b
72	1. c	2. d	3. d	4. b	5. d
73	1. b	2. c	3. a	4. b	5. d
74	1. c	2. d	3. c	4. a	5. d
75	1. d	2. a	3. b	4. c	5. d

3-2 Reference Sources

76	1. d	2. c	3. d	4. a	5. c
77	1. b	2. b	3. a	4. c	5. d
78	1. c	2. a	3. d	4. c	5. a
79	1. c	2. b	3. d	4. a	5. a
80	1. c	2. a	3. b	4. b	5. d

Unit 4 Final Reviews

4-1 Final Review (I)

81	1. b	2. d	3. c	4. a	5. b
82	1. a	2. b	3. b	4. d	5. c
83	1. c	2. a	3. d	4. a	5. b
84	1. a	2. b	3. b	4. d	5. c
85	1. a	2. c	3. a	4. d	5. b
86	1. d	2. b	3. a	4. a	5. a
87	1. d	2. a	3. a	4. b	5. c
88	1. c	2. b	3. c	4. a	5. d
89	1. b	2. a	3. d	4. c	5. c
90	1. b	2. a	3. b	4. d	5. a

4-2 Final Review (II)

91	1. a	2. c	3. d	4. b	5. c
92	1. b	2. d	3. c	4. b	5. d
93	1. d	2. a	3. c	4. a	5. d
94	1. d	2. a	3. b	4. a	5. c
95	1. d	2. c	3. d	4. b	5. a
96	1. c	2. c	3. d	4. a	5. a
97	1. d	2. a	3. c	4. c	5. b
98	1. a	2. c	3. d	4. a	5. d
99	1. c	2. a	3. a	4. d	5. c
100	1. c	2. c	3. a	4. c	5. a

英語閱讀技巧完全攻略 1

Success With Reading

二版

作　　者　Michelle Witte / Zachary Fillingham / Gregory John Bahlmann

協力作者　Anna Kasprick (11, 29, 39, 57, 61, 66, 69, 85) / Owain Mckimm (72, 87) / John Calhoun (13, 65) / Catherine Jensen (14, 40) / Evan Gioia (31)

譯　　者　林育珊／劉嘉珮

審　　訂　Treva Adams / Helen Yeh

企畫編輯　葉俞均

編　　輯　呂敏如／丁宥暄

主　　編　丁宥暄

校　　對　黃詩韻

內頁設計　鄭秀芳

封面設計　林書玉

製程管理　洪巧玲

發 行 人　黃朝萍

出 版 者　寂天文化事業股份有限公司

電　　話　+886-(0)2-2365-9739

傳　　真　+886-(0)2-2365-9835

網　　址　www.icosmos.com.tw

讀者服務　onlineservice@icosmos.com.tw

出版日期　2024 年 3 月二版再刷（寂天雲 Mebook 互動學習 APP 版）

郵撥帳號　1998620-0 寂天文化事業股份有限公司

訂書金額未滿 1000 元，請外加運費 100 元。

（若有破損，請寄回更換，謝謝）

國家圖書館出版品預行編目 (CIP) 資料

英語閱讀技巧完全攻略（寂天雲 Mevook 互動學習 APP 版）/ Michelle Witte, Zachary Fillingham, Gregory John Bahlmann 著；林育珊，劉嘉珮譯．－ 二版．－［臺北市］：寂天文化，2023.06–

冊；　公分

ISBN 978-626-300-197-8（第 1 冊：16K 平裝）

1. CST: 英語　2. CST: 讀本

805.18